# VAGRANT PRINCE

by

## JACOB KILGORE

# CONTENTS


Constantyne's Letter ..................................................... 1
Sapling ...................................................................... 3
The Church Is in Flames ............................................. 9
The Storms of Life ..................................................... 18
Drifting ..................................................................... 24
Money ...................................................................... 31
Drink to Forget .......................................................... 38
A Blessing or Curse? .................................................. 42
Delerium ................................................................... 47
A Friend .................................................................... 56
Judith's Pain .............................................................. 61
Off to the Country ...................................................... 66
Sybil ......................................................................... 72
Wood ........................................................................ 77
The Powder ............................................................... 82
The Axe ..................................................................... 87
To the Sky ................................................................. 91
The Fires Are Lit ........................................................ 94
Trauma and Recovery ................................................ 102
Poor Ed .................................................................... 114
Street Trash .............................................................. 122
Breaking Bread and Bloodletting ................................ 127
A Wild One ................................................................ 137
A Deal with a Swordsman ........................................... 143

Dark Days ............................................................ 151
Possession ........................................................... 158
Heroism and a Bullet for Louis.......................... 168
Coligny and a Brief Peace.................................. 176
Hell on Earth ...................................................... 186
The Hills of the Slaughtered ............................. 194
Heartache and Departure................................... 203
White Sand .......................................................... 208
A New Hope, New People ................................. 213
The Intruder ........................................................ 220
A Vision and a Skinsuit ..................................... 227
Exodus ................................................................ 234
Jubilation ............................................................ 243
The Cat Pounces ................................................ 247
A Spiritual Wound Is Now Festering................. 256
Barbarism Shows Its Face.................................. 259
The Source of Lucy's Suffering ......................... 268
Revenge............................................................... 273
Despondency ....................................................... 276
The Floating Coffin ............................................ 281
Thomas the Tyrant.............................................. 285
Showdown with Lexington.................................. 289
It Unravels........................................................... 294
Home at Last ....................................................... 300
Iona ..................................................................... 303
A House for a House .......................................... 306
Purge ................................................................... 310

*This is dedicated to all who supported me, and to hard times. We could not be who we are without both of these. For true friends we must be grateful, and we must not thank that which made us suffer, but be thankful for what we've become.*

—Jacob Kilgore

# Constantyne's Letter

**W**HAT WE DO IS VILE BUSINESS, but I've sworn to God, this Earth, and to England that I will perform my duties 'til death, gathering any resource available to ensure we remain as masters of our world. I will be cursed if I do not stay true to this, placing my body and soul in service with no reservations. May my flesh revolt against me if I do not uphold the sense of justice defined by my country. By this I live, as a spearhead on the sharp tongue of my ruler. May she rule by the sword, for there is no other way in this life. Just as the wind blows and the sea is wet, armies will clash for land and glory. Therefore, remorse will only lure our enemies to ravage us, to start up the war drums and work up a hunger for violence, rather than to be at temporary peace when fear is mutually felt.

I have been sent here to this northern kingdom to inflict shame on peasants. It gives me no happiness to do this, but peasants will never respect too much tolerance. We knock the lords from their seats of power. A few throats cut to save the masses from all out war. This is our destiny, a strange lot to be placed here in charge of enforcing morals contrary to reason. I gather my pay by this occupation, so I do not question the ways of the world, made by our Lord, who decides we should be continually cut down like our life-giving grain.

—Constantyne Landsman

# Sapling

THOMAS CALLS, "Look father! Look!" lifting a woven basket before his face. His feet tromp downhill over the light spatter of mud. He nearly trips himself several times as the great mass of delicate-brown objects lead him down the worn, stone-scattered road.

"Careful, careful. What's the hurry?!" Thomas' father asks, securing Thomas' shoulders. He brings both his son and the massive basket to a stop. It is evident that he is a working man by the caked dirt and straw all over the wide sleeves of his shirt. He kneels before his son bright-eyed with a jolly smile.

"Look at what we have here!" Duncan exclaims, raising one of Thomas' hazel treasures toward the horizon. He shuts one eye and rotates it over and over in his hand.

"It has been some time since I've laid eyes on ones this fine. Did you gather all these on your own?" Duncan asks.

"No. Mary helped me."

Thomas stares high as a shepherd passes with his flock and reclines under the shade of the birch grove. Their hands motion in greeting with wide smiles.

"Well, better be off. Allen will be missing these, I'm sure," Duncan says.

"They are ours," Thomas says innocently.

"What is that?"

"They are for market. He let us have 'em," Thomas says, staring to his father's face.

Duncan twists his lips into a smirk in hearing this and says, "Well, alright then."

He leads Thomas back down the long dirt path, basket in hand.

Thomas and his father stroll up to Allen's house. It is a humble home with little care for excess extravagance. Pretty rose bushes line the outer wall of the front gate. Mary greets them with a girlish skip upon seeing them. She is dressed in her best frock. It is the color of nut with a border of auburn at the bottom. For a beauty of fifteen years of age this look is very suitable. She kisses Thomas upon the cheek and motions for them to follow inside.

"You're just in time. Supper's warming on the fire as we speak," she says.

Thomas' mother Annabel appears from the side of the house with a beaming smile and says, "Welcome home dears."

Thomas' parents meander the walkway through the bushes arm in arm. Mary takes Thomas' hand. He takes hold of her fingers and whispers to her, "May I feed the sheep?"

She nods, smiling.

Allen herds his flock among sprigs of harvested grain. The wool is thick on these simple creatures. It bunches up like clouds. They baa and bleat as they consume what is left on this muddy, fallow land. A lamb suckles from its mother, struggling to keep hold as she steps from stem to stem nibbling. Far off, a golden sea of barley shines radiant in the sunshine. It waves gracefully, helpless to the will of the wind.

Allen peers away from his bleating company to see his joyous visitors. Proudly, he approaches Duncan and pats him on the back.

"Haven't worked too hard, have you?" Allen asks.

"No, I enjoy it."

Thomas rips up small handfuls of straw and shoves it toward the slender mouth of a little gray sheep. It takes hold and munches its meal swiftly. Thomas slaps his hands on his knees and giggles.

Allen falls deep into thought, gazing off into the sky. Calmly, he says, "I fear that there may be gray clouds approaching."

"What do you mean?" Duncan asks perplexed, seeing the sky to be perfectly clear.

Joy fills every face on market day. Blankets lie on the spring grass along the old Roman road that links Musselburgh to Clyde Valley and beyond, displaying goods of every kind known to these people. Frolicking children devour honey cakes and play games of chase. Their squeals are heard, along with their constant laughter, filling the ambiance of sound, mixing in the chatter of buyers and sellers.

Ale and wine are in most every hand. Freshly killed game such as venison and birds are sliced and served. Salted beef lies in slabs ready for the taking. Fishermen display a rich assortment of delights such as oysters, crabs, salmon, herring, and mussels. Vegetables are scarce but seaweed and moss easily take their place in stews.

Thomas and his family have no problem getting rid of their goods. Customers' eyes light up when they see Annabel's sweet cakes topped with cream and freshly picked berries, especially with such lovely ladies as Annabel and Mary serving with glimmering smiles and entwined heather strewn through their braided hair. Also on display is Annabel's handiwork: fine wool blankets woven from Allen's own flock. And the eggs disappear quickly, for they are a rare commodity. Who does not enjoy such a pleasure?

Allen's fine cuts of mutton are displayed on an old table with many years of abuse upon it. Jagged cuts are carved deep, dyed red with blood. Various innards sliced and seasoned lie steaming in a black pot. A poor couple graciously motion to Allen and he serves them a helping of the soup in trenchers in return for a small sum.

"Such a fine day it is," says Duncan.

"I agree," returns Allen.

"I must thank you for your gift to my son. He enjoys selling them."

Thomas takes an egg in each hand and passes them to an elderly man, receiving coins in return.

Allen returns to slicing with a tingle in his cheek.

English cavalrymen mounted on chocolate steeds gallop past. All eyes seem to be nervously drawn to this alien presence in their town. What do these invaders want?

One of the riders, appearing to be of higher rank than the rest, speaks to a mutton salesman on foot. He lifts a hunk of lightly charred meat from the display table and tears out a fatty piece with his teeth. He then unrolls a paper and delivers a few phrases. The salesman appears to plead with the captain, offering him more meat, but the offer seems refused. At this, the middle-aged merchant falls to his knees begging.

The captain turns from him without showing emotion and slowly rides up to Allen. He takes out the list. Looking directly at him he asks sternly, "Are you Allen Sinclair?"

Allen replies, "Y-yes."

"Come over here," the captain demands, waving his hand once toward himself. He speaks to Allen, the words being a mystery to the rest. After a moment Allen returns to his meat, appearing slightly shaken, but attempting to be productive and charming as usual.

It is nighttime at the Sinclair household. Annabel stirs the pot on the hearth. Allen removes a smoking side of lamb from his small oven, the meat full of rubbed spices, bubbling with its own juices. He places it on the table in the center of the room with a grin.

Duncan's eyes widen. He says, "This is too much. How could we ever deserve such treatment?"

Allen speaks solemnly. "You are my friend. That is enough." He sits and says, "Now let's enjoy this gift and be thankful, for our lives will never be the same afterward." This last part he says with a shaky voice, tears restrained.

Duncan takes hold of his shoulder, attempting to console him. "It is not true!" Duncan says, gripping his shirt. "We are healthy. We are happy. No need for such words."

Allen peers into his cupboard, saying, "We have milk; we have butter; we have all sorts of meats and breads. Take all you can." He faces his company. "Any item you can carry, please, please. You will need it!"

"Whatever do you speak of?" Duncan asks.

"I was poor in youth and poor again I shall become," Allen answers. "My home is not mine any longer and you cease to be in my service. Soon toil will again be our bread, but please eat up while meat still lies before us!"

Hands and mouths work in unison, filling up on steaming mutton, fresh, hearty bread, and a soup filled with mussels and various animals of the sea. Almost forgotten are the words Allen just spoke. The hearts of these happy, simple people are warm in each other's company, content and wanting of nothing else in the whole world.

Allen asks Duncan, "Have you any place to go?"

Duncan freezes, lacking an answer.

Allen sadly says, "I wish the best for you. Mary and I will understand the troubles the poor bear very soon."

Allen and his daughter share a sad glance just as torchlight appears through the front window. They rise and take bags in hand that they prepared beforehand. Allen opens the front door to see a stern-faced soldier staring silently under flickering torch-light. Several soldiers clad in armor stand wielding pikes behind him.

Thomas clenches the loose material of Mary's dress, stricken with fear, unsure of what is happening. Mary kisses his cheek and quietly tells him goodbye. Mary and Allen exit their house seeming empty, letting little emotion escape.

More soldiers enter and compel Thomas and his mother and father to pass through the doorway. Halberds pointed at their backs, they pass over the grassy hills in the darkness. Behind them, torches are passed by the overhanging thatch, lighting it ablaze. Allen's house erupts in orange flames.

It is a long way to venture in the dark, and Duncan feels the slender point of the weapon infrequently poke his back. Fear for his family rises up in him. Every time one of them stumbles he imagines one of the English halberd spikes will slip right into a kidney of his wife or son.

"Please," Duncan begs the nearest soldier. "Have caution with your weapon, sir. My family is all I have."

Still they continue on, staring at their feet as they pass over stone and rut. Thomas' eyes land upon the new sight of orange spots floating within the night's black horizon. The duke's manor and other scattered residences around the perimeter of the town are now nothing more than campfires.

Duncan says, "I ask you man to man. I'm sure you have a family of your own."

"No more," a voice from behind tells him, and so he obeys.

As they are led into town, the place feels alien. The clamor of the cavorting soldiers echoes through the narrow roads. The harshness of it is unsettling.

On their left they pass a tavern that has been overtaken by lower ranking, bedraggled sorts. Inside they are crammed shoulder to shoulder. A barrel of ale is drained and mugs passed all around. Outside, a bottle of cheap whiskey is guzzled by two local girls. They make rounds hanging on each man as they stumble about, cackling, and hollering their thoughts into each ear.

"Come… drink with us," a wasted brawler says, yanking on Annabel's arm. He tugs her toward him, but a lieutenant swiftly knocks the butt of his weapon upon the man's head. At this, the drunk is waved off, a command he surely obeys. As the march continues, he plants himself in the corner and massages his aching head.

Finally, they reach the center of town. Here sits their humble, stone-built church. From the single tower an object is being swung about, occasionally colliding with the structure. Upon nearing closer, Thomas sees the "object" is an upper class elderly man. A rope has been tied to one of the many jagged castellations which jut from the perimeter of the tower. The other end is wrapped securely around his ankles. With his arms tied behind his back, he can do nothing but holler through the shirt that hangs over half his face. "Ohhhh ho ho! Oh, please! No, no, no, no!"

A number of sergeants and raw recruits take turns rushing at him, lifting him high, and pushing him with oomph. As he flips, swings, and spins, the lot of them lob anything from fruit to heavy stones right into his soft body. A young brat clears them away for a moment and, with a running start, rushes toward him with a heavy oak bucket wrapped with iron bindings. As physical laws dictate, the man predictably swings back, and as he does, the bucket is thrust from the hands of the young soldier. The corner bangs straight into the man's forehead. "Aooowowawow! Oh please, no more!" His wild moaning fills the mob with great laughter.

The lieutenant takes out a key and unlocks a side door of the church. Inside, townspeople are huddled in the dark. They skitter away like cockroaches at the sight of the soldiers.

The lieutenant tells his men, "Put the boy in here. We'll take these two up the hill."

Annabel says, "I want to stay with him."

"Up the hill with you," he tells her.

"Will he be safe?" she asks.

"He will, as long as no one starts any trouble."

# The Church Is in Flames

CONSTANTYNE WRITES a letter to himself. He grips the end of a tattered old stick, transcribing his thoughts with no intent to ever pass them off to another. In this personal meditation, he is hateful in his want of privacy.

Lexington pulls open the flap of the tent, flashing in the torchlight. The way he holds his eyes and brow reveal his astute-ness, though, just the same he holds his tall frame low as to show respect to his superior. The entrance flap falls into place, allowing the shadow to rest, and Constantyne is once again in his solace, feeling the peace brought by the one lit tear of flame warming the milky white walls.

"What is the temperament of the people?" Constantyne asks.

"They are not happy," Lexington replies.

"Is there a riot?"

"It is contained as for now," Lexington says, nervous for the outcome. His curly locks of hair hang low before his face. He looks more like a minstrel than a military leader.

"Care for a drink, soldier?"

"I best not. I've got my duty to perform, sir."

"You don't turn me down. Remember that."

"Yes, sir," Lexington says, showing his eyes for a moment.

Constantyne lifts a small jug and pours slowly into a small, graduated glass.

"You find this nowhere else. The people stock these in caves along the beach. I prize nothing ingestible more than good Scotch."

Lexington receives his glass and nods gracefully. The scent inflames his nose immediately as he lifts it to his face.

"Thank you," he says after swallowing.

"It is for sipping," Constantyne says. "Savor it."

Musicians enter. Gladness falls over Constantyne's face.

"I am permitted this enjoyment when off at war, for my head. It turns me inside out."

"Oh?"

"The vibration helps calm the pain."

"Would not silence be preferable?"

"I am particular."

Constantyne removes his thick leather coat and sets it upon his chair.

"Please sit," he tells Lexington. "It is no time for stressing. Please sit."

He motions to one of two chairs along the boundary within his tent. Lexington seats himself and sips from his glass.

The twang of the lyre plays softly, accompanied by a pair of violins and a flute.

"What do you think of the execution of our campaign?"

Lexington noticeably stalls in answering.

"It is fair at best. I have my criticisms."

"Of what?"

"One is rarely quite free to set things as they should be. There are always others' hands in the mix."

"And what does your hand wish to do?"

Lexington thinks it over for a moment, then replies, "I think people want respect more than anything in life."

"And what of it?"

Lexington says, "The people we trample, they care nothing for those who rule them."

"You forget your occupation."

"If we stop after we rip their lords from their thrones…"

"And who do we recruit for these jobs?"

"Who?"

"Hungry dogs."

Lexington is at a complete loss, stunned, forgetting his train of thought.

Constantyne follows up, "Dogs must be fed; don't forget that."

Lexington struggles to organize this idea and at the same time spills out words, "But the end result, sir."

"How long have you been in command?"

"Four yea—"

"War time, for God's sake."

"This is my first."

"And this is what I mean. Good sense will tell us one thing, but humans are mongrels."

"We can try," Lexington says with less confidence. "With minimal fighting… this occupation can be won."

"It can. But try to stop them from pillaging. Can you do it?"

"I don't know."

"We work in this world, not in books."

Lexington's gaze lowers. He says, "The common peoples' simple happiness. We step upon that and we have nothing. Only anger, chaos."

"You remind me of myself at your age, though slim for war."

Disheartened by this, Lexington replies, "I assure you, though muscles refuse to grow from my bones, I more than make up in strength of will."

Constantyne laughs and raises himself to pour another shallow helping. "I asked only because I knew the answer would please me," he says smirking. "It is love and spirit that saved me more than once, led me past the blades and missiles."

"And me. For true virtue, beauty unadorned I strive."

"I've heard that somewhere."

"It's a classic."

"I requested a few books to keep my mind off all this mess. I enjoyed a few lines here and there, but I don't care for feats of memorization."

"Neither do I."

"Go around quoting things and I'll label you what I want."

"Utility is for those who aim to put it to use."

"Enough," Constantyne says coldly. "You think you know anything by stuffing your nose in a book? Try that talk before your men; you'll have a knife in your back."

Lexington's throat constricts.

Constantyne sits firm in his chair, his spine straight against the backrest. His attention goes to the flow of the night air, uncon-cerned with the boy in the room. Still as can be, he breathes, wholly concentrated on all that is around him.

He says, "Take advantage of that youthful vigor. When you age your idealism shrivels; your world becomes smaller."

"I see," Lexington says sipping.

Constantyne rethinks his coldness and eases the tension in his face and shoulders. He says, "But perhaps you need it. I took in things that helped form who I am when I was your age, and so you are wise to do the same."

After a moment, with greater caution Lexington says, "I appreciate this perspective."

"Good, good. My body is stiffening, as is my mind. It is not fitting for us old ones to dictate how the new flesh, dealing with the life and death of the world, should think and feel."

Lexington nods as to acknowledge the point and sips again.

Constantyne lifts himself and paces. He stops upon reaching the opposite side of the tent and stares into the shadow that clings to the boundary. For at least a minute's time only the music, most notably the harmony of the violins, is heard ringing out.

Slow and paced, Constantyne speaks, "I've always heard a lot of wasted words, people talking about philosophy but not committing it to action. Or even worse, becoming so caught up in the ideas that they shrink away from life and become pale and morose. I cannot afford to risk that."

"It's the practicality of it that has allowed it to endure."

"No more of this talk—"

Constantyne prods his temples with his thumbs in a vigorous, gyrating motion. The pain is evident as the teeth and muscles of his face tighten at regular intervals.

"Are you all right, sir?" Lexington says, leaping from his chair.

"Fine, fine," Constantyne says faintly.

The violinists ring out sweetness that keeps Constantyne's mind focused. The triumphant flute in its constant upward sweeps flows through him as a vision of elated children leaping for joy in a green field. Their happiness numbs the agony. He feels the calm being poured over. At times there are lapses in peace, though. He imagines a long metallic object like a spit used for roasting pork breaching the soft meat in his head. The steel and blood enter his mental vision, sharp edges dripping red. The spongy organ is laid there, ready for victimization every moment. Heaven claps aloud a warning as each side wrestles, fingers clenched.

Constantyne rises to his feet. The swell in his head flows to the front part of his brain. Quite an adept at controlling his mind, he uses this pain, transforms it into exuberance, and is determined to make the most of this moment, even though it is only a stroll for urination.

His words spill onto a sort of tablet which he can see faintly in his mind's eye:

"Here is my life, a churning swell of misery and ecstasy, forlorn, morose, glad and proud, though I must view my accomplishments as though I'm a shade, dead, always inflicted with epileptic tremors of depression in recounting my moments of glory and all the regretful actions I performed without any power to press my hands and fix them like an artist can. There is no standing back to observe. The first brushstroke is the last. I will be remembered by the fate of all the horsehair which by one stroke of my wrist were physically free to go their own way. That is why I drink. My actions are nothing. By my mind and my mouth I hope to push things in a better way, but to toss a ball, am I the stones it happens upon?"

"Through a heroic pee, I feel it is leaking, which electrifies my soul. My little church in my head. The prayer and meditation in a drunk mind, the pressure and relief in the bladder, the high noted pleasure in the tip of my penis, and the coinciding singing around the corner from my eyes. It is—"

"My Lord!" Lexington says frantically, standing in front of two soldiers. "Forgive me for rushing upon you, but there is something terrible—"

"Tell me," Constantyne says, raising his pants and tying them snug around his waist.

"Though we commanded with strict orders... Sir—the church is in flames!"

Constantyne loses all feeling in his limbs. His mind reels with pain once more. To him the fires are roaring high, feeding on his hair and scalp like a halo sent from the devil.

"I am finished," Constantyne says.

Lexington becomes alarmed in this momentary weakness in his commander.

"Fire!" he screams. "The living bodies of those who sought to seek refuge in a holy sanctuary! They are scratching at the walls, Lord! Your soldiers fail to douse the flames that eat at all four sides! Your clarity will save their lives as well as your reputation!"

Focus comes back to Constantyne's eyes. The blackness of the night and the coolness of the air soothe him. His person condenses to a dagger blade in the center of his mind and protrudes from between his eyes. From this he storms forward, his breathing controlled and his heart full of murderous blood.

They both bolt full speed to the center of town and see the bell tower of the church above all the other structures swirling and glorious with flames sending righteousness toward heaven. The soul of the town is writhing in agony like an animal rolled over, bones snapped by a passing cart. There is death within. A pleading is being uttered to God.

They reach the foot of the structure and Constantyne sees his armor-clad soldiers, some having stripped themselves of their protection, frantically trying to contain the fires consuming it, as well as the houses that circle the structure on the boundary of the smooth-stone road.

Constantyne roars, "Leave those cottages to burn. If the fires rage or die out I don't give a damn. Take up your blades and free those entombed in the church!"

They immediately begin their task. They cooperate to toss buckets of water on the flames while others rush in and hack away at the great doors. Soon both the locks of the north and west doors are hammered loose so occupants can be rushed out to heave their lungs free of smoke.

In seeing the bodies piling before him, being carried out on the shoulders of soldiers, Lexington notes that most must have submitted to the fire and had accepted their fate within it. With a head full of poison, the vision of returning to Earth is only numbness for them.

It is when the soldiers brave the upper story that the real guilt begins for the rescuers: people not so much led, but dragged out, their skin warped and bloody black, gazing out from unfamiliar, torturous shells, from eyes that know better days. The forms come from both doors, semi-stiff, encrusted shadows of the models of society: Women come out like black pigs and so do their children. Some have life in them, humming elegies of pain. Some are frozen. The corpse of a priest emerges with his vestments melted, the adornments, the drape around his neck shrunken and charred. He is laid to accompany his flock, many of them fingerless and with the personalities in their faces homogenized.

In seeing this, the citizens rise up in hate. This is why Constantyne had ordered the church to be untouched. He knew in this time of religious strife a church should be a sanctuary. Now all is lost.

The knights, their armor reflecting the orange firelight, rout the oncoming peasants. Their hearts sink in this task. A hole in the earth seems to open up in committing these actions and they find themselves firmly in the pits of hell where these actions belong. Blades disembowel men, women, and even the young who have the heart to revenge their loved ones and ransacked livelihoods. A sort of kindness remains in most eyes that run forth, eyes not so accustomed to coldness and slaughter.

In the morning Thomas awakes, his back against a hard surface. The daze of sleep slowly fades and he notices his hands tingling with pain. He positions his right hand before his eyes, digits spread, and cannot recall how the tops of his fingers became covered with pink and rubbery nodes.

The orbs in his skull soak in the puffy tufts of white as they pass in front of the baby blue sky. He lies not wanting to move, knowing not why he is hurting. He touches his scalp and feels the bristly nubs of hair along the crown ridge. The dry ripples of skin over his forehead and brow flake in places like autumn leaves and are mushy like past ripe apples in certain other spots.

Thomas forces through the agony and lifts himself, first rolling on his side, then pressing against the dry soil with his feeble palms and forearms. He grits and bears the pain of tearing the sealed-over scabs within the crooks of his elbows. With a weary head, he manages his balance and stares along the line, to body after body of his townsfolk, fifty or more black and rosy faces, many cooked through like yesterday's bacon. The remains of the church, half a staircase and three pillars ashen-toned, lie smoldering not farther away than Thomas could throw a stone at this moment.

Constantyne paces down the line next to Lexington with soldiers in tow. Thomas, though a bit frightened and empty of spirit, stands as well as a newborn fawn may and takes in Constantyne's words: "I must wash over this error with charity, flood them so that when one speaks of this, the power of the words of cruelty and barbarity are diluted."

"What do you have in mind?" Lexington replies.

"I must bear this upon my own back. I must invite those that lay here in agony as my guests."

"I disagree that it is necessary."

"I told you. I am particular."

"If that means crippling you from future good deeds, by weighing you down—"

"I never said I was to be always trusted with rational thought. My heart takes over."

Thomas sets his eyes on the faces of these two and remembers them well. To him they are faces of evil—one broad and sturdy like stone, the other long like stretched clay.

Constantyne asks, "Who set fire to the church?"

Lexington thinks on the question and says, "Some goddamned fool, that's all."

"That will be the question of my life. This will be why my superiors will doubt my ability. I will forever be making up for this failure."

"Surely, it will pass from people's minds," Lexington says. "There was nothing you could do, no way you could know."

"And so it is. The things that have the most power over us we have no power to control."

"Yet we must suffer and bear the blame. It's true."

As Constantyne returns to his tent, he once again takes up his pen and pours his thoughts out in the form of written words:

Curses I accrue from the mouths of the poor. Needless to say, I will answer for what I have done. My ships came from the sea without warning and unloaded steel-girded men charged with violence to burn and violate the little they took pride in. I should think now, now that it is too late, that I should have put the fear in those under my power. I should have been observing with not a single moment's rest like in the old days.

I bring the battered, shamed folk into my newly acquired properties as I felt I must. I silently question this blind sort of suicidal, false-morality. My superiors know this air of kindness will wash over our present worries, but you cannot escape the consequence of neglecting a wound. It is as kings who thought they could wed the daughters of rulers they'd crushed. Only time will tell when a knife propelled by vengeance will show itself. No sort of title can save us from these things.

And so, besides my war duties, at home I must now be on guard, policing these vagrants who, no doubt, will dip into their shallow wells of intellect and turn my streets of bile and filth into an even greater slum. It is by this duty my life will become hell. Their villainous minds will create horrid tactics upon their fellows. The retched will fester all around me like a creeping skin disease. I see it coming: corpses in the streets, pockets picked clean. This is why kindness is not possible for those in my position. The crude, uneducated poor must see a face they hate to remind them of the barrier they need, for toil is their element. God put us in our stations and it couldn't be clearer. We act out our roles like actors on a stage. The low-bred suffocate with too much freedom. It is a fact of life. They do it to themselves. Any surplus is squandered. Just as fish need water, the impoverished need hardship.

—Constantyne Landsman

# The Storms of Life

THOMAS SLEEPS HALF-NESTLED in his mother's arms. It is a bizarre sort of sight, for he is too large in size to be cradled. The deeply felt wrongness has developed a need in him to feel protected. To lay eyes on his singed scalp—that explains his want to curl up like a small child. It is also the confusion he feels in others, of why they are here on this ocean away from home. Everyone seems distraught, and this brings on a spell of melancholy. As they stepped aboard this vessel, as their feet pressed onto the hard boards, they were prisoner to the sea and subject to the fate of those dictating the direction it headed. This alien feeling found its way into Thomas through his toes. It slowly inched up his calves and into every part of his body. Where is the soft earth, the cool mud of the pastures in which he would sink his feet? It has been taken. Still too young to fully comprehend the circumstances that are soon to form his fate, he feels the unwelcome displacement as a churning swelling of sadness.

"Mother!"

"What, dear?" she answers sweetly.

"Where are we going?"

"We are going to a new home."

"Because they took our old home?"

"Yes."

Thinking on this Thomas says, "Can we ever go back?"

"No," Annabel says faintly.

"What will we do there?"

"We will be English."

Thomas thinks on this idea some time. Will he forever be English?

The rise and fall of the world underneath them has sent aloft an air of nausea, along with the spray that has clung to the passengers for the past two days. The exodus across unfamiliar waters is spent in sleep for those who are lucky. Many are racked with fear at this sentence, often wringing their hands as those who await a noose for their guilt in charges of theft. These pastoral folk are to see fields no more. Their skills are to be squandered, thrust into the throng of the reeking cities of Britannia. Their annexation will be forgotten, lost to the pages of history, but the worry on the heads of these people is very real to Thomas.

Thomas has slept through the hottest hours, unconscious to the momentum of this vehicle. Prone, yet still drifting on, he wakes intermittently to see the same sights: people cast by boredom, the occasional bird, and gathering gray clouds filling the blue sky.

Once again he relaxes into slumber. Those cheeks, once soft, pale and unblemished, now display tragedy and an oncoming infection to those that pass. Caught up in dreaming, his lips hang slightly apart. Brown strands of hair stand tall above the blood-clotted bald spots, hiding and revealing again what was done to him. They wave and whip more every hour, increasing with the growing intensity of the sea breeze.

As the dimming effect of evening sets in, the gust has had time to grow in strength, now battering and nearly wrestling some weaker ones to their knees. It has brought on such a chill that all of the passengers have retired to the lower level, bundling themselves away.

The creaking merchant ship is pressed by the water churning beneath it. The fluid, when it trickles can bring such calm, but in such a quantity, when set in motion by the power of great winds, it is filled with the power of a god. The boards are pulled by the force, nearly cracking to pieces as it sails. Thunder rumbles a low boom and the sound of rain is constant. It is a mystery of sound in the absence of light, save for when a bolt of lightning illuminates the waves surging upon the hull.

These families sleep in a small room below. Their square-topped hats cause them to appear as though they belong to one order. Thomas cowers in fear as the crash of thunder sounds about all around. His eyes widen. He stumbles up the staircase to the top deck and peers into the charcoal sky and sea, amazed at the commotion.

The weather-worn door opens and he creeps out. He holds his arm over his face. The door slips from his grip. It slams open against the outside wall. He is startled so terribly that he jumps, shocked into alertness. As his constitution returns, he forces himself against the wind, grasps onto the side, and makes his way.

Two helmsmen grip the tiller, trying to keep control of the helpless vessel in the chaos of the storm. A skinny young sailor's voice cracks over the bass of the waves pummeling the ship. The scrappy red cloth he wears about his neck flaps wildly as he screams, "We're losing it!" His knuckles clench as to not be ripped from the world.

Thomas stares across the dark horizon, struck with wonder despite the danger. Soft moonlight occasionally dances upon the deck as gaps in the cloud-clumps pass above. Suddenly, a great wave rises. It carries him across the deck and slams his shoulder into the sidewall, while his belly is lifted by the rising water. Thomas leaps to his feet, fighting against gravity and the force of the rising vessel, finally gripping the rigging and ropes in the center of the deck. There he clings as the boy with the red cloth about his neck is carried by a wall of water, helplessly surged to and fro. The poor young fellow tries in vain to remain low, gripping anything he can. He yells, a continual yell for help and for mercy from God and the world. His fingers press against the ridge of wood that frames the perimeter, but a new wash rushes over and easily lifts him. He screams for the elder shipman to help, but the focus must be on the tiller and the safety of the passengers. All this companion of his can do is continually force his shoulder into the mighty construction of board and hinge and fight against the forces of nature. Finally, a slight balance of the ship goes in the favor of the boy.

Thomas calls to him, "Rush here! Fight it!" holding out his arm.

The boy scrambles against the slippery surface, feet and hands getting what traction they can when he is not outright swimming.

"My hand is here!" Thomas hollers. "It's not far!"

Another wave envelops the ship. The boy screeches with all he has, with curses, stomping through the waves as they rush over him. The great angle shifts everything, so Thomas must hang with both hands and knees tight around the swinging ropes in order to not lose his life. It is a terror for the boy sitting beneath him in the pool gathered at the sidewall. Thrashing at the edge of death, staring into pitch black waves, terror is cast hard in his features.

"I'll go for the door!" the boy calls. He stretches out his hands, pushing off the sidewall as the ship rocks. He collapses into the surface yet again. Crawling fully submerged in the icy streams of fluid, he feels the stinging cold enter him. His sense of touch is stolen through numbness, so he pushes as best he can, though he feels his limbs are not his. He tumbles and is throttled repeatedly into the hard deck.

The helmsman yet again forces the tiller against the violence and gives his shipmate another chance at life.

"Here boy! Give it yer all!" he yells.

For a moment the boy's fingers clench the railing, but as he jerks forth a step, the vortex of wind and water rips his fingers free. His ribs slam, then he falls into the deep, sinking farther and farther among the churning depths. A few peaked screams are heard, then all is silent. He slowly drifts downward and feels a salty mouthful of seawater rush down his throat. Above, bolts of electric light reflect through the swirling liquid.

Thomas' mind is not on the boy, for he is still clenching to the bundles of ropes, still tossed about with no sign of relief.

Early in the morning hours, as the purple hue transforms the skyline, Annabel awakes. She rubs her eyes and waits for her sight to adjust to the darkness. She begins to see the outlines of the families all around, but no Thomas. Her heart speeds a little. Duncan opens his eyes and notices her alarm. She tells him the reason for her worry and they both rise, taking up a lantern, searching among the clusters of sleeping people lying upon scattered hay.

"Thomas," Duncan whispers, looking over each face he passes.

Annabel starts off the other way, calling his name, searching in even the smallest spaces, lifting blankets and annoying other passengers.

They move to the top deck, searching hopefully around the mast, past the billowing sail, ducking under the loose rigging, only to see a few portly sailors and a sleepless old shepherd with tufts of sideburns gazing into the motion of the waves. Duncan notices something strange about the demeanor of the captain. He is pacing erratically and is speaking to the helmsman in a frantic manner while tugging at his hair.

Duncan and Annabel approach them not quite sure if their words will seem strange or even be acknowledged. After all, there was not much space to get lost on this small ship and the worries of poor folk were not often regarded as worthwhile anyway.

The Captain stops as he sees them. "Yes?"

Duncan says stuttering, "Our son. He's gone missing."

The captain looks to the helmsman with dread, fearing the worst.

"What is it?" Annabel asks. "Do you know something?"

"I don't…" the helmsman starts, clears his throat harshly, then continues, "I don't want to go and say—"

"Tell us, please," she says.

"I don't want to say something if I can't be sure, bringing you sorrow for no reason."

"Just say it," Duncan says.

"The storm last night took my apprentice. Just before the waves rushed on deck I thought I saw a boy come from below. But when the waves cleared I saw nothing and wondered if it was a flash of madness."

"If I were there I would not have stood by," Duncan says.

"Believe me, I hate myself for it, but there's nothing I could have done. Weather like that has no mercy. I had to fight with all I had so that it didn't swallow the ship whole and take everyone."

"What can we do?" Duncan asks.

The captain says, "You can pray. That's all I know to do. I'm sorry."

Truthfully, Thomas is very near. He hears every word they say. In the center of the deck, under bundles of rope he lies. As the rains stopped, crewmen went to work at repairing torn sails. Someone placed a box of rigging atop Thomas' serpentine cover for ease of accessibility. Buried under the iron and wound cord, his arms remain constricted. The weight on his body prevents easy breathing. It prevents audible speech as well, for his chest is pressed powerfully. He woke suddenly as this force was placed upon him, but could do nothing, for the act was done once he realized anything. He is buried, and so, as if he were a ghost he hears their sorrow-filled speech.

"What was he doing out here?" Duncan asks the helmsman whom has no more replies to give.

Annabel says, "We know how curious he can be... He'd climb over any fence, often getting chased by dogs. He'd discover something new to scale and get himself scraped up in falling."

"We were so tired, but we should've watched him," Duncan says. "What kind of parents are we?"

Though Thomas is not strong, he struggles through the hours, wiggling under the great mass. He can, with the utmost strength he can muster, slide and jerk. The fibers press hard into his cheeks and he pushes the smallest distance off his heels.

Night returns, and with it another spell of rainfall comes. Thomas' struggle suddenly becomes desperate. This tight space holds in the drips like a good washtub. He feels the moisture draining under him through his hair and under his neck. Frantic, he jerks, scraping his belly and shins, though it seems as if he were making no progress at all. The water can be heard pelting harder now, and soon it soaks all his back.

He calls aloud, "Mother!... Mother!" as the liquid splashes inside his ears.

The progress is slow, but now he knows he has not struggled in vain. The rain now strikes his forehead. He wrenches his face past each ripple pressing upon him and juts his mouth as far as it can reach.

"Mother!" he wails so many times. "Mother!" he calls as he jerks his shoulders, one after another. "Mother!" he yells, till the helmsman hears and peers in.

"Boy!" the helmsman says wide-eyed. "Don't you worry!"

With great effort, the helmsman lifts the wooden box containing the rigging. "Can you move?" he asks Thomas.

"A little!" Thomas answers, pushing with his fire-scorched elbows.

A team of crewmen see the helmsman struggling and rush to help. As their hands work in lifting, the helmsman tells the smallest one, "You—rush and tell this boy's parents—their son is alive!"

Moments later, as Thomas' parents' venture into the open and they begin to be soaked, disbelief still fills them. The helmsman calls out, "Oy! Over here!"

They slowly step over. The heavy ropes are lifted, piles of it at a time, and Thomas is yanked free. As he is placed on his feet, his breathing is noticeable and relief is awash over his face. Duncan and Annabel take hold of him and look to each other in astonishment.

# Drifting

ALONG THE MOUTH of the river Thames, wharfs extend the full breadth. Some great ships rest with their mighty sails concealed, though many take in wind again and set off across the sea. People scurry in every direction. A frail workman lets his side of an ornamented chest slip from his fingers and crash upon the dock. As he frantically lifts the object, placing a broken leg within before anyone can see, his superior at the head of the line barks, "Get a move on it! We don't have all day!"

Wide-mouthed smiles are seen on the faces of many cluttering this old dock, seeming most strange to the passengers of Constantyne's ship setting foot here for the first time. Duncan and Annabel are no different. They are tired, as is their son, who is asleep in his father's arms. Annabel steps toward a merchant selling little mullets which he bakes in a miniature oven. She waits for the fish and an accompanying bread roll. Duncan, drawn to follow her by the lure of the nice smell, lays Thomas upon a bench not far away. He stands beside her, peering back to his son from time to time.

Inside the iron latch they can see the glow of the food and the small sticks placed inside. Smoke drifts out as small talk is had throughout the cooking process.

Eventually, the merchant says, "Just about done," and takes up a thick cloth, opening the oven's latch. He places the fish atop the bread, using it as a sort of dish, and says, "Well, enjoy and be safe."

Duncan and Annabel turn and see Thomas sleeping. Instead of waiting for him to wake, they slowly nibble on their meal. There's no rush. They must wait anyway for information on which house they are to be appointed to.

After a time, Annabel asks her husband, "What if they don't look for us?"

Duncan says, "We'll see their man. He'll come calling when the time comes."

Annabel tells him, "You should go. You know how most things are."

"They'll see us," he says.

"Get up and stop arguing," she growls.

"Can't I sit—"

"No you can't," she says, not even looking in his direction. "You don't take risks with our family!"

Standing abruptly, with a timid wave of his hand he says, "Fine. I'll stroll among the crowd," and steps backward and away.

It's there among the crowd that he finds that Annabel was right. Not immediately, but after a wait which is met by the change of morning pleasantness to the heat of the post noon sun. The representative of the housing distribution begins passing around scraps with a number and location written on each. It is this ticket that holds his family's future, a future that would not have been acquired if he had not been forced out of his trust in other's responsibility.

Duncan returns to Annabel flashing the ticket. "You were right," he says smiling to her. She says nothing, but seems happy. He lifts Thomas and they follow with the crowd.

As they pass a pub, women in fine dresses chat. A team of boys with holes in their gloves chase each other around the various structures, letting fly giddy laughter. Duncan and Annabel raise their heads as a great commotion is heard. Dozens of people step hurriedly past. Many who shared their sea voyage ask questions of those crossing past and are then led by them in the direction toward the shipping docks.

Duncan stops a dirty-faced fellow and asks, "What is the excitement about?"

"They found a boy, floating in between some boats."

"A boy? Is he all right?"

"I don't know," he says, waving them to follow and find out.

They follow him past rows of ships of all sizes. After turning a corner, they see half a dozen sailors working on a bottle of rum while others work on nets and hooks. They pass fish being beheaded, scaled, and finally fried up, surrounded by an impatient, hungry cluster of folk.

Duncan tells the man, "That ship we were on—a young helmsman fell overboard."

The dirty-faced man replies, "Well, that's not a pleasant thought, now is it?"

They turn corner after corner, passing piles of driftwood stacked along a building, broken tables and chairs, and two embracing lovers with their hair disheveled, quite unhappy to be disturbed from their privacy. They come upon a short stairway that descends to a flat stone platform lined with vessels.

Duncan and Annabel see the crowd gathered and forcefully pull the onlookers apart, squeezing to the center. There in the water, between two boats, Abraham, an old sailor, treads water with the junior helmsman collapsed in his arms. The soaked white hair and beard hanging stringy in the old one's face and the way he struggles awkwardly in the water cause him to appear as a swimming cat.

"My God!" Annabel bursts.

As several people assist Abraham in lifting the body from the water, Duncan sets his son down and puts his hand under the base of the dead boy's skull. They lift and set the corpse down like it is a basket of eggs. It lies prone, curled. The chin is set gently, resting over the right shoulder. It is soaked and ghostly white: stark death on the bed of stones. Wetness surrounds the space. The face is plump, saturated. The arms lay limp, collapsed almost pathetically like the limbs of a dead squid. The sunken chest and bony arms do not at all fit what Thomas remembers. And there he is—Thomas—standing over the boy whom he recently shared words and cares with.

With sorrow and shock on his face, Thomas tells his father, "I saw him fall. Out of the ship."

"You want to stay with him for a time?" Duncan asks him.

Thomas nods, staring into his father's eyes, then stares back to the boy and sits with him.

Abraham stands guard over the body, as if the waves that had given this tumultuous baptism would beg for him back. Thomas' head bows. His small hands folded in reverence seem very innocent. He still has in him a child's awkward honesty.

Annabel asks, "What can we do?"

Abraham answers quietly, "Best let everyone find their peace. I'll contact the authorities soon enough and tell them what I found."

She settles her hand on Thomas' chest, feeling his heartbeat while he mourns. They let him sit and have whatever time he needs for this.

The three of them make their way along the water's path.

Annabel says, "We must find a transport up the river,"

As they enter a busier center of commerce, Duncan asks around. Meanwhile, the clashing of cymbals can be heard just past the buildings before them in a market square. The lively music excites Thomas, brings him out of his exhausted state. The tune repeats with a preposterous melody going up down, up down, up down, with a few higher notes and a few low; then it begins again.

Passing through the alley, Duncan leads his family to a wall of people. A choir of farcical, juvenile revelers crashes in every so often over a symphony of chaos-infused country violin. It seems as if the players on stage are children at rambunctious play rather than professionals, yet the energy and presence is compelling, drawing out smiles on the faces of Thomas and his mother and father.

Duncan tells Thomas to climb upon his shoulders, kneeling. Thomas rises high above the crowd, now seeing the carousal for what it is. A man, if he can be called a man, frolics front and center with a face painted like a lady's, though more extravagant, as if he dripped on a whole case of rouge, the cherry shimmering on an oval of white. He poses like a dog, tongue out and all. He raises his arms in the most exaggerated fashion, the hole in his face spread most cavern-like, its walls painted red like the raw ring of flesh of a slaughtered lamb's throat. This actor heaves to and fro, displaying nothing in particular, but swaying with an arm extended to the left or right in turn to the rhythm.

His white plastered face and frills about his neck make it seem as if he is mocking the Queen—it is so hard to tell for sure since the words are mostly unintelligible.

Frail-figured in corsets strapped over large pantaloons, the actors advance toward and away from the actor in white, center stage. They sing their nonsense songs as Annabel lifts herself upon her toes to catch a glimpse. Just then, the main actor feigns repeated shows of bashfulness. He wipes of his forehead with a handkerchief and blows kisses, this last act being repeated for minutes at a time. This causes the viewers to feel tension in that they expect it to end briefly as all the other actions do, but it continues for several minutes, causing them to become uncomfortable and confused. For the finale, he combines all the moves in order, adds in a flash of his pale buttocks, and pulls down his frilly woman's underclothes: shimmer, rump, shimmer, rump, over and over.

Annabel, as many others do, looks away, embarrassed at their vision locking with the cleft undercarriage. Peals of laughter erupt from the crowd. She tries to cover Thomas' eyes, but he is entranced in a fit of chuckling that she cannot bear to break up so soon after his sudden reemergence from death. He is caught up in this vision so foreign to one such as him, a country boy. He has never seen a performance such as this before, so this is quite stunning, to say the least.

The actors on stage take turns shoving handfuls of cake into the mouth of the blushing fem-aristocrat. All the while, money is tossed in their direction, much of it pelting them and resting on their perched backs and shoulders. The dainty man-queen takes a timid bite, then is slapped hard, a blow which results in much gyration. He plays as if dizzy from all the abuse, yet still desiring to be fed. Thomas applauds along with the rest of the crowd, caught up in the spectacle, of being one with many.

"Shall we go?" Duncan asks him.

Thomas nods.

They observe people leaving, some calling to those with oars, shoving and pulling themselves forward, fighting others like them to occupy the ferries. A hand lands on Duncan's shoulder belonging to one with streaks in his hair the color of gray burnt wood.

"In need of a ride?" he says.

"Yes, please," Duncan says, handing him two pence. They then carefully step into the small, wobbly craft.

The craft drifts along the great passage of water, the ripples revealing the green river scum caked on the brickwork. Small boats like theirs pass carrying people of various rank, but mostly the lower classes. Many hold ladies being courted: couples arm in arm with teeth showing in eager smiles, most likely discussing the details of the dress and comedy they had just seen.

Thomas scans over the sun-tinted ripples and the scattered crafts bobbing. The direction of this giver of life winds like a snake, so what appears to be on one bank is on the other.

A wide, rounded vessel floats just behind, carrying piles of boxes. Atop those, figures stare out into the complex lines of the rigging and sails. The shapes of the structures along the riverside seem fitted together on the whim of each builder, often offset and in various shades of wear.

The ferryman stops the movement by planting his oar hard before himself, and shifts the craft into a crevice built into the waterway for such a purpose. Duncan thanks him and they climb out, careful to step wide onto the outcropping of dock, for the space closing and opening between the rim of the boat and stretch of wood seems it could be an awful pinch.

They locate the house in the heart of Dartford where their landlord's tenant manager stays. Duncan knocks and receives an agitated, belligerent holler from within.

"Who is it?" the voice calls.

Sounds of defecation ring out.

Duncan, taken aback by this, is unsure if he should reply.

"Take your time!" Duncan says, red in the face, hoping he said the right thing.

"I'll be right out!" the strained voice sounds, followed by the resounding treble of wet splatter.

Humphrey, a round sort of person with a wiry, unkempt beard exits his home and leads Thomas' parents down a narrow, muddy road. He pats his stomach and says to them, "Sorry about that there. I had a bit of a party last night. The beer turns the contents of my bowels into a shit-storm." He laughs at this alone, opening his shirt a bit wider in his sudden intestinal relief.

Duncan leads Thomas by the hand. The boy struggles as his body begs for sleep and has sent him into a groggy state.

The houses they pass are stacked three stories high, casting darkness into the small space between. They are crammed together to such a degree it seems that an earthquake must have crushed the walls into this close proximity. The wood in these structures is so neglected that collapse is a real fear. The remains of older dilapidated houses from centuries past still sit planted firm and deep, lining both sides of the road as jagged foundations to nowhere.

The stench of urine, feces, and discarded animal carcasses burn within their nostrils.

A family sits in the dirt on the side of the street in semi-shadow. A boy Thomas' age stands with his head lowered, his eyes moist as if crying for days. His mother holds out her hand to Thomas' father and says, "Spare that we could eat? I beg you."

"Wish I had a bite myself. I'm sorry Miss," Duncan replies.

They walk further, seeing a boy and a girl playing with sticks in the settled water on the side of the road. As they pass, a woman empties a bucket full of waste into the street. Annabel leaps to the side, surprised and angrily says, "Did we leave our home for this? What for?"

Humphrey, taking insult, making known his status tells her gruffly, "Stop yer' complainin' or you'll end up in the streets suckling a baby with the rats!" He grumbles and continues on.

Nervous, Duncan says, "At least we have a chance. Maybe we won't starve to death here."

Humphrey coldly hands Duncan the key to the house and says, "Keep this safe—you lose it an' you're gone. We tolerate no nonsense. An' you best be in by lights out, ya' hear? When the lamps are snuffed your door is locked tight. I'm tired of hearin' it from the watchman that my tenants are disobeyin' and havin' to be drug down to be locked away for the night. We don' wanna make that happen, do we?"

Duncan faintly says, "No," not wishing to make trouble.

"Good then, well eh—"

Humphrey's belly rumbles. With a slight nod he sets off.

Duncan and Annabel lead their son into the dark cover within their new home, retreating speechlessly. A great weight gathers on both of their hearts.

# Money

OR A MONTH Thomas watches his parents struggle to make the rent. The crowded city creates a sort of frenzied competition and a steady sense of desperation among the poor. If one is lifted by circumstance, say by a very fruitful season, it is possible for them to permanently be lifted to a higher status of poverty. It is not often seen so clearly as this, but there are numerous strata among the poor, states of being in which the quality of life of these wretched souls are as different as lives are between the Crown and their servants. To be in the midst of this one may be reminded of the stark difference between the poor who have become accustomed to going without food for part of a day and those who often miss several days.

Thomas is only just beginning to get a real grasp of these divides within society. What he knows firsthand are the pangs within his gut. His body calls more desperately for food at night than for sleep. As time goes on, it seems more and more ordinary, the stars in his vision and the dizziness he feels when rushing about with neighbor boys. With limited food to go around, their desire for roughhousing decays.

Duncan leads Thomas through the market, instructing him as he propositions meat sellers for employment, making known his years of experience as a shepherd and butcher. At last he is accepted to be put on for a few days the following week slaughtering hogs and presenting cuts fresh according to buyers' tastes. Just as he feels relief to finally have some promise of money in his future, Duncan notices a small wad of beef fat clenched in Thomas' fist. Immediately fearful of punishment, he promptly leads Thomas by the arm to return the stolen morsel and humbly asks for forgiveness.

Upon reaching home, Duncan carries Thomas into the small room, lies him down on the straw mat and tells him, "This isn't the life I thought it'd be. And I'm sorry for that, son."

Duncan brushes Thomas' hair away from his eyes and says, "But just as God gave you another chance in that storm, we have a chance at life here."

Duncan, upset, puts his hand on Thomas' shoulder.

Thomas tells him, "An angel saved me."

Duncan says, "I believe it with all my heart," and kisses his head softly.

Standing in the doorway Duncan says, "Poverty makes a man desperate, makes you do things that are beyond you, things God looks down upon. Never steal Thomas, never hurt anyone—you must work for your gain honestly, you hear me? No matter how hard it is."

Thomas whispers sweetly and truthfully, "Yes, father."

"God will be on your side if you do right."

Thomas listens intently.

"Always listen to your heart. God is there—he will lead you. Now say your prayers."

Duncan makes a good impression on those he works for. His diligence and knowledge prove useful, though the wages are slim. If there is a large quantity of meat to cut and sell, they need him; otherwise he only receives a few hours oftentimes or nothing at all.

"What we need is to get a spot on a farm. We did well at our old home," Duncan says to Annabel.

She replies, "It's different here, we have to realize. There are many more people. We can't be sure of anything. We can't assume it will be the same, but I think it's worth a try."

The next morning Annabel readies Thomas for their outing to the local Anglican Church to hear some words of hope, of communal cares, to remind herself that she is not alone in these hard times. She fits on her bonnet over her rolled hair, fidgeting with it until she is finally secure that it is properly in place. She knows that the aristocratic ladies will be watching for err in a common woman's way of dress. She cannot risk slipping in her obedience to the state ordered decree and end up in bondage. The Crown dictates what one may wear, how they may wear it, and what items may accompany. One must never step beyond the borders of their class.

Just before they leave their home, Thomas places on his head his fitted cap. Holding his mother's hand, he steps with her into the frosty air of this wintry Sunday. For Thomas, the world does not extend much beyond that of his mother and father. He desires nothing more than such an excursion as this, to the damp church rebuilt through the ages over weathered foundations, to be huddled in a blanket on his mother's lap.

He hears the words of the preacher, the words spoken relating the story of Moses: the plagues, the slavery and the boils seem very real to him; he sees this every day. The idea of God punishing people—those who deserve it, what an idea! The Angel of Death electrifies his mind with grandness. God's power is something to tread lightly under, but to be on God's side! Why would anyone go against God knowing how he punishes those who do? It seems so easy to Thomas, pondering this question while resting his head on his mother's lap: just follow God, love—it is so easy, but still people do not. This he could not figure out at all.

"Wake up Thomas, we're here," Annabel says.

Thomas raises his head from his mother's lap. He recalls a blurry moment of leaving the church, but what surrounds him does not make sense. The sky shows forth, the sun free of the structures blocking the skyline. His back lies on the hard bed of a hay cart; before him he sees several poor folk, some in youth, some longer in years. Their faces are filthy. Their voices culminate not into words, but to Thomas like a sound that a wagon wheel might make. They step off onto the soil and filter down the road.

Thomas does not recognize the scenery around him. A team of workers in the midst of an expansive field rake up loose rye grass into a bundle higher than they are. The freshly cut blades waft in the smell of life, the freeness of the country. He smells the sweet scent of manure riding on the wind. Immediately a memory-flash sends his heart beating faster—he thinks his parents have brought him back to the farm he had been born on, the only place he considered home. In his mind he is away, finally away from that cruel city, to the life before boarding that ship. He is back to the life in which his parents were happy, when his father tended the needs of Allen's farm, keeping the sheep in pristine condition. His mother worked the wool, cleaning it and working it into beautiful woven articles for market. Thomas had no idea of what money was then, that it was possible to be poor. The land provided all they needed. Since Allen was kind and giving, it had completely slipped Thomas' mind that they were of a low social status.

Thomas smells his shirt. The dry hay that clings to it reminds him of the bread topped with sweet butter Allen's daughter Mary would make. He remembers her kissing his cheek and always calling him kind names. He thought of her as his older sister. "Where was she?" he wondered. Why were mother and father in no rush to get back to their home? And where are Allen and his sheep? Thomas learned to walk while studying his father tending those animals; wishing to feel the lamb's softness, he sprung up at once and has been in motion ever since. He knows these sights and smells as if they are a part of him. They must be home now. If this is true, then why are mother and father acting so lazy?

Thomas leaps from the cart and rushes toward an old, gnarled oak tree. He lets himself swing freely from a low hanging branch, taking in the massiveness of the world before him, the cascading hills that lay cluttered, propping up trees, sprayed with the yellows of the horizon. Duncan helps Annabel to the ground and they make their way to the foot of the tree. She sweeps sprigs and dust from Thomas' back and sets down a bundle wrapped in a handkerchief. They set themselves on a large, flat root—a perfect seat. Annabel unfolds the thin cloth. She motions her hand sweetly and says, "Come dear, Thomas, try this."

At the call for food he answers readily. Thomas seats himself in the untamed grass strewn with acorns with his mouth open wide; the moistness of the earth seeps to his skin. His mother removes from a small jar a preserved sugar cherry and places it on his tongue. At once he loses the drive to wander. The sweetness captivates him, fills his senses with an overwhelming tart, the flavor of happiness. Annabel places another in his mouth once he has savored the first. He radiates with joy. Never had he known such goodness. His mother, the messenger of this God-sent wonderfulness, is a saint.

They lie in the patch of green all afternoon enjoying the happiness of nature. The three, used to the ache and suffocation the close quarters of city life can bring, revel in closeness now: Father, mother, and son. Throughout the day their backs press into the cool, wet earth, while they study the labors of a blackbird fluttering in the branches, and honeybees so meticulous in their occupation among the honeysuckle.

Thomas follows his parents from house to house. Duncan asks if he can be of service, making it known his skills in a field and with animals. Annabel offers to help with washing or mending of clothes, cooking or cleaning and so on. Just before sundown an elderly woman named Sarah accepts Annabel's services and allows them all to stay in her barn. She has not much more to offer than food and shelter, therefore placing the weight of responsibility to earn money on Duncan's shoulders. This excursion to the country was not a holiday. The purpose in traveling far from home was a desperate attempt to find work, as it is near impossible to acquire in the city, being crammed shoulder to shoulder with desperate folk.

As Sarah cannot easily keep up with what has to be done around her house, Annabel is never without work. The dust has piled seemingly on everything, save for Sarah's favorite chair, an Italian Sgabello, an ornate work in which a cross is designed into the back. It is not the most comfortable place to recline, having no armrests and being of a peculiar slenderness in the seat, but its rarity hints that her family must have been wealthy at one time.

On the first day, Annabel spends the whole afternoon scrubbing clean the exterior of the house which had become caked with dirt. The originally white stucco is now tinged with filth and cobwebs to the extent that it appears as if it had been abandoned. The crossing timber framework on the exterior had accumulated so much dust in the corners that one hand cannot collect it all in a single grasp. The stucco has collected enough material that it appears to be a steep-sided cliffside covered with miniature bird nests.

While Annabel is busy, Thomas wanders in search of the prettiest wildflowers to fill vases for his mother and Sarah. He enters the house again and again with bundles of daisies, white elders, blood red poppies, yellow cowslip and irises, towering violet bugles, tiny wood anemones, red clover, and soft clusters of pink yarrow with their little white knots in the centers.

Duncan stands among more than thirty who also wish for work. There are limited spots, so all here covet the positions dearly. Several figures work scythes upon the flowing sea of grain in the distance. The men waiting push forward, crushing each other before a noble wearing a white jerkin fitted over his burgundy doublet with gold embroidery, slashed to fit snug around the waist. He wears a black leather codpiece and a rounded hat of the same color with a peacock feather stuck in, standing high above his head. The noble calls out while pointing at random: "I'll take you, you, and—the short one right there."

The chosen make their way beside a hedge. The noble waves the others off.

"That's all for today. There's always tomorrow!" the noble says.

Most of those remaining stay still for a time, unsure of what to do. Duncan draws a weary look across his face, his eyes glossing over with moistness. He steps toward the one in charge and asks, "My Lord, might you know of someone—"

"I know what you're going to ask. No, it's all the same around here. Your only hope is to be more desperate than the rest."

"I am desperate. I have skills with shearing, raising, and slaughtering animals. My wife and child can work a field. She can knit, make, and mend garments. We only ask for the smallest compensation."

"Not that kind of desperation," the Lord says. "You're not the only one from the city. Not the only one with a family or offering special skills. Travel out farther into the country, farther away from familiar surroundings than others are willing to go. That's the only way. Just keep trying."

Duncan nods and slowly turns around. He follows the other poor lot silently, for they have no words they care to share.

For a week Duncan attempts to acquire work but only manages to be admitted to one half day piling hay onto a cart. The pay received for this labor will be reduced to even less as they will likely have to pay for their ride home. Meanwhile, Annabel makes Sarah's house shine. She washes all of her clothing by hand and even knits her wool stockings for the coming winter, because she has been so hospitable. Sarah shows her thankfulness by sending them home with a sack full of bread and cheeses. She also gathers a pile of seeds from some old dead flowers Annabel had cleared from her bedroom and places them in a small locket held tight by an interlaced metal clasp.

Sarah presents this gift to Thomas. She tells him, "One day your family will have a nice, big house in the country like this one. There you can plant these seeds and remember how it was when you were young." She embraces Annabel, her eyes moist with tears both for thankfulness and for her own loneliness. She says to her, "You will make it, dear. Life is hard, but I promise you God will ease your pain."

Sarah disappears into her house and hands Annabel two dresses and a bag containing a small number of household items. She tells her, "Use these or sell them to get by. Please take them. I wish I could have offered you more." She enters her house again and exits with the flowers and a vase. She presents these to Annabel, telling her, "Put those in your house. Make it look beautiful like you made mine. Remember me, won't you?"

Sarah gives each of them a hug and waves them off. "Come any time. If you are in need you have a place here," she says. They nod and thank her again, then wander down the road in search of a ride.

Now, back at their home, Thomas' parents argue hour after hour behind their closed door while Thomas sleeps near the smoldering fire glowing in the hearth. The smell of cereal wafts through the room out of the kettle that contains the remains of supper. Duncan opens the door and sternly says to Annabel, "I will not be shown up, do you hear me?! I am the head of this household and I will not be shamed this way!"

He thrusts himself out the front door and slams it behind himself with a great crash. Annabel stands in the half darkness of the bedroom doorway. She rubs her wrist as if it had been yanked violently and wipes the tears from her eyes. Thomas wishes to speak, to ask his mother what is the matter, but before he can she turns and shuts the door behind her. In his childish ignorance he finds himself completely lost as to why this has happened.

# 7

# Drink to Forget

THERE IS A HOUSE five down from Thomas', next to the corner on the left, in which the occupants are heard carrying on just about every night. They are friends of Humphrey, who must receive a considerable cut off their rent, for they never seem to be needing to head off to work, or anywhere for that matter. There is always a circulation of people coming and going from that place to take part in the revelry, the dancing and drinking, to howl all night, singing rounds to the accompaniment of the twang of the lyre and the piercing whine of the flute.

Thomas sees his father coming from this house the second morning after his sudden departure. Dawn shows its royal purple up above the array of black triangular rooftops. Through the gray fog that settles in this small tunnel of houses, he watches his father place one unsteady foot after another, managing to keep his balance, despite the network of rain-molded ravines. Duncan sleeps though the afternoons and arises with an aura of gloom that settles on every inch of their house.

When father leaves, the darkness leaves with him. It hovers about him, following him like a storm cloud, churning his turmoil. As Duncan steps out the door every day when the sun still stands bright and yellow, the darkness lifts more the farther he gets. Thomas loves his father, but the truth is that he seems to be only bringing sorrow to his family most recently.

Mother, in her simple sort of love, is a relief. When she strokes his hair the world around disappears. Nothing else matters. Every day he helps her water the flowers grown from Sarah's seeds. They had been placed in two old rickety boxes Annabel found by the roadside. Her little effort in patching the holes with rolled up hay allow the boxes to hold soil just fine. The flowers are an extension of her ability to bring a feeling of joy to a drab, dreary life. Thomas helps her water them, taking great care in his attempt to mimic her ability to nurture. Most of the flowers never grow at all, or sprouted from the soil but then wither in having to grow in almost total darkness. What harm is there in giving them a chance?

The blue-purple bugles flourish, their green mass of leaves filling the house with a sweet mint-like scent. A few yellow irises survive as well, also being lucky to be tall and have the ability to grow at a slant, taking in the partial sun. A few daisies also grow, though they are noticeably weak, their petals discolored and drooping. Annabel tends to these every day, despite many being in poor condition. She speaks to them even, coaxing them on. This causes Thomas to see them as being his companions too. This caused him cheer. As he dances around the room and sings to them he has something to hope for. For their determination, she decides, they deserve the chance to live and not be uprooted. Those that look unsightly don't ruin the image of the rest. On the contrary, they better it. To see the flowers lean to such a degree seem to be an unspoken show of yearning, a wish to return to the wilds of nature and bask in the sunlight.

Thomas is awoken in the middle of the night by the sound of the carousing going on down the block. He quietly gets to his feet and exits the house, careful not to awaken his mother. Slowly, he shuts the door and leaves barefooted. He can see the warm yellow of candlelight beaming and wavering on the building opposite from the one his focus is on. Cackling erupts from several voices. Wasted singers peal out and instruments play off-time on the second floor. The dark plays on Thomas' fearful mind, and so causes him to be more agile, rushing to the source of light. He peeks through the window, seeing Humphrey engaged in telling some story to his companions. His voice sounds as a belligerent hollering, followed by the ever constant cackle.

Thomas carefully opens the door, hoping no one would notice. He slips within and hides beside a plush chair, spying a woman in the room opposite to the one Humphrey is in. Her hair is hopelessly in knots and her legs are clenched in a tight hold around a burly soldier with blonde, curly locks. Her blush is as red as a butcher's work-floor. She pulls him on top of her, her hands thrashing his hair, giving him sloppy tongue kisses all over his face. He loves it.

Humphrey grabs Thomas and grumbles, "You're not supposed to be here!"

Thomas stands dumb in confusion.

"What do you want? You wanna see yer dad? Shit, this is no place fer kids!"

Humphrey grabs Thomas' arm and roughly leads him upstairs where a drunken chorus is erupting in perpetual song. Thomas sees his father sitting on a crate in a state of delirium, his head swaying in a stupor, barely able to keep from falling. Humphrey pats Duncan on the shoulder and leads him stumbling toward Thomas. He is so drunk he can barely see straight.

"Hey you, fella! You got a visitor!"

Duncan's head bobs and jerks in his attempt to focus against the force of his spinning vision. His eyes close and he nods off.

Thomas sits patiently, as innocent as ever, not knowing why his father would leave home to be so miserable.

"Buddy, your son's here! Wake up!"

Duncan jolts to attention. He allows the vision of his son to register in his mind. He cannot believe the embarrassment he feels. He can't believe this is real. These worlds are supposed to be separate. He's the father, the responsible one. Why, why must this happen? He tells Thomas as kindly as he can, "Go home son. I will see you later." At least he intended to vocalize those words.

Humphrey leads Thomas back to the stairs. Worried, Thomas looks back to his father who has one hand planted on the ground. Humphrey pushes Thomas on, attempting to console him. He says, "It's all right, son. All men need this sometimes."


Annabel sleeps with Thomas curled beside her, his limbs sprawled every which way, having kicked off the blanket that covered both of them. She hears the bedroom door slowly open. Duncan enters still stinking of alcohol and says, "Hello, love."

He packs up his few extra shirts, his pipe, and a few of his favorite books into a blanket and neatly ties it in a bundle.

"Whatever are you doing?" she asks.

He says, "My family will have food on the table tonight. After all, we are not stray dogs," and storms out determined.

She rises to her feet and catches him before he exits the front door, lightly tugging on his shirt sleeve. They embrace for a moment, then kiss. With a look she expresses her worry and care for him.

"I will be back soon," he says and departs.

# 8

# A Blessing or Curse?

THE CLOTH MARKET is filled with folks in great need trying to sell their wares. A straw-covered peasant holds a small chest before a merchant and trades it for a moderate sum. Duncan faces a merchant who looks over the objects before him and ponders their worth.

"They are not in very good condition, you see," the merchant tells him with a pale, blank expression on his face.

The merchant contemplates a moment, then drops six copper pennies in a bag. Duncan takes the bag in hand and makes his way back where he came. A beggar creeps just behind him, sweating profusely and breathing as though he were a dog panting; his hair lies stringy down his face and his mouth lies open and desperate. He appears shaky and violently ill.

"Spare a penny that I might buy a speck of bread?" the sickly beggar says.

Duncan stops slowly, cautious of the beggar's behavior. He shows a downcast look in order to attract pity while he holds out a trembling hand.

Duncan reaches in the bag slowly. Suddenly, the thief in disguise snatches the bag away as quickly as an adder and dashes within the crowd, disappearing with skill. Duncan frantically chases in the direction he saw the thief run. Looking high and low, he is nowhere to be found.

"I have been robbed! Somebody please help me! Stop that theee—!" He quits his effort, knowing his words to be in vain.

Duncan strolls, dragging his feet, feeling desolate. He presses his hands across his face in great frustration. Collapsing flat on the dirt road, staring at the sky, he mumbles words to himself and to God, almost as a mantra, "Oh God, what am I to do? What am I to do?"

He wanders throughout the day, contemplating how he can return home with nothing. He knows Annabel will understand. It is his foolishness that worked up this pride, causing him to place such a weight of expectation on his shoulders. It is his own self-hatred that brought him to this level of desperation. But is it so wrong to want to provide the basic necessities and not allow his wife and child to continually starve? Feeling drained, he seats himself in a patch of weeds beside a wall on an empty side street and falls asleep.

Duncan dreams of returning home with new clothes for the three of them, and in one hand a goose, in the other a bottle of wine. They wrap their arms around his neck and kiss him dearly. As he lays down his goods, he pulls an orange out of his pocket so his family can enjoy its sweetness.

He becomes alert as he notices the sound of something scratching in the soil. A healthy-looking, white-feathered chicken emerges from behind an old, cracked wagon tiller, pecking at the ground just ahead. Disbelieving his senses, he rubs his eyes. With this little feathered answer to his prayers still in his sight, he quietly gets up and stalks it. With silent strides, he nears it and scoops it into his arms and nearly flies down the road back home, grinning and laughing for joy all the way.

Is it stealing? No, it must be a gift.

From time to time Thomas visits Abraham and Gilbert, the sailors who had found the drowned boy. They promised Thomas, because they had taken such a liking to him, that if he ever brought them worms he would receive a sum in return. Thomas loves this responsibility, being able to hand his mother a small amount of earnings to help bring a bit of food to the table. He takes a pot shard out of a special hiding spot and a jar the sailors give to him to refill whenever they "use up the contents". He uses the pot shard to dig in the moist soil. The spaces alongside the houses have no shortage of worms because they love to churn through human waste. Thomas, being an innocent youth, is unaware of the possible hazards of such an occupation. He cleans the worms as best he can with his bare hands, even washing the little creatures in the settled pools in the road. If Annabel knew exactly what he was doing to become so covered in waste-saturated mud, she would put a quick stop to it, but she is busy with her own work weaving cloth and does not have time to bother with her boy "playing in the mud." She wipes him clean and washes his clothes, demanding he not do this again. He always promises and says he is sorry, but knows deep down getting dirty is a small price to help his family.

Thomas finds his way to a table where Gilbert and Abraham slice knives through sea bass and pike.

"Hi there! What're you doin'?" Thomas says.

"Oh hello, Thomas. Jus' another day's work," Abraham replies.

Thomas reveals his jar full of worms to Abraham.

"What's that ye got—ah, wonderful! Thomas has got us another batch of worms!"

Gilbert sets down a fish and steps over to Thomas, humoring him by taking the jar in hand and praising the contents as if it was pure gold, "Oh wow, so lively these are! These'll be sure to bring in the fish! Now what do ye think this would be worth?"

"At least four pennies, I think," Abraham says.

"Four? Here's five, son. How's that sound?"

Thomas nods his head enthusiastically in agreement and takes the money. He studies the sailors as they go back to their work gutting fish. Thomas stretches high to get a better view.

"Why don'cha let me try to catch fish some time?!" Thomas says cheerily.

"Sounds fine by me," Abe says.

"Really?" Thomas says smiling.

"Don' see why not."

Thomas rushes home as if on air. He passes the beggars and the starving children along the way. He stops in his tracks as he sees the woman from the house across the street being carried dead. Her wide-staring eyes and protruding jaw cause his face to be emptied of color. She is wrapped in a sheet and placed in a wagon. He slowly backs up, sliding his feet closer and closer toward his door, trembling. Thomas enters his house to see his father holding the live chicken in his hands. It flaps its wings and lets out a few quiet clucks. Duncan turns around toward Thomas.

"Look what I have!" he says laughing happily. "I prayed and God provided for us!"

Thomas' growing apathy refuses to let the tears come forth. His clacking teeth and desperate eyes give him away, though.

Duncan says, "What's wrong? Has something happened?"

"That lady," he says. "God killed her. He made her sick and she died."

Duncan is shocked to hearing this. He attempts to comfort his son by saying, "Sometimes... God just takes people and we don't know why."

Terrified, Thomas says, "He's going to kill us, too"

"What's that? Why would you say such a thing?" Duncan asks.

"It's in the Bible."

"Oh, that… But you see…"

"An angel will come… and kill us!"

"But God's people were fine, were they not? Because they believed."

Thomas sobs, becomes frantic, and hides under the table. Shuddering he says, "Please kill the chicken. I'm not moving from here!"

Annabel, in hearing her son's words, is disturbed.

Duncan, not knowing what his son is getting at, since he was planning on killing the chicken anyway, takes a large chopping knife and a bowl from the side of the room. He slowly sets the squirming chicken on a small wooden table. The chicken's neck hangs over the bowl.

With a heavy chop of the blade, the chicken's head seems to pop off of its body, save a small strand of skin. Only a slight screech is heard before the head bobs to the side. Blood drains from the chicken's gyrating torso as Duncan severs the last tendon with a sawing motion. A small bowl full of blood sits on the floor. Duncan picks it up and places it on the table.

Thomas is somewhat terrified at seeing the chicken's body lie limp on the table before him, but finds new strength within himself. He takes the bowl and heads for the bedroom door. Before the door, Thomas scoops a handful of blood and smears a vertical line, which runs all the way to the floor.

"Now you do it," Thomas says to his parents with blood drenched hands.

Duncan and Annabel stand perplexed. Duncan says confidently, "That is quite all right. We'll be just fine."

"No, you have to!" he says, becoming more emotional.

"Thomas!" Annabel says, kissing him on the cheek. Wiping the tears from his eyes she says, "There's nothing at all to worry about."

After roasting the meat over the fire, Duncan and Annabel begin eating.

Thomas feels compelled to sit in the corner and concentrate on the floor. Images of his mother and father play before him as if he were in a dream. In his mind they are afflicted by an oncoming black cloud, and after it passes they are ill. He breathes heavily as he is taken closer, hovering over them as they drag their feet in a stupor. The fear forces him to fight to retain focus. Slowly the swirling vision of doom dissipates and he becomes more aware of where he is and his surroundings. He rises and joins his parents at the table.

His father asks him, "Smells good, doesn't it?"

Thomas grimaces, jutting his lip forth and furling his brow. Keeping the ugly glare firmly set, he rips a juicy drumstick free with his dirt-and-blood-caked palm and fingers. He loses his will to put up a fight with the first bite. He didn't realize how long he has gone hungry. He smiles to his parents and wipes his mouth, causing it to be far dirtier than before. Duncan and Annabel return a loving smile and continue eating breast meat from their trenchers.

# Delerium

CONSTANTYNE, in that he is the owner of these properties, he must visit Humphrey, at minimum, on a monthly basis to make sure everything is in order and to collect rent. He passes Thomas on the road. Thomas' hands are filthy and has a deep redness smudged over them. Concerned, Constantyne asks him, "What have you been up to?"

Thomas replies, "We marked our door."

"Marked your door? With what?"

"Blood."

"And why is that?" Constantyne says, imagining his property stained and defiled.

Thomas answers timidly, "Because God wants us to. He will send his angel and we need to be ready."

"Or what?"

"He will kill us."

"Oh really? Do your parents believe this?"

"Yes."

Constantyne lets the boy pass and continues to the house of Duncan and Annabel. He knocks and soon Annabel answers, slowly swinging the door open. With a glance Constantyne sees no red stain and is in one sense relieved.

Annabel kindly gives a slight bow and says, "Welcome. Is there something the matter?"

He asks her, "May I ask you of a matter concerning your son, miss?"

"Yes."

At hearing this, Duncan rises from his seat and stands before Constantyne, greeting him with a nod.

Constantyne tells them, "Just a moment ago your son told me a disturbing story about how you all slathered this door with blood due to a belief that it would save you from a heaven sent plague."

Duncan says, "Sir, I have no idea about this which you are speaking of."

Laughing, Constantyne says, "I figured, in seeing that this wood is clean. Still, perhaps I would be going too far to say you should be concerned, though there was something in his conviction that startled me. There was no sort of play, but only the utmost seriousness."

Annabel says, "Do not feel odd in telling us this. I have noticed a strangeness in him—"

"Ever since the fire, I've noticed it," Duncan says cutting in.

"Yes," Annabel says, continuing. "I know my son better than anything in this world. And I know being trapped in that church strangled out some part of him. I thought it was a miracle that we found him alive, but what emerged, a piece was taken from."

Constantyne takes this all in and finally nods in respect and to show appreciation for the tribulation they have silently borne up to this moment.

He says, "I have known him to be generally kind. I wish him recovery with all my heart. Let us work together if we can do anything at all."

They thank him and he backs out of their doorway with a slight wave.

Several times that day, Constantyne passes Duncan and Annabel's house in checking up on some tenants. An unmistakable smell of rot catches hold in his nostrils upon each stroll. The scent intensifies suddenly around a certain spot, and so, in letting his nose lead, he arrives before Duncan and Annabel's house. His eyes dart about as he stands there, looking for what it could be. He overturns some remnants of broken tables and chairs and sees there two toes of a chicken sticking out of the loose soil. Taking up the shattered leg of a table, he shovels with the sharp end and reveals a whole chicken. None of it was cut up to be consumed, although its belly has been torn open, the marbled intestines and various organs lying coiled outside the body.

A week later another strange thing occurs. Humphrey, while patrolling the streets late at night, sees a figure lurching along the wall. He spies from afar before possibly inviting a confrontation and notices the person vigorously scratching his face. He can see he is hunched over. His jaw jerks nervously side to side while every so often garbled words spill forth.

The words echo through the silent streets and must be disturbing those who occupy the houses. Humphrey sends a servant to visit Constantyne's house and bring him. Even though he may be unhappy to be woken at such an hour, and the strange person may be no harm to anyone, it is better to be wary and avoid a mishap.

Constantyne arrives in a carriage accompanied by two soldiers who bear swords but no armor. He disembarks and strolls up to Humphrey who stands waiting patiently.

"Thank you for coming, my Lord," Humphrey says.

"It's no matter," Constantyne says, signaling his driver to hand him the lantern hanging near him. "Lead me to what you speak of."

The hazy yellow glow from the lantern bathes the vicinity. It lights little more than their torsos, the features of their faces, and the nearest cobblestones. Humphrey enters the alley. And so they venture into the filthy yellow and stark black shadow. He stops suddenly and holds his arm out to block the others from moving farther. They hear an erratic rustling and a sound emitting that expresses suffering.

They all carefully inch closer and see the figure hunched over on its knees. It slowly, perhaps in a way to express some painful emotion, pounds the ground with its fists. Constantyne steps forward, followed by his guards, with light footsteps.

The sound of mourning and torment come from the lips of the one huddling before him. As Constantyne steps very near, the person turns his face to him. It is Thomas. His face has been scratched deep. His nails are bloody. Constantyne is taken aback by the sight.

Quivering, Thomas says, "My skin is burning."

"Stop it! You're hurting yourself."

"It burns," Thomas says.

Constantyne slaps Thomas' hand away from his face.

"Stop this!" Constantyne says sternly.

Thomas replies with words muffled, "I can't stop it. I can't."

"What can't you stop?" Constantyne asks him, now with more compassion.

Thomas presses his head hard into the crook of his left arm. A moment later he utters, "There's screaming above me—of children, of girls and boys, of men and women—"

Constantyne says, "Thomas—"

Thomas speaks, shaking, filled with hatred and sadness, "I can still feel the pain. I gave myself to the fire… I was dead."

Constantyne notices his heart beating faster. He doesn't know what to say.

"I was dead. I don't want to be here," Thomas says.

Constantyne knows the boy is right to feel this way. He inflicted this upon him.

"What can I do to help?" Constantyne asks.

Thomas breathes hard. He says, "Make them go away."

He coughs.

"You shouldn't be out here," Constantyne says. "It's dangerous."

"I scare my mother when I get like this. She has enough to worry about."

"I'm sure—"

"I hate you," Thomas says with his nostrils flaring.

"I know you do."

Duncan packs up some clothes and a few small loaves of bread. He looks in on Thomas who still has scratches covering his face and is in a state of delirium.

"Goodbye son," Duncan says. "Your father's got to make money."

He kisses Annabel and heads out the door, determined to make life easier by following the advice he was told on their last trip to the country: travel farther than others are willing to. He will return every so often with any money he receives, then relocate his wife and child if the situation is significantly better in another place.

Thomas misses his father. The void in the home makes him realize how much of a difference he makes. If he wishes to share something new he saw or ask a question only his father could answer, Thomas will often rush home in his usual way only to find an empty seat.

One day, as Thomas' scratches are beginning to heal, two boys see him and approach. They ask him, "Hey, what happened to your face?"

They laugh and point.

"You fall or somethin'?" the orange-haired one says.

Thomas attempts to ignore them.

"What's wrong with you?" the brown-haired one says. "I think he's broken up here," he continues, pointing to the side of his head.

"Go away," Thomas says.

"What's that?" the orange-haired one says laughing. "Look at his eyes. There *is* something wrong with him. He's off somewhere else."

They push him, but Thomas catches his balance and keeps on walking.

"What's wrong, scab-face?" the brown-haired one says. "Turn around," he says pushing him from behind. "Turn around," he says again and again pushing him each time.

Suddenly they have enough and both start punching him in the side of the head, in the ribs, everywhere. Thomas scurries away to evade the blows. As they chase him down, he holds up his hands in front of his face and throws a heavy punch. The brown-haired boy easily dodges and counters. Blood streams from Thomas' nose. He swings wildly, landing a few, but receiving many more, finally getting knocked to the ground by a hard strike to the chin.

The orange-haired boy tries to kick him, but he pulls on his leg making him hop to keep balance.

"I'll show you, you—" the brown-haired boy says, kicking Thomas in the ribs. Thomas cowers to protect himself. They get in a few more shots before a merchant pulls them apart.

Thomas encounters these boys every few days, and a similar finale results each time. They strike and he gets bloody. That is, until he begins to notice weaknesses each of them have. The orange-haired boy only blocks from the front, so a good hook can get through. The brown-haired boy leaves himself extended and his arms remain down too long after punching. In having plenty of practice, Thomas teaches himself to lay his weight into his strikes and to stay loose so as to maneuver around their attacks.

Finally, one day it is obvious: Thomas is better at fighting than they are. He smashes his fists all over the orange-haired boy's jaws, then pounds him square in the nose. Then he takes the air out of the brown-haired boy by shooting a blow to his stomach after watching carefully for when he would attempt his clumsy strike. As the boy is choking for breath, Thomas charges him and slams his head repeatedly against a brick wall, hoping that would make them decide to quit picking fights with him.

"Who looks fucked up now, you bastards?"

Thomas only ends up celebrating his victory for a few weeks' time, for his father returns quite ill.

"I got caught in the rain far from town. I was soaked and freezing for hours after sundown," Duncan tells Annabel and Thomas.

Annabel watches over Duncan who is shivering with fever next to the hearth. She saturates his forehead when his body goes hot. When he goes cold, he drags his crippled legs to the fire and clasps his knees just out of reach of the flame. He loses his chicken supper in the first hour, plagued by convulsions to vomit once the jolts start to shoot through him. His is a frog, croaking out yellow bile. By the time the second hour arrives, his eyesight becomes a blur with white stars flashing randomly. In the third hour his stomach swells and he feels an agonizing pinch in his gut. Sitting on a bucket with the world swirling, he releases constant bursts of diarrhea that, to Annabel's great fright, are filled with broad swirls of shimmering red blood.

Thomas awakes from his pallet mat of straw to hear his father moaning outside. Still sleepy-eyed, he opens his door wide enough to poke his head through. He spies his father lying by the fire writhing in pain and quivering. Annabel rises from his side and calls softly to Thomas, "Your father is sick. Come on."

Thomas groggily enters the main room with his mother.

Duncan moans, "My bones ache."

Annabel declares, "Let's be off."

Fifty-some sick people line up before a makeshift hospital formed by a series of sheet-built-tents behind the Dartford Priory monastery. Many people lie prostrate on the ground. All anyone knows to do is to offer a place to rest. The nuns provide a few kind words to the sick to allow their time to pass easier. Some people sweat and shake violently. Duncan is soaked with moisture. His eyes appear sunken in and he holds his head as if in severe pain. Thomas notices a small stain on the back of his father's pants and the foul, sharp odor he knows too well. He also recognizes that his mother is appearing weak, shivering as Duncan did earlier.

Duncan, delirious from the pain pressing on his bones, looks as if he would gladly welcome a bludgeoning to ease his suffering.

A black-clothed figure with tight, pursed lips ahead of them turns his head and says, "We waste our time! We are damned to taste death!"

A physician yells something far ahead and continues down the line. Again the figure speaks, "Hear my words! Repent of your sins for none shall escape! Our Father has sent plague to swallow up the sin festering throughout our merry England!"

Ahead in line, a fellow comforting his sick wife turns and violently grabs him by the collar and says "Shut your filthy mouth, or I shall send you to your maker before your time!"

The physician stands before Thomas' family and tells them, "I am truly sorry, but we have not one bed left. It would be best for you to return to your homes."

The figure in black goes mad at hearing these words. He says, "It is true. We're a hopeless lot! Prepare for judgment! We shall meet our lord soon!"

Duncan, Annabel, and the couple ahead in line appear distraught. Thomas peers through the trees and sees bodies being unrolled out of their sheets and into a mass grave.

Duncan asks the physician, "Perhaps tomorrow there will be room?"

The physician stops cold. Two pairs of physicians carry two dead children past Thomas' family followed by a crazed, weeping woman.

They all very slowly return home. Duncan and Annabel embrace each other upon arriving. Thomas motions to open the front door.

Thomas' mother tells him, "No, son. We need you to catch us a nice, big fish so we will feel better again."

Tears stream from Thomas' eyes. "I don't want to!" he says crying aloud.

Annabel tells him, "We need to lie down. We are ever so tired."

"Mother! Daddy!" he says, reaching out.

They back away from him. Thomas throws a fit. He motions to hug them.

Duncan snaps, "No! Go on! Get away from here! We are sick. You must not touch us!" He lies down and prays.

Annabel backs into the darkness saying, "Go on. I love you."

"Mother! No!" he says heartbroken with tears gushing from his bloodshot eyes.

"Catch us a big fish so we can grow strong again," his mother tells him as she shuts the door behind her and locks it. Thomas bangs on the door.

"Momma! Father!" he says, tiptoeing as high as he can, unable to glimpse through the windows. He turns away and wanders down the road.

Dockside, Thomas is mesmerized watching the men at work. Thomas speaks to the sailors as they ready their gear and unload a large catch. He wanders to his friend Abraham who is busy cleaning fish.

"Hey there lad," the old sailor says. "Why don't ya try this out?"

With the sailors' guidance, Thomas chops the head off of a fish and slices it along the belly as the fisherman shows him how.

"Not bad at all for the first try," Abraham says. "You should sail with us today."

"Really, can I?" Thomas says with a smile.

"Sure," he says. "We always need another hand on deck. I'll teach ya how."

"What d'ya say? You ready, son?" Gilbert squeaks, still busy slicing.

Excitedly, Thomas replies, "Yes. Yes, I'm ready,"

"Then take this. You'll need it," Abraham says, handing him one side of a net.

Thomas fumbles with it, half carrying, half dragging it as he enters the fishing boat. The old sailor shows Thomas how to use it. He holds it before his face, explaining the process. He stands focusing into the water hoping to catch sight of life down below. Gilbert, slurping a mug of ale, guides the boat though a stretch of sea.

He drunkenly says to Thomas, "I need a hand over here, son."

Thomas tries to keep his balance, carefully making his way to the sailor's side.

"Go on," Gilbert says. "It's not going ta steer itself."

Thomas places both hands onto the tiller and Gilbert takes a mighty swig from his drink. After a quick swallow he says, "Aye, looks like we have a new captain. Hurray for Captain Thomas!"

Abraham says, "Nicely done. You'll make a fine sailor."

Thomas smiles and stares across the surface of the sea while holding firm onto the tiller. Though he falls occasionally as the ship tilts, Thomas enjoys every minute of it.

Later, as evening falls, Thomas pulls upon the netting.

"How's it feel?" Abraham asks.

"It feels heavy," Thomas says. "Is that normal?"

"Nothing can be counted on," Abraham says, lifting the net. Thomas and the drunk lend a hand.

"Not bad. Not bad at all!" Abraham judges.

"Ha!" Thomas says jumping about. He feels the wet scales as he holds on tight to the lines of the netting. The fish spray him with seawater as they flop about within.

Having been out for longer than he realized, Thomas feels a chill, noticing the curtain of black spread overhead. He carries a fat fish in a wrap like a baby while hurrying down the road, struggling not to drop it. All the way the dampness over his skin intensifies the coldness. His legs gather speed as his mind centers on the image of his mother tending a fire. Reaching his house, he kicks the front door as a way of knocking. He kicks again and again.

He yells, "Mother! Father! Open the door!"

He listens with his ear up to the door. He kicks and kicks but no one answers.

Thomas says loudly, "I caught a big fish for us to eat! Mother?! Open the door! Where are you?!"

Humphrey approaches Thomas holding a lantern.

"What's the matter?"

Thomas says, "They won't open the door."

Humphrey asks him, "What's that? Did you steal it?"

"No, I caught it," Thomas says, struggling under the weight.

"They won't open the door? Hmm, I wonder what the problem is," Humphrey says as he fumbles with his keys. He finds the one he's looking for and opens the door. He enters the dark house. The creak of the bedroom door is heard and then a sudden expression of disgust emits. Humphrey rushes out of the house, leaving the doors open.

"Don't enter there, whatever you do!" he says, bolting down the street. Thomas stands perplexed. He slowly stretches his neck to see only darkness. A bit orange of light from the fire illuminates the next room through the open bedroom door. He lurches farther inside and peers within to see the stone cold faces of his parents. His mother is prone, face-down on the straw mat.

Thomas shrieks, leaps out of the front door, and throws the wrapped fish into the gutter. He runs wild down the street and bellows like a dog. He collapses in the dirt. His cries are hysterical.

# 10

# A Friend

AFTER LOSING HIS PARENTS, Thomas went the way so many children do when they have no other means to get by: Crime as a means of survival. At first he was tolerant of the behavior he received as a beggar. Being smacked or receiving verbal insults seems to be just part of the production line. Doing odd work never quite works to get him far enough ahead of his hunger.

Thomas is now running with a boy named Charles. Neither can remember exactly when they first became friends because it was more of a gradual thing. They were focused on stealing loot from market stalls, filling their stomachs. They both recall the other making an impression, Charles striking Thomas as unusually clean for a boy on the street. His clothes were washed and his face was scrubbed. Even his hair was trimmed regularly, how, Thomas had no clue. Thomas struck Charles as particularly filthy, even compared to the other boys they spent their time with. His hands had a perpetual layer of dirt and grime upon them and when he would place them in his mouth to eat, Charles made sure to face the other way.

It's difficult to say why people choose the friends they do, but Thomas and Charles seem to be of the same mind, run in the same mode, and share a unique strength of will. It was after hearing his account of his parent's death that Charles took to him. Thomas led him to a riverbank and shared some thick beer as he told this story:

"I couldn't help myself. All I could do was call out to express the deep sadness I was feeling. The sound of my own wailing echoed back. I thought it a shameful sound, so I quit. My mind fogged over and a pressure overtook my muscles, twisting them. My throat constricted, and deep in the air pipe throbbed a force reoccurring. The rush of fluid through my veins set my whole body and mind into a frenzy, of lunatic anxiety. Now numb, I wandered back to the old house. The light still flickered within. On clouds I walked, guided by God to this place of non-life, protected by the spirit in the form of madness so that the toxic effect of the experience may have trouble climbing through."

"Each step past the doorway seemed a venture into a chasm within the underworld. I hoped fervently, even as I gazed on their pale, motionless forms, that they would rise. As my perception of the world twisted in spirals I contorted my body, bending over and crouching like a badger. I crawled to my mother as reality slipped away. I slid my legs out, scraping my knee on the pebble-strewn dirt floor, and lay beside her. I knew I must be imagining it, but I felt I could perceive the slightest movement in her. I held my hand in front of her mouth. In keeping it there I swear I felt a breath, almost impossible to perceive, but in this mindset I suddenly felt empowered, capable of sensing what was not possible before."

"My father gave off a cold vibration, the whole corner of the room frozen and infecting everything nearby. I saw these phases of deep oceanic blue and black wafting off and sensed demons lurking in the most concentrated pools of sadness and fear. I knew I must save my father from this leeching of his soul. In an instant I became paranoid and twisted around toward the door, my eyes locked on the portal left open to the world. I stared into the open street and swallowed hard, unsure if someone had crept in during the briefest loss of concentration. I stepped quietly so as to not make a sound, then I tackled the door shut as quickly as possible."

"My attention went immediately back to my father."

"'I must save him', I thought. 'And I must not allow this possession of his body to grow and consume my mother.'"

"I sprinted silently and gripped my father's wrists and pulled him out of the ungodly tar and grease. The body was stuck firmly in this. The force needed to pull him out of this hole took every grunt and force of muscle tension I could muster. Finally he was out of the grip of the devils, but they wouldn't be long in returning. 'What can be done?' I wondered, while my father's body still dripped with the awful sludge."

"'The fire,' I said to myself. 'The fire,' I thought, mouthing the words, recalling that the Admiral and Humphrey would be there soon and would surely disgrace the bodies of my parents. They must be dealt with respectfully. They must be allowed to have their bodies consumed by nature without shame."

"I rolled the body of my father into the open flame, curling his legs and folding his arms to what seemed to me a comfortable sitting position. The cloth caught fire quickly, and then the hair ignited. I did not wait to watch the horrible end; I just knew my father was saved and would rise to heaven without any barrier. Then I knew I must rescue my mother before those fools barred my path of escape."

"'I will heal her,' I muttered to myself."

"Her body was drenched with sweat."

"'Speak to me mother. Don't go,' I said into her ear as I wrapped my arms around her rib cage, dragging her with the best of my ability. I let her rest as I swiveled the door on its hinges, opening the house to the world. My senses came alive as the coldness of the breeze and the minds of all those living nearby immediately became aware to me. I turned to take up my mother again and noticed the whole room was tight with smoke. The fire was blazing and hot."

"I slipped out with my mother, her bare heels dragging on the loose gravel. Her ribcage protruded so sharply. My fingers grasped onto the ridges of flesh-laced bone. I never noticed before how she must have been withering away. Her arms were like sticks, swinging like branches on a tree accosted by wind. I always saw her as beautiful and full of health, but at that time it seemed she had suddenly been carved hollow."

"I hurried as I saw the forms of the Admiral and Humphrey approaching, their shadows rising and falling at a faster rate as the smoke sneaked out in more abundance. I felt no worry though, for as I slunk against the buildings in the shadows I sensed no fixation of us in their minds. Their focus was on the house, so we safely escaped around the corner."

"Through the night I dragged her down the streets, softly speaking to her, unable to catch the dripping tears that fell from my eyes and rolled down her chest. I smelled the sweet oil on her skin and the nutty warmth of her hair, the same from my earliest memories, of being submerged in her scent whenever she held me. I gripped her, stumbling backwards, aimless, without hope or place in this open sore of the world which I had found myself drowning within."

"I arrived here at this riverbank, right on this spot. The rushing flow of water was the only thing that felt familiar and inviting to me. I could think of no other place to go. I lay my mother on the sandy mud and collapsed beside her. My body throbbed with pain as my mind began to achieve focus momentarily. My limbs were mush after all the blind exertion. I stared to her, still believing that I could see the sand move ever so slightly before her mouth during odd moments."

"I woke in the morning, surprised to find myself here. Immediately I was filled with a terrible rage in seeing my mother laying still, all illusions of her returning to life being futile. Also, I was enraged my mind would not focus, a dumbness swimming within it, making ordinary thoughts and movements impossible. I focused on her form again, the swirling images, pissed that my hope of an honorable burial were lost. I could not muster an ounce of spiritual strength, my body also lost to me, sapped of vigor and even the ability to cry."

"I pulled her up, the body now stinking. I held my breath and refused to look. In a very unceremonious manner I set her on the edge of the river—there next to that old boat. I filled her clothing with all the large stones I could find, and dumped her headfirst."

"I wandered as the fool of the world. My mind had left me as the most incapable creature imaginable. Often I would find myself suddenly strolling among the city people, unaware of how I arrived, or too often collapsed in an alley beside half eaten rats or old rotten slivers of bread. People treated me with the most unabashed expressions of horror that came through in the slightest flashes to my distorted consciousness. I was diseased. I knew that. My disease resembled that which my mother and father had, but why was I still standing?"

"In my mind I knew something of who I was, but lacked the ability to translate that to the outside world. I was led to a room within a prison and was allowed to rest and take in food that was not as bad as before. After a month in this cell, the haze finally began to wear off. My mind cleared up some, though I was still incapable of functions much beyond expelling fluids and being a cauldron of pain. The sickness receded little and tormented me constantly. I was allowed to vomit in the provided containers, actually making it in a greater amount of time as time went on. My survival was a wonder to the guards and doctors. They expected to toss my corpse within a week, but since my refusal to die had sustained, they nursed me partly due to their curiosity. This scientific-based fascination was more awe that anything, for it had no grounding in anything they knew. One day I was released back to the sun-drenched city. I felt blank but I was alive."

– 60 –

# Judith's Pain

IN THIS LIFESTYLE one must be extremely observant of the laws that send those caught for thievery to hang. Even begging receives harsh penalties. Both Thomas and Charles received thirty whacks from a wooden club for being caught receiving money in front of a popular pork restaurant. The boys wish they could strut like the lavish rooster-men, with the cloth around their upper arms and thighs puffed out as if tight with air, shimmering in the light with radiant thread. Everyone knows the most ludicrous-looking are the most willing to thrust forth the talon sitting in the sheath at their sides. In case the plume soaring from the crushed velvet cap upon such a head or the pomp he exudes does not sufficiently warn others of the individual's unrestrained ego, a point stuck in the belly will make sure the awareness is made. It is surely a society of poultry.

A woman who used to reside on the street not far from where the boys settled found her neck broke in a noose the year before for stealing eggs. She was only one of many who suffered death for a crime in a life that offered no alternative. Suicides are common. The deaths of children are frequent. No one wants to be a prostitute, but when one suffers starvation for years on end their mind and body is affected and something in the emptiness in the gut transfers to the spirit. We lose the will to really care. This is how one succumbs to have her body lost to the possession of lechers who dream at night how to better defile a whore's body.

Everyone knows someone or knows someone who knew someone who received the death penalty for stealing. How else can the poorest class make it besides by begging or stealing? Every one of them would love to work rather than suffer this, but how exactly should the quality of life be uplifted when it's difficult enough just to scrape together something so that hunger pangs do not torment them in sleep? It is evident that they are captive in a country that holds them prisoner, a country that forces laws on them that are so contradictory that it is evident that they are not even meant to make sense. The assumption is finally made that the laws are meant to support the rich and the reasoning declines as one attempts to apply official rule of order upon those who are barred from cooperating in that civilization. Reason declines because the existence of the poor is a reality the lawmakers wish was only a bad dream. It is something that can be ignored, and if one sees the poor on the street they can easily turn their head.

A group of girls stop by and see the boys on occasion, most of the exchange consisting of empty talk with nervousness weaving a near impassable barrier between the sexes. Usually the encounter consists of the girls seating themselves some safe distance off, but not so far away that the opposing camps cannot overhear the other's secrets if they strain hard enough and make sure to shush their comrades. With enough courage one slips into the ranks of the other, most notably Charles whom the girls take the most liking to. It is a nymph, a thin girl named Judith who catches his eye, and who has small sprouts of breasts pressing against her soiled, worn-from-wear dress. Her hair hangs in an impossible web of knots, the blonde mixed with faint strands of strawberry.

Judith peers through the crowd, piercing the fog of noise churned up by the other girls with her quiet pleasantness. She is still, neither smothering nor rebuking the boys as the others do. She fails in attempting to mime the traditions these girls practice, of letting fly any thought that comes to mind, of performing acts contrary to reason out of a fear, as though the universe would judge if they broke character. Mob rule and nature dictate, so the girls hedge Judith farther and farther away. This makes Charles all the more infatuated with her, for he senses he can be a source of comfort, and he very much loves to be able to shelter the warmhearted from the cruel world. He speaks softly to her.

It feels easy since she responds more like a friend than a girl, the rest of them seeming more like something alien like seabirds.

Charles and Judith soon begin disappearing off together. Her hands cling to him as if he would drift off like a leaf in the wind. Her wide, innocent smile spreads under squinting, joy-filled eyes. Charles is an on-and-off tenant among the urchins. The rest of the time, when he gets word from a relative, he meets with his family in their travels, performing rituals field to field to help raise the crops throughout the countryside. When he returns, Judith stays with him, her head on his chest in a cluster of fleas and friends. In the mornings often someone comes to fetch her. She never speaks a word of what occupation they require her for, his youthful innocence allowing him to oblige and let her leave out of duty to adult authority.

One morning Charles fixes a breakfast of porridge for himself and Judith. He carries the bowl through street after street to where he knows she stays. He knocks but receives no answer. Pushing the door open, he quietly lets himself in. In a room lit by one candle, women of vastly different ages sit in rows and stare at the ground. Since the window has been covered with plastered black wool so as to block out the sunlight, a morose, eerie mood is about. The wrinkled face of an old woman is cast in the heavy, wavering orange glow. The crevices seem as cascading valleys lit by an encroaching fire consuming the countryside. Several other women, some in their thirties, some in their teens, sit solemnly with all promise and hope stricken from their faces. They seem to be awaiting a fate they cannot escape, knowing they will be consumed by a beast, but have become tempered to not fuss about what is inevitable.

Charles ascends the stairs hearing a faint moaning come from the closest room. As hesitation takes hold of him his mind becomes alert to the chorus of groans sounding from the many worlds-in-wood down the dark hall. Pushing the door ajar, he sees the faint outline of bodies engaged in an act of raw gouging, like a person attempting to bore the core out of an apple. The man's hand is perched on a woman's buttocks as he lays into her. Her curly brown locks sway with her swinging flaps of breasts with in near perfect unison.

The scene frightens Charles, so he retreats and approaches the next door.

It is quiet. He slowly pushes the door open, hoping not to be heard, and there he sees the small frame of a little girl. Her small, stick-thin legs he follows to the pale twin hills of her buttocks. The thin ivory slope of her back lies still in the bed. He does not recognize her, but somehow he knows this is his sweet Judith. Peering through the crack in the door he overcomes his senses. He never wanted to view her this way, so cold, so sterile, a hateful image.

Pushing farther inward, he is paralyzed by fear. There stands a tall, stout figure with black curly hair hanging in his face, wiping clean his penis with a handkerchief. With his pants hanging loose on his rump, he takes care to rub his flaccid prick free of fluid, lifting it, and methodically stroking the underside as well. Charles steps in.

Surprised, the stranger asks with authority, "What is it, boy?"

Charles continues toward her not saying a word, though terrified of the great power before him. A bit demure now, the titan swiftly covers his pubic hedge and puts on his shirt. Now that the rush of adrenaline is making his head spin, Charles acts almost unconsciously. Seeing Judith's dress within the darkness, he lifts her up, slips it over her head and covers her body. In a daze she sets her legs onto the floor, following him, not yet aware it is him.

Outside the door she looks to his face and is overcome.

"No," she says struggling to return to the room. "I need da go back."

She pulls on his arm from blind reaction, but she is much smaller and weaker than him. The severe disorientation from alcohol consumption reduces her thrashing to aimless stumbling. He grasps her and plants her on his shoulder, digging his side into the wall as not to fall, taking each step down the stairs carefully.

Huffing a strained whine she says, "What are? I…" She then falls silent.

She seems to have gone back into a daze, staring to the floor. They pass the line of women without much notice and slip out the door.

"It hurts so bad," Judith says curled in a heap, resting her head on Charles' lap. A forest of legs passes by them on this busy street. Merchants call out, advertising their wares. Her eyes lie closed, clenched in pain. His arms surround her delicately as if she would burst like a bubble if he gave too much force. Sickness fills his chest and rises up as a poison burns through his throat. His eyes water as the evil that was thrust upon this poor innocent thing in his arms overwhelms him with visions. She presses her fingers repeatedly across her frail pelvis, massaging her soreness incessantly like a poor creature tormented by a skin disease. Did he possibly have the right to intervene so that she did not wear herself raw? Her legs twitch involuntarily from the pain as if she were suffering from cold. All he knows to do is to hold her, despising the passers-by on the road, cursing them if they dare look her way.

"Does your head still hurt?" Charles asks.

"No, it hurts down here," she says with her hands pressed on her pelvis. "It feels like he punched me a thousand times."

"Poor g—"

"It's all bruised, and there's blood."

"He will get punished. One day, you hear me?"

After half the day is passed sitting in that spot he says, "We need to get away from here."

He raises her up. She shrieks in pain and whimpers with each step.

"I'm sorry," he continues amid her sobbing. "This place is filled with sickness."

Through her tears she chokes out, "Where? Wu—We can't go anywhere."

"I have family. Would you like to get away to the country?"

She ponders the idea for the briefest moment, then silently nods, revealing some of her old joy.

# 12

# Off to the Country

WAGON WHEELS ROLL over unsteady earth. Somehow Thomas and Judith manage to sleep, their bodies resting on wood and their heads on pillows of hay. Charles stays alert, watching over the passing fields, paying close attention to the figures sowing seeds, tossing the contents of their bags over the bare soil. The sweet smells of spring ride on the wind, reminding him of growing up in this expanse of soil and plant-life. So happy it makes him to be free again, to be far from the human feces marinating in streams of piss. Pollinated floral delights are a relief from the constant musk wafting from the hordes of bodies he passes constantly.

He knows the signs of where his family resides almost by instinct. They work only a small string of plots in the countryside of Newbury. There are a series of bridges traversing the spider-webs of rivers, those being the river Lambourn which is a tributary of the river Kennet which branches off the Thames. Charles is looking out for one special bridge, one that would be overlooked by anyone else, but this old, rotted wood he knows will lead him to his mother and father. It is not often he is able to see them for, since they could barely feed themselves, it was arranged that he live with his uncle and learn the craft of woodworking. Charles knew well that he was unwanted by this graying recluse who was finished wrestling with the energies of others, who only wanted to whittle away for the last of his days.

The country houses finally give way to that mildewy bridge grown over by hanging trees. He asks the driver to halt his horse's progress, handing him a sixpence as they stop. Charles wakes his companions. They stretch out the kinks in their backs and begin down a long road between muddy fields, some with teams of horses pulling plows, preparing the life-giving earth for another season.

The day is spent wandering the road leisurely while Charles' eyes remain fixed like a fox sniffing out a mouse, his brain struck into alertness. It all works in efficient cooperation: tapping dormant memories to lead him to familiar territory. The heat has worn them down beyond the point they care to stand, so they wander down toward the stream that runs alongside the road. Under the cool cover of the slim poplars in rows, they carefully step down the muddy slope that must be under water at times when the level is higher. Removing their shoes, they step in fully clothed. The bottom is covered in stones that are, for the most part, worn into friction-softened, rounded edges. The farther they step in, the more surprised they are to find how the mud rushing through the water obscures how deep it is. Charles grasps onto Judith's hands tightly to keep her from getting swept away like some free-falling leaf.

The flow runs past, the surface diverging around their bellies. Thomas lets his feet up every few seconds and allows the force to drift him a ways. He dunks his head, letting chunks of caked dirt wash away. The cool, country air makes him feel as refreshed as ever, almost reborn. Charles plays a game with Judith, letting her hands go every few seconds, letting her float hopelessly away for a brief moment. She grins each time, half exclaiming from delight but also to chastise him out of the fear of drifting off for good.

The radiation of the sun warms their faces and shoulders, while underneath the surface is cool, almost unbearably so, especially if they stand still. A sense of heavenly glee grows within. The wind rushing through this miniature ravine stimulates their nerves to tingling, bringing the differing temperatures to a climax. They take it in, absorbing nature's ecstasy.

"Where is it? How much farther?" Thomas asks Charles, still feeling the radiance.

Charles does not attempt to answer. His mouth pinches shut. He stops and breathes in heavy, waiting to be criticized for leading them blind. Thomas just closes his eyes and floats.

Charles says, "Don't worry, I'll get us there. What are you waiting for?"

Thomas is focusing on something, concentrating. His breathing slows. He can feel the ripples lapping upon his skin as if the liquid all around is part of him. He feels some sort of power channeling into him through this liquid swirling with mud. Slowly, almost unconsciously, his legs take him before Charles. He rests his hand on his shoulder and closes his eyes. Thomas surges at odd intervals. The way his mouth gapes wide, taking in big gulps of air then releasing them, startles Judith.

Charles and Judith stand immobile in the face of this startling trance that has overcome Thomas. Suddenly his eyes flash out of the daze and Thomas says, breathing heavily, "Yes, brother. Ha, I know where it is, where they are."

"What did you—" Charles stops and shares an acknowledgement of bewilderment with Judith.

"I have no idea how, don't ask. But it called to me. It was lost in there and I fished it out."

Having no clue as to what to say, Charles and Judith stand silent, shivering slightly as the breeze brushes by their skin. The water droplets run off their shoulders and down their arms, evaporating as they step farther on toward the horizon. It runs down their legs wetting their shoes.

"C'mon. Let's go, it's not far," Thomas says, leading them across the field to their right. He smiles exaggeratedly as if he had caught onto some clever joke and wraps his arms around his companions' necks. They walk on, somehow trusting Thomas' guidance. He takes them over a hilly, rut-covered field of rye. They skip through a grove of apple trees and pass down the tunnel formed by the bunches of clustered leaves. They each take a piece of fruit in hand and bite into the clean, sweet taste, filling themselves with a delightful flavor their tongues are so unaccustomed to. Thomas leads them past all this, guided by a force of will that passes to his mind visions from Charles' childhood. These flashes of memory related to these locations settle in him as if he had gone to and from here daily.

Eventually, they come upon a field of sprouts in which a manor sits in the distance beside a main road leading to the city. Past the fledgling span of young crops, far off on the opposite side, one in which the protrusions of green are just slightly higher, stands half a dozen shacks made of rain-worn wood.

Charles at once exclaims a shout of joy, "I don't how you—lets go. I'll introduce you!"

He waves his friends on to follow, so they let their footfall land upon the well-trampled track of moist dirt scattered with high weeds.

Charles kisses Judith and tells her, "They'll love you, don't worry."

She smiles at him and grasps his arm, biting her lip in her nervousness. The sprigs of grass pass as their feet take them onward, the rows of green passing by in streaks of color. The structures may seem sad if you are divorced from this lifestyle, but these young ones press toward them as if they are to greet royals who house themselves in some exotic locale.

Thomas stands before the first house and knocks on the door. A man and woman whose heads are topped with gray and white hairs peer out in confusion. Charles explains their reason for knocking. Pete and Mary invite the young ones in and provide them some porridge. Taking this rare chance to offer hospitality with the utmost seriousness, they sit the young ones upon their bed to feast upon bread mush, which is flavored with the essence of a rabbit haunch. The meal is wonderful to these young ones who are as used to those who made this to acquiring a taste for nothing, of water and nothing. The rich, but sparse, gamey meat lathers their tongues as they lay each morsel on. The grainy beads of rye bring on a spread of bitterness, which lays a heavy, and quite pleasant, compensation in chewing. It is a soup of two ingredients, typical of the lower classes, something these three find satisfying.

Charles asks Pete and Mary, "Do you know people by the name of Sybil and Nicholas? They are my parents and I have not been here for some time."

His hosts strike up their eyebrows as if it were not a surprise to hear these names. Pete agrees and says, "Yes. They are surely two doors down, no question."

The young ones finish their bowls without rush. When the food is eaten and words fail them, Charles excuses himself and his friends to leave and seek his mother and father.

Charles steps out of the house and sees before him the dilapidated shack his parents call their home. Suddenly filled with disbelief that he is actually here, he opens the door slowly. Sticking his head in he calls, "Mom? Dad?"

He pushes it open more. Knowing it is Charles' voice right off, his mother Sybil rubs the sleep from her eyes and says, "Charles? Hello?"

Lit by the rectangular glow of the incoming light, Charles' parents, having nodded off, try to focus as their eyes adjust. Quite overcome with the sight of their son, they become alert and ecstatic.

Sybil throws her arms around her son and showers him with kisses.

"My son, my son," she coos.

Her freeness of spirit and the outpouring of love overshadows her appearance: The dress spattered with dirt, two round spots where her knees press; her eyes, worn deep from years of stress; and the ratted hair atop her head that has such an amount of dirt about it, as on her face, that it can hardly be conceived to be blond.

His father Nicholas picks himself out of his chair and stands, exclaiming for joy. His scraggly beard hangs below his grin, chaotic as paths of sheep with no shepherd. The legs of the old seat bend as his weight lifts. His own legs resemble these, slim to the point of being emaciated. He wobbles like a drunk stork, but soon gets his footing and pats his son on the shoulders.

"I cannot believe it!" Nicholas says. "What have we done for such a blessing?"

Sybil notices Thomas and Judith standing coyly outside their door. She says, "Who are your guests? Come in, please. You are all welcome."

Charles introduces them and his parents insist they seat themselves, somewhat shamed they have nothing more to offer in the way of hospitality.

Sybil kneels and chats with Judith. The young girl blushes and overflows with nervousness. Her responses come out mousey and strained, her hands clenched, and her feet do a dance, one stroking on the other as her eyes dart upwards, contemplating each word.

Thomas sits himself in Nicholas' seat, not wanting to seem rude. The legs of the seat bend under his weight. Thomas has to steady his torso almost as if balancing on a taut rope, for any leaning makes him feel as if the whole of it will twist and fall to pieces under him. He stands to remove himself from blame and embarrassment before this occurs.

"Ah, damn it all," Nicholas says. "We've had that thing for near fifteen years now. I've mended it best I can, but it's not good enough."

Thomas inspects the underside of the chair, seeing layer upon layer of resins placed through the years. Some are black, some brown, and some range from yellowed white to clear. Anytime Nicholas would come across a material that resembled glue he'd apply it and hope for the best. Such substances included tree sap, tar, syrups from various rotted sunk-in fruits and vegetables, and every byproduct of animal carcasses he could get his hands on—the most successful being the ground bones and hooves of a cow he made into a thick gelatin.

Sometimes the repair may last more than a year, but in time the legs loosen in their sockets in having a force set upon them, and scrape out the glue, sometimes sending poor Nicholas at once to the earthen floor.

Thomas unloosens a knot from a thin, old, worn rope that once bound the two left legs solidly. He stretches them hard together, attempting to wind the two ends and make it tight again.

"Are you of the woodworking craft, son?" Nicholas asks Thomas.

"Can't help you there, father. That's your boy's thing," Thomas says grinning wide, awaiting Charles' response.

Charles sends a swift kick into Thomas' bent over rump. Thomas does all he can to contain his chuckling.

Nicholas, now that the issue has been brought to his mind, asks Charles, "How are you getting along with my brother? You getting a hang of it?"

Charles, hating to lie, tries to keep it simple.

"It's not too bad," he says.

"He's difficult, I hear you," Nathaniel says, sensing uneasiness in his son's voice. "But you don't want to end up like me."

"Don't say that."

"No matter what, you must be grateful to learn a craft. Without it you are lost in this world. I'm sorry we sent you away, but you must understand. You don't hate me, do you?"

"No! I love you both, quit that talk."

Charles kisses his father on the cheek and then his mother.

# Sybil

ACROSS THE WIDE field of dirt seven families spread out, a woven basket slung around each neck. They reach their hands inside and toss a sprinkling of seeds upon the earth. The motion becomes an unconscious act as Thomas takes a step, tosses, take a step, tosses, all the way across farther than he can even see clearly. Whenever one reaches the edge of the line, he or she turns around at the border and starts off seeding the next row and the next after that.

By the time a week has gone by, the seeds have been set. Another job must be done, that of harrows being put to use to turn the soil, covering the seeds that they may grow. These are dragged across quite easily because the ground had already been broken up by a plow pulled by oxen the previous month.

Sybil, Thomas notices, works as any other. But she seems to oversee the serfs—that is, besides Edmund the reeve whose job it is to watch over the workers and manage sales of product. Edmund was a serf until promoted to his position by the earl. He always did a fair job and was well liked by those who worked the land, so he was never replaced. Sybil's job is different though. While he oversees practical matters, keeping the people working, Sybil's actions cause a yearning in Thomas to develop. He senses something oddly familiar in the way she goes about things like a dog that has been kept with humans throughout its life and has suddenly been introduced to those of its own kind. Thomas' senses are on alert when she goes by.

Sybil patrols the surrounding fields, chanting words and splashing drips of water here and there on the dry soil. The small amount of moisture that is flung about could in no way satiate the thirst of the seeds waiting for a real rain. Her actions are more of a ritualistic formality, like a priest of the Roman church wetting members of his flock with holy water.

Charles and Judith live almost as a husband and wife. He comforts her. He lets her have the blanket at night if she shivers, and performs a greater share of the labor. She keeps his mood pleasant, always kisses his cheek and adores him. She helps Sybil with meals. Many of his memories of her go back to watching her stir a pot of stew of swirling vegetables. He imagines his life with her continuing until they are his parent's age and beyond. At meal times she fills a wooden bowl with eatables and brings it to him, so careful not to spill and burn her fingers. As she places it before him, she radiates with the utmost love.

Day after day Thomas finds he has nothing to do. He works when there is work to be done, but otherwise he wanders the dusty roads winding through in his mind. He often sits outside the house and contemplates the coolness of the breeze that sweeps across his sweaty, damp forehead. When it rains he often takes to drenching himself. He wanders the length of the field and back, letting his patched-up shoes sink deep into the layers of mud.

He often sees Sybil watching over the workers, guiding them, or engaged in her watering of the crops, such a slight watering, Thomas thinks that it seems a worthless activity. Finally, something in it intrigues him. He always lets her be when she is at her odd business, chanting, often like a sick cat she sings. For one thing, it frightens him, although there is nothing outwardly threatening. It is mysterious like the ways of adults he is still figuring out, but this, what she is doing he cannot even get a finger on what the purpose of it may be.

On this particularly sweltering day, he sits on the doorstep and watches her lug that old bucket around like always, spreading water upon the sprouts of grain. He feels all of the sudden, for whatever reason, that he needs to help her by holding that weight. It is an oncoming force that compels him, just as whenever something slips from a girl's grip and falls upon the ground. He knows it must be him that picks it up. He rushes over and says simply, "Let me carry it for you."

She lets him, and from this point on, whenever he is not occupied with work duties, he is beside her holding that bucket. He can see close now the process she acts out. She holds in her hand a branch of fennel, the long stalk of green ending with bursts of leaves that appear to be more like multitudes of stems that have exploded like a blast of gunpowder. A few tiny yellow flowers have bloomed here and there. She dips the end into the water again and again, flinging the stream that spreads into the air every which way. She ends up drenching Thomas and herself before they are done, a few drips at a time. It is fine, he concludes. He takes it with a bit of humor and actually enjoys it most of the time. It is better to be of some use, he feels, than to watch the day go by so slow staring into nothing.

On a day covered with the haze of fog and hints on oncoming rain, a woman meets both of them in the field. She is panting. The sweat across her face and chest is thick like diluted butter.

With a tinge of hysteria she pleads, "Follow me! I beg you! My lady is having birth complications!"

"Can you see the baby at all?" Sybil asks her.

"No. She is not opening up."

Sybil nods in understanding. She says, "First you must follow me."

Thomas and the servant follow Sybil to her makeshift shed, but as they approach the door she insists they stay outside and wait. She quickly returns with a small clay pot that fits neatly in her palm.

Thomas asks, "Should I leave this here?" motioning to the bucket of water.

"No, we will need it. Hurry," she says hastily.

After a sprint down a long country road, they approach the house of the baron. Upon reaching the open doorway a teenage servant girl screams aloud, "No, no! You must not step into the house with your shoes caked in mud!"

Thomas feels as if his arms cannot hold the continually jostling weight of the water any longer, and this girl's delay almost makes him unhinge. The master of the house, the baron, cries aloud and says, "Why do you wait about?!" At once he is made aware by the look upon his servant girl's face.

"Please go!" he bellows. "Up with you at all cost! Please help my dear Liz and my child!" he says near fainting.

Sybil and Thomas shoot out at once, smattering footprints of mud across the floor, and fly up the stairs built from old, bleached oak.

The woman's screaming can be heard booming from the room before they enter. The sound is like one would make while a saw is dragged through her body. Thomas, upon entering the room is stricken cold and silent. After looking straight at this rawness of womanhood, full in its saturation and oozing of blood, he clenches his eyes tight. Thomas tries not to hear the horror wailing, crying from fear, her deep mourning that life is leaving her and her child. She goes into wild throws of unconscious pulsing of the muscles in her loins, far beyond exhaustion, trying with all her might to push it out. She can feel the blockage. Something must be lodged somewhere. She's been trying for hours despite this feeling that something is wrong. Her energy has been leaving her the more her blood has been draining.

Examining Liz's vagina, Sybil at once recognizes the problem. Looking inside to the dilating cervix, she can see the baby's shoulder pressing through. The head must be pressed in another direction.

Sybil yells to Thomas, "Pinch some of what I have in that jar, hurry. Place it in her mouth."

Thomas does as he is told. His legs and fingers do not want to cooperate, but he fights their protests, opening the lid and holding a bit of the dried, green herb between his fingertips. He feels it would be a violation to place it in the young woman's mouth while she gapes from the pain, though he fights all thought and drops it in. He returns to a chair by the window and stares hard at the floor, wishing to be away from here.

Sybil keeps a close attention, and after a few minutes contractions of the uterus continue and the baby loosens some. The woman seems to convulse as her body responds more and more to the ingested herb. Relief is evident in the woman's face: her pointed nose lowers, her teeth unclench. Her release eases the tension in the entire room. Sybil reaches in as far as she can, correcting the baby's alignment. With more and more pushing the young one eases farther and farther, closer to birth. Not knowing how, Thomas finds himself standing next to Sybil, watching a baby's head clothed in an amniotic sac slide out of the mass of red pulsing flesh and the drenched wall of hair. Soon Sybil has the slippery child in her arms, fully clothed in the membrane of its caul.

"You are a lucky one," Sybil says, proud for this newborn.

She tears the caul open, ripping the cherry-streaked, translucent bag down the center of the child's body, revealing a squirming being crying out to the world. Sybil takes a cloth and cleans the baby, then hands it to Liz. While the new one is adored completely, Sybil holds the caul toward her. Spreading it outstretched she says, "It is this which allowed him to breathe. You both would be dead now, do you realize?"

Liz nods thankfully for a moment, and then returns her attention to her son. Robbed of energy, her eyes grow heavy. Her servants enter, placing the little one in a soft bed, wrapping him in warm blankets. They leave him by the bedside and watch over mother and child.

Sybil and Thomas descend the stairs and are approached by the anxious father, the baron.

Sybil speaks first, "They are fine. You have a healthy son."

Elated, he kisses her on each cheek and noticeably desires to leap up the stairway, greet the new member of his family, and wrap his arms around his wife, so thankful she is alive.

"She needs her rest," Sybil says calmly.

"Yes, yes of course. Please sit. I will treat you well," the baron says, inviting them to sit at his dining table. He claps twice and instructs his servants to slaughter a pig, for there will be a celebration, all invited. Thomas and Sybil dine on fruits, nuts and delicious juices while they wait for the pig to slowly cook in a blend of apples and fragrant spices. In short time a servant returns with a troupe of musicians whose playing makes the waiting luxurious. When the food is ready, the table is loaded. After the baron and his honored guests, the servants take seats at the table, save for those who take turns watching over mother and child. Thomas bites into the soft pork dripping with rich juices. He slides each mound free, skin included, relishing every movement it makes upon his tongue before it practically gives way like butter between his teeth. It is, by far, the best meal he has ever had. After a time he sits dazed, confounded, for before this moment he had no idea such flavor was possible.

# 14

# Wood

WHILE OCCUPIED IN HIS THOUGHTS, Charles hears a great crack across the room followed by a thump. His father sits on the ground in a piteous condition, rubbing his tailbone, reeling from a sharp pain as evidenced from the poor look on his face. Charles rushes over and helps his father to his feet, seeing the chair leg had, after all this time, cracked through. It lies in a pile, a pathetic ruin of what was once a family relic. He can tell there is a sense of loss within his father, in knowing an age has passed—that of patching up this old inanimate companion and seating himself upon it like he always has.

"You all right?" Charles asks.

"I'm fine," Nicholas says, trying to brush off his sullen reaction.

"I'm surprised it lasted as long as it did."

Biting his lip at this, Nicholas finally blurts, "I suppose I should sit in the dirt."

Charles holds his tongue so not to bring out any more of his aging father's melancholy. They both stand silent, staring into the deep blues and purples of the dawn coming upon them.

Nicholas says, "We could do it. We can make a new one."

"Father, you don't think I know enough—"

"I recall learning a few things from my brother. I know how to shape wood."

Charles considers his father's feelings and how they have been apart for so long. He concludes that even if they lack the proper tools and the knowledge to form an object such as they seek to make, at least he could try for the father he loves.

Charles says, "I haven't learned much—"

"That's all right," his father says smirking, "a crooked chair is better than that old wreck I've been resurrecting."

Charles' tension loosens now that his father has relaxed. He says, "I can ask around for some wood."

Charles asks door to door for wood that would suit their purpose. One by one they all turn him down, having none to give. Pete and Mary, his parents' closest friends greet him with a warmer welcome. Sorry to be unable to provide him with wood, Pete instead offers him his axe so that he may be able to choose his own wood from the source. The elderly people then sink back into their usual mode of chatting with each other, allowing Charles to be on his way.

Behind the row of fieldworker's houses lies a deep, untouched oak grove. Charles steps within the cover with the axe resting across his right shoulder, seeing before him all the stout, deep-grooved trees. Their strong branches reach like the upraised arms of workmen, the sinews well developed from holding aloft heavy merchandise, never resting. The array of leaves forms clusters that block out the sky for the most part, forming before him over hill and slope a wall of vibrant green, but sunlight breaks through the windows, the places where the perimeter of one tree and another do not overlap. In these places a very particular shape emerges in the light, that which is outlined by the unique rise-and-fall lobes that form the edges of the oak leaves, which make all of the various configurations within the line of sight seem to move very slightly as if they were alive.

The darkest places, those not broken by a clearing, play a particularly eerie effect on the mind. Here and there the twittering of a bird up in the boughs or the sudden rustling in a patch of bushes takes Charles by surprise. Fluttering moths appear when they pass into the streaks of sun rays containing swirling dust. It almost appears that they are being drawn upward by the light, their papery wings given lift by the force of this golden illumination.

Charles scans around for an adolescent sort of tree, not too small and not too large. Most he sees are very ancient and greatly gnarled, spreading out in wondrous and twisted configurations. This causes him to recall his grandfather on his father's side whose face was just as well grooved. The memory is crystal clear of when he would wander the small house on holidays, chomping on his favorite tart that grandma would make, the flaky crust littering the ground with each bite. The way these old trees let fall their acorns onto the moist forest floor and how the old, rotten ones feel remind him of those ancient days.

Most of the oak seem as if they respect the space of others, not encroaching into the private space of their neighbors, but some violate this law altogether, their trunk jutting from the earth in a horizontal direction like a restless sleeper kicking their partner out of bed. He wonders, in seeing some fallen among their brothers, if it would be prudent to just chop up one of these rather than putting forth the effort of felling one rising proud and healthy yearning for the clouds.

Scanning across his field of vision, Charles skips over a shorter, more flowing shape among the shadows in the veil of green. He glances quickly back, as it strikes him as being alarming. He is drawn to the alien nature of it. From the pinnacle of this shape it slopes and frames a face with two eyes he can make out staring cold and frozen into him. Charles passes through a cluster of trees the size of a man's arm in order to flee. He clenches tight on the handle of his axe now. His eyes are wide like an owl's, watching within the darkness for the strange figure. Crossing over a solid wall of bush, he peers down an open row clear of trees. There he sees a figure just like the other—no, this one does not have its head covered, but is topped by standing growths—a crown of foliage? Charles, now frightened beyond all measure, circles around, realizing an overwhelming feeling of claustrophobia in this jade prison. He had never seen such figures like these wild men. He speeds past trunks and low hanging branches, stampeding upon ferns, stones—every sort of thing seems to block his path. There stands another figure, and another! They stand as still as the trees, but make themselves present in the force of their demeanor.

To elude what he reads as a boundary line, Charles cuts a sharp right. There he sees many more of them standing side by side, never moving at all but seeming to follow him like his own shadow. The more he runs, the more he becomes frantic, and the worse it seems to get. This realization seems to eat away at his hope of escape. Suddenly his body is struck by a seizure followed by momentary blindness. He falls suddenly, collapsing hard onto the ground. In his mind he fights for control, but his body will not obey. There he lays, the world coloring itself again, while figures wearing long-hanging, ratty cloaks surround him.

From the mystical, stone cold figure standing directly at his feet, an astoundingly eloquent voice emits. "You are the child of Sybil, are you not?"

Struck with shock, Charles gives a slight nod. His muscles return to his control more and more.

Charles asks, "How did you strike me down? Did you poison me?"

"We are capable of far more than that," he says, with his long, stringy auburn beard rising and falling with each word. "Your mother insisted you follow the new way. Therefore, you must leave us."

"What do you mean? Please explain. I've never understood what it is that she does."

"And that is the way it must be," the mystic says simply, knowing that Charles will soon see.

Charles stands. Before him, among the numerous figures of this forest tribe, from the boughs of the trees hang countless bodies of young males about his age in various degrees of decomposition. A rope hangs from each neck, but there are also numerous stab wounds through each chest with wide, gaping holes exposed revealing they were robbed of their organs. The faces are smashed in as well. Most have stuck expressions, as if the horrors felt at the time of death were frozen in the tendons of their locked, screaming jaws.

Charles clamps up. He fights the urge to faint, though he can feel the dizziness pulling him. Past the tall, cloaked figures and the corpses he can see families: men, women, and children, going about their day as any other people would. Some look his way, holding their young ones, until Charles, this threat, has left them somehow. Most are dressed in a similar garb, that of some sort of wiry, weaved material, very rustic in appearance. Those few families who appear to hold a higher status, as evidenced by that particular laxity of character that results from fewer episodes of stress, wear what appears to be the fur of deer.

Charles notices one of the warriors holding his axe firmly in both hands. A part of his will surrenders at this point. His life is completely at the mercy of their whim.

The same mystic speaks again in his clear, eloquent tone, "You will be cutting down no trees. This is our forest. We do what we can to keep invaders out, as you can see. It is only because of your mother that your blood has not been spilled and your heart, liver, and kidneys have not been burned on the fire as a sacrifice to our gods."

In hearing this hint of being released, Charles' spirit soars. His legs become a little less feeble. Still, the gaze of the circle of bearded mystics cuts holes right through him. Their cold eyes look upon him, all in unison, as prey. Wide, gray-black streaks, perhaps from the ash of the fire, mark each of them from under their eyes to the bottom of their jawlines. Several of them have donned their hair with ornaments of the forest, leaves of oak, strings of berries on the branch, and bones of various size and shape. Each of them has a furious, absolutely mad presence.

Charles pushes past his fear, daring to speak. "Is there nothing you can tell me of my mother?"

The mystic takes a moment to gather his thoughts, respecting the risk Charles has taken in speaking openly. He says, "Know that she is respected. You should be proud to have sprung from her womb. But she chose to cleave herself from our people."

"Did that have to do with me?"

"It was unclear, but I do suspect this. We are of a dying age. She chose to live on the verge of starvation and toil for the outsiders who bow before the cross. She must have had good reason; otherwise, she would have cut her own throat than sink so low."

Charles nods. Though still afraid, he has a deep appreciation for this knowledge. He says, "If she is of you I must be as well. It is good to look upon my people. I look on my family, though I am ignorant of who my cousin is and who is my mother's mother. Know that even though I return to the cities that overflow with food and riches, no one I know sees the abundance. Though my friends cry out the name of Christ when in pain, no one is free."

This warm-hearted, frank expression causes the mystic to soften in his appearance. He steps before Charles, places his hand on his shoulder, and says, "I've never before considered. But since you speak honorably, and since you are one of us, if those people fail to provide a way for you to flourish, I will allow you to make this your home."

Charles considers for a moment, and then answers thankfully, "I appreciate your offer. But I feel I've been possessed by a sickness acquired in the city. That is, no matter how miserable I become, I am compelled to strive to the point of madness. I could never live in a village."

The mystic nods respectfully, "Then you must be off."

"Farewell," Charles says, wandering back, never turning around once.

# 15

# The Powder

THOMAS AND SYBIL return to the house with sweat beading from their brows.

She says to him as they stop before her shed, "I can feel it in you. What I have. You can hear inside people sometimes, can't you?"

His eyes lower, not knowing how to take hearing this so bluntly. He says, "Some days I can feel it."

She places her hand atop his head and closes her eyes. After a moment she smiles and says, "Yes, I can feel it calling out. You have a chance to be very powerful and live a grand life. But know that the people of the world don't look kindly on people like us. No matter how many you help, there will be those who wish to shrink from life, and they see your kind of gift as a threat. Because of this, if you follow where it guides you, you will find much suffering."

Still not knowing how to react to all this, Thomas only nods in response.

"You say that you have trouble making use of your gift," she says.

Sybil unfolds a cloth revealing the caul.

"This will bring it out of you, allow you to harness the power."

The translucent membrane glistens in the sunlight. The amount of blood still draining off of it gives it the appearance of the sinews and fat of a slaughtered animal.

"It is extremely rare for a child to be born wrapped in this. These are sought after far and wide, especially by sailors for their ability to keep one from drowning. You will not only have an increased awareness of what lies in those around you, but also a superior ability to lead, even when lost in the wilderness or at sea."

Sibyl unlocks the door to her shack before the eyes of Thomas. For the first time he can see the numerous rows of jars filled with solutions, powders, and the dried limbs of animals. She unfolds the caul, stretching it over two feet wide, hanging it on two beams to dry.

She tells him, "It will take three or four days to become stiff. When that time comes I will ask for a blessing to be placed upon it and contain it in a vial for you to wear."

"See?" she says showing him an old stone carved into a half-cylinder, quite worn, bearing the rust and blue corrosion of time. "You can see this has seen sun and rain through the seasons of many lives. This has been passed along the hands of our family for hundreds of years. On its face you can see the runes," she says, pointing at various details. "Those configurations of lines have more power than to direct speech. It is the god-given language of the people who lived here before this country was called England. This rune brings power and offers protection from weapons. You can still see an outline of a ship sailing on the waves underneath. This will make one a powerful force in life, but it is nothing without the caul."

"I don't understand," Thomas says. "How could this save anyone? It's just a rock."

"I wish I had time to teach you more. But sadly, I don't. I feel a very powerful force of darkness coming on and I fear everything will change. That's why I give this to you without much in the way of guidance. Believe me, I will do what I can."

"Tell me something, please. I will be lost. I have no idea what you are talking about."

"When you desire the power you should seek it alone, because once someone speaks, your connection with the spirit is broken. I doubt you'll be around others you can trust like those I know. If you are, you're lucky."

"Is there anything else you can say?"

"No. It comes from experience. It wouldn't even make sense. But I will guide you in this. Once I place the caul inside, always keep it on," she continues.

"Never remove it no matter what. It will protect you from such a great number of things. You will need protection; I can feel it already."

Sybil picks out an orangish-red powder and removes two pinches and places them in a small bowl. She then pours a small amount of water and mixes it into a paste with a small spoon. She scoops half of it and swallows it down. She then instructs Thomas to do the same, which he does, albeit snorting and choking.

"Good," she says. "This will give you the strength to help us tonight. There is much to do if we are to build up our power."

"What do—"

"Don't worry. I will explain."

Thomas feels a stirring of emotion, as if the substance he ingested released a tap of pride and enthusiasm. He feels a great energy surge, making him feel ready for any task, although there isn't much of a task to speak of at the moment.

Men and women of surrounding fields and the four families who live on either side of Charles' family meet with Thomas and Sybil. They eat dry oat cakes, sitting in a circle in the dirt. Each has a cup of water that they occasionally sip from. These people's eyes focus on nothing in particular, seeming to contemplate something within. Though he feels compelled to stand and take charge, of what he knows not, he stays silent and follows the mode of the rest. In letting himself forget about that business of—what was it? His mind turns inward, causing him to remember back to times spent with his mother and father, stirring in him a rising tension. An acute sense of loneliness washes over. It is so unfair, he thinks, that he should have to lose his family and be on his own with no one to rest his troubles upon. In this thought he focuses on his mother's face in his mind, saddened that the vision seems incomplete. What did her lips look like? And her nose? It is a vague image, not at all satisfying or vivid enough to bring her back to him. He feels as if he had failed her somehow. It's the least he can do, in his mind, to keep their memory alive. It is such a profound feeling of loss in him, the void left by the death of his parents. Finally he concludes that it is not his fault he cannot remember, but his mind which must be a terribly insufficient organ if it cannot properly do its job to keep their memory alive in him.

Sybil takes a small, slender clay jar from a small pocket of her dress. The object fits neatly in the fold of her palm.

She says to Thomas, "Do you wish to join us?"

He nods his head in agreement.

Continuing, she says, "Do you concede to engage yourself in the initiation rite?"

A bit confused, he stalls.

"This is very important. I'm glad you take a moment to think on it. Certain parts of nature open us up to understand something within us. You must be ready. Don't decide now."

Music erupts with a nod of Sybil's head. To Thomas, something odd must be going on in the heads of the others. They play their traditional instruments in a much more vigorous way than usual, plucking madly upon lute strings and jamming bows upon fiddles. After a song ends they all rest and fall into a deeper spiritual focus than Thomas has ever seen.

Thomas nudges Sybil, and asks if he could try.

She lifts his chin so that he will remain open and submissive. With as little motion as possible, Sybil twists out the cylindrical cork and lets one drip fall between Thomas' eyebrows. She instructs him to rub in the oil. He does so, supposing that this must somehow be an important act, though he only feels awkward. He knows not what to do. Everyone stays silent and still. "Am I supposed to say something?" he wonders. Suddenly warmth comes over him as if the sun had poured honey-like syrup into the crest of his head. The feeling flows through him and rides his veins. In breathing he feels the force culminate and recede in him. God is with him, like never before, manifest in a pure overwhelming love in which he has to clench onto his pants like reigns in order to guide himself along the tunnel to heaven or wherever he is going. He is not sure. He can only focus, not daring to be distracted. His back slackens and he begins leaning, so Sybil and others gently, very slowly lay him on his back.

Thomas is awash in an ocean of milk. The soil beneath him takes him in, molding to his muscles. The white essence of the sun's light envelops him and everything, purifying it all. Sybil starts the others in a chant by beginning it herself. Thomas' mind reaches out to each syllable. Each tone uttered is met with streaks of luminescence visible in the blackness of his closed eyes. At first their voices seem to him like those he used to hear while in church with his mother, but these sounds are sweeter, stirring in him a greater feeling of spirit than those off-key, droning songs ever could. The words they say must be of a different language, for he is free to be unhindered by meaning and only feel. The farther he travels, the more he is absorbed. To higher and higher planes he is lifted, carried by their words. He sees angels up there, slender-bodied beings radiating pure love, though lacking wings. They acknowledge him without any sort of motion, but somehow he knows. Also he sees many smaller people, flooded with glee and lightness of spirit. They are like little plump candy children. The colors that shine forth change erratically, shifting between the vibrant shades of a rainbow, seemingly without method to timing or reason. They drift through an airy mist of whiteness that seems to be filled with life in of itself. It lifts and has weight; a thick consistency propels Thomas' spirit farther.

It is night and Thomas wakes. He sees that the others lie sleeping around him covered with blankets. A sudden rush of appreciation climbs out of him for he realizes that he was watched over. Standing, he notices that some of the swell still drifts through his head. His vision carries across the field of grain colored with a wash of lunar glow. The grains shift in unison with the slight wind that passes. He has never realized its beauty before now, the warmth of the gold that shows on each strand as they bend and are lit for such a short time the mind can hardly realize. Looking skyward, the array of stars seems more sharp and precise than ever, each streak of piercing light formed with such clarity of design, pressing into his mind, passing out his eyes. The grandiose beauty overcomes him and he feels tears falling from his eyes uncontrollably. The feeling is somewhat embarrassing for he feels exposed like he did once when unable to hold his urine in the marketplace at the age of seven. He is glad to be free to smile so widely and let his eyes drink in gulps without embarrassment, since everyone is asleep. He takes this moment in deep for himself.

# The Axe

There is a knock on the door.

Nicholas approaches and asks, "Who is it?"

A weak, wavering voice answers, "It's me Nick. It's Pete."

Nicholas opens the door, greeting his neighbor with a smile. He says, "Welcome, friend. It's a sweltering day. Please come inside."

"Yes it is," he says, noticing the sweat beaded on his forehead. "It's been a week. I was wondering if you were finished using my axe."

Pete's eyes fall on Charles, whose tongue is caught, unable to speak.

Nicholas turns and speaks to his son, "Did you borrow an axe from him and fail to return it?"

Charles remains stunned, not knowing what to say. He knows he cannot tell the truth.

Again Nicholas asks, "Tell me, where is the axe?"

"I lost it. I'm sorry. It's out there," he says, pointing toward the forest.

"Then we'll get it right now! Put on your shoes!" Nicholas says.

"It's so far in we could never find it. It dropped from my hand when I fell down a very steep hill moistened by the rain. I looked for hours and never saw it again."

Nicholas says to Pete, "I am shamed by this. Believe me, we will repay you for its full worth."

Charles says, "Yes, I take full responsibility. For a start I will be your servant. Whatever you ask, I will be at your service."

Pete thinks it over and says, "Well, I didn't intend on making this such an ordeal. But I suppose it is fair to have you do some light labor for a time."

"Thank you for your understanding," Nicholas says, glaring at Charles

"Thank you," Charles says. "I will be over within the hour."

Every few days, Charles knocks upon his neighbor's door and asks Pete or Mary if he can be of use. Their house becomes immaculate in its cleanliness and orderliness. He takes their clothing that needs washing and, with Judith's help, they take it all to the river and scrub the stink out of everything. The elderly couple happily sits in their house in their undergarments, waiting to try on something fresh.

Judith, though, is not content in working off the debt. She is sure that if she looks long enough she will eventually find the axe. Once everyone is asleep, she takes up a candle and creeps out the door. Every slope and valley is scoured. With her little feet she scatters piles of dead leaves. She pokes her head within the many patches of bushes. She quits each night when her body grows weak and sleeps through the day when she can.

As the months pass and the grain reaches over a foot high, a peculiar act is performed. Sybil wakes Thomas and takes him to a field, a different one each time, seemingly in rotation. Each time the same people arrive, as if it is part of a cooperative organization. Sybil always brings close to her the serf who is in charge of the field they are currently gathered. In this ceremony, at the dead of night, groupings of both sexes gather together. The shirts of the men are removed, and the women, oftentimes their wives, rub the men over with glossy oil, covering every spot of exposed skin. The application is voraciously sensual, in order to arouse the libidinous male energies. Once the kissing of the neck and thorough massaging of the muscles has been performed, Sybil distributes fennel stalks to the women, a much larger and robust version than what she uses in her water ritual.

Now that they have been aroused, the blood properly energized to the point of blushing, the women violently whip them with the fennel in order to force out that fertile power into the field. For over an hour they take a beating, bleeding profusely, but in good faith that their sacrifice will bring forth abundance. Sybil applies healing herbs afterward, and supplies them a drink to numb the pain, since some of them find themselves shaking from the blood loss.

Thomas, beginning as a voyeur to these activities, is eventually pushed to be involved, being whipped a total of five times upon fields in the surrounding area.

Whenever an animal is found among the seas of grain, it is chased down with an incredible fervor. Anything from rabbits, rats, quail, snakes, all sorts of creatures that nest in the ground and make use of the fields as cover, are taken up and proclaimed as the "spirits of the field." Thomas thought they must be speaking in some sort of way that connoted play or lightness of heart, a play at seriousness. This brand and degree of superstition is supremely unknown to Thomas, for the people who ordinarily conduct themselves in a rational manner let sense take flight at the sight of a creature scurrying around.

The animals have their neck constrained and their belly slit open by Sybil while they are still breathing and squirming. She reads some sort of omen in the organs pumping with life. Occasionally she severs parts of their insides and chews them raw. A space is cleared in the soil for combustible materials to keep a fire from spreading to the field. A small pile of sticks and brush are lit, and the body of the animal is consumed in the flame, while all meditate on the strange, water-trickle-light foreign words Sibyl chants to the sky.

Judith takes to slipping out in the daytime as well as the night whenever she can. Whenever there is no work to be done, especially when Charles is busy helping his father in some manner, she is away from the openness of the land adapted to the cares of people. However, Charles becomes suspicious eventually.

"Where are you always off to?" he asks.

"I'm taking a walk," she tells him.

This answer makes him quite suspicious, so after having enough ambiguity, he takes to following her. Upon each venture she travels farther within the depths of the green world than the time before; therefore, by the time he begins tracking her, she is entering into the heart of it. This shakes him for the incredible danger she unknowingly puts herself in. He catches sight of her as she is wandering the perimeter of a deep, rain-cut ravine.

"Judith!" he says, seeing her figure far off. She is greatly startled, circling around, unaware of where the echoing call came from that carried her name.

He approaches her and she calms, but is at a complete loss how he could find her out here.

"What are you doing?" he asks her.

"I'm looking for the axe," she says innocently.

"You've got to be careful. There are very dangerous people who live out here."

She knows not what to say.

"I don't want you to get hurt," he says.

"I'm trying to help you."

"I know. But I don't care so much about some axe."

# To the Sky

SYBIL, surrounded by nine of her companions, those who are the most adept in at her craft, lead Thomas into a shed housing tools of the field. The meeting has a particular auspiciousness to Thomas in the way that everyone holds themselves. One may think they are preparing for a meeting with a prince. This building was constructed with a lock on the inside, a puzzling, but oh-so-slight detail. Sybil involuntarily shrieks and clamors about, sometimes screaming at her helpers as though she were possessed. Words are spoken here and there of something in the way of battles. Sybil explains it matter-of-fact to Thomas, that she is to fight those who wield dark forces in the land of Verona—a far off city he has never heard of.

Sybil rests her hand on Thomas' shoulder and tells him, "What the church fathers fear from witchcraft is absolutely sound. It is us who battle with it, our kind that stave off its curses."

A call for prayer is announced. So many beings are invoked that Thomas cannot keep track. Gods of vegetation are sought for, along with gods of the earth. Gods of the sky are called upon for safe passage into their realm. She regards these beings as if she passes them on the street each day. With a screeching peal, she lets loose her call for nymphs and deities to help her in her battles across the skies. She beats her chest violently, as never before seen by Thomas. She scratches into her flesh with her long nails, bleeding in long streams, staining her ragged dress. This frightens Thomas, for he is not so sure she will not attack him.

Sybil's companions attempt to take hold of her in this ecstatic state and pour the contents of a wide brimmed jar down her throat. She protests, as if they were assaulting her, striking them hard in the face if they in any way hesitate. She screams as if being murdered, which finally causes Thomas to fully cower in the corner of the room, wishing to be far away from here. A portion of the concoction is swallowed down by her, and then the rest slurp in turn, finally ending with Thomas, who is approached in his fearful state. He calms as they approach, surprised at his own reaction, for he reasons that nothing harmful has happened as of yet.

For a time of unknown span, Thomas is in a state of nausea. He is lost to this supposed rise of spirit. He is angered in being tied in this prison of twirling, always spinning vision, which corrects itself many thousands of times. It's as if someone made him overly drunk and forcefully shook his head from side to side. Vomit erupts on the bare soil, the involuntary upheaval discharged upon a spider stronghold that covers various tools, a rusted pick, and old cloths tossed away. He peers up to see several of the others vomiting as well, but with small buckets to catch the horrible stuff. He sees one just the same before his left knee, which he must have missed in his anxiety. Thomas raises it to his face and lets the thick spit that has gathered flow, settling on the flat silver bottom.

As comfort comes back and the sick feeling recedes some, Thomas begins to feel the great throbbing in his head, of the blood working overtime, of the smallest parts of his brain stimulated far beyond their normal capacity. This ecstatic rush causes him to immediately recline in the most restful position he can situate himself in, so that he may take leave of his arms, his head, settle his rump and shoulders, and drift off.

Thomas focuses on his spirit lifting as it swims above his body. It is there he plays, giddily laughing. He is really on the ceiling. The bodies of the others he sees below. They look so odd with a few bald spots and bad angles on their guts and shabby clothing. The humor ends as he really looks to himself down below. Through the swirl of deliriousness he focuses and sees the ugly face, the puke splattered down the maw and shirt, and thus takes a dive. At once the vantage goes back to his head, and his spirit makes rounds in an arc above, and one through the earth, just as the Sun does each day and night. It is this rotation which tortures Thomas all though the night. Round and around, warped is all vision and thought. Spurting out bile into the bucket is the focus of his whole sick being. Wave, wave… surge! He notices two of his companions have awakened. They are laughing, for they have dropped bits of cheese on the soil. As their hands reach, Thomas sees the clumps lie within a pile of shards from a broken clay pot.

"Duh pot… bu duh…" Thomas blurts with a burp.

The two young men look to him, giddy with the cheese pressed between their fingertips.

Thomas tries again. "It's sharp. If you eat it, it will cut you!" he says, slapping his belly like a senile ape.

"It's alright," one of them says, already chewing.

The sick vision of the tiny jagged edges flowing, scraping through the innocent pink of the drugged men is the last Thomas has this night.

Thomas wakes inside the shed, surprised to be in such a static place. He stands, though disoriented. Sybil's remaining companions help her rise to her feet.

Someone takes out a key and unlocks the door and they exit. The mood is of devastation. Sybil and her closest companions, in one way or another, thrash about as though they have no minds, as though they haven't fully returned. The fiercest devastation is seen from Sybil, who beats her hands into the earth as though these appendages were of no more use, as if she were beating to death a person who had sodomized, tortured, and desiccated her child. She is mirrored by her closest followers. It was an absolute loss for Sybil. Something went very wrong. Drips of rain fall, followed by a downpour. Sybil orders everyone to perch themselves atop the roofs.

"What happened?" Thomas asks.

He receives no answer. Sybil stands cold as stone, staring into her field. The people exit their houses as the rain soon shows its intention to resemble that which filled the lungs of Noah's contemporaries. Having to lift his pain-filled frame, Nicholas is quite unhappy that the piercing slope of his rooftop is to become his seat, rather than the soft-cushioned one he dreamed of building with his son. Hard, fat drips fall, smacking into each face regularly. A secondary thought enters Nicholas' mind, as it does within that of his neighbors' once the constant moisture becomes an accustomed and tolerated feeling. In looking to the field now drowning, there will be far worse effects than of momentary discomfort.

# The Fires Are Lit

THE GREAT RAINFALL takes Charles and Judith by surprise. They are drenched within a minute. Stuck within a vast expanse, with no real cover, they huddle together against a tree. The rain continues to pelt the world around for hours upon hours, unrelenting. The soil becomes a slick mud. Water gathers and flows in streams, growing more and more in its force. Where the land slopes downward, floods begin to rush. This forces Charles and Judith into a tree to escape being carried off and perhaps drowning in a ravine. The water flows under them, quickly rising to over a foot high, carrying loosely held foliage and even heavy stones slipping through the mud.

Sybil acknowledges her loss and takes the punishment from the skies quietly. After a full day of sitting on their hard, thatched rooftops, after most of the material possessions have surely been ruined by the saturation, some of the houses begin to come apart. The front of Pete and Mary's house goes one way, while the back remains anchored. After hours of hearing the creaking wood sound out, being pushed to the limit, the construction breaks free, leaving half of the back wall standing. They drift with it, still sitting on their roof, watching as their flimsy, hay-padded beds float down the stream and all of their clothing is carried off, submerged in the flowing mud. Their house drifts for no more than fifteen feet, then trips up and topples over, sending them both hard, sunk into the mud. They receive help from several people, but they are not the only ones to drift away. As the rain continues for over a week, three more houses are uplifted. People survive on little more than a mouthful of food a day. They are filled with despondency, watching the grains they had worked so hard to nurture drown. At times the water level rises above the field, remaining there for some time, disguising the space as a great, glassy lake.

Charles and Judith huddle together on a wide branch. A cold wind blows in and arrives during nights as a horrible frost, an icy hell. To endure this requires the utmost of both their wills. Each of them, by the second day, succumbs to sickness. They are horribly chilled, sneezing relentlessly and feel their limbs sapped of life. Each time day arrives, they make a new attempt to venture, but they sink, the mud halfway up their calves. Because of this, and the unrelenting return of the rain, they must quit their attempts each time and find a new tree to roost in.

Hunger compounds their weakness far more than the sickness does. Their spirits settle into emotional silence as the reality of death nears. The gray atmosphere brings this on all the more. They try to sleep as much as possible to escape this feeling, and in order to expend the least amount of energy.

As the rain gets worse, they must remain in a single tree. Charles tries to stay alert, for in the gathered bundle of foliage underneath them, food is occasionally snared. If he hangs on tight he can climb down and pick out worms and on occasion nuts. Thankfully, on the fourth day a small brown bird is wrapped up there. They feel ill in eating the raw flesh, but at least it hadn't completely gone foul due to the low temperature of the water.

On the fifth day, while sleeping high in the branches, Charles wakes upon hearing the sound of numerous feet sloshing through the soupy mud. After inspecting them, he is not sure whether or not they are friendly. He doesn't care at this point.

"Heeaaay!" Charles calls loud and desperate.

The group of seven stop, flabbergasted to hear a voice in such an environment.

The closest one speaks. "Who is that? Speak up!"

"We're just two kids, caught out here when the rain surprised us!" Charles says.

"My Lord!" the leader says. "How terrible. You mean to tell me you've been stuck here since this began?"

"Yes, for five days now," Charles says weakly, climbing down to greet him. "The floods were so dangerous we couldn't leave."

"You are hungry I assume!"

Charles' face is as white as that under a tabby's fur.

"Yes," Charles says with conviction. "We may have starved if this lasted any longer."

The leader unlatches a clasp on a small bag that is slung around him, hanging on his side. He reveals two mounds of soft bread. Judith, in seeing these, climbs from the tree with incredible speed. They each take the food in hand and consume voraciously like greedy dogs. Charles notices now that the men are all armed with long swords. Each of them has their pants rolled up above their knees so as to not soil the fine material, that of wool dyed burgundy.

"I am Nathaniel," he says.

Charles, while munching the last bite, introduces himself and Judith with a full mouth.

"What are you doing out here?" Charles asks.

"We hope to find those who make their home deep in these woods and destroy them."

"Oh," Charles says, seeming unfazed.

"Have you seen any sign of those who call upon the devil?"

"I have no idea."

"That's good. From what I hear, you would be dead if you did."

Just then, Nathaniel tries to take a step. He laughs light-heartedly in thinking his shoes were somehow caught in some sort of pressure due to the mud. The others notice the same thing, but fear grips them as numbness fills their legs, works up their bodies, and crawls the length of their arms. At once, in the distance, the tall tree-men Charles had seen before stand cold and unflinching as if they had appeared out of nowhere.

Judith becomes frantic and tromps in the direction that those who had fed them came from. Charles follows, knowing that although he had been spared by the people of the forest once, he may not be a second time. The warriors of the city holler and squeal as the forest mystics confront them in unison with long, slender swords drawn. Madness overtakes the men of the city in being confined, though tied with no ropes. They can still scream, and their limbs move very slightly, but only with the mental command of the utmost frantic jerking.

As the men of the forest approach their invaders, each receives one swipe across the throat. At once the victims holler, but then and gurgle and struggle for air that won't come as the flaps of their necks spurt pure red. As they collapse, the liquid draining from each man becomes diluted in the settled pools the tone of chestnut.

In the process of this, Nathaniel is faced by their leader. The distraction of conducting the paralyzing spell delays Nathaniel's execution long enough for him to clench onto his pistol and raise it far enough upward. He shoots the mystic in the foot as he is stabbed three times in the neck and belly. One member of Nathaniel's party, the farthest in the back, so far has not been harmed. He regains control of his limbs as the mystic becomes distracted. He runs for his life wild and crazed, but is cut through seven times by unseen attackers, desiccated beyond belief.

"Run, run!" Charles says to Judith, whom he sees in the distance staring his way.

Judith's nimble legs carry her through the mud, though she must often jolt like snared prey to not allow each step to be surrounded by the soupy friction. While Charles trudges behind her, attempting to quicken his pace, she turns her head.

"Don't stop! Keep running and never look back!" he screams.

Charles' body stiffens and collapses to the soil, just as he saw happen to the others. Helpless, though conscious, he is dragged over foliage, rocks and all, his head knocking on everything as if his skull was a plow.

He sees Nathaniel being dragged along with his companions. Nathaniel's eyes move and look over Charles' expression of agonizing pain. From the gaping wounds leaks blood from his back. A trail of strawberry-stamped footfall is left behind over stone and earth on this travel which seems to never end.

Finally, the forest men reach the village with their captives. It is a relief to Charles, even though this is likely their place of execution. Nathaniel and the others are tied to trees, constrained ropes slung around their necks so that they may be hung on display. The breastbones of the conquered are sawed from the bottom up, slowly severed, the shells cracked. Chanting in a language unknown to Charles, they carefully place their hands in each cavity and cut loose organs, lifting them to the sky. They set the guts in a large iron bowl set above a roaring fire. Along with this, bundles of pine needles are brought continually by a train of women. The scent of burning blood and pine lifts into the air.

After this is performed on the last of Nathaniel's party, Charles feels his limbs regain mobility and he is brought his axe. The mystic tells him in his eloquent manner, "It is the highest honor, son of Sybil, to sacrifice a still living man. Crack his chest in two without splitting his organs and bestow upon us all an unsurpassed blessing."

Charles feels his legs are strong enough to stand now. He takes the axe firmly in both hands and wonders what he is to do. Nathaniel moans as his back pours its fluids through the ravines of the bark, through the accumulated crust. The rope around his neck is made taut, so that he will be strangled while simultaneously disemboweled.

Charles, thoroughly caught up in the experience, hears the mystic whisper, "Right down the center, boy. Not too hard, not too soft."

Charles and Nathaniel lock in a gaze. At Charles' first thought of subverting the plan, the Mystic screams out in a great fury. Charles steps forward, already feeling his body stiffen. He lifts the axe high overhead and swings it far higher than he was instructed, landing an angular hack into Nathaniel's temple, splitting his skull, quieting his mind in an instant.

Charles can feel his body stiffen inch by inch. Before he loses all control, he plants his left hand against the tree and chops his smallest finger through. As the axe blade is lodged and the tiny digit bounces here and there, Charles' mind erupts in pain. This disturbance of mind somehow separates him from the Mystic's control as he had hoped. He runs, roaring in agony. He spins around and sends the axe flying in vicious spirals. His legs carry him from his pursuers; his subconscious somehow noting the elevation and barriers of the oncoming terrain, for his conscious awareness is gone, filled with fright, pain, and deliriousness from blood loss.

Charles does not stop running until, greatly relieved, he reaches the city of Newbury. As he enters the streets, he receives concerned looks due to his ghostly white appearance. He is bleeding profusely and is covered in mud from head to toe. The focus of judgment is deflected from him though, as Judith approaches with townspeople she met in the city square, and begins hysterically clamoring on about madmen of the forest wielding the powers of witchcraft and slaughtering a team of warriors. Charles wishes to stop her, but he knows not whose side he is on, if any, at this point. He has no idea what the implications of her words are soon to bring. People are immediately astonished at this and provide them with clean clothes, hearty meals, and a warm fire. Charles' finger is singed on a metal plate heated red hot to stop the bleeding and to seal the wound. They provide him an elixir to numb his agony and allow him to sleep. Unbelievable relief hits them both. Judith spends day and night nursing him, stroking his forehead and saying kind words. This feeling of goodness causes Charles to free himself of any hints of worry.

As the rains stop, the worry of the people transfers from their own wetness to that of the crops, which were either torn or destroyed, buried in mounds of soil. Most of the crops, if still standing, have been drenched for so long that they have become infested with a bluish-green mold and are thus inedible.

It is the fate of the wielders of magical arts, that they will be loved by people as long as they retain their ability to attract good fortune. Sybil and her retinue are well known in Newbury, and though they are not followers of the Christian path, people thought well of them since, regardless of what strange acts they performed out in those fields, the harvest was always plentiful. One may think a Christian is free and wholly against such practices, regardless of the outcome, but religions are not at all uniform in this way. People of this land have had a long history with such wonder workers that belief in such things are as settled in them as knowing that the sun will rise. It is this belief that paves the way for these wonder workers to be accused of wrongdoing, for if their actions are responsible for abundance, they are also the cause of destruction. It is therefore the word going on around town that they have been robbed of their harvest by the willful malevolence of the witch known as Sybil.

As the hate rises in the people, they begin making connections between Sybil and her companions and the people of the forest who have slaughtered countless numbers of their fellow citizens and have filled them with terror for as long as they can remember. The people have been put in such a despicable mood due to the effects of the downpour that they have vowed an all-out attack on witchcraft. Sybil and the others who reside in the shabby living quarters beside her are rounded up and brought into town.

Soon after, Thomas visits the jail. Sybil is sitting against the wall, covered in shadow.

"Hey. Hey, it's me," he calls to her.

At this she stands and wanders over, more ragged than ever.

"Hello there, Thomas," she says, muted of feeling.

"Why didn't you grab your things and run?" he asks her.

"I have no desire for anything these cities can offer me."

"So, you'd find a way. I know you could."

"My way is done. They've already killed me."

Thomas, at first, finds this to be lacking in heart, but then relents and says, "Yes. I… guess it's not truly living if…"

After a moment she asks, "Where's Charles?"

"I don't know. He disappeared when the rain came."

"It's best for him to stay away from us—and you too. I feel they only want to punish us, the faces they recognize, but you never know what people will do when vengeance is in their hearts."

He nods and reaches into her cell. They clasp palms. He tells her, "You are strong. Stay that way as they come for you," and then, when he feels he can be of little more help, he is on his way. He crosses over to the main road and slips within the gathering, cantankerous crowd in the city square.

As the heat of the high afternoon sun strikes, Sybil, Nicholas, Pete, Mary, and the eight other workers of the field under Sybil's leadership are all strapped high above the crowd screeching with hate. Thirteen piles of sticks are gathered, one before each pitiable individual. The crowd is filled with an ecstatic fervor, a feeling of justice in doing away with those who desire to do evil. Elbowing his way through this wall of fury, Thomas sees Charles and Judith and makes his way to them. These three young ones seem to be the only ones taking the side of those accused. The noise is deafening. An official wearing a black doublet lined with shimmering emeralds and matching green tights speaks, but his voice cannot be heard over the cacophony.

The fires are lit. The dry wood is consumed within a moment and the screams are already heard as the feet of Sybil, Nicholas, and the others are cooked. Standing beside Charles, Thomas feels this great crime forcefully in his gut.

Charles stares hard at the back of a man in front of him who raises his arms cheering, "Burn! Burn, then burn again in hell!" Locked in blind, hateful fury, Charles thrusts his elbows hard into the man's back, leading him to retaliate. Charles pushes through, clawing viciously at those in his way, squeezing closer and closer to the front. Thomas has no choice but to support his friend, and so, despite the madness he surmises taking on a crowd is, he goes in anyway. Charles reaches the base of his mother's pyre. She is screaming mad, ungirded by sanity. He is gripped by no less than five guards just as he was about to leap before the sloped terrace of flaming wood and attempt to set his parents free. Thomas' legs carry him almost unconsciously toward the pyre. He throws the logs, fire and all, with such alarm as if he thought it would save his own parents. He is quickly overtaken, beaten into unconsciousness by some club.

These peasants disappear under excruciating torture, cooked alive as the voyeurs soak their eyes full. Roasted, pouring grease as the flesh of a pig may under such heat, they die slowly, blackening, imploring their organs to cook through so life will at last leave.

Thomas stands over Charles who is lying in a crumpled heap of sadness upon the ground. Charles peers upward, sickened to see the wall of charred skeletons. He hides his face as black smoke drifts their way from the ashes of the pyre.

"C'mon," Thomas says, pulling Charles to his feet. "Let's get away from this place."

Charles replays in his mind how he broke through the frenzied crowd who were celebrating a fervent lust for his parents' death. He recalls the applause that intermittently grew in fervor as new layers of their flesh sloughed off, furthering the metamorphosis. He heard a woman in the crowd repeatedly saying, "Send the witches to hell!" one of the many mantras of the day. He wrestled with common citizens to try to get to his parents. As he stood before them, staring into their eyes, he could do nothing. All of society was a devil. Though he kicked and bit the guards like a wild beast, he failed to stop them. He wonders what more he could do. He desires revenge. In his young mind he incinerates every statesman, every member of the various religious orders he passes by on the street. Though his basic demeanor is calm and cool, his deep-seated hatred causes him a great desire to strap every fool to a pile of sticks and char their flesh in an inferno. He would light whole country on fire if he could.

# Trauma and Recovery

**T**HOMAS, CHARLES, AND JUDITH return to their haunts on the edge of the Thames, oppressed by an unending hate and an itch to disembowel these people who heralded such horrific murder. A long, sad time is had in riding in a wagon transporting pigs. Months pass, and still Charles fails to recover from the trauma. He is dead to the world. Seeing Charles gutted of the desire for life so unrepentantly casts Judith and Thomas' happiness into stone.

Watching him in this misery brings Thomas back to when he saw his own parents stiff and dead. He once thought he was the poorest, most lonesome person around. Now he finds there is no end to the number of wretched souls with stories immeasurably heartbreaking, telling of such cruelty that his parents' withering seems nothing at all.

Charles often screams at night in his sleep, then wakes, staring into the darkness, realizing he is in this world. In the dizzy state of waking, he realizes that he has returned to where he was been trying to escape.

One particular night, Thomas raises, intent at all costs to help his friend and to relent without retaliation to whatever sharp words or lashing out Charles inflicts in his boiling over. Charles lies with his face half buried in his straw pillow, breathing heavy, weak from the exhaustion of releasing so much emotion. Thomas stands over him and taps him on the shoulder. Charles slaps his hand off of him violently. Tom tries again and receives the same reaction, only harder. With a smirk, smacks him quickly several times on the shoulder.

"Get off!" Charles yells.

"Hey, listen."

"Get off me! Don't fucking touch me!" Charles says, throwing out his legs, kicking at Thomas. He covers his head with his thin blanket.

"Quit wallowing in here, friend. I've got something that might help," Thomas says, holding up a bottle of half-drunk sour wine.

"Where'd you get that?" Charles says, peeking his eyes from his cover, his eyes widening in seeing this, trying to focus in the small amount of light.

"I, uh, found it," Thomas says with a slight laugh. "Took only a little here and there, trying to make it last. But now's a perfect time to squander it. What do you say?"

"Okay," Charles says, cracking a smile.

They both toss on a few items of clothing for warmth and wander to the beach. There they sit in the damp sand and speak their minds, sharing heart to heart while passing the bottle back and forth. Each drink triggers the urge to puke, and getting a gulp down requires pounding their fists into their thighs to direct the unpleasant feeling elsewhere.

Full now, in a drunken stupor, Charles says, "My mother. I will never see her again. My father; what could he do? He was so weak already."

He tightens his jaw, breathing slowly and meditatively.

Thomas, sipping from the bottle says, "They needed someone to blame, those selfish bastards. To make themselves feel strong, they crush those they feel are different."

"After all the years of working for almost nothing. One thing goes wrong and the people who have benefited, they cry for murder when they're hurting. I want to run through their town and cut all their throats. Watch them squirming, struggling to breathe. I want to teach them that it's not so easy just to cast blame. That it hurts."

"Here," Thomas says suddenly, untying the knot in the rope holding the caul around his neck. "This is better suited for you, I think."

"What is it?" Charles asks.

"You mother gave it to me. She said it will protect the wearer and guide him on the right path."

"No," Charles says. "It was meant for you. She wanted you to have it."

"You know that she loved you. She kept you from such things to keep you safe."

"I have never seen such a thing with my own eyes," Charles says, holding it close. Thomas glimpses Charles' small finger of which only a stub remains.

Alarmed, Thomas asks, "How did you—?"

"Never mind that. I'll tell you another time," Charles says, lying back on the sand, resting his head on his crossed palms.

Both boys wake intermittently in the morning hours with urges to vomit. After a time, the sun's rays become too much. They leave pairs of footprints from the royal purple sunk in puddles sprayed from their surges.

Thomas and Charles dodge this way and that within the clusters of people in order to escape an angry, portly gentleman and his servant. They chase just behind the boys. Thomas has a small purse in his hand. The two boys hide behind a merchant's cart until they see that the two angry fellows have caught sight of them and are once again in pursuit.

"Where to?" Thomas says.

Smiling, Charles says, "Do not worry. I know a shortcut."

Charles tugs on Thomas' shirt, and they speed down the nearest corner and scram down an alley. Within the dark, the boys see the two run by. They watch them disappear around the next corner and run off.

Passing down a series of alleyways, Thomas and Charles slip through a passage covered by a cloth flap and enter into a small chamber in which five others around the same age reside. Robert, Henry, Jack, and David play cherry stones by dim candlelight, while the last, Edward, lies on his side with noxious chemicals wafting from his direction.

Charles says, "Still content on playing games I see. Well, we picked up some real loot!"

Edward says, "So what? I earned my keep. I worked all day," letting out a raspy, loud cough.

"You all right?" Thomas asks him.

"Yeah, I am not supposed to breathe in the poison. But I can't help it," Edward answers.

After a time, a feeling of claustrophobia builds in Thomas and Charles. They step outside and wander wherever their legs take them. They stroll over cobbled roads, crossing through the many dark alleys as a patrolman passes by. Inevitably they reach the seashore once again and stand barefoot before the calm waves. Thomas wraps a blanket around himself. They sit on the sand and stare at the sea for over an hour. Charles stands and brushes the sand off of his clothing saying, "Why don't you find some shelter?"

Thomas stares ahead for a moment and answers, "This is the only home I've ever had. I can always forget my troubles here."

Charles takes out an old wooden comb that looks as if a carriage or two had run over it. Deep scars are carved into the sides and several of the teeth are long missing. He runs the remaining teeth through his well kept hair. He has been teaching himself to cut his own hair for the past year, preferring a short-cropped style, letting the strands sit neat under his wool hat.

Thomas lets himself go ragged like most other street urchins. His hair is a tangled mess hanging across his eyes and it is filled with dirt and other refuse. His face is covered with caked mud, as are his clothes. Under his long fingernails is a black paste, telling of his frequent excavations in garbage heaps and hiding his money in the earth like a dog buries a bone.

Charles takes off his coat and soaks it in the small waves lapping upon the beach. He scrubs it hard into the sand, hoping to remove some of the filth. The smell and the grime seem to be magnetically attracted to those who sleep side by side with the cockroaches. Charles wishes to minimize this effect as much as possible.

"Why do you even bother?" Thomas asks.

"Even though no one may notice, I notice," Charles says.

"It is just going to come back like it always does."

"Maybe so. But I keep telling myself that this is temporary. I feel that if I accept that I am trash, I will remain trash and will be more and more chained to this sort of life as I get older. You don't think we will be like this forever, do you?"

"N-no."

"The dirt and the smell slowly take over your mind and suddenly you believe that you belong here. I don't belong here. I believe that if I treat myself like I am a lord, one day I will be a lord. Those who run such a poor society that allows so many to suffer—they are the trash, not us."

Thomas contains his feelings for a moment, finally admitting, "I can't

Charles. I just can't make myself believe it."

"What's the problem? Why can't we have what they have?"

"I don't want to be a lord. I just want to live on a farm like the one I grew up on."

Charles, seriously confused by this statement says, "A farm? Now, how are you supposed to afford that?"

"I've been saving."

"How much you got?"

Thomas empties the contents of his pouch into the sand, all of it equaling about four pounds.

Charles, not wishing to condescend in response to hearing his friend's dream, forces himself to voice with an unemotional tone, "You know how much a farm costs, don't you?"

"I know."

"It'll take all your life to save that much."

"If that's what it takes," Thomas says, letting his sadness slip out.

"Someone needs to find a real job."

Thomas sits for a long time wondering what can be done to make some money.

Thomas stands before Gilbert and Abraham with his head lowered. He forces out, "I can't survive digging up worms anymore."

Abraham's eyes rise from his pile of fish guts and says, "Oh no? What is it you're trying to say?"

"I want you to teach me to fish, to man a ship. I have no craft of my own."

"We don't take on apprentices, kid."

"Please, I beg of you. I'll do everything. You can just sit back and order me around. I don't ask for much, believe me."

"Do you understand? We're too old to go through all the trouble of teaching someone new. Please understand, Thomas."

"Don't pay me then. Just bring me on so I can learn."

"It don't make sense. You gotta eat; it won't work."

"No?" Thomas says, scooping up a handful of fish guts. He pops fish hearts and kidneys in his mouth and chews them down raw. "I'm hungry, see?" he says, shoving in the whole handful of bloody intestines, gnashing them in his teeth.

Abraham becomes alarmed, fearing customers may be scared off by Thomas' hysterics. "Have you fucking lost it, boy?" he grimaces, imagining what it would feel like swallowing down that bile and blood. "I blame myself for encouraging him when he was young."

"So you will?" Thomas says.

"We'll see if you can handle it," Abraham says, annoyed.

"I will. I'll show you. And no playing soft like when I was a kid. Make me a true sailor. I want to become a master and net the whole sea for you old walrus fuckers."

"I suppose it does take a dose of madness to fall into this life."

Thomas' head spins. His stomach is hollow and fatigue reels his body. The muscles in his arms are clenched tight from the constant strain of the rigging and wrestling the tiller. The rocking of the ship fills him with nausea and causes his abdominal muscles to contract, trying to send up food that is not there. He leans over the side of the deck, his throat constantly making a sound like a frog, "whulp, whulp," as he spits out thick lemon colored streams of stomach acid.

He peers outward into the abyss. Amidst the sun's gold reflected on the concave ripples of the glassy sea stands a figure of black. Thomas doubts his eyes, but the shadow remains, its obsidian head poking above the horizon. Despite the churning waters it remains still. Thomas wonders what this thing could be. He is not afraid, only curious. Is this figure here for him, or is it the ghost of a sailor who died on this spot? As the ship rises and falls, it drifts from the silhouette among the waves. Distanced now, the figure heads straight for England.

Thomas suddenly feels an itching sensation, not on his skin, but a sort of irritation in his heart. This anxiousness culminates in a vision of swirling sardines, the sparks of their small brains showing themselves before his mind's eye to be in the place underneath where the shadow had stationed itself. Thomas becomes alarmed that the ship is sailing past this point.

He calls to Gilbert, "Turn the tiller! Out there!" he says, pointing his finger aloft. "I can feel the fish squirming just at the surface."

Gilbert and Abraham look to each other quizzically in hearing what they conceive to be nonsense spoken from the mouth of a delirious, seasick boy, but they have no alternative plan. The tiller is turned and the net is dropped once they reach the spot. As the anchor is dropped, they immediately see the silver glistening as the school flows and scatters. Ultimately many are caught in the snare. In no time their net is near bursting, to the astonishment of all. This action is repeated day after day. With Thomas being guided by the unknown spirit, record hauls are loaded early in the day, allowing them to retire before lunch and enjoy some free time.

After a few months of this, while Thomas is busy mending torn netting, Abraham and Gilbert approach him. Abraham tells him, "Thomas? Stand up, please."

"What is it?" he says, awaiting criticism.

"You have a gift for fishing… and, well…"

"What's wrong?"

"Nothing, boy. It's just… we're too old to do this any longer, but it's hard to quit doing the only thing you've ever done."

Gilbert cuts in, "We want you to get your friends to be your crew. Take over for us."

Thomas twists his face in hearing this.

"It's just a fishing boat, Thomas. You can handle it," Abraham says.

Thomas mumbles, "I don't know… how to do many things still. I'm—"

Abraham says, "Well, there's the offer. If you make up your mind, let us know."

"Alright."

Thomas leads his companions to the lonely fishing boat bobbing in the waves. They climb aboard, one after another, and he unties the rope securing it to the dock. The boys chat about nothing special as the vessel slowly floats down the Thames. Finally, the sea is in view. As the land fades away and blue is all they can see, Thomas calls for them to be quiet.

The boys absorb the daily instructions on proper rigging and maintenance as Thomas repeats himself, sometimes sternly if they do not listen. Benjamin, a plump, but beefy young man, proves himself to be fully capable of steadying the ship under the choppiest conditions.

Jack disobeys and removes a grime-covered whiskey bottle from his jacket.

Jack says, "Let's celebrate, boys! We can learn later!" and makes rounds pouring the liquid into the open mouths of his companions.

"There's work to be done!" Thomas yells.

"What's the big rush, huh?" Jack calls out among the cluster.

Thomas' teeth press in his fury. His anger boils as he stares hard into his crew frolicking about the deck. He pushes Benjamin aside and forces the tiller the opposite direction.

"Hold onto something," he tells Benjamin and Charles.

They turn to him quizzically. The ship tilts, rocking the port side upward at nearly a 45 degree angle. The young hooligans are taken by surprise, slamming against beams and falling in a pile against the sidewall. Two fall overboard before Thomas steadies the ship again. Ben and Charles cautiously release their grip on the mizzenmast.

"First Mate?" Thomas yells.

Charles rises, rubbing his elbow. "Yes, um, Captain?" he says, finding the words strange, addressing his friend in such a way.

"Lower the anchor so we can lift these good-for-nothings."

"Aye aye, Captain," he says, rushing to and releasing the anchor. Ropes are lowered and the two struggle through the open sea, grasping onto the lines and raising themselves up one arm after the other.

"You will not disobey me again. Is that clear?" Thomas calls to them.

"Yes, Captain!" they yell in unison, standing at attention.

"We will not be taken by surprise like that again. Is that clear?"

"Yes Captain!"

"It is we who are in the business of surprising. We are not to take this lightly like amateurs."

Day after day, Thomas and his companions wake early, fitting into their stations like the organs of this sea vessel. A sense of pride adheres to their hearts. Whenever they introduce themselves, it goes as such: "I'm Jack, carpenter under the leadership of Thomas Ashcroft," or "My name's David, boatswain of the best fishing crew in the city."

This dropping of status is most prevalent when meeting other seamen in passing or in a tavern. The esteem that is gained from these sea-weathered cod-heads is far above the disdain they received scraping the streets for sustenance. This status stating is an almost regular part of speech with the girls who the boys meet. It works astonishingly well on them, as if blurting out of one's station on the ship is the natural and biological answer to questions such as: "What do you want?" and "Oh God, what now?"

Nearly half of the dozen boys manage to somehow snag a girl, bringing fresh fish to share as well as expendable money. It is funny to Thomas in a way, feeling this game to be awkward to him. He sees his friends turn into some sort of family men. They are still awkward and youthful in the movement of their limbs and their way of speech, but otherwise acting out the traditions of carrying "home" food and coin in turn for kisses and affection. Home would, alas, be a moment sitting together on a crate, or having a bite together somewhere. At best, some time may be spent off at play with a girl. Thomas, knowing these young brats, he always suspects their tales of exploit must be elaborated and concocted, but still he wonders and feels envious. No matter how his feelings of inferiority tug on him, he always feels that the act of bragging and falsely boosting the greatness of one's achievements an act far beneath him.

At the end of each day of work, Thomas approaches Abraham and Gilbert and places before them an equal share of the money made and a plate of food. This is an act of thanks for allowing them to use their ship and equipment, as well as appreciation, a nod to the instruction bestowed and to lives spent in service. Thomas often stays by the side of Abraham and listens to his stories of storms and bureaucracy spliced in with faint memories of friends and loves known long ago.

A fruitful day is had. Thomas leads his companions to follow a frenzied mass of herring north up the coast, following them until they take rest in a small cove nestled by cliffs underneath a manor donning a towering chimney. Smoke rises from the house on this chilly day. The boys drag their nets on each side, filling them with the fat, slippery creatures.

Feeling completed as far as his momentary goal is concerned, Thomas orders the ship sailed back to dock after a brief celebration, so that the fish may be sold fresh for suppertime. The halo of tangerines and violets pours into the atmosphere, sloughing off the layers of the sun as the bells of sundown ring. The yellow sphere has reached the horizon which signals that work is done. The wet mass of netting drains off the salty water as the sea life is brought in. Another day of waiting and diligence is over. They now head back home.

Thomas heads into Abraham's dark shelter built completely with driftwood. Abraham lies silent on a bed consisting of a quilt and some worn out clothing. Thomas lays his hands on the old sailor.

Abraham says, "You will have to seek for a captain to work under."

"I will never be able to."

Abraham lies silent. He finally, after a span of contemplation says, "The government will take my ship. I worked for it, but still somehow I have no right. It will be taken for use for the Queen's stores."

"Nothing is as it should be. Damn them."

"All of you will have to work under another master, commanded by a captain."

Thomas continues, "I cannot be told."

"You will suffer then," Abraham says.

"I know it could be no other way. By this time I would be lonely and empty without that feeling."

Thomas sits and holds onto his hand for the rest of the day, and for hours each day following this sharing of woe. Gradually, the grip becomes more and more delicate, and finally life leaves altogether.

Thomas and his friends have become desperate. Their means of survival is taken from them, and the girls are far gone, save for Judith. Representatives from the Crown declare that Abraham had no legal will, and so his ship is taken for the government for their own benefit. The boys are told to leave without protest or face severe punishment.

At a complete loss of what to do, they spend each day loafing on the dock, the sun baking them into a dumb stupor. Suddenly, a large crate crashes from the deck of a ship before them, its contents spilling out like an avalanche. A barrel-bellied sailor speeds away past dingy boys. The crew of the ship chases after them, but stops short as passers-by take up the contents of the spilled cargo for themselves. Thomas knows not where to set his focus, because his comrades pile goods into every conceivable space of their shirts. A great tower of muscle, he assumes to be the captain of the ship, overlooks them with grim menace and branching blood streaming from his balding scalp. "After them!" he yells to his crew. The few who follow cannot catch the young boys who scatter down various streets like a churning swarm of flies.

Judith's behavior strikes Charles as queer. Although she heaps insults upon those who come to drag her back to the house of prostitution, at other times she speaks kindly with them if they happen to pass by. She speaks highly of herself, of how she has repented of her old ways, vocally scathing her old self, though her manner is, as it slips through from time to time, inconsistent. She disappears at times for days, and has been caught on more than a few occasions with more money than Charles brought her from fishing. He tells her she has no need to soil herself in that way, but she makes every excuse in the world why she may need to return. As soon as his job was lost, although there is plenty of money left, it is difficult to find her much of the time. The oddness of her behavior wells up in him, for he has such an abundance of free time in which to spend with her. There is no reason for her to go there. She denies everything, feeling great insult in his asking, but he knows something is not right. She is either with another boy or she has given in and has sunk herself in that horrid lifestyle.

Judith meets with Charles and his friends one night at a tavern called The Golden Boar. When he sees her, there is no elation in him. It is as if a screen has been pulled over her figure, filtering out the color and light he once saw. He is cold to her, answering very abruptly with matter-of-fact answers, purposely holding in his feelings so that they don't get stepped upon or contaminated by her filth.

They sit silent for the most part, then at some point after they are both sufficiently drunk, he gets up to buy himself ale. Bound with Simon in a conversation of fleeting worth, Charles notices a lecher in his thirties with reddish-brown, unkempt hair falling out from the sides of an ages-old felt hat. He approaches Judith, looking to her with eyes sunk into caves of ash. She smiles and touches him on the chest affectionately. Two friends of his leer at her: their measures of her worth can be assessed in their wanting looks. What they know about her, if not known firsthand, must be informed by a vulgar tale. The lecher goes in for a kiss, but is pushed off. By his third attempt she gives in, clouded by her drunken state.

Simon notices that Charles' attention has been distracted for some time, and to his shock he sees why.

"My God! What is this?" Simon says.

"The stupid girl knows only abuse."

Charles fights the tears, though a few rest upon his eyelids. He knows well what business she attends to in her disappearances— he is not stupid after all—but he never wished to have to watch. Now it has finally reached an apex and the flood pours over, unstoppable. His friends now stand by his side, their mouths agape, calling out a need for vengeance upon this man who violates poor Judith. With a light touch Charles signals Thomas, Benjamin and others to stay put.

Judith clenches onto Charles the moment she sees him, hanging around his neck. She is horrified with what she has done, reviled with herself. Her face is pressed into his shoulder, her tears drenching his shirt. His eyes gush now, remembering this feeling of being close to her being pure and untarnished. He can hear the cackling of the degenerates behind her, mocking him. It is clear to him what he must do. He forcefully removes her arms from around his neck, pushing against her efforts, seeing the disbelief in her eyes. He presses them down at her sides and leaves her be. She is a pit of black misery. To him, their two figures seem to separate at breathtaking speed, though they are caught with breath tied up in their throats, immobile.

Judith shudders, her lip quivering. Her eyes are frozen, scarcely blinking. She wants him to forgive her so badly.

Simon cuts in and says to Charles, "Take her. We can leave you two alone tonight, let you work it out."

Benjamin agrees, saying, "Yeah, we can sleep outside. It's nice tonight."

Thomas agrees as well, in the belief that things will be well again. "Come on girl," he says. "Let us take you away from this."

Charles shakes his head in solemn disagreement. He coughs and takes a deep breath, gathering his strength. "Let her cry, boys," he tells them.

He guides his friends with a wave of his hand. From this stuffy tavern, into the open air, they follow him without protest.

Once they are under the cover of stars, far from the stress and noise, in disbelief Thomas speaks out, "Y-you're going to leave her?"

"I've done all I can do," Charles tells them.

Charles wanders down the dock, followed by his closest friends, passing rows of ships under the glow, wanting to be as far away from her as possible.

# Poor Ed

UPON ENTERING a patch of countryside, Thomas notices a large circular gate. Within the enclosure curious noises are emitting. Perhaps two hundred people are calling out with murder-lust in their voices, as if there were an execution commencing. Even more curious are the intermittent hoots of excited dogs along with the call of a much bigger creature. Thomas pulls himself up the side of the barrier and peers within.

In the center of an arena, a large brown bear is latched to a short tether, swiping at two mastiffs. Both dogs tear into the bear's chest and rip flesh, causing it to gush blood. Two more of the trained beasts latch onto vital organs in the bear's neck, shaking their heads in an effort to tear something open. The bear's eyes show its valiant spirit as it attempts to slash its claws and pierce the flesh under one of the dog's ribs. The muscular yet agile dogs do not care if they are injured. Knowing the dance, they take a step back, then leap upon the bear as they were trained to do, taking it to the ground and tearing into it. The beast swipes in vain, unable to defend itself. Thomas is sickened and frightened by the sight and moves through the tree line once again, peering backward from time to time.

There in the clearing, he sees the figure of Edward waiting impatiently amid the drifting fog. He calls to him, "Why didn't you wait for me?"

Edward says, "Let's go," his raspy voice carrying across the distance. "They have surely started the boilers by now!"

Thomas pushes himself, sprinting across the field. Suddenly, a waft of a horrid stench fills his nose and lungs. "Fucking ass fucker! What—?" Thomas says choking.

"Now you know why they are forced to construct their mill such a way from town," he says, muffling his frog-like voice.

"Bury the shit! Oh! I will be sick," Thomas says, holding his shirt over his nose and mouth.

They meet the road. Thomas can see the far-off destination with its several billowing streams of clouds rising.

"Keep a fast pace. I intend to win their favor," Edward says.

"What for?" Thomas asks, his voice muffled through his shirt.

"Admittance in the dyers guild would be the greatest honor. If I show my desire, I feel I can rise in their esteem."

Thomas sighs and acknowledges the logic. "I can understand that," he says.

"I know you can. This is the way out for me. It's something I can do, something for the beauty of our country. For the people, for our churches, the paintings that sit in the houses of the rich."

"Do they acknowledge this work?" Thomas asks.

"They push us off five miles if that answers your question," Edward says laughing.

As they reach the mill, Edward explains the various processes, "See, the leaves of the woad are plucked from two-year-old plants and are carted here in the early morning. They are placed in these circular troughs which are ground by these grinders."

"How long have you been working here?" Thomas asks.

"Almost a year," he says faintly, focusing on his work.

Thomas looks over the construction, which is made up of two great beams with a sturdy pole in the center. This hangs over the shallow pit full of the deep blue mashed material. Three wheels each as tall as the boys are pulled by one horse each, tearing up the material with the long bars of wooden teeth. Workers churn the material with skinny rakes, ensuring all is consistent. Here and there they mix in manure as a mordant.

Edward says, "You will most likely start rolling. Once the woad is pressed into the consistency of clay, we roll them into balls over a slab of wood, ensuring all moisture is removed so that they do not rot. They are then left here to dry and ferment for days."

The finished balls of woad sit on shelves in the open air specially made for the purpose. The gradation of these long planks reminds Thomas of a playhouse, the dye material being unusually patient spectators. The smell arising from these reminds him of the retch-inducing sourness when uncovering something dead with its moisture preserved.

Edward gives Thomas a board. They both plant the wood upon their bent knees to provide support, then set themselves to pressing clumps of the blue material over the surface. Their fingers dig in, staining them blue, the spaces under the fingernails inevitably being packed tight with the stuff. By giving force to a ball, a bit of moisture sloshes forth. The reek that releases soon saturates their skin. Half the day is spent at this, until a supervisor approaches Edward. His face is covered in pink and purple splotches, something that results from nothing else but severe burns.

He says to Edward, "You know how to run the kettles?"

Edward nods, trying not to stare at the peeling, rubbery skin on the face before him.

He continues, "I need someone over there. My best cook's gone ill. You think you can handle it?"

Edward agrees proudly, "Yes, I've been watching them closely."

"Good. There'll be a bit of extra pay in it for you, then."

"Thank you, sir."

"Take your friend as well and teach him what you know. Now be off."

They hurry to another production of dye. Thomas' eyes water upon approaching, and he senses it is somehow more toxic than the previous operation. Here madder root is crushed much the same as the woad. A fire is kindled under a copper kettle four feet in diameter. Edward takes to carrying one shirt at a time on an oar, dipping it into a batch of the red solution composed of madder diluted in water. After a time, he dips each one into the caustic bath of salts. Edward is very astute, never letting his mind get distracted from keeping the process in a precise balance, despite the acidic burn that sticks to his throat every time he approaches the kettles to do his checks.

Thomas is much more irritated by this discomfort that is erupting into a great swelling and rawness deeper and deeper into him as the hours pass. Still, he delivers blocks of wood to feed the fires at Edward's command. He does his job washing the finished cloth and hanging them to dry, determined to complete his day of work and receive his pay without argument.

Edward and Thomas let their feet lead them unconsciously down the dirt road as evening approaches. They attempt conversation, though it is difficult now that their throats are flaring with pain. Thomas heaves up mucus from his throat and spits into the soil. It shines in the dying light, black goo highlighted with reds. Thomas stares back at it as they pass.

"You know what that means, don't you?" Thomas says.

"What?"

"I'm done working in that shit. People don't spit up black, Ed. I'll rather go without food for a month than have that running through me."

"You've got to be tough—"

"We've got to be smart, friend. There will be other jobs."

"Don't worry. This happens sometimes. If I rest it'll go away."

"I don't—"

"They won't make me breathe that in forever. They see how capable I am," Edward says, rubbing his rugged hands together, scanning over the stains of purple up to his forearms.

"They don't think," Thomas tells him. "You see it their eyes. You've got to care for yourself, because no one else will."

"But I want to be strong. I can't give up."

"Run with us, brother. Together we'll be strong. You don't need to prove yourself to some cocksuckers who don't care if you live or die."

Edward continues to leave every morning, despite barely being able to breathe. His innards feel inflamed and his stool comes out as black and red as Thomas' spit. Thomas spends the days following his work as a dyer spitting and analyzing the appearance. By the fourth day it begins to come out less black, and the ache in his esophagus and lungs lessens.

Edward, on the other hand, returns soon after his morning exit a few days later and lies down to sleep. The seriousness of his failure to work is made more aware to the other boys as he spends day after day coughing up the most noxious bile. Blood shoots forth in his vomit hour after hour. The boys take turns feeding him small bits of food. They provide water, which he takes reluctantly. They pray over him frequently, for they are so alarmed and humbled by this collapse of their friend's body and spirit. To their gladness, he recovers some.

As the sun rises, Thomas wakes Edward to feed him a bit of porridge.

"Wake up, friend. Time for breakfast," Thomas says, lightly shaking him.

"I can't… eat," Edward says. His face is a stark, chalky white.

"Try a little," Thomas tells him, placing a dab on the end of the spoon. Edward takes this bit and rubs it around with his tongue.

Thomas dips a tin cup in a bucket of water.

"You thirsty?" Thomas asks Edward.

Edward is still smacking the remaining porridge stuck around his mouth. With a dazed look, he shakes his head.

"Here," Thomas says as he drips a little water at a time into his friend's mouth. "A little more food this time, okay?" he says, filling half the spoon this time. Edward gets it down just fine.

Edward mumbles, "I want to get up for work tomorrow. Maybe if I rest…"

Thomas tries to ignore this statement. He says, "I'll leave the food here. And the water. Take care of yourself."

The next day Thomas returns to the hideout after sleeping on the beach. Charles and the four other boys are sitting in a circle. Thomas carries a lukewarm bowl of porridge before Edward, who lies in the same spot as before, aching all over.

Thomas asks, "Ed, you didn't work today?"

Edward breathes raspy, answering slowly, "I can't breathe. I couldn't go."

"Good," Thomas says. "Get that place out of your mind."

Charles says, "So you're saying you're not joining us?"

Ed says, "I don't like stealing. Regardless, I cannot in my condition. Sorry, Charles."

"I was joking," Charles says, patting Edward's shoulder. "Get your health up."

"Can you handle feeding yourself?" Thomas asks Edward.

"I think so," Edward says, whispering.

Thomas stands and declares to his comrades, "Let's get on with this. The game is Robin Hood. Steal from the rich. The team with the smallest loot buys dinner out of their take. Got it?"

Behind a street butcher, Charles digs through garbage and finds parts of a lamb. He dips his hands in a ball of gelatinous blood and fat, smearing it across his face. Thomas and Charles make their way down the road, trying not to seem suspicious. A well-dressed man beats a poor family with a walking stick.

"Let us be away from here," Thomas says.

They run up the next street. Charles points to someone in a faded red outfit. Thomas says, "No, too poor."

Charles points to a gentleman in a blue doublet. A gown trimmed with bear fur is draped over him.

"How about him?" Charles asks.

Thomas answers, "No, he obviously is trying too hard. He must have spent it all on that fur."

They turn around a corner and see a noble up ahead wearing a fine black doublet, a short black cape, and an elaborate ruff around his neck. Instantly recognizing a prime target, Charles says, "Ah, there it is. His purse is 'bout to burst."

The boys step quickly before him, Thomas behind and Charles just ahead

Charles says to him, "I beg you, help me sir! I was assaulted just down the road by a band of Catholics!"

Thomas steps behind the man, following each step. Thomas has a horn sheath on his thumb and a small knife in his hand. The purse dangles from the man's waist, just below his cape.

Charles continues, "I am in desperate need of medical assistance! Please sir!"

The noble sidesteps him and says, "Excuse me, I must be going."

Charles speaks, now waving his arms, "I beg you, please help me!"

Thomas snips the purse free by pressing the knife to the horn sheath. It falls gently into his hand.

The noble pushes Charles from his path and says, "Filthy wretch—move out of my way!" and keeps moving past.

Thomas and Charles smile to each other. Thomas pats Charles on the back and they head the other direction.

Thomas and Charles recline on a bench at the inn. The other four boys stroll in.

Charles says aloud so they all can hear, "I will have the lamb and—what is your taste?"

Thomas says grinning, "Duck. I'll have the duck."

Robert says, "That is too much!"

David holds Charles' shoulder and inspects his face closely. He asks him, "What is that, blood on your face?"

Robert, now inspecting close as well, says, "Were you hurt?"

David says, "It is not his blood; I know that."

Thomas sits proudly. He places the stolen purse on the table and says, "Well, boys? You have any chance?"

Taking a seat up close, Jack says, "Show us—show us what you have there."

Thomas pulls a penny out of the purse and says, "Penny…"

"That's nothing!" Jack exclaims.

Thomas pulls a shilling from the purse and feigns pride over it.

Jack says, "Still, what's the confidence about? I don't see—"

Thomas pulls a crown out of the purse. They unanimously voice an ecstatic scream.

Thomas sarcastically says, "What is it? It's just a crown."

Charles, pointing to their four bags lying on the table, bursts out laughing, saying, "You mean you cannot beat a measly crown? With all those bags?!"

Leaning on the wall outside their hideout, Thomas munches on a drumstick. He says, "Good thing we saved some for Ed," and enters. Inside, the boys huddle around. Thomas makes his way to Edward.

Thomas says, "Ed. Edward."

Thomas shakes Edward's shoulder and Edward's body flops face first on the ground. Thomas jumps back with fright. The other boys are struck breathless. They inch forward slowly.

Thomas screams, "No! God no! Get up, Edward!" He rises, places his hands on Ed's cold face, and screams.

"Poor Ed," Charles says. He hangs his head low.

All of the boys become very quiet.

The boys stare over Edward's body lying on a dry, leaf-strewn field as Charles digs his grave. They decide to bury him in this spot since the shade of the willow tree hanging overhead seems pleasant. The wait for the hole to be dug is agonizing. Jack tries in vain to rub free the bluish-purple stains deep in the grooves of Edward's palms. He is stained with the shame that ended him.

Charles stops and says, "I think that should be fine."

The others nod in agreement, seeing that the grave is about four feet deep, and it is long enough for the body to lie.

They all take hold of their friend and gently lower him down onto the water-drenched soil intersected with roots of various sizes and colors.

Charles piles the loose dirt high on the still face, feeling it as an almost rude gesture. He wants Edward to react, but he does not, which cuts him deeply. He continues filling in the hole, patting it down hard every so often.

Thomas, kneeling at the grave, takes up a fistful of dirt and says, "This is what he gets for trying to live honestly?"

They stare at the grave somberly.

Jack speaks from the heart. "I always liked him. I never saw him do anything wrong at all."

Charles appears agitated. He wants to make a grand speech and inspire his friends, but he is at a loss for words. An uncomfortable silence remains there, hovering. They cannot stand it, so, save for Thomas, they all leave.

Thomas, in the cover of foliage, collapses beside the trunk of a walnut tree and stares blankly. Over an hour passes before Charles looks for and finds Thomas. Lying on the earth, clutching his knees, he barks loudly, "Leave me alone!"

He remains in that spot despondent, feeding on nuts when his stomach complains. He wanders back to his living quarters early the next morning only because thirst becomes too much.

# Street Trash

**F**OR TWO MORE YEARS Thomas and his companions play out the same routine, that is, until they see Lucy for the first time. This petite girl is a few years younger than them. She has a strong pension for candies, pretty dresses, and having her black locks curled. She conceals her sweet demeanor with a vicious tenacity. Brought up in affluent society, she has every means to satisfy her physical comforts, though she has no freedom to choose which direction her life will take within that world. She has a burning inside her bosom to break free from her bondage, to lead a heroic life. "But alas," she says to herself again and again, "only in storybooks."

Thomas and his five friends stroll down the same block that she is strolling in her search for dresses. David snips her purse without her being aware and tosses it to Robert. Looking downward, she notices that the purse is missing and immediately suspects the boys.

"Where is it? You better give that back!" Lucy demands, grabbing Jack by the collar.

"Hey guys, I think she likes me!" Jack says as his collar is pulled, choking him.

The boys stroll just ahead of her.

Jack flashes his index and middle fingers at her. She gives short chase, insulted at this gesture.

Lucy angrily hollers to them, "My father gave me that! He will have you hung when he finds you!"

Jack flashes a small knife to her from his belt. She bolts backward in fear and runs to her father, who is negotiating prices at a nearby market stand across the way. The boys slip away before she can point them out. They step through a series of complicated streets, only to be confronted by another group of boys. These are the Red Feathers: Leonard, Francis, Simon, Anthony and Roger, terrorizers of Fleet Street. They stand grimacing with arms folded, attempting to appear tough.

"Look what we have here," Anthony says.

Fearless, Leonard steps forward into the center of the action, saying, "You think you're a challenge for us? Don't make me laugh!"

Charles says, "Talk don't win battles!" charging toward Leonard, connecting a solid punch to his face. Leonard goes down and Charles continues laying blows into him. Francis, a nimble French boy, turns and tackles Charles.

Benjamin sees this and punches Francis hard in the stomach. Leonard gathers himself and sends three quick blows into Thomas, just as he is tackled by Jack. They lay in a violent pile while the rest fight it out on their feet.

Roger and Simon team up on David. Jack slashes Roger with a knife across the meat of his thigh, which sends him bending over in pain and screaming. Jack kicks him in the face and David beats Simon to the ground. A watchman runs toward them a block away and yells, "Stop right there! Hold it!"

A surly wretch under the effects of fermented drink runs to the boys and tells them, "Come now, all of you this minute!" This is Barnaby. He jumps back half behind the corner of the wall and waves them to follow. Jack looks to Charles with a look on his face, which seems to ask, "Are we sane to follow this man?"

"That's right, with haste!" Barnaby calls out.

The boys follow him quickly and slip inside a side alley. They race through the back street, continue for about ten feet, and enter a small house. The boys stand around the secluded main room. Leonard angrily approaches Barnaby and says, "What do you mean bringing them here?"

"You fool. You are on the same side!" Barnaby says, throwing up his arms.

"We are not. He cut Roger in the leg!" Simon says, pointing to Jack.

Barnaby asks Jack, "Did he deserve it?"

David says, "They teamed up on me."

"How are you ever going to get ahead if you keep fighting amongst yourselves!" Barnaby says.

Charles says, "He is right. We cannot fight over scraps forever."

Roger crosses his arms and says, "Fuck you and fuck all this joinin' up talk. I don' need—"

Barnaby cuts in and yells, "Fine! It doesn't matter what you think, but the job I have in mind requires all of you." He scans over the group of boys continuing, "Now does anyone here know their way around a chimney?"

"I do, sir," Charles says.

"Good. I will need you first," Barnaby says.

Later, as the boys sit around the small, darkly lit house, Charles and Barnaby step into the room covered in soot. Charles slides the house key from his jacket and shows it to all.

"Look what we got!" Charles says.

"Up on yer feet!" Barnaby bellows.

They make their way to a large estate two blocks over. Tromping across the lawn and washing themselves in the fountain upon the front steps, this ragtag group of filthy boys appears very out of place. If anyone were to see these street urchins marching upon this land as if it were the territory of a foreign enemy: tulips stomped underfoot and sacks intended for carrying off loot in hand, the authorities would be notified at once.

Barnaby slips the key into the door. It turns with a click and the vagrants enter, filled with awe in the presence of riches they've previously only imagined.

Barnaby says, "Fill them to the brim boys!"

Jack fills his bag with a blue and white porcelain Chinese angel statue and a candelabra chiseled with a beautiful leaf motif. Roger fills his bag with a Swiss clock carved with the image of Christ surrounded by a company of angels and a silver dinner set. Upstairs, David, Jack, and Simon fill their bags with ruby, diamond, and emerald encrusted rings and necklaces from inside a large dresser.

Richard takes a large mirror, the frame of which is layered in gold leaf. Charles and Thomas fill their bags with fine China dishes and silverware decorated with stylized gold patterns. Thomas cracks open a case, finding a large Persian knife decorated with letters that appear as wide, elegant gold swirls, the hilt glimmering with jewels. All he knows is that it looks deadly and expensive. As Simon takes hold of a candle set, his vision shifts out the front window to see the owner of the house inspecting his tainted fountain, then continuing on toward the house.

"He is coming! Everyone hurry and escape!" Simon calls to the burglars.

The invaders filter down the stairs and through hallways to reach the back door in order to escape. Charles and Thomas see Barnaby with a full bag in his hand, waiting in the front room.

"Go on boys! I'll hold him off!" Barnaby says.

The owner of the house opens the front door and sees Barnaby standing before him.

"What in heaven's name are you doing here?" the owner of the house asks.

Barnaby picks up a chair and beats the house owner over the head with it, knocking his tall crown hat to the floor. The house owner collapses violently on his side, his perfect hair disheveled, lying across his face.

"No, please, please stop!" the house owner screams.

Barnaby continues to beat the house owner in the head with the chair.

The house owner screeches helplessly, trying to shield himself in vain.

"No! Stop it!" Thomas yells.

Barnaby beats the house owner again and again upon his head, until he ceases to move. Barnaby turns toward the boys with the bloody chair in his hands.

Gazing at them like a wild dog, he howls, "I thought I told you to leave!"

Thomas and Charles rush out the back door.

Back at the safe house, the boys sit around the main room.

"What do you think he will pay us?" Francis says.

"It has to be fifty pounds a piece we stole!" David exclaims.

Curious, Thomas asks, "Why? How much do you usually get?"

"Not much. Just enough to get by on," Francis says weakly.

"Why would Barnaby deserve that much more than you?!" Thomas bursts.

Francis says, "He is the leader. He organized the whole plan," swallowing hard in sorrow.

Thomas marches across the house. After a moment of pondering he asks Francis, "Didn't you risk your neck just as much as he did?"

The whole cluster weighs their eyes heavy on Francis.

Slowly, Francis mutters, "Yes."

Thomas says confidently, "It was Charles who risked himself the most. What did the old man do, but nearly get us charged for murder?"

Just then Barnaby opens the front door. He enters wearing a brand new velvet hat and takes a swig from an expensive bottle of Irish whiskey. He says,

"I want to congratulate you boys, well done!"

Barnaby places his hat on a table and speaks again, "Do not think you are done yet! A merchant ship sets forth in three days. We will be on that ship!"

# Breaking Bread and Bloodletting

**THOMAS AND CHARLES** stroll down the market road and see Admiral Constantyne and Lucy speaking to a clothing salesman.

"That's the old landlord I told you about," Thomas says, fingering the knife at his side.

"And look who his daughter is," Charles says.

"I know," Thomas says, nudging him.

"Do something," Charles says.

Thomas tells him, "Hold still. I will," and signals Charles to stay where he is. Thomas speeds off and stands before Admiral Constantyne and Lucy.

Immediately upon seeing him, Constantyne shows a glad smile and says, "Hello there, my boy!"

Thomas nods but barely utters a sound.

Constantyne continues speaking. "You look mighty dirty. Haven't seen your parents in some time, then?"

Thomas stares off.

"I think they'd be missing you quite a bit."

Thomas ignores the words and instead says, "Might you have some work?"

Constantyne is choked by tragedy of this boy's mental decline, but realizes the futility in trying to explain the truth to him. He restricts himself and says, "Certainly."

"It's for my friend," Thomas says.

Charles greets him with a nod.

"All right, that's fine. You come too," Constantyne says.

"No, I'll be busy," Thomas says matter-of-factly.

Constantyne senses strangeness in this, but lets the boy do as he pleases.

"When will you be ready?" Constantyne asks Charles.

"I'm ready now."

"Right. Let's be off, then."

Lucy throws a fit, saying, "But father! You promised!" stomping her feet.

"Dear, we already bought three dresses."

"It is not fair. I blame you, trash!" Lucy yells to Thomas, folding her arms and showing her teeth.

Constantyne says, "Lucy! Mind your mouth around company! You are to act like a lady, you hear?!"

"I don't care!" she screams, as the three of them step down the street.

Barnaby and the boys sit on crates, watching a merchant ship being loaded under the night sky. They rise to their feet and make their way before the ship. Barnaby stands before the Merchant Captain and says in an official tone, "The word is you intend to sail northward."

The merchant captain says proudly, "That is correct."

"Might I make use of your ship in order to bring these orphans to better land?" Barnaby asks.

He holds up a purse full of coins in front of the merchant captain. The merchant captain takes the purse and says, "Right! Come aboard then."

Barnaby turns to the boys and winks.

"You heard him," he says. "Up with you."

Charles and Constantyne exit the manor and follow a path to a storehouse down the hill. They enter the doorway. Shipping supplies line the shelves. Charles notices piles of packaged gunpowder in the corner. The Admiral motions his hand to the chimney cleaning supplies between two racks and says, "I shall leave the door unlocked for you tonight. Here are the tools you will need for proper cleaning."

"I see," Charles says, nodding his head.

The Admiral says, "Supper is on the table as we speak, so let's break bread and then you can get to your service."

Charles ascends the stairs with a maid to fetch cloths. The maid opens a drawer and lays stacks of cloth napkins on top. Just outside Lucy's room, he hears yelling. Charles places his ear to the door in order to hear the words more clearly.

"I will not!" Lucy screams.

Her mother, Grace, orders her, "You will go downstairs and properly address our guests!"

"I do not care about them at all!" she screams as loud as she can.

Grace chides her, "You will not get a chance like this again. Lexington is the son of a very prominent family in town!"

"I don't like him!" Lucy screams, followed by the crash of a glass object against the far wall.

"I'd like to see the scoundrel who does catch your eye," Grace says with a mocking grin.

"I'll be more like a dog than a wife," Lucy says.

Her mother laughs aloud. "You think you're not dependent on wealth?"

Lucy says confidently, "No. I'm not. I'll make my own way."

"There is no other way," Grace says. "You cannot change who you are."

Lucy storms out of the room. Charles leaps, falling hard on his buttocks. She sends Charles a dirty look and descends the stairs.

Finely dressed guests are seated at the large dining table in the center of the room. They are fellow seamen and members of another rich family.

Lexington enters, accompanied by his beagle. His clothing is pristine. He holds himself with great formality and gives off an air of sophistication. He approaches Lucy and says, "Hello Lucy, dear," taking her hand softly. He slowly kisses her middle and index fingers, and glances into her eyes. She grimaces and pulls away. They then make their way to their seats.

Charles sits quietly near the end of the table, enjoying himself as beef soup is served. Admiral Constantyne sits at the head, while Lucy sits in front of Charles. Chatter fills the room as guests and host alike wait to gorge on the cuisine, keeping in mind proper manners.

Lucy breaks in. "Why does the servant get to sit at our table?"

"Lucy! I will not tell you one more time to mind your mouth!" her father scolds her.

"She is quite right. He offsets the table considerably," Grace says.

Lucy says, "He makes me ill. I cannot eat a bite as long as he sits here with us!"

Grace motions to the servants and they pull Charles' chair out and escort him outside.

The Admiral says sternly, "Very well then. You shall not eat either! To your room with you!"

Leaping to her feet, Lucy says, "How dare you embarrass me like this in front of company!"

The Admiral rises angrily. He points to the stairway and screams, "You embarrass yourself! Up with you!"

Pouting, she slowly turns, stomps the length of the stairs, and enters her room.

His poise returning, the Admiral seats himself and says, "I apologize for that. I spoil her far too much."

At this his guests nod to acknowledge his admission. They eat slowly, tending to sip more than chew. When they do, the meat is broken into miniscule bites so that they will not eat with their mouths full.

They spend the evening discussing politics, Lexington's beagles, and the meal. The view is splendid. The cliffside that the property is built upon overlooks the roaring waves of the North Sea. Constantyne's beautiful ships, some made for leisure, some built for war, are lined along his personal dock. The guests stroll Constantyne's garden and feel much bliss sipping wine and listening to the tones of a lyre and flute.

In time, the guests make their way home. Charles helps clear the table as Constantyne and his family ready themselves for bed.

Barnaby and the boys stand on the deck. As the dock nearly disappears from sight, Barnaby struts to the captain's quarters with Francis and Benjamin, barging into the room. The captain is at his desk. He rises up startled, saying, "What is this about?"

Barnaby holds a gun against the merchant captain's back as Francis and Benjamin tie him with rope and muffle his voice with a tightly knotted cloth wrapped around. Barnaby takes a set of keys off the desk and harshly states,

"Just keep yer mouth shut and maybe you'll live to sail again."

Exiting the captain's quarters, Barnaby tells Francis and Benjamin, "Keep watch over him."

Barnaby makes his way back to the other boys.

He says, "Roger. Pete. C'mon."

Barnaby motions to Roger and Simon to follow him and they descend to the lower level. They head down a long passage until they approach the door at the end of the hall.

"This is the hold where the good stuff is," Barnaby says.

Barnaby tries a number of keys until one fits, then he opens the door. Upon sticking their heads in, they see several chests surely filled with riches, several other smaller boxes labeled as various spices, and fine clothes and weaponry laid about, all for the taking. David enters from the top level down the hall and says, "There is a commotion above! Hurry!"

Barnaby quickly shuts and locks the door. They speed down the hall and ascend the stairs. On the main deck, two crewmen stand before Francis and Benjamin with knives drawn.

Francis says, "I told you, the captain happens to be busy at the moment!"

Benjamin orders the crewmen, shouting, "Stand back!"

Barnaby and the young thieves crowd around the entrance to the captain's quarters. The captain's muffled cries and the pounding of his chair is heard knocking on the hard wood floor. Barnaby slides out his rapier and slays both of the crewmen, their blood spilling onto the deck, filling the air with the rich smell.

The boys are alarmed at the sudden violence. Barnaby enters the captain's quarters and stands before the captain with his gun drawn. The captain releases frantic muffled screams.

Barnaby yells, "I thought I told you to hold still!"

His finger squeezes the pistol's trigger with the wrath of the devil himself. From the captain's head, body matter spatters across the room onto the far wall. The lifeless husk collapses with a heavy thud, still strapped to the chair. Staring down at the blood-soaked form, Barnaby says, "Such a terrible waste of rope."

Working through the night, Charles moves most of the bags from the storehouse to various locations in the Admiral's house, fifty-three in all. Again and again, he exits the storehouse with a sack of gunpowder under each arm. Slowly edging the side door open with his foot, he enters the Admiral's main hall, pouring gunpowder along the floor as he slowly steps backwards across the full span of the room. He stacks the rest of the sacks in the chimney with a pile of full bags reaching his chest. A large pile lies under the dining table and continues along the red brick of the front wall. Charles exits the window at the end of the second story hall, reaching the roof, and adds another sack of gunpowder to a line of bags stretching across both sides. He meticulously covers every room in the house with a thick layer of the black powder, finishing by filling an empty room upstairs and calmly steps out the door and rests on the front lawn.

Barnaby has all of the crew and other occupants of the ship rounded up in the center of the top deck. Several of them pray with their children.

"There's no need to kill them!" Thomas yells in desperation.

Barnaby says, "True. If they went overboard, there'd be no mess to clean up," stomping toward the crew, raising his rapier. He continues, "If any of you haggard dogs wish to live another day, I shall give you a chance—cast yourselves into the sea, or feel the cold steel of my blade!"

He swipes at a passenger with his rapier, tearing at his flesh, causing him to holler and leap away.

"How could you?!" Thomas screams.

The whole crowd erupts in a frenzy and leaps overboard into the cold water. Barnaby swipes his rapier in the air and holds Thomas back with his gun. "Get! Get!" he says to him.

Overboard, the people slap at the water, moaning and coughing.

"When do we get our cut of the loot?" Thomas asks, trying to keep his balance on the unsteady craft. His eyes appear very serious.

"I shall give you your shilling in the morning," Barnaby says, dismissing him.

Thomas steps forward declaring, "We acquired far more than a miserable shilling apiece!"

"You got taxed," Barnaby says, thinking nothing of Thomas' protest, entering the captain's quarters and shutting the door behind him. Thomas holds a cold silence. His anger grows as the old dog's insult echoes in his head over and over.

Thomas wakes around dawn, sore from sleeping on the hard deck. At the edge of the ship he sits meditating on the horizon and the rising sun. He watches a school of carp have breakfast in the morning light. Wind flows through Thomas' hair as he steadies his footing. He turns and enters the captain's quarters feeling very anxious.

Barnaby sleeps in a large bed fitted with layer upon layer of sheets fit for royalty. Thomas grips his knife in hand and prepares to stab him. Barnaby opens his eyes and raises his gun, as if he was prepared. Thomas slices Barnaby's wrist. Barnaby flings his hand upward and fires the shot into the ceiling. Thomas slices at him, forcing Barnaby to dodge and leap upon the bed.

"You will pay for this, boy," Barnaby says with blood gushing from his wrist and sleep still in his eyes.

Barnaby motions toward his rapier which rests in its sheath against the wall. Thomas blocks the path, standing in front of it. Barnaby leaps from the bed and slams the handle of his gun against Thomas' head repeatedly.

They wrestle for a moment, and then Barnaby kicks Thomas hard in the teeth. He then stomps on Thomas' ribs over and over. Thomas swings, but Barnaby grabs his fist and slams the butt of the gun across Thomas' brow, opening a gash that immediately gushes blood. He writhes in pain. Barnaby slowly steps forward and slides his rapier from its sheath. He turns toward Thomas, who is pressed into the room's corner. Glaring at him from above, Barnaby points the long needle to the eye of his prey.

Delighting in the chance to spill blood, Barnaby says, "You mean to overtake an old man of the sea? Just who do you think you are?"

Thomas quickly lifts his shirt and reveals the Persian knife he found as he was robbing the mansion. It flies from his hand and lands an inch into Barnaby's fleshy neck, serrating muscle and opening a tiny slit in his jugular. He lets out a howl one would expect to come from some sort of large ape. Blood gushes from the wound as he grasps and leans on the rapier that is stuck fast into the deck. Thomas rushes to the door and turns, witnessing a torrent rushing from Barnaby's neck.

Petrified, the once-confident tyrant takes up a shirt from the floor and presses it to the wound. The item is quickly filled as if a pitcher of liquid were poured forth. Barnaby screams to Thomas, eyes wide, "I beg you, do not leave me! I will give you anything!"

Triumphantly, Thomas tells him, "Why should I? I shall soon have all I want!" He exits the room as Barnaby's screeching carries to every ear on the ship.

Thomas locks the door to the captain's quarters and holds tightly to the key. The rest of the boys stand petrified at hearing Barnaby's screeching echoing within. Benjamin, in his astonishment, lets slip the mug of beer he had been slurping from. It falls to the floor with a clomp and rolls to the side of the ship, spilling out its contents.

Thomas, with his face battered, streaming with blood, announces, "Any who cares to leave now may do so. But if you choose to sail with us you must swear your life to me and this ship!"

Benjamin asks, "What just happened in there?!"

Thomas answers, "The same that happens to anyone I find that abuses their power. You can be assured that you are in good hands. I swear everyone on this ship shall receive an equal share of all that we acquire! Any quarrel with that idea?"

No one makes a sound.

Thomas calls out, "Right! Set sail!"

The boys stand quiet for a moment. Jack takes a few steps forward from the middle of the ship and tells him, "No one knows how to!"

"What was that?!" Thomas says puzzled.

"Not one—" Jack says.

"We'll make due. Pretend it's a fishing boat."

The boys wear swords fitted in sheaths on their belts. Benjamin attempts to steer the tiller, slowly getting a feel for steering a ship as large as this. A large flame is seen in the distance. Several of the Admiral's ships are burning. Charles is waving both arms overhead to signal them.

The anchor is lowered, yet the merchant ship does not completely stop. The wind passes into the sails, causing it to glide into the rocks near the shore. Charles calls, "Follow me; we don't have much time. Where's the old man?"

"I'll tell you later," Thomas says, his feet carrying him toward the house.

The boys quietly enter with large bags in their hands. Jack and Richard fill theirs with items from the mantle. Charles and Thomas climb upstairs and quietly enter Lucy's room. Thomas swipes a figure of a swan made of solid silver, perched on a large ruby, framed with goldwork off of her dresser. He stuffs this object into her mouth and ties a handkerchief snug around it, gagging her. She wakes and flails about. Charles quickly binds her arms to her body by winding and tying rope around her. She thrusts her leg and kicks Charles directly in the face, sending him backward. Thomas and Charles take firm hold of her arms and legs and carry her.

"Why don't you get the legs?" Charles asks.

"Quiet," Thomas whispers as he struggles to carry Lucy's flailing body.

They descend the stairs, constantly slipping and regaining balance as she thrashes about.

Reaching the ground floor, Thomas tells the rest of the boys, "Let us be out of here."

Lucy is taken aboard the ship and locked inside the captain's quarters. She fills with fear at smelling the fresh blood and notices a smear as if a body were recently dragged across the floor.

Charles takes a thick branch and wraps it with a white cloth one of the servants would use when cleaning. He lights it by holding it to the flame of one of Constantyne's ships. He transverses the gardens which separate the shipyard from the manor with torch in hand. The Admiral and his wife exit their room and descend the stairs, terribly startled in having to climb over piles of black powder. They are in their bed clothes. All of the boys approach them with swords drawn, some with guns. Thomas points his pistol toward the Admiral.

"Thieves, common thieves! What have I done to deserve such treatment?" Admiral Constantyne says, turning his head to Thomas. "And you, you spawn of the devil! How dare you bring evil to my house?!"

Thomas says, "I am no common thief. I seek revenge for a crime you have committed against me. That is all."

The Admiral asks him, "Crime? It is the way of the world. "

"You came to my city and laid waste to it. You have stolen everything from me and I shall do the same to you."

Constantyne loses his composure and directs his speech like a thrust knife. "I know you. I saw the workings of this in your skull long ago. But you will not best me! You will be crushed!"

"I want you to have the pleasure," Charles says, handing Thomas the flaming stick.

The Admiral screams, "Low bred animal! Know your place!"

Thomas says to the Admiral, "I cease to believe your insults any longer. You found it easy to inflict pain on me, so I shall do the same!"

Thomas holds the torch aloft as the other boys speed away toward the ship. Thomas tosses the flaming stick inside the Admiral's house and leaps off to escape on the ship. The flame catches the gunpowder afire which engulfs the floor, igniting the sacks of gunpowder in the chimney, causing a concussive burst. The brick wall framing the front of the house erupts, tearing into the Admiral and his wife. They are thrust to the ground and seared with flames.

The sacks of gunpowder in the upper back rooms explode, blowing off the parts of the roof in those areas, and the house collapses in on itself. Grace lies face down, motionless. The massive octagonal chimney pot cracks into pieces, rolls down the collapsing roof and crashes with great force. Constantyne lies under burning rubble with a large piece of jagged wood lodged in the side of his arm. He struggles to free himself as his house burns beside him. His right leg is crushed flat by a heap of bricks. The Admiral's sailors rush to him and lift him from the burning wreck.

Constantyne orders, "Go after them! Cut their throats!"

As they chase after the boys in vain, a mustached sailor pats the fire off of the Admiral's back telling him, "Your ships are on fire."

The Admiral madly screams, "Put them out then, fool!"

The sailor calmly says, "It is too late for that. They are gone."

# A Wild One

THOMAS SAYS, "Let's check on her."

Benjamin and Jack follow Thomas into the captain's quarters. Lucy is nowhere to be seen in the dark room. They search high and low for the girl, but find not a trace. Then, Benjamin spies the untied rope among the bed sheets and holds it before his companions.

Thomas asks his friends, "You took the old man's rapier when you locked her in, didn't you?"

Jack and Benjamin look to each other, knowing full well they tossed Lucy in and locked the door as fast as possible. They look toward the large wardrobe in fear and back toward the door. In a flash the tigress leaps from her hiding spot among the captain's clothes, rapier thrusting through the air like a marlin. The boys leap for the door.

"What are you afraid of, you lily boys? 'fraid of a girl?" she says, jabbing at Ben. He ducks just in time to dodge a swift attack, the sword blade cutting straight through his wool hat. The boys skitter out the door as she removes the skewered cap.

On the main deck, boys scatter in confusion.

Thomas calls to Francis, "Get me a sword."

Francis slips out the sword from his sheath and hands it to him. Thomas stands ready for the vicious girl to emerge from the room. Lucy kicks open the door and marches toward him.

Thomas tells her, "I suppose you deserve a fair fight. For all your cunning."

She charges him with ripe confidence, the blade aimed at his throat. Thomas rolls and strikes at her. She deflects the attack, coming back with a triple thrust which he escapes with a backward leap. Both adversaries' chests heave from the exertion. They await the other's next move like dueling wolves of rival packs, surging with adrenaline.

Both blades thirst for blood. In a flash each finds what they seek. Sharpened metal tears open each wielder's arm. Both stand focused with streaming red pouring down from straight cuts. The onlookers are cheering, filled with excitement. Lucy backs away, reaching down to pick up a heavy pulley. She tosses it overhand, letting it plummet hard into Thomas' right shin. He falls hard, letting his sword fly far across the deck. The crew looks on in horror.

Lucy charges him, striking her blade straight for his heart. Thomas spins around and catches her from behind the waist, slamming her head against the deck with a loud thud. On top of her back he secures her wrists. Thomas pulls the bones of her fingers in painful positions contrary to their usual motion. The hand is stressed until it opens, letting the blade free. She screams all the while.

Thomas holds her down as other boys take her arms and legs in a firm grip. "It's not fair!" she screams.

Thomas says, "Not fair? Was it fair when you landed that rigging hard on my shin?" Thomas orders, "Someone get me some rope! We'll do it right this time!"

They tie Lucy so that she may not move an inch. They carry her to the captain's quarters and lay her in the bed. Simon, Benjamin, Jack, and Francis run downstairs and emerge later wearing the fine clothing of the former passengers and rolling a barrel of ale up to the top deck.

The boys drink while Benjamin, thoroughly under the influence of ale, sings a ballad while playing a tune on an accordion. Others swing their mugs in time and slowly learn the words. Simon and Henry dance as David attempts to play a lute and Jack and Roger swing around the main mast in merry, drunken fashion.

Later, as the boys lie about the ship asleep, Thomas wakes, fills his mug full of ale, and staggers into the captain's quarters. Lucy lies on the bed tied and asleep. Thomas steps over to the left side of the bed, crawls in, and wakes Lucy. She is alarmed as he pushes the mug toward her. She turns her head away from him.

Thomas unties her hands from the bedpost. She punches him over and over. She bangs his head against the hard wood and they both holler in their fury. He kicks her off and she goes flying backward.

She strikes at him, but he dodges and exits the room, locking the door. She reaches onto the ground and grasps the mug, confused by the kind gesture. She drinks what is left within it.

One month later, Constantyne is brought his rough-hewn leg made of wood and iron. He lifts the stump that remains of his right as shipmates secure the series of straps to a belt tied about his waist. His pants cover this, so only by the limp could one tell there is something wrong.

Constantyne tries out his new appendage as he hobbles across what was once his dining hall. Amidst the black ash he tosses aside broken dishware with his gnarled cane. Outside the perimeter of the manor, carpenters saw wood for the reconstruction. Others work at clearing the debris. Grace follows behind Constantyne and asks, "Does it suit you?"

He lifts his pant leg to show her the wooden pole sticking out of his boot and says, "It'll do."

"Why are you dressed?" she asks him. "It looks like you're planning to head out."

"I am to visit my fellow admirals and discuss plans for a voyage to retrieve our daughter."

"What chance do you have to find her? Think it through!"

"I will not sit here while my daughter is captive!" he screams.

"I won't sit here either!"

"Then stand if you must, pace even," Constantyne replies. "But what is done is done. They have shaken us. They have brought us to their level, and we sink as far as they desire."

Grace rails, "We are not cowering. No. For our rules they will bend. They will bend even if they are across the world."

"I will find this out firsthand," Constantyne says.

"And what am I to do?" she says to him.

Silence sits on their tongues for a moment. His shattered limbs cause him to resemble an old, shaky man past his time. Half his body is broken, though his exceptional brightness of mind and the fire roaring through his sinews allow him to lurch on, regardless of the pain.

He kisses his wife's hand, and, for she knows the way of things, especially in her corner of the world, she responds with creaks in the corners of her eyes and mouth to show him some gladness. She responds as honestly as she can. He is honorable. He is as honorable as any fanciful knight of myth. He is real, and so it seems lesser. She knows he is leaving. Her time will consist of sitting. No nobility to speak of. It is hard to be grateful in times like these. His goal: to seek out their daughter from thieves. So faint and disheartening is this life's substance.

Overlooking the shore, the Navy Royal headquarters appears as a seaside palace. Surrounded by hedges fashioned into various geometrical shapes, framing clusters of bluebells, the garden is an ocean of beauty. Any who wish may spend their afternoon in the center of it, reclining beside the finely wrought stone fountain topped with cupid, his arrow taut on the bowstring. Beauty is the ideal in the design. Even the doorway, framed by a marble Romanesque portico, was inspired by a temple of Apollo built in the reign of Octavian.

Those inhabiting the building are not discussing such lofty, carefree matters. Three Admirals sit behind a heavy oak table facing Constantyne. In the center, the Admiral of the Fleet speaks, "Since you are incapable of performing your proper duty at the head of a ship, you shall receive pension in return."

"I wish to sail on my own accord," Constantyne says, a strange declaration to hear from a man whose body is as broken as his.

The Admiral on Constantyne's far right looks up from his papers, saying, "You are free to do so, though you must use your own funds to lead whatever venture you have in mind, you understand."

Constantyne says, "Very well."

The Admiral of the Fleet says, "We trust you still have such funds, now that a large part of your estate is burned?"

"I shall sell off the property I own. The east side housing block shall go to auction. My other houses in the country will be sold as well," Constantyne says.

The Admirals appear disturbed.

The Admiral on Constantyne's left says, "You mean to lose near all you have for this—expedition?"

Constantyne nods, "These brigands have taken from me that which I love in this world. I intend to do everything I can to take it back."

Lexington, standing off against the shadowed wall, steps forward and says, "Sir."

Constantyne asks him somberly, "What is it?"

"Upon your approval, I wish to set forth as well."

Constantyne turns disinterested. He tells Lexington, "This is not your battle.

Your place is here, defending our Queen."

"I am shamed as well! I have been greatly dishonored!" Lexington says, bowing his head. "I will be damned if I let those vagrants steal poor Lucy and do God knows what with her in the middle of the damn ocean!"

"Well then," says Constantyne, "if it is for honor's sake, then so be it. Those vermin well need a lesson in how the world works."

Lucy is secured with a rope tied around her waist, the opposite end knotted around a high beam. She attempts to scrub the deck with a block of coral.

"Ow! It's too rough!" she says, massaging her fingertips.

Thomas throws a piece of bread at her.

"Stop it! Why do I have to work?" Lucy complains.

Thomas tells her, "Because you are the slave. And it is fun to watch a spoiled brat work hard."

He laughs as Lucy continues scrubbing.

She scrapes scum off of the deck with her teeth pressed hard in anger. "I have never been treated like this in all my life!"

Lucy rises and pulls toward Thomas, attempting to hit him, but the rope is too short. Jack and Henry attempt to tie rigging in order to secure the sail. Cannons explode below deck sending cannon balls into the sea. Henry falls. Charles and David shoot guns at a loaf of bread which sits atop the side railing. Due to being imbalanced by the rocking ship they miss terribly.

Lucy laughs so hard each time she sees their failures and finally falls flat on the deck, chuckling. She points her finger at them, yelling, "You are the worst pirates I have ever seen! Let me try. I will show them how to use a pistol!"

Thomas says, "Shoot a gun? Girls do not shoot guns on my ship!"

"I cannot do much worse, now can I?" Lucy says.

"Give them time, give them time! What we need is more guns, definitely more guns!" Thomas says smiling.

"Good. Maybe you will all shoot yourselves," she says.

Thomas looks at the compass near the steering tiller. "Ben! Head south!" he calls out.

Lucy says, "What do you want in going south?"

As Benjamin rotates the tiller, Thomas says "We are going to sell you as a slave to the Spaniards, of course."

"I am the only daughter of an Admiral!" Lucy exclaims.

"Yes, a perfect selling point: the fresh virgin daughter of your enemy to do with as you please!" Thomas calls out, taunting her.

Everyone cheers, save for Lucy. Benjamin continues to watch the compass carefully, holding the tiller in place, adjusting it slightly from time to time as they make their way. Thomas pats him on the back and gazes to the unseen destination across the sea.

# A Deal with a Swordsman

**C**ÁDIZ, **SPAIN**. Dock workers hammer tar into the hulls of great warships. Thomas observes the busy folk, rushing about the deep-bellied merchant vessels that dwarf his own.

"What will we do?" Benjamin asks.

"I suppose we should look for an opening, tie our ship there, and hope they don't take us to be their enemy," Thomas says.

They drift along this dock for some time, in no hurry. Benjamin, at the rudder, keeps their progress a smooth one.

"There," says Thomas, as he sees a space that could fit their vessel with room to spare. "Men, heave to. Ben, guide us into that space."

They do so. As the sails point in the direction of the wind, their speed slows considerably. The anchor is dropped, and immediately eyes from the dock turn to them. Voices call out words the boys cannot understand. Thomas is not dismayed, though.

Thomas says to his crew, "Let's wait this out while we get some food in us."

They do so, stepping off their ship amid the clamor.

Thomas orders Simon, "Go find us some fish, and something to get us drunk."

He hands him some coins and he is off. While waiting, Thomas repeats to the cantankerous workmen, "Go find your master." He uses every hand signal he can think of to get the message across and to quiet them.

First, it is Simon who returns with baked cod and two bottles of mildly sweet sherry wine. Such a delicious treat it all is, flaky, yet moist and fresh. The wait for the bottle to come around and meet the lips makes the wash of citrus tang all the better. While they are busy consuming, the master of these men, Marcos de Aguilar Romero, approaches. He says, "They told me you were Englishmen, but I see you are boys. I… take it you are trying to make it in some way as merchants?"

Thomas approaches Marcos and bows, "I apologize for our intrusion. We are new to this, I admit, but we do have money and nice goods if you care to buy or trade."

Marcos says, "I don't often see boys arrive alone, far away from their home country. Where is the man in charge?"

"He," Thomas tells him, "is at the bottom of the sea. Where he belongs."

With a raised eyebrow Marcos says, "Oh? Well, I don't care to know. I'm only curious about what concerns me. Is business your only goal?"

"I take risk in saying this, but we are in Spain, after all. In hope, in an assumption that you have no loyalty to England, especially when our countrymen raid and sink each other's ships in the name of profit and gaining the upper hand—"

Marcos laughs, "You're quite a speechmaker, lad. I've learned to speak your tongue for the sake of trade and sales, but if you fling words at me like that, I'll be lost, I admit."

"Yes, well…"

"What is it, boy? Do you want something more?"

"Yes. If it's possible," Thomas begins. "A certain admiral, an English admiral, is out for my blood. Is it possible to outfit this ship with cannons?"

"That we can do, but I can't believe you can afford it."

"Have a look at our hold, what the rich left behind. Tell me it's not sufficient."

"Very well. If I can take your money, by all means. If you intend to make this ship armed for battle, you'll also want it streamlined for speedier sailing."

"Yes," Thomas says, nodding.

"This will take time, therefore… enjoy yourselves. My country is beautiful. Drink more wine, meet some girls… now is the time slow down. Forget your worries. I have several houses in Jerez, which is not far away. It is so luxurious, the surroundings beautiful. Let me see your goods, then spend some days here strolling the beaches. After that, see me again and we'll get on with our deal."

"Fantastic," Thomas says, bowing again. "I am very thankful."

After a brief time, Thomas leads Marcos onto his ship. Before heading down to the hold though, Thomas stops and tells him, "I having something that may be of special interest to you." At that, he directs him to the captain's quarters. Marcos is shocked to see this young girl confined here. "That English admiral—this is his daughter. I wish to sell her."

Lucy barrages them both with insults. Her hollering and kicking about startles Marcos. He clears his throat in reaction to the shock of this sudden revelation. Regardless, he turns to Thomas and nods.

"We need not move her. Know I will keep her fed, clean, and unharmed. She's our asset, after all," Marcos says.

In their new locale, the boys take to lounging and filling their cups with sherry from Marcos' own vineyards. A barrel of the delicious stuff is on hand at all times, with a tap inserted so that they may simply press and have their fill.

Their first night there, Marcos gave them a tour and had his cook prepare boiled cigalas. They ate the creatures, dipping them in a light sauce made with oysters, lemon, and freshly picked herbs.

Wonder soon developed, and so on many days they would pass through the hills or into new towns. They found several castles built through the ages, some more recently and very much in use. Upon the discovery of a new market, a boy would arrive back at the abode with delightful food items, such as meat from the black Iberian pigs that comes in so many varieties: fresh cuts, spicy sausages, and even the prized leg of one acorn fed and cured for four years. The stay here is luxury beyond their wildest imaginings, from the freedom from obligations, to the meals professionally prepared, to lounging and nibbling varieties of cheeses and drinking wine in the arms of beautiful local girls.

One day Marcos arrives and announces their ship is ready. At this, they pack and ride along on horseback.

Strolling down the same dock, none of them recognize their ship. Extraneous sections of the deck have been sawed down for the sake of speed and four cannons are now installed on each side. It is painted black with an outline of blood red. The words "Blood of God" are painted on the aft.

"It is unbelievable, no?" Marcos asks.

Thomas answers, "It is a dream," his eyes transfixed on his beautiful sailing vessel.

"Do you accept the name, Captain?"

Thomas nods and smiles.

Both of them peer up toward the blood red flag flying over the ship.

Marcos says, "Actually, I am extremely proud of their work. Does the flag suit you?"

"Don't be lukewarm about what you are, I guess," Thomas says, laughing to himself. "I guess I'm a pirate."

"Speaking of that," Marcos says, "We have found a buyer for your slave girl. The deal will be done tomorrow."

"That's great. Everything is wonderful, thanks to you."

Thomas' crew gulp drinks and converse happily in a local tavern. They sing songs and dance merrily through the night. Two beautiful Spanish girls take Charles and Jack by the hand and sneak out with them.

An aristocratic Spaniard wearing frills of burgundy stands tall above Benjamin. He introduces himself. Ben, being as congenial as he is, pats him heartily on the back and invites him to share his bottle of wine. The two enjoy each other's company greatly, and in a few hours time their minds fill with such a stupor that the Spaniard nearly forgets his purpose.

"I must speak to your captain," the Spaniard says, standing wobbly upon his feet.

Amid the clamor, Thomas' mind wanders off to a place of silence as it often does. To Thomas, the collision of mugs makes no sound. The mouths swinging on their hinges are those of mutes. He feels the sails above his head propelling him towards the arms of fate. In his vision the wind is on his face.

Benjamin approaches, blackening the room from Thomas' point of view, blotting out the light of torch fire with his girth.

Benjamin says, "Captain. This is Diego de Cervantes."

Diego bows respectfully, "Diego will do."

"What is your business with us?" Thomas says.

"I am in need of transport."

"Perhaps. You must assist us in return."

"But of course. I am at your service," Diego says, bowing.

"What do you know about warfare?"

"There is none better with a blade in Spain."

"If you are so talented, then why must you lie low?"

"That is precisely why I must ask you of this favor," Diego whispers. "They want my head, you see."

"Then we have something in common," Thomas chuckles. "I assume you have a destination in mind?"

"I know of a priest by the name of Agustín de Zárate. He is doing God's work in the new country."

"What is there to want in this distant land?"

"It is said to be untouched by the hand of greed. The natives live in solemn peace as God intended."

"Is it true? There are people still unblemished by sin?"

"The towers of Babel are nowhere to be seen. They live among the meadows and forests of the natural world."

"Do you know the way?"

"I shall procure the necessary maps as well as a navigator."

"What do you think, Ben?"

"It would be nice to rid ourselves of the threat on our heels," Benjamin answers.

"I agree. If we may escape from this evil, we shall all be reborn. Diego, if you serve me by passing on your skills in battle to those I command, you will find yourself welcome."

"It will be my pleasure, Captain," Diego says.

Thomas leaves the tavern and crosses town to the docks, boarding his ship. He enters the captain's quarters with chicken cuts in a bowl and a mug of beer. He sets it on a table by the bed and unties Lucy.

"Why do you untie me?" she says.

He says, "I do not feel like feeding you by hand."

She looks downward.

"Go on; you must be hungry," he tells her, motioning her to eat.

Thomas moves to the other side of the bed and takes his boots and armor off. She takes the bowl in hand and eats with her fingers.

With food stuffed in her mouth she says, "I actually prefer being a captive. This is the first time I have ever felt free." She takes another bite and says, "Why did you steal me?"

He answers, "To get back at the Admiral. Revenge for stealing everything that meant anything to me."

"What do you mean?" she says innocently.

He tells her, "Your father came to my city and destroyed everything."

"I am sorry. I hate him as well," she says, laying her hand on his shoulder.

"Even the smallest items in your house could have fed us well for over a month," he says, staring blankly.

"None of those things mattered, for our family was greatly unhappy," she says. "We did not even enjoy what we had. How sad is that?"

As Thomas becomes consumed in thought, Lucy takes up an iron rod she had been hiding under the sheets and smashes the end into the side of his head. All goes blurry for him and his feet disobey as if he were drunker than he was. He lands hard into the wall and gets a sharp strike to the ribs, the skinny end of the weapon sliding into the crevice of two bones, pinching the meat. Thomas lunges at the blur mad as hell, clenching his hand around the first thing he feels. He crushes her throat without mercy and forces her back, slamming her head into the tall oak bedpost. She lifts the rod, but he catches it, twisting her wrist far beyond the point her joints stop. The skinny end lands into her this time, jabbing sharply into her soft, tender belly. She erupts, expressing the pain streaming through her and bolts, kneeing Thomas hard in the testicles. In a flurry she lands an open palm into the left side of his throat, then swiftly goes at his eyes with fingers outstretched.

There is a hard knock at the door, and Benjamin calls out, "What's that noise?! I hope that's not what I think it is!"

"Come hold down this girl!" Thomas says, tackling her to the ground, trying to constrain her strong, flailing legs.

Ben rushes in with Simon. The three boys hold her limbs the best they can and lift her to the bed.

"You better sit here or we will fucking kill you," Thomas says, still aching from the blows he had just received. "You will be lucky if I sell you with only toes missing."

Thomas slides out Benjamin's sword, pointing it steady, and lets his companions tie Lucy as she takes his threats to heart. She shakes both from fear and the adrenaline rush.

Benjamin looks to Thomas to see if he will be needed, but Thomas gives a nod and they leave, closing the door. Lucy cries like a little, innocent girl. Thomas is still and takes in how she must feel, to have been kidnapped and all. She didn't know that he didn't want to harm her, but his intentions weren't pure, after all. She fell into his path for vengeance as an innocent victim.

Lucy says to him amid tears, "Are you really going to sell me?"

He must answer truthfully. "Yes. Your family is shit and you must pay."

"I will be a servant with no rights, and I will be a whore. Does that make you happy?"

"Yes," Thomas says. "It is only fair that you suffer like my friends and family have."

She looks to him, sniffles, clears her throat, and says, "Come here."

He knows neither what she means nor if he can trust her.

"Unbutton my bodice, slip your hand inside. It's okay."

"W-why? No," he says turning his head.

"I'd rather you take me first, than some old man, than whatever lecher who tosses a few coins to use me."

"Shut up and leave me be."

Thomas stares blankly at the scared girl with her hands tied behind. She breathes heavy and many of her swirls of black hair are pasted to her forehead with sweat. She looks to him as if waiting for something, not afraid as before, which scares him more than ever. His sight falls on the delicate features of her face, the soft angles of her nose, the bright white in her eyes outlined with slender black brows. The line of his vision then deviates, over her chest, her waistline and hips, causing him to feel like a criminal. All while she watches him, judging in ways he knows not.

Thomas approaches her and slowly pulls the bow apart at the top of her dress. He draws out the string from each loop until each side of the pink satin shell hangs free.

"Go on," she says, half terrified, half curious. "Feel me."

Thomas slips his trembling left hand in the flap, feeling the tender, silky mound of warm fatty tissue, pressed with the indentations of the crumpled material. He scoops the small thing in his palm and looks at her. She is flushed and alert to his every sensation.

Lucy rises as far as the ropes will allow and stares to him. He kisses her and they melt into each other. His hand strokes up the underside of her thigh.

"Pull it up. Pull it up," she says as she stretches her buttocks up, pushing off on her small feet tied at the ankle.

His fingers grasp around the layers of frilly white cloth and pull it off of her. He sees her soft mounds of buttocks upraised as the cloth is lifted. A bloom of small black hairs spread over blushing lobes presses together between her bound, skinny legs. He lifts these long limbs filled with the softness only a girl possesses. He gazes long, never expecting another chance at something so wonderful. He works his fingers over the spongy, moist flesh. It is glorious to him.

Charles wakes in the morning to the sound of Lucy berating Thomas and of objects hitting the walls. Her head pokes out the door, her hair frazzled and unkempt as he storms out.

Charles stops him and says, "Why does she think she has the right to speak that way here?"

Immediately recognizing Thomas' demeanor is that of a beaten dog, he knows he has given himself over to her.

Charles continues, "No, of all things! You know better! She's a mad bitch! He's here right now to purchase her… like we planned!"

Lucy belts out, "Are you speaking about me?! You're lucky I'm not presentable for company! "

"Fucking Christ," Charles says to himself.

Thomas is shamed and hangs his head low.

She goes on and on, mocking many, especially Thomas. The old Spaniard dressed in dusty finery from twenty years past loses all interest after hearing her barrage of words. He turns, followed by Marcos, who tries to beg for forgiveness for wasting his time.

Charles says to Thomas, "What do you mean in keeping her? She will lead to the downfall of us all. She's already beyond mad."

"We were wrong about her."

"That's not fucking good enough! And I know what you're getting at— you're not getting our throats in a noose over your desire for some fucking sex. If it's a cunt you want I can find that!"

Lucy begins yelling again, something about "cleaning this mess up," and Charles shakes his head in disgust. Thomas goes to her and fists exchange, first from her, then his defenses, until it is a full on battle.

# 25

# Dark Days

NIGHT FALLS. Benjamin plays an Irish song on a lyre. He sings slowly and sorrowfully:

In days so distant
I was a child
Health was fair,
the weather mild

The glades so green
bore my weight
The lush valley
moistened glade

Into the earth
my feet did fall
Dreaming of gifts
that fate bestow

# JACOB KILGORE


Hal-lay-loo-yuh
We did sing
and carry on
Hal-lay-loo-yuh
My thoughts were nothing
Love was strong


Several of the boys lock arms and sway. Some clap their hands to the rhythm.


Infinite days to come
it seemed
The orchard bloom,
the lift in me


Joy of youth
I never feel
Now I'm old
and feel the chill


Mother, my comfort
you did bring
Found in you
my everything


Many voices now join in as the chorus comes.


Hal-lay-loo-yuh
We did sing
and carry on
Hal-lay-loo-yuh
My thoughts were nothing
Love was strong


Long for your touch
tender arms
Your embrace
a soothing calm

# VAGRANT PRINCE

Words in me
from your lips
A warmth now gone
my emptiness

I heard the call,
board the ship,
My will to find
a life in it

Hal-lay-loo-yuh
We did sing
and carry on
Hal-lay-loo-yuh
My thoughts were nothing
Love was strong

Bound across
the raging sea
Failure found
its home in me

Loss whispered
among the waves
Life passed by
just as a day

Such is life
It passes from
Mother, dear
now you are gone

Hal-lay-loo-yuh
We did sing
and carry on
Hal-lay-loo-yuh
My thoughts were nothing
Love was strong

I, a man
lost among
the figures of
the city throng

You are gone
mother, true
Where's the goodness
that I knew?

Hal-lay-loo-yuh
We did sing
and carry on
Hal-lay-loo-yuh
My thoughts were nothing
Love was strong

Several of the boys fall under a spell of melancholy as they drink. Thomas lets his face fall into his hands, morose as ever. Memories flash through him of his childhood in Scotland. He remembers his beloved mother and father, and the calm, happy times spent with Mary, Allen and the fuzzy sheep. It seems so long ago that he lived among green pastures, far away from the death, the putrid stench, and the starvation of the city. Thomas lifts his head and sees Jack sitting with Lucy beside the stairway that leads to the tiller. He notices Jack touch her breast. His anger surges as he sees them kiss. Thomas stands and stomps directly over to them.

"You think I am blind to this? Your sitting in the shadows taunts me to quarrel more so!" Thomas screams, enraged.

Thomas shoots two guns and blasts a hole in Jacks chest. The music and singing stops. Jack clenches in pain.

"You monster!" Lucy says, leaping back in horror.

Thomas stabs Jack in the chest and drags the knife, causing it to gush.

He turns and says to all, "I cut a fish; I cut a man. It makes no difference!" Thomas cleans the blood off on his pants. He says, "You forget who is the captain! Any who disagree with my decision shall receive the same!"

All stare in shock. Thomas grabs Lucy, drags her to the railing and ties her up.

"Play on!" Thomas yells, entering his quarters as Benjamin starts a new song.

In the morning the ship is anchored. Jack's body is wrapped in a white sheet and is held by several boys as it half hangs over the edge of the ship.

Benjamin says solemnly, "He was a good sailor. And a good friend. May God rest his soul."

The boys send Jack's body into the sea. They meditate on the moment.

Thomas notices three blurry objects appear on the horizon out of the corner of his eye. Two companion ships sail in triangular formation, positioned behind the lead. He extends his telescope. In straining his eye, he identifies St. George's Cross atop each warship.

Lucy, recognizing them at once, says, "Those ships are my father's. I am sure of it! Turn around! Turn around, you stupid fools!"

Lucy rushes and takes hold of the tiller, trying to pry Benjamin's hands off of it.

She screams, "I can't take this anymore! It's so filthy here! I need to wash and have some real food! I don't care if I hate him. You're no good!"

Thomas, Simon and a few others wrestle her away.

Lucy yells, kicking and screaming, aiming her taunts at Thomas, "Let me go home! I can't stand you! You're stupid, you stink, and you're bad in bed! Stop being a crybaby; you deserve what you get!"

They put her away in the captain's quarters and tie her to the bedpost as before. She is in such a furious mood that she thrashes the heavy bed along the floor, the great clamor being heard outside.

They hurry and unfurl the sails. The vessel swiftly widens the distance. Night falls and the three ships are highlighted by the moon's glow. For three days and three nights, the Admiral keeps after Thomas' fleet with murder in his eyes. With the full energy of his being, he meditates on their slaughter. The little he sleeps, his dreams consist mostly of draining the blood out of Thomas' severed head. It is all he has left in life—to destroy Thomas is his only wish.

Thomas awakes on the third morning of the pursuit to the sound of the watchman calling out, "Our destroyer closes in! Ho! He is upon us!"

The ship is still at full speed as Thomas emerges from the captain's quarters. He blocks the sunlight from his eyes and sees the dark haze creeping from where sea and sky meet.

"We must be rid of this menace. It fills me with the chill of death," Thomas says tired and aggravated.

Thomas rallies his companions, Benjamin, Charles, and Diego to follow him to the lower deck. Charles stands firm in his footing, untrusting of the strange demeanor that engulfs Thomas.

Thomas turns to Charles and says, "Now! Why to do you stall?"

Charles, despite the wobbling of the craft, stares resolutely at his friend. He says, "I suspect strangeness in you."

"You what?" Thomas charges angrily. "If you weren't my closest friend, I'd cut you through right now!"

Charles says, "Our chance of survival lessens with our captain distracted! What is the madness you are set on?"

"Follow me and find out," Thomas says.

The four disappear into the lower level of the ship. Charles sees Benjamin and Diego tie the legs of a pig and take it in their arms. Thomas carries a chicken. He says to Charles, "Help the men up the stairs."

"What is this?" Charles asks.

"Just trust me."

"We're not in the days of the Bible. You're gonna get us all killed."

"I'm you're captain. Remember that."

"I always questioned that story—the first one you told me about your parent's demise. I think the only true part was about your mental decline."

Thomas turns his head toward Charles, his eyes spread wide and furious like twin suns. Unconsciously, Thomas slips out his blade and thrashes a heavy overhand sweep toward Charles. Charles thrusts himself to the floor, still in reach, suffering an inch deep layer of his arm flesh flayed.

Thomas calls out with fury, "Don't tempt me when my heart is set on blood!"

Thomas and his two helpers appear with the live creatures in their grasp. Thomas holds a chicken and Diego and Benjamin together hold the fat pig to the bewilderment of the rest of the crew. At Thomas' order, Benjamin returns to the lower deck, momentarily glances at Charles and his gushing wound. Benjamin wraps his arms tight around a stack of kindling, holding aloft a blazing torch, and sets up the stairs again.

Thomas slips his knife from his belt and says, "We beckon our Lord to help us in our desperate time of need."

Thomas holds the auburn feathered creature aloft and slits its throat. Streams of blood shoot forth and gush upon the deck. Thomas lets the red flow into the black-green of the water, settling in a red blotted trail. Benjamin nurses a fire within a buckler, as ordered. Thomas parades around the main mast, makes a full circuit, and returns to the aft. A circle of blood is formed on the deck, creating an ominous feeling. Thomas holds the lifeless body aloft just as he had before, this time drenching himself, squeezing the body of juices, soaking his hair and face, the remainder staining his clothes in rivers of rust-red. Feeling the task completed, Thomas flays the chest open and spills the guts into the fire, followed by the rest. Black smoke soars upward, accompanied by a sweet smell of burning fat and flesh.

The pig is brought forward at Thomas' command. Thomas slashes the beast's throat as it screams terribly, gurgling blood through its torn pipes. The animal kicks wildly, but soon the struggle weakens and then stops altogether. A heavy rush of glimmering red flows from the severed neck, washing over the feet of the observers. The liquid ripples to and fro with the rocking of the ship. A bucket is held before the laceration and is filled to the brim.

"Come! Anoint yourselves!" Thomas yells.

Though hesitant at first, the entire crew one by one dips their hands into the bucket and smears the warm, red liquid on their faces.

Down below, Charles, shaking from blood loss, tears at his shirt with his dagger and rips free a long strip of cloth. He seals the wound with this, cutting free several more strips as the material becomes soaked. He can hear Thomas' words bellowing above, "We beg you, Lord! We are at your mercy! Save us from this evil so we may do your work in a new country!"

Thomas takes the bucket and slowly drips the contents over the edge of the larboard side. He makes his way with great intensity down the starboard, dripping blood off the stern, and dripping forth the remainder as he returns to the bow. He flays the body of the pig and places it upon the underside of an overturned table. It is covered in lamp oil and set alight. The blazing sacrifice is then dropped into the sea to drift, its scent floating aloft into the welkin as a gift to the Lord.

As night falls, black clouds manifest on the horizon. Perhaps this is an answer to their prayers. A torrent of rain pelts the wooden hull as the vessel is enveloped in black, obscuring the vision of their pursuers.

"The death scythe is lifted from our heads! We are saved!" Benjamin yells as he struggles with the tiller among the soaring waves.

# Possession

ONSTANTYNE STARES into billowing fog. Soaked through, he yells, "Keep at them!" Rain and thunder are all around. His pair of vessels cut through the sea. Undeterred, Lexington continues on at the head of his prow, brave as ever. His tall, spindly form is silhouetted above the rest, undeniable despite the obscuration.

Constantyne's building umbrage catches hold of all around him. The free valiance he had exuded so far on the voyage catches in his throat as a realization of failure; the futility of action strikes his awareness. The storm had drained away the worth of the strength in his arms, in his crew, and cannons. He is left as a boy in a man's body, full of self-doubt. Onward they sail, for a day and more, until finally the sunlight shows through, and the cruel horizon holds no prize.

They are alone.

Constantyne lies in his bed, wondering what would happen if their voyage bore no fruit. This devolves to mere swirling images of his ravaged daughter, his depressed and lonely wife, and his own withering body floating upon the sea. At this he slinks away inside himself.

Now their vessel bobs about the waves, heading in no direction. Its captain has locked himself away in isolation. The non-order still stands. They are in a constant state of consternation.

With the increasing bouts with sickness, and the danger of boredom and aggravation in this small space, the crew considers the risks Constantyne brings to them. They wonder if he is so far gone that perhaps a new captain may be chosen.

Every so often Constantyne reemerges. Lumbering out of his quarters, he seats himself upon the deck. He stares, focused out there on the wide world, as the fury turns bits of him at a time to stone. He falls into booze at times. He makes it his life's ambition, regardless of the detours, to trample the world. It is so large: his enemy may mix among the rest, hiding, committing crimes, shaming him, mocking him from a country far-off. When his thoughts are cleared, he returns to his room, shuts the door, and lies in blackness. The food stores run low and the men quarrel amongst themselves. Their hunger exacerbates the frustration and cuts short their tolerance for the anxiety and lack of direction they must suffer. Their lack of confidence in the captain begs for a disruption of order.

It is too much. It's better understood through his own thoughts:

"I've lost her. I've lost her, my daughter, my blood, my love. I failed as a father and as a husband, and I failed in my vow to remain unbreakable."

"What am I but a defense line to the precious, the defenseless? I am nothing on my own. A crumbled wall amidst a desert, a relic of an aged country whose citizens are bones and dust. I am a shield lying beside a slain warrior."

"Out there somewhere is my daughter. I am worthless. Constant are my thoughts to seek her out, rescue her from those barbarous men before they ravage her, as I only imagine. It saps my will, my mind, to think these vile thoughts."

"What a poor world we've had fashioned for us. What sort of God set the world to this violent method? Only an animal, a dumb beast could manage the crippled thoughts that manifested this endless muscle shredding, flesh consuming hell into form. God must be a lumbering, hair-matted creature so crumpled in its black pit of a heaven. Only the most despondent, vindictive, spiteful-from-weakness bastard could imagine our lives set into motion this way."

"And so I must pick up the pieces off the floor from where God dropped them. The world is a mystery. A largely uncharted, wild wasteland."

"I have no energy to wander the waves in vain. Of all the ports, all the hovels they could have found themselves, where could I start? No guess is better than the rest. I am wretched. Though I feel a seed of hope, I leave it lying still, not yet planted, cast within a shadow."

"I hear them outside my door complaining, questioning my judgment, criticizing my state. And why not? I must blame myself for all the wrongs that have befallen those around me. Still, I have earned the right to refrain from calling out orders. I have followed the rules of this world and have gained the clout necessary to stand my ground, to stay my will."

"After all, not all battles are won by giving in to flights of emotion. On the contrary, most things in life are bettered by long contemplation, by ostracizing oneself from all humanity. The thoughts are what matters. The proper decisions are what make the difference between a worthless life and one worth envying."

"I have not the spirit to stare those fellows in the face. I see my food stores running out in short time, and I have no better plan. I see only regret and severe melancholy in my future. I'm a little shriveled version of myself, the one I was not long ago. Occasionally I'm asked to show my face, but no longer am I feeling confident to answer to my name. Who I was required honor."

"I ask silently for patience and pity, collapsed in my sheets, from these fellows, restless, weary of the joy and cheer stolen daily by the sun's rays and the stench of the deck below. I ask so heartfelt, for I do not think it long that I have before I must admit my failure. I lay my body down and pry the cover of one of Lexington's old books and fall into the words. Perhaps I can escape."

Constantyne is collapsed in a daze on his well cushioned bed, staring into a book entitled *Accounts of Ancient Kings,* which contains accounts of the sea raids of Olaf Tryggvasson, the Viking commander and the nearest thing to a prince they had, turned king of Norway. The king of England at the time, Ethelred, was a coward, and had insufficient resources to counter anyhow, so the wealth of the country flowed to those who worshiped Odin. England, as the world knows it, would be no more if it weren't for an ignorant-of-the-laws Christian fortune teller, the ultimate contradiction, whom Olaf happened upon.

The fortune teller told this lord of the seas that a portion of his men would mutiny. In short time, so they did. Therefore, Olaf returned and asked the man how he was in touch with such power. The fortune teller told him that his god was the god of gods.

A Viking respects anyone who can back up their word, man or god, and in also recognizing the strategic advantage of uniting with and dominating the Christian powers in England, and what would be France, Olaf converted and inherited the belt of kingdoms that would surround and strangulate the neighboring countries.

And so, England survives today, and Christianity with it, due to the acts of this sorcerer, whom under Moses' rule would have had his head crushed with stones. The contradiction sets in Constantyne's skull as he weighs it on the scale of his conscience.

He feels he is no less a contradiction, raising the icons of the cross while dehumanizing people at a militarily disadvantageous position to his own. This is the sort of thing that got him into this mess.

The wave of the candlelight plays with the shadows on the page. A few more dates, a few more wars, and the lids of Constantyne's eyes lower without conscious thought.

His body lays still, the great form still masculine and forceful, though collapsed. Hours go by and still the fire sways.

Lexington, in a stupor of depression, his spirit cut down by the abrasive mood and general nastiness of those around him, sits and writes in his journal:

"I feel sick at all times, but I feel free, liberated from the feeling my feet must endure in being sunk in solid ground. I laugh a jolly laugh as my body is carried off, how far? I know not. Laughter fills my soul, though I stand alone. My fellows, those stationed under me, drink the caustic broth, and finally I've tried it—with great exuberance I've let my dimples give way to smiles for the first time. They curl back and I'm ready to spit forth my love-embrace, the flesh and cares of comrades."

"It's not the first time really, but it's my first to lose it. And they saw a hole in my sail, so I called one sailor by the name of Mark to be raised up and hung to death to think he could spill false rumors about me from his mouth. I was quite free initially, in that I believed my companions would find some value in my word, but once we left port for some time, their angst was aimed to grind on me all the more."

"My want is to have some red ribbon wrapped as lightly as possible around the man before me, but all know the vileness of our occupation. This should take several years to give way. This should surely take time for the haunches of the creature to be shoved some miles, flung off the cliff to the stones below."

"My teeth are shoved clean along the roof in laughter, and I glare in one place, in a dark doorway, gleaming over the wood napes."

"We chase him. That is our main focus. All eyes on the sea, struck on the villain."

Constantyne wakes and his head is spinning. A spell of nausea has overtaken him, swelling in his head, throat, and belly. He rises from his place of rest to find his eyes have lost the ability to see, save for swirling blurs of the candlelight.

"I'm blind. I'm blind," he says to himself, unable to take in the objects around him.

Gone is the wardrobe across from him, not four feet away. He feels as a cup filled to the brim; his mind sloshes about, the feeling of illness spilling over. Like a deer caught in the jaws of wolves, his struggling is done. What can he do but wait to be carried further in his descent? He could not imagine it would be this terrible. Nothing is worthwhile when one's mind is gone.

Constantyne collapses on the bed, surrendering to the loss of his vital sense. Open-eyed, he takes the darkness in. His limbs quiver as violently as those of a man twice his age whose mind has collapsed. Perhaps life's events have brought him to this stage early in life. This notion is a horror to him.

The soft plush of the cloth beneath brings some relief. He bunches it up in his fists and grips it, imagining the wadded fabric to be the strangulated necks of dogs. He clenches the life out of them, forcing the points sharply into the loose skin till the bones inside dully crack.

Nothing could make him want to die more than to be blind. "Where is my gun? Where is my knife?" The ideas shoot out and dissipate, failing to connect in his brain properly. In his confusion, he presses himself up, lurching on the edge of the bed like a troll gazing out of its hillside cave into the vast, inhospitable world before it.

He feebly reaches downward and plants one palm, then the other, and slides, pulling his exhausted, crippled body. The raw dough plunges suddenly in a heap to the floor.

There he lays for hours, unable to bear the nausea that is further stimulated by the sensation of the liquid light being carried into his pupils. Knowing it is there bothers him still. The yellow-orange penetrates his skin. It tries to slip under and through his eyelids, but he covers them and hides his face. Collapsed and moaning, he wishes he could die.

Constantyne, after a span of time unknown to him, raises his head and notices a pinhole of light gleaming on the opposite side of the room. The shimmering, how it pierces through the blur in his vision, entices him. The way the gleam is focused in one small, flowing spark is magnetic on his curiosity. He climbs over to it with hunger in his belly and piercing pain in his wrists, elbows, and forearms.

There in the reflective glass of the mirror, a vision comes into focus of a shadowy cavern the same dimensions as the walls and various objects around him. Now focusing harder than ever, with his eyes spread wide, he follows a figure lit by cauldrons of fire on either side. The fashion of the figure is noticeably simpler, that of the century before, and his lower half is submerged in water, the ripples occasionally being visible as golden, shifting arcs.

The man cast in shadow, his hair falls in thick curls, is styled similarly to the Spanish fashion. Unearthly, gray-white spirals outline every curve, swimming like smoke, yet solidified. The eyes of the vision are not his own. The sunken, pain-filled, weary image inside the mirror stares from a bodily frame of much bulk. Who is this stranger?

Immediately upon focusing on the image, the center of Constantyne's vision seals over again. He is desperate to see. It's as if it was all a cruel trick—only the delusion of a dying brain. But suddenly, fingers clench around his shoulders tightly. Out of reaction, his hands fling forth, yet touch nothing. Fear sweeps though him for the briefest moment.

"What is—?" Constantyne says as a sudden rush of light transforms his surroundings to the blues of the sky and sea. The warmth of a noontime sun bakes his neck and the taste of salt settles on his lips. In looking below, he sees two intact legs hovering over the waves. It must be a dream. By will alone, he finds he can drift as he pleases. Ascending to the height of the clouds, he can see the faint haze of land. Towards this he flies, arms outstretched and joy streaming. The yellows of a sandy coast come into view, and after nearing this some more he can see some square-edged, seemingly man-made constructions on the left side of this landmass. It is a wharf, with grand boats docked as far as he can see. No people are there, though. None at all—but wait! Off in the midst of it, sitting with his legs hanging off the side of a dock, is a man.

Constantyne descends, but decides to try to plant his feet on solid ground, as to not scare the man to death. He goes around behind him and sets down upon the dock. It is like walking in mud. As he half trudges, half floats, he calls out to the lone man, "Hello there! Might you tell me where we are? I seem to be lost!"

There is no answer.

As Constantyne steps just beside the man, he says, "Hello? Can you hear?" After a moment he tries again. "No? Nothing? Must be me, then."

He huffs in frustration and looks about. Just then he sees a figure in the sky off to the right. The man nears Constantyne, setting down on the dock beside him.

The man says, "Hello Constantyne. I'm the man in the mirror. Recognize me?"

Constantyne replies, "Why, yes… I do… Hello."

"My name is Arthur, and this fellow hunched over here… well, that is me too. That's me in 1465."

"Why can't he…? I mean…"

"I can help you track down those pirates who stole your daughter."

"Yes… I beg you."

"I will begin with some narration… I was sitting on the edge of the dock intensely staring into the rippling water… as you can see." He motions to his old self as he says this. "A young boy with blondish-brown locks found this sight all too curious."

Just as Arthur finishes saying this, a boy just as he described comes stepping up the dock.

"He stood nearby, thinking he was clever," Arthur continues. "Nervous as could be, he inched closer as his wonder grew. Before he knew just how hopeless his spying strategy was playing out, he spoke."

"What are you looking at?" Jeffrey asks Arthur.

Arthur raises his head and shows a slight smile. He says, "What I am looking at is not a subject fit for little boys."

"Why?"

"Well," he says, trying to find the right words. "When a man grows old, he begins to hear a voice."

Jeffrey is lost to the meaning of the words. He stares off to some kelp floating on a ripple.

"Men must pay attention to this voice before it is too late," Arthur says.

A grain of interest sprouts in Jeffrey's chest. He asks, "What does it say?"

"It says many things."

"Like what?"

"You really want to know?"

Jeffrey nods, unsure about this ominous lesson.

"If I tell you," Arthur says, "you must promise to listen to the voice that speaks to you."

He knows not what to say.

Arthur says, "There are so many possibilities how a man's life may turn out. You must not believe that you know what is best. The voice will guide you."

"What does it sound like?'

"It is very quiet," Arthur says. "So quiet that most never even know it's there."

"What does it teach you?"

"What it has to teach I am too old for. But you son, for you it is not too late."

"I'd like to know."

"Do you promise to listen?"

"Yes, I will try."

Arthur then stares off in a trance.

"Why are you looking into the water?" Jeffrey asks.

"I am staring into the world of my other self."

Jeffrey leans over the edge of the dock and peers into his own reflection.

"Would you like to hear his story?" Arthur asks Jeffrey.

He shakes his head excitedly and sits with his legs hanging over the edge.

"All right, then. This is a story of my other self. A story that seems as real to me, perhaps even more real than the life I am living now. His life plays out over and over. I can see it, the ribbons all intertwining, piecing it together again."

"What is he like?" Jeffrey asks. "Is he—"

"I will tell all I can. It is the slightest things that make one life different from another. You see, I lost my family when I was about your age. But my other self did not. His mommy and daddy were quite healthy."

As Constantyne hears these words, the world around has the matter sucked out of it. He wakes in his quarters lying on his side, full of inspiration. A smile finds its way to his face and he rises up. He takes his cane leaning against the wall and manages to stand. He is beginning to see again.

He takes his quill, dips it, and scribbles into Lexington's history book a message that presses upon his mind. The words flow without strain around the border of the original text. It goes on like this for hours, until finally he feels emptied out.

He quickly jerks the knob of the door and invites himself into the sunlight. The core of his vision has returned, and the shakiness is minimal. The crew is startled by the brightness about his miserable face. Constantyne orders them to signal Lexington, for he wishes to share a word.

Lexington sits before his superior, full of hope and trust. He decided long ago that such unaccounted for events in one's life are to be treasured and glorified. What's even more, his life aboard his ship had been utter torture, and any release from that ordeal is dove upon.

Constantyne does not know where to start once the crews of his ships gather around him in so great a number. His body is weak and his faith is brittle, so his lips stop in order for him to plan his narrative strategy most wisely.

Constantyne announces, "I want to tell you… that I feel our suffering is over! My mind went deep and finally drunk its fill. I sunk into a horrifying delirium. I feel it was real, but how can I prove?"

The grungy captain has captured their attention. Sitting on an old box, he continues, "You may not believe me. I may not believe myself. But in my waking life as well as dream, I witnessed unbelievable things, and we not are in a position to turn any of that down. In my mirror, a dead man showed himself to me. I knew not what was the significance, but soon I believe I was overtaken, and in my dreaming state it became much clearer. He told his story to me. He was a man as any of us, yet his soul was cut like paper due to decisions he fell into."

"This man's name was Arthur. He lived a life of few vices, relatively free of struggle. His eyes were on the goal, to catch the haul. Off to work he would go. When the time would come, the men were off to the tavern, then back home for a span of sleep. 'It was a practical life' he would say to himself, safe and surrounded by the company of kind fellows, kindred sent from the halls of heaven to share their company in this time on Earth."

"No children did he leave behind; no house filled with the chatter, the high tones of laughter, the resonance, the chorus singing his praises, their arms wrapped 'round daddy's neck. No wife was there to call his name; no response when he came to his cramped, damp quarters. There was no echo when he came home to his lonely bed, save for the reverberations of the ebb and flow sounding through the hollow under the boards beneath his feet like a massive cello. Every morning he would wake in his cold bed, greeted by the familiar smell of sea salt."

"May God forgive him for his trifles. I do not think he harmed a soul all his life. He was a lonely man, but aren't we all much of the time? When he arrived to me, I was not much startled. I was fully lost in my bodily impairment, and so when he appeared and spoke to me I was in no position to rise up and become afraid. On the contrary, he came to me in the form of a dream, so the strangeness adapted to my understanding much easier."

These statements set a few unnerved sailors on edge. A commotion erupts among them. Are they to stand more of this loony admiral's hallucinations? Lives are continuing on the shore. Babies are born, marriages are being held, holidays are celebrated, yet on these vessels, life is pure humiliation. This poor, transvestite mimicry of rituals aren't enough.

"Here, men!" Constantyne calls to quiet them. When this is not enough, he hollers, "Silence now!" and raises himself with fury. He hobbles within the center of his companions and says, "I noticed something of value in the specter's words… He mentioned a few things that are anchored in Thomas, our prey. It was something about the death of his parents. Thomas mumbled some nonsense about that as well."

"I believe that the ghost of Arthur Robinson reveals itself to those of a collapsed mind. Perhaps it takes to those who become completely open to it, like the boy Jeffrey in the narrative he spun. I feel there is significance in this. Thomas was ill in the head. He began uttering nonsense and threw my life into chaos as a result. Therefore, I believe he had succumbed to this same parasitic ghost, and now I am bestowed with its curse and blessing."

Before Constantyne, the others stand with their eyebrows set low in confusion, and there is much wandering of the eyes and biting of lips in trying to piece together the words they just heard.

Constantyne tells them, "I understand your feelings on this, but trust in your captain. Despite the setbacks, the ailments I had been tormented with have become our greatest boon."

Constantyne orders his ships to be sailed toward France, for he feels the heart of his victim like a wolf smells its prey. The creature tears across the plain of the world, pulsing blood, hair on edge, beautiful.

# Heroism and a Bullet for Louis

THE BLOOD OF GOD travels up the Loire River, a winding passage through Nantes, France. Cathedrals and châteaux the color of ivory greet Thomas and his crew as titans ruling over mortals. The massive façades display imposing spires with numerous grand arches. One after another they are overwhelmed by the creations. Finally, they arrive at the docks and step off the ship. Above stands the Cathedral of St. Simon and St. Paul. High-standing alabaster city gates arch over the crowds passing through in clusters. Though haggard, the crew of Thomas' ship strolls proud and noble.

Charles is immediately brought to a doctor. Daily his wound is washed, healing herbs are applied, his bandages changed, and he is fed nutritious food and drink to help him along. Warm blankets and kind words are given, which work wonders, despite the sickness that lingers through the healing process. After three weeks, he can tolerate lying on his back no more, and he decides to accompany his fellows in their training as best he can.

One by one the crew filters into a lively pub. They down gulps of ale and feast on a variety of meats, soups, and breads. Benjamin plays an upbeat song, as those listening twirl and clap in time. Simon engages a girl, holding out his hand. The girl takes her invitation and they join in a festive dance. Thomas and Lucy sit together, singing along joyfully, and Henry is off in the corner swapping saliva with the pub-maids daughter, having a crafty grope.

Diego whips the crew of pickpockets into a force of efficient soldiers, as well as educating them in the knowledge of the working of a ship, opposed to the large amount of guesswork that was done before. Day and night, feet are heard tromping through drills, and hollering echoes upon the deck as blades clash. Form, discipline, valor—this is what Diego instills upon his students. Slash, lunge, parry—these maneuvers become more natural every day as the boys diligently perform their tasks, the motions sinking solidly into their minds.

The leadership also improves, due to Diego's experience as a commander. His insight moves both Charles and Thomas to excel in their abilities. Under this reformed organization, the crew achieves quality of skills they never thought themselves capable of.

Below the main deck, a team of boys race to load cannons. Another team packs, while yet another set are positioned to aim and set fire, igniting them. Four black cylinders blast their contents into the sea.

Charles emerges from his rest and yells, "Double time! I want these loaded and ready to fire! We send out two for every one they send!"

The boys shoot at dummies lined on the side of the ship. The dummies break apart as the shots fly and hit their targets. Behind them, others practice sword fighting with skill.

Thomas oversees them from the main deck. At the top of his lungs he calls, "Drop the targets!"

Barrels are dropped into the ocean.

Thomas yells, "Lower the sails!"

David and Simon unroll the sails atop the mast. Francis and Simon fasten the sails below. The ship gains great momentum.

"Turn us left!" Thomas calls to Benjamin.

Benjamin fiercely presses against the tiller.

"Aim! Fire!" Thomas orders, as the cannons blast off and explode the floating barrels.

As night falls, Diego instructs Benjamin in the use of a cross-staff. Shaped like the Christian cross, the edge is aligned with Polaris in order to ensure the ship is headed in its proper path across the Atlantic. Diego tests him by pointing to various destinations on his map and having Benjamin draw up a proper plan of navigation.

Originally they had not planned to stay so long in France, but things change. With the money that was distributed from what was found in the ship's hold, everyone falls into a new state of existence. They take up living in permanent housing, befriending locals, and settling in with some business dealings and getting a gradually better grasp of the language.

Thomas strolls down an alley where several entrepreneurs have rolled forth carts to sell delicious morsels. The smells of chicken grease, mint, and saffron flow into his nostrils. He is not far along when he sees a familiar neckline. The blonde hair has been snipped at the slightest angle. He knows who this is. This is Charles, dressed immaculately in a doublet lined with stripes of bloody-rich-burgundy on black. He is seated on a small, wobbly stool, sharing words with two common fellows. Upon a small, lightweight table between them sit two dishes holding squares of spinach tart and poached eggs filled with custard. As Thomas brings himself into view, Charles' words are cut short. His hand, upraised to give emphasis, is momentarily frozen.

"Hello, friend," Thomas says. "Enjoying yourself?"

"Yes. Why not?" Charles answers. "Good food, new friends…" He says this while motioning to his companions.

"You look fantastic… Very healthy," Thomas says to Charles.

After a somber pause Charles says, "Gentlemen… This is my captain…"

At this, the men stand and give an awkward, though nervous bow. Thomas tries to give the best bow he can.

Thomas breaks into a grin and asks Charles, "Care to run off to the seaside?"

Charles answers slowly, "Well… I'm enjoying their company."

"Perhaps later?" Thomas says with a big grin.

"Will you stab me if I don't?" Charles asks, gripping his wrist. He holds his fingers spread wide. The bandage wrapped around his hand, and Charles' unflinching expression sinks Thomas' hope of reliving the past.

Thomas steps off without a word. He knows the sin he committed. In hand, he does not let this go. The guilt he sucks in as he wanders street to street.

After a somber stroll through many winding streets, Thomas spies Diego within a crowd. He is amid sellers of strange wines made by peasants. Thomas waves wildly to make his presence known to him. Diego continues bargaining, seeming a bit tipsy.

Diego calls out to Thomas, who is still separated by the cluster, "It is a wine… made with the comb of bees… some are still in the bottle! And… there are cuts of apples… grapes… I suspect it tastes like shit, but I must have it!"

After a time, Diego jerks his way through the crowd with his prize in hand.

"Hello, my friend. How are you?" Diego says in a jolly manner.

Thomas' forces his enthusiasm. "What is your lesson this week?"

"Defensive techniques. Will I see you soon?"

"In the morning."

"Good, good. How's the form look? Let me see it," Diego says, stepping back to give him room.

Thomas takes a side stance.

"Take out your sword."

Thomas does as he is instructed. He points the blade with a straight, outstretched arm. Diego drunkenly sets down the bottle of honeycomb wine and suddenly feigns an attack. Thomas blocks and presses it to his left side.

"Now pretend you have a dagger in your right hand," Diego orders. "I'll come at you again."

Diego strikes slowly again. Thomas blocks as before, then steps in with his right foot and thrusts his imaginary dagger into Diego's neck.

"Again," Diego says.

Thomas does so.

"Again."

Diego stands straight and relaxed once more.

"How's my progress?" Thomas asks.

"Better. Keep up the footwork."

Thomas nods.

"How long has it been since you've seen your wife?" Thomas asks.

"Already three months have passed. It's a lifetime in my mind."

"Isn't there any way for you reunite? Summon her here perhaps?"

"I know of no way. They'll have my head if I set foot there."

"Dare you tell me for what crime you are wanted?"

"It's for my liberal use of a dagger in place of words. Death lay in my wake, though my only remorse is for my wife's solitude."

"You must find a way," Thomas says, taking a step back in the direction he was headed.

"I see you mean to be going somewhere. I won't stop you," Diego says.

"Yeah, Lucy's in one of her moods. I know what shuts her up."

"Bribing her? My god—" Diego says, both of them now parting further with each word.

"I know what keeps her here. We all have our price."

"It's a high one for her," Diego says, now distant.

"Yeah, well—you're right about that. But that's how it is," Thomas says, mumbling the last words mostly to himself.

Thomas enters his house. Lucy, seated at her desk scribbling something, does not turn to see him. He nears her cheek to kiss it, but she swats him away.

"Just one kiss," Thomas pleads.

"I don't want it. I'll be leaving soon," Lucy says frankly.

"With what? You didn't earn a thing."

Thomas lifts the two new dresses he just purchased, one pink, and the other deep green. Struck by his silence, she briefly sees the vibrant colors and raises herself. She takes them in hand, and holds them up before her body, comparing them in a mirror.

"You like?" Thomas asks her.

She nods happily and kisses him.

"These always remind me of the time I interrupted your shopping day with your father. I'll forever be making up for that, won't I?" Thomas says, cracking a smile.

She nods again and says, "Yes you will."

"What have you been doing?" he asks.

"I'm writing a letter."

"To who?"

"To myself. It's something I picked up from my father. It helps me think."

She leads him over to the desk to see.

"It's just my thoughts," she says. "It's nothing. Why don't you try?"

"I'm not sure how," he says.

Lucy takes a quill and dips it in ink. She slowly writes "Thomas" at the top of her letter while saying the letters as she writes them, "T-H-O-M-A-S. Thomas, see?"

Thomas takes the quill nervously, saying, "H-How do I start?"

Lucy smiles with compassion, "Poor dear. You draw a line from here," pointing to the top, horizontal line of the "T". She then draws another line going down, then quickly finishes the rest of the word. "Like mine, see?" she says, pointing to the letters she wrote.

Thomas copies the letters, his penmanship as sloppy as a child's. The "O" looks more like a square than a circle. Lucy Laughs in a girly way, hugs him, and kisses him. Quickly and quietly she whispers in his ear, "Good job."

As evening rolls around, Thomas and Lucy stroll hand in hand down to the shopping district. Thomas has an uneasy look on his face. He quickly draws his rapier and thrusts it behind himself. The tip of his blade points at the neck of a young vagrant boy. The boy's face is frozen and has his hand extended, as he was attempting to steal Thomas' purse.

"Do not hesitate, boy," he tells him.

Thomas takes one of two small purses at his side and tosses one to the boy, then continues strolling down the street hand in hand with Lucy. The boy shivers with fear and skitters away with his knees wobbly and unsteady. Lucy smirks and nudges Thomas.

Thomas and Lucy indulge in finery, having their hair washed and brushed. They have their hair cut in the latest Parisian fashion. Lucy tries on a beautiful, midnight blue dress in a high-class boutique. The dress is fashioned in the latest style, having a low, square neckline; a constricting bodice, molding to her exquisite figure as a corset would; and a ruffled skirt gathered at the waist. Thomas meets her, wearing a black and burgundy doublet with a large black frill around his neck. He clasps a glimmering diamond necklace around her neck. They both pose in the full-length mirror before them, astonished in their transformation.

"Is it a dream?" Lucy says, glowing with happiness.

"Yes, it must be," Thomas says, kissing her on the cheek and embracing her around the waist.

Lucy and Thomas stroll proud in their new clothes. Someone speeds down the road dodging careless shoppers. A nimble black-haired Frenchman has a bloody gash on his right shoulder. Two guards chase behind him with spears in hand. One fires and shoots Louis in the leg, sending him to the ground screaming. The guard raises his spear. Thomas steps forward and blasts a pistol shot into the guard's face. He lies dead and bloody, mutilated on the cobbled road.

The second guard thrusts his spear at Thomas. Thomas thrashes. His sword swipes with might against the strike, knocking the guard off balance. The guard, falling backwards, raises his pistol. Thomas dodges and the shot flies by, crashing through a shop window. Thomas lunges, piercing through the guard's kidney, sending him to the ground, quivering. People scream in horror, some running away.

Louis lies on the ground, moaning in pain. Thomas takes his hand and helps him up. Louis staggers on his injured leg and says, "Thank you, Monsieur. I owe you my life!"

Louis uses Thomas as a crutch. He says, "We must hurry. You are no longer safe. There will be more of them very soon."

Thomas and Lucy hesitate.

"Come with me," Louis says. "I will keep you safe."

Louis knocks on a door of a small house. He screams, "Let me in! It is Louis! I am badly injured!"

The door opens. Louis quickly enters, followed by Thomas and Lucy. The hearth holds an inviting fire. Two finely dressed Frenchmen sit with glasses of wine, their heads turned from their conversations to the newcomers. François, startled at seeing Louis' injury exclaims, "How did this happen?"

"I was attacked! These two saved me!" Louis says, cringing from the pain.

The other Frenchman supports Louis on his feet and tells François, "Do not worry. I will find a doctor for him."

"Thank You. I know he is in good hands," François tells him with folded hands as if in prayer.

François approaches Lucy and Thomas with a bottle of wine in one hand and two glasses in the other. In rough, accented English, he tells them, "Please, make yourselves comfortable," waving his hand toward open chairs.

Thomas and Lucy sit, warming by the fire.

"This wine is from my own vineyards in Navarre," François says as he pours wine into their glasses and hands them to Lucy and Thomas. Lucy takes a sip and is delighted.

"I love it!" she says.

Thomas takes a sip and agrees.

François smiles and tells them warmly, "It is my pleasure to serve those who would risk their lives for one they do not even know."

Thomas takes another drink and a look of seriousness comes over his face. He says, "But I wonder why aristocrats, such as you, must hide?"

"It is true we are nobles in our lands in the south, but our religion is persecuted here," François says.

"Oh? Which—" Thomas asks confused.

"Protestants."

"Oh, yes. We've heard things, seen things. But we've managed to ignore the trouble, till now."

François lets fly from his mouth with great tension. "They suffocate us. They hate us and strike us down with impunity."

Thomas and Lucy each take sips, listening intently.

"We shall soon attend the marriage of Henry of Navarre to Marguerite, daughter of Queen Catherine of Medici. Perhaps this bond will end the slaughters, the civil wars that bring ruin upon us all," François says.

François tends the fire. He takes a long drink from the bottle. The glowing embers illuminate his face as he turns and says boldly, "We are to be one country again—uniting in the glory of God, as one people."

"It shall be a wonderful day to see this," Lucy says with cheer.

"Then you shall! Be my honored guests. What do you say?" François asks.

"Yes, of course!" Thomas says, shining like the sun in the glow of the fire.

# 28

# Coligny and a Brief Peace

LUCY SAYS, "THIS IS SO LOVELY!" peering outside, seeing the countryside pass.

"Indeed," François says. "I believe that the heart of France lies not within walls of any palace, but in the hearts of the common people."

The sound of the horses' clomping sets the mood, one of joviality. At a gentle pace they go. Peasants pick grapes on both sides of the carriage caravan.

François says, "I propose, for good luck, we all throw something valuable out the window. With this gesture we can set the standard."

"For what reason?" Thomas asks.

François answers, "We can cut off our greed… in a small way."

Lucy says, "But maybe a person could pick this object up and something terrible would happen as a result. Perhaps this person will be murdered."

"Yes, perhaps," François says. "But if the objects are lying out in the field… I think the secret will be kept well. These lucky ones who come across this wealth wouldn't dare tell. Think of the secrecy on those lips. Think of what would be at stake for them."

Thomas says, "It is not a great sacrifice for me to give. I did not work for any of it."

"It is the spirit that counts," François says, slipping a ruby encrusted ring from his finger. "It's the spirit to sacrifice the want for gain… in the hope that peace will come from tomorrow's marriage."

At this François tosses his ring far out into the vineyard.

"Very well," Thomas says, staring at Lucy. He removes a ring dotted with sapphires and she follows by unclasping her necklace glittering with small diamonds.

"To peace," Thomas says.

"To peace," Lucy repeats, and they both toss their jewelry out the carriage window.

Later that night, François' carriage arrives at Admiral Coligny's house. Thomas exits the carriage, followed by Lucy and François.

"Cannot my companions join us?" Thomas asks.

François tells him, "Admiral Coligny has but limited room at his table for special guests. They will thoroughly enjoy themselves in our accommodations. Do not worry."

François knocks on the front door. A servant opens it and invites them inside. They enter Coligny's dining room to see Coligny himself seated at his table dining with four other guests.

Upon seeing François, Coligny stands to his feet, shouting aloud, "François! I am so happy you have arrived! Who are our guests?"

"This is Lucy, a fine, gentle girl of refined spirit and taste," François says.

"It is a pleasure," Coligny says, bowing in a gentlemanly manner.

"And this gentleman goes by the name of Thomas Ashcroft," François says, holding his hands directed toward Thomas. "He risked his life to save Louis from certain death."

"What nobility!" Coligny says with his eyebrows raising considerably. "A man of true character!"

"Thank you," Thomas says modestly.

"Please sit," Coligny says, holding his arms before the open seats. "We have already begun our feast, but there is plenty. Do not be modest; what is mine is yours."

Seating herself, Lucy says, "Such a wonderful array of dishes. What do you call this?" pointing to an elaborately dressed meat.

"Chicken galantine," Coligny says, licking his lips and pulling free another strip of meat. "Fill yourselves friends. I know your stomachs must grumble after the travel you have undertaken."

Thomas, Lucy, and François fill their plates. A servant fills glasses of wine for them.

Coligny holds his wine glass aloft toward Thomas. He says, "Thomas, your sacrifice is an inspiration to us all."

The rest of the company do the same and take sips to give honor to Thomas.

"Here, here!" François calls out, holding his glass toward Thomas.

"You speak too highly of me," Thomas says, peering downwards bashfully.

"I do not believe so," Coligny says intensely. "Louis breathes as a result of your bravery. You risked your life to save another—one you had never seen before. Is this not true?"

"Yes it is," Thomas says.

Coligny says, "Your modesty may be a bit too much. But the willingness to give is lost among us, and this is why our civilizations are filled with hate."

"Indeed," François says, saddened to be reminded of the truth.

Coligny looks to François, asking him, "Do you believe the wedding tomorrow will erase the feelings of hate? The vows of revenge sowed in times of bloody civil war?"

"I have faith that people can change. It will be difficult, but there is a chance," François says intensely.

"The problem lies in the fact that we keep so much for ourselves and allow the peasants to suffer. It's not as simple as charity, either," Coligny says.

Thomas says, "This is so in every country. The poor have no other choices but to revolt or simply die."

"And so all must live in turmoil," Coligny says, wiping his forehead noticeably stressed. He takes down a sip of wine and ponders. Finally, he speaks his mind once more. "It is a peculiar truth, that one does not have anything if it is not shared."

Massive white pillars line the walls of the Notre-Dame Cathedral. Curtains of fine red cloth sewn with gold threaded illustrations line the walls throughout, outlining the stained glass windows decorated with motifs of the saints. Light soaks through the many colors shimmering a heavenly glow upon rich Parisians within. At the head of the church hangs a colorful statue of Christ crucified. Cardinals and Bishops are seen from afar, their white and red points jutting above the heads of the people.

Thomas and Lucy stand amongst the crowd near the back of the church. Charles and a number of others wait outside to save themselves from struggling within the crowd. A finely dressed young boy kneels on the ground facing the back of the church playing with a wooden toy horse. The boy mumbles to the horse, rocking it in his hand in a mock trot.

Cardinal de Bourbon speaks the rites of marriage, unintelligible to those as distant as Thomas. Lucy lifts herself on her toes, but still cannot see those up front. Thomas looks to people lined along the walls, then to the boy who continues playing.

A choir erupts in song, and the crowd becomes alert to the notes emitting. Choir boys move in precession down the aisle, followed by the leaders of the church in stunning red and gold. Behind them, members of the royal line follow, surrounding Marguerite de Valois and Henry of Navarre, side by side. Though the aristocracy attempt a gait of formality, the newly married couple stride empty of affection, stiff as wood, filled with uneasiness.

"There! I see them!" Lucy says.

Thomas and Lucy peer through the crowd and witness a brief glimpse of Marguerite and Henry. Marguerite is adorned with a dazzling, bejeweled crown, glimmering brightly with multitudes of diamonds.

The sound of drums, flutes, lutes, and other instruments fill the air of the palace courtyard. Young people dance merrily, some in pairs, and others prance in line hand in hand. A young girl chases after a boy and tackles him to the ground, giggling, and forces a kiss on his cheek as he squirms.

At a long table, lords and ladies dine on sweet cakes and other desserts. Crystal glassware is filled with red wine by servants. A spry lad scoops lemon tart from a dish and shoves it into a ladies mouth across from him. She laughs aloud with her mouth full.

Coligny speaks to Charles IX in a friendly manner upon the steps leading to the courtyard. People all around clap along to the music cheerfully as the dancers pass. Thomas and Lucy do the same. Charles stands by nervously. Thomas hands him his wine and says, "Looks like you need this."

Charles tips it back and starts to drink. François pushes him into the circle of dancers from behind and laughs heartily. Wine spills down his throat and he falls into Anne, a beautiful brunette French girl, as she is dancing. They lock hands in order to not fall. As she lays eyes on him though, glee arises in her and she tugs him near. They begin swaying together, light-footed. As they twirl, he looks back to François with a smile.

"It is a joyous day," François says. "Everyone lives without a care."

Thomas laughs at Charles, saying, "This is what I have always dreamed of."

"Can it be—we shall have a united France?" François says.

Louis dances without care, throwing his arms into the air. By accident, he kicks up dirt upon the shoe of the Duke of Guise. The Duke thrashes Louis upon the ground violently, bloodying his lip.

The Duke glares at him and scolds so all can hear, "How dare you soil yourself upon me, you vermin?!"

Louis wipes the blood with his palm. In seeing it he is enraged. He leaps up, only to be held back by Coligny.

Louis struggles with him and says, "Let me go!"

Several of Coligny's guests stand by his side, yearning to fight. Coligny holds his hand toward them, signaling them to stay back. He speaks so all can hear, "Is it true, the first drop of blood has so soon been spilled? The dam has broken through, and soon shall flow as the sea. Such fools to believe we can hold a torrent of hate with a loveless marriage!"

Fog rolls in as Coligny's carriage slows and halts before his house. Thomas and Lucy sit on one side, Coligny on the other. Coligny waves them to the door, telling them, "Guests first, please."

Thomas steps to the ground, then turns. The blue haze of the moon illuminates the night. He supports Lucy as she descends the steps, one hand gripping hers, the other on her hip. She leans into him as they stumble to the front door.

"Poor thing. You are exhausted," Thomas tells her.

Coligny exits the carriage and swiftly reaches the front door.

"It was a long day," she says with her eyes half closed.

"Yes it was," Thomas says, kissing her forehead.

Coligny unlocks the door and holds it open for them as they wander inside. Thomas helps Lucy up the last stairs. Coligny follows behind and tells them, "I must attend business tomorrow morning, but I beg of you, please enjoy yourselves."

Thomas and Lucy stop several feet before the balcony in the middle of the room.

"We do not wish to be in the way."

Coligny says, "Make use of what you wish to fill your comfort. It is nothing."

"Why is it that you make such effort for us? I do not understand," Thomas asks.

Coligny stands before Thomas. He rests his hand on his shoulder. His words fall cold as stone, "I am constantly surrounded by liars and traitors. It is not often I can trust anyone."

Thomas says, "Is there any hope of peace in this country?"

"I fear the worst, unbelievable suffering," Coligny says, filling with bitter emotions.

Thomas feels empty. He speaks with hope still clinging to voice, "I so strongly wanted to… make life better in some way. I did not consider failure."

Thomas leads Lucy onto the balcony and sits with her on a bench. His hair gently flows in the breeze and the moon shines on his face. She sleeps with her head on his shoulder.

Coligny leans on the bench beside Thomas and says, "It is already a failure to be born human. It is inherent in our nature to always be pulled toward a decline. Therefore, it is a triumph to fight this and to live this life as nobly as one can." Strolling around to the railing, he continues, "It is tiresome to stand beside those who never developed further than the spoiled child they were born as. To stare in the face of the fools who run this Earth. Never should we falter, whether they tear us limb from limb and rip every bit of skin from our bones!"

Thomas says, "Then we can never succeed?"

Coligny slams his fist, saying, "How can any succeed when everyone dies? To win is therefore all within your belief of what that means. Nobody wins in this life. There will always be an unconquerable horde ready to crush you. The only question is how you will go down."

Thomas lightly caresses Lucy's hand as Coligny's eyes follow the people passing below.

Thomas quietly replies, "That is why the fools continue being who they are. In their minds it is they who live truthfully! In their minds it is they who are the heroes!"

Coligny says, "Therefore, it is up to you. What will you live for?"

Filled with a bittersweet sense of nostalgia, Thomas says, "The only thing I have ever asked is to be treated with dignity. I will fight to my death for this."

"I would not have you risk your life. This is our country, not yours," Coligny says.

Thomas breathes the cool air deep into his lungs. He says, "I felt for an instant today a sense of belonging. I will not hesitate to sacrifice all that this may last."

"Then you will stand by my side. Help me unite this land," Coligny says.

"This is too high of an honor," Thomas says, shaking his head.

"Nonsense! Our ideals will be a reality or our blood will drain through the streets!" Coligny screams, his voice carrying far.

A baby is heard crying down the road. Coligny steps backward and calms himself.

"Alas, it is late. I must rest," Coligny says, making his way inside. Thomas helps Lucy stand. With small steps they enter the dark room and he seats her on the bed.

"Good night to you, Thomas," Coligny says closing the door.

Thomas slides down Lucy's dress and pulls it off.

"Good night my love," he tells her.

Thomas kisses her on the mouth. She hugs him close and kisses him on the neck with her eyes shut.

"My daughter," Constantyne says. "She is here in this city!"

A servant nods, "Yes, sir. You will be with her in no time."

"I will. But I don't like this business she involves herself in, these people she surrounds herself with."

"There is word," says the servant, "that they wish to do harm to the royal family. There is much shouting and bad air. They mean to ignite a revolution while they are still in town for the wedding."

"I live for order. I believe the people should respect their king and not try to arrive at their own solutions to how a country should be ruled. Everyone to their station, I say. Let the people work to keep the wheels in motion. Their calamity is a crime, an act to trip up the legs of production."

"What do you mean to do?"

"We will find the leader of these cretins and put a stop to him. When it all quiets down, I will take my Lucy in the midst of their mourning."

"I know him, sir. He is the Admiral Gaspard de Coligny, Lord of Châtillon. But I must say, he is not hateful toward the crown. He is good friends with King Charles and is an important bond between the two powers in this country. It is because of him that the Huguenots are kept at bay."

"I do not trust such a cowardly sort of behavior, tip-toeing around one's own kingdom so as not to bring on the children's tantrums. It is the common people that should be wary of arousing their King's anger, not the other way around. This is not my land, so I will do as I please. It is my summation that my plan is sound—that if we silence this Coligny, I will have my moment to run home with my daughter. I care for nothing else."

"Very well. Today he is to meet with the King. I will take you to a place that crosses his path."

Coligny calmly makes his way past cheerful people. He passes a salon. Within, people converse while others have their hair styled. He passes a bakery. A customer is handed a large loaf of bread while several fresh ones are lifted, steaming out of an oven.

He passes a meat market. A bound cut of pork is carried past. Through the window a butcher hacks a large hunk of beef ribs. He looks up and smiles and waves to Coligny. Coligny waves back happily. Street vendors sell all sorts of sweets, one providing fine sandwiches as well.

People fill inside the many varieties of clothing boutiques, trying on hats and other sets of fine clothes. People enjoy cakes while reclining on the base of a grand fountain. Children chase each other and birds chirp in the trees.

Thomas and Lucy lie in each other's arms. The sun shines through the window, illuminating the room. Lucy opens her eyes slightly due to the light striking her face. Thomas wakes as well.

After a moment Lucy says to him, "When you are alert I want to ask you a serious question."

Thomas feels stunned and dreads what may come, but still tells her, "I'm awake."

"Why did you kill Jack?"

"Because you're mine," he answers.

"Yours? Your what?"

"You were my slave, remember? We had a deal to sell you, but I saved you from being given to that old man. The deal was that you are mine."

"But he was your friend," she says stroking the sheet covering her leg.

"You both knew very well what you were doing. You were both trying to get at me for different reasons. If I hadn't done what I'd done I would no longer be captain."

She asks him, "What stops me from running out on you when you're not watching me?"

"Nothing. You're not my slave anymore."

"What changed your mind?"

"I like you, I guess."

"Oh. I see."

"So why don't you run out? Walk out of here right now. I'll even give you the money."

"Right now," she says. "I find this sudden rise in social status very impressive."

Coligny sees Louis on the other side of the street. They wave to each other. Louis purchases a chicken breast from a street vendor and crosses the street while munching on his meal.

Louis says, "It is good to see you! What a beautiful day it is!"

"Perhaps it is an omen—such cheer in the air. Shall we shall not lose hope, after all?"

"Never!" Louis says, laughing and taking a large bite of his chicken.

Lucy kisses up the length of Thomas' throat. He smiles, taking in the pleasure. She strokes down his bare chest and kisses it slowly several times. She climbs on top of him and they stroke each other's faces and kiss passionately.

Coligny and Louis stride side by side.

"What is your business?" asks Louis.

Coligny says with an official tone, "We are to discuss grievances with the King."

"Concerning?" Louis questions, interested.

"Concerning the Peace of St. Germain. To ensure that our striving is not in vain," Coligny answers.

"May fortune lay in God's hands," Louis says.

A great blast sounds from the second floor building of a nearby house. Blood explodes from Coligny's left shoulder. A lurking figure escapes into the shadows within the window. Coligny screams and falls on his knees, gripping his wound, reeling in pain.

"God help us! He has been shot!" Louis calls in a panic, as he drags Coligny to the side of the building. Many citizens rush to find help, while most stand alarmed.

Coligny lies shirtless on an operating table. He grits his teeth as the doctor attempts to pry free a bullet lodged in his scapula. Coligny screams madly in pain and shakes uncontrollably. The pain, far from weakening Coligny, has only filled him with rage.

"Fools! They should have aimed more true, for my death would take the place of thousands!" Coligny says, tightly closing his eyes. Through the pain he blurts, "For now their lust for blood is raged and they hunger is merely aroused!"

The doctor grips the bullet and slides it out slightly.

Coligny screams with all his might, "Woe to those who lurk in the temple of sin and mock peace, calling it the play-toy of the effeminate!"

The doctor pulls out the bullet and drops it in a metal container.

He casts his curses upon all, vehemently howling, "All you that hear me now: your bodies shall litter the streets and will rot in a most gruesome manner!"

# 29

# Hell on Earth

T HE HALLS OF THE LOUVRE echo with the sounds of Huguenot bellowing. The brethren, enraged by the attack on their beloved leader, spew forth hateful decrees. Several wave their hands angrily in the air as they voice themselves. A consensus cannot be reached, but much of the talk calls for revolution. A distinguished Huguenot arrives, followed by several of his armed soldiers.

"The shot came from a house of Guise! We must repay the favor!" he says, drawing his sword, attempting to pass. He is stopped by an elderly aristocrat named Theodore, calling for the mob to come to their senses. Pushing and shouting ensues. Amid the ruckus, the distinguished Huguenot grabs the old man by his collar and thrusts him upon the floor. Cowering, Theodore manages to evade the stampede, only to feel the wetness of warm saliva upon his cheek. He catches a glimpse of the haughty grimace of his defiler glaring down at him.

Anne scrubs the floor with a damp cloth. Hysterical shouts echo from Queen Catherine's room. Anne continues scrubbing, despite the noise. Inside, Charles IX nervously fidgets with the cloth of his cape as Catherine stands beside him dominantly. She is hard, and her face is worn from years of stress. The Duke of Guise and her advisors stand near.

Catherine screams, "The assassination was a disaster! They mean to do us great harm. The Protestants have become as a mob of hornets!" She paces about the room in an uproar.

"What would you have me do?" Charles IX asks, feeling helpless.

Charles IX stands and wearily leans against the bedpost. Catherine lightly touches his sleeve and says, "The coldness of death approaches. Your old mother shall be slain," she adds, hoping to arouse pity.

"It is not true!" he yells.

"Your blood shall be spilt as well," she says. "Their anger will only be calmed by the sight of our severed heads, our spurting blood!"

He embraces his dear mother. Stroking her hair he tells her, "Dear mother, stop this wicked talk! Sit and drink your wine and forget, that this foul day may pass."

Charles IX picks up her wine glass and hands it to her. She screams, "Our eyes will not see the sun of another day, lest we hasten to action! They devise their plots as we speak!" She causes the wine glass to crash upon the floor. Charles IX lies his head in the nook of his arm against the wall, weeping.

Blubbering, he says, "Life is unfair!" He pauses then sobs again. "Why must we always struggle?!"

Catherine shakes him powerfully, shocking him to alertness. She slaps him hard across the face, roaring, "Speak like a king! Not as a boy! This protestant disease shall tear our country apart! None will survive! Our holy France shall lie with its throat slit!"

Charles IX thrusts himself on top of the bed, holding his face. He hollers, "Then… it must be done! If death must be struck, then do not miss one throat that they may return in vengeance!" Striking his fist into the air, he rises to his feet and addresses his company. His eyes betray his lunacy as he screams, "We must slay all who may harbor resentment and a foul mind toward us! Kill them all! Slay all of them, young and old, so they may never rise against us!"

Catherine halts, stunned, but shows a slight smile. She says, "Then Coligny too must be slaughtered! None shall survive to weep the dead."

"Not him as well," Charles IX says. "It cannot be true! Shall we have no friends in death?!" He wails terribly. His pain is heard through horrific screams, muffled into the padding of his bed.

Anne sits near the door intently listening. She hears Charles IX scream, "God grants no mercy upon us! Hell awaits us all!" followed by the sound of steps approaching the door. Anne, extremely alarmed, leaps up and drops her cloth. Anne moves for the staircase. Marguerite leaves her room. She commands Anne with one word. "Come," she says, beckoning her.

Every inch of Anne's body yearns to fly down the staircase and flee for her life. She composes herself, not wishing to arouse suspicion. She turns to Marguerite and follows her into her room.

Marguerite seats herself in an oak tub. Anne lifts her hair and scrubs her neck. She spills water over her back.

A knock is heard at the door. Anne grabs a towel and covers Marguerite. The door bursts open and Charles IX enters.

"How dare you barge in here?!" Marguerite scolds him.

Charles IX nears her, telling her softly, "Sister, you must not leave this room for the remainder of the night."

He kisses her slowly on the cheek twice.

"Why?" she asks.

"It is very cold out," he tells her.

They share an erotic kiss, stroking lip upon lip, staring into each other's eyes. Anne slips out of the room. She descends the main staircase in a fright.

At the bottom of the stairs a lord asks her, "Where are rushing to?" sensing her fear.

Anne jumps at hearing the voice. She says, "I must fetch for my lady. No time to waste," and continues running. The lord shakes his head in disbelief.

Anne reaches the street and speeds as fast as her legs can take her. The street is brightly lit. Anne passes boys wrestling in the street. She passes ladies slowly pacing and conversing. She passes a horse drawn cart filled with building materials. She passes many beautiful houses.

"I want all of the gates sealed!" the Captain of the Guard orders. Thrusting his arm forth, he calls out, "With haste! We shall snare our prey inside these city walls and slaughter them like caged animals!"

Soldiers split in four divisions, toward each direction of the compass. Traveling, they all reach their separate destinations and quickly fulfill their orders.

Anne walks hurriedly. She nears a carriage whose horses wander without order. The driver is dead, with blood covering his shirt. Inside, a couple lies dead with blood covering their faces. Anne stays low and moves carefully near the canal. She passes by the Louvre. Two civilians stab swords into a portly old woman and kick her into the canal. Anne huddles low and hides in the shadows.

Outside the Louvre, the Captain of the mercenaries stands with his troops, girded with steel armor, their brilliant blue uniforms and gleaming pikes. There are no better at cutting throats in all of France than these members of the Swiss Guard. They stand frozen at attention with black berets firm on each head. The Captain speaks with a slight accent. His second in command stands beside him.

The Captain says, "The orders are simple, spare not a life. Cut them down sans mercy. May their screams ring through the night!"

The second in command salutes properly and stiffly nods, calling out, "Aye sir!"

"That is all!"

The second in command leads his troops to the left entrance of the Louvre, the Captain to the right.

Inside, the halls are empty. Not a sound is heard. Within a room suited for lodging, several Huguenots sleep in fine beds. A candle flickers. The door opens, and a silhouetted figure steps in. A Huguenot rises groggily due to the light in his face.

A soldier thrusts a pike into his neck. Blood spurts and an explosion gurgles from the throat. His hand thrusts upward in pain, then falls at his death. Another Huguenot rises. A soldier slashes his pike across the Huguenot's neck, spreading it wide open. The head falls backward, limp, revealing the spine within. Blood gushes out of the head onto the body and splatters onto the wall, glimmering in the candlelight.

Inside another room, Theodore, the elderly Huguenot, wakes and leaps up at seeing a soldier before him. The soldier slashes through his gut with a sword.

"I warned you, you fools!" Theodore calls as he holds his wound and flees. The soldier cuts through the back of his neck, causing him to fall dead. The remaining Huguenots wake at hearing this commotion. Immediately the two soldiers pierce pikes deep into their bowels and stir them around.

The Captain enters a room with two soldiers and finds a Huguenot on his feet. The Captain blasts him in the chest with a shot, sending him to the ground, curled in pain. The soldiers stab him with halberds, then attack two other Huguenots.

Three Huguenots stand in a corner, frightened as another across the room is stabbed with a sword. Two more soldiers enter with pikes. A Huguenot grabs his sword from the ground and stands defensively. A soldier lunges his pike into his neck. The Huguenot swipes his sword with his last breath, but its reach is far too short. The other Huguenots are cut through.

Shouts of might and wailing ring through the halls. Within a long hallway eight Huguenots stand as sheep, shivering with fright in their bedclothes. Three of them hold swords before their faces. They are surrounded by four soldiers on each side. A Huguenot swings his sword downward, but is caught in the gut by two pikes and falls to the ground.

Another Huguenot swings his sword wildly, clashing with the soldier's weapons, sending them back. As he deflects the two pikers in front of him, another Huguenot clashes with a soldier beside him, yet gets stabbed in the shoulder. A piker knocks the sword out of his hand as another disembowels him. The first Huguenot is stabbed repeatedly by multiple pikes.

On the other side of this cluster of Huguenots, soldiers cut through two of them, causing them to fall bloody and dead. The last Huguenot among them, grasping a sword nervously, lunges and gets his belly slashed with a pike, spilling his guts onto the floor. He drops his sword and falls onto his comrade, both screaming madly. A soldier grabs the wounded Huguenot by his hair and decapitates him. He throws the bloody head gushing with blood at the Huguenot he fell into. Covered in blood, he shrieks in terror and flees. The soldier stabs him in the back, sending him down dead. The rest of the Huguenots are slaughtered mercilessly.

Throughout the halls, blood gathers in lakes of red. Bodies lie in great piles with gaping wounds, revealing their insides. Soldiers wander, searching, streaked with bits of shredded muscle and organs, stepping over the dead. They gather the corpses in piles. Two Huguenots lie dead, suspended on pikes. The second in command spies a Huguenot within a pile, barely alive. He quickly takes a halberd from a fellow soldier and decapitates him.

Outside the Louvre, dozens of Huguenot nobles and soldiers clash with spears at each entrance. Beside them, an old couple beat a teenage protestant with clubs. He rises to his feet, but is beaten upon his head until he falls silent. A priest and two middle-aged women attack a young couple. The women stab them with pitchforks and the priest stabs the girl in the back with a knife.

Anne rushes down the street in the shadows. She enters a crowded neighborhood. Mobs of Catholic citizens crash in the windows of houses and leap inside. The front door of a house bursts open and a peasant is forced out. His throat is slit and he is tossed to the ground.

A woman with a crying baby in her arms is brought out of the same house by two workers of the court. She screams as she sees her husband lying still on the ground. The baby is taken and slammed into a stone wall, until its skull is compacted. She is pushed onto the ground and shot in the back of the head.

Anne gasps and cries at seeing this, struggling to keep from screaming.

Stopping beside a house to catch her breath, Anne witnesses a horrific scene through the side window: Four soldiers smash every object they see. A dead boy lies face down on a table. Inside the bedroom a dead grandfather lies limp in a chair with his throat slit. A lieutenant rapes a woman on top of a bed as she screams in horror.

Anne runs mad in fear across the city square. The ground is covered with dead, eviscerated bodies. Large pools of blood gather by the corpses. Other streaks of blood run across the ground along with organs and items of clothing. A dead baby lies limp, lacerated, and bloody. Several dozens of dead bodies stand impaled on various bundles of pikes piled together.

Anne stumbles over bodies in the shadows. Three Catholic nobles stand over a headless corpse covered in blood. They carry on in a jolly manner as an impoverished peasant strips the bodies of clothes. A Catholic noble charges by on horseback with his sword raised overhead followed by two dogs. He chases a frightened young woman. The dogs tear into her and he swings the sword down hard into her skull. Two filth-encrusted commoners grab Anne and put knives up to her throat. Anne lifts the Catholic styled crucifix around her neck.

"Catholic. I am Catholic!" Anne screams.

The one with the knife tells her, "I do not care," grinning and laughing sadistically.

"Help! Stop!" Anne yells, running away.

A noble rides up to them on a horse. He asks Anne, "Do you not work for Marguerite?"

"Yes! Yes!" she answers him desperately.

The noble tells them, "She works for the Queen. Do not lay a scratch upon her, you rats!" He extends his hand to her. She grabs it and climbs upon his horse's back. The noble has blood streaked across the cloth on his arms and chest.

"You must not be here. I will take you as far as I can," the noble tells her.

"Thank you," she says to him, exhausted.

Anne is deeply saddened by the scenery that passes her: A blacksmith carries a little dead boy over his shoulder and throws it near a pile of corpses. A young blonde woman lies dead with only a bloody cloth around her legs. She is nude and has a wide open gash across her face. Her belly is split open with her intestines and much blood spilling out.

Several nobles mounted on horses invite three noble boys to take up spears.

A father, a mother, and a little girl are brought before them. One boy repeatedly stabs the little girl to death as her parents empty their lungs with voiced anguish. The boys giddily slash and lunge at the two people, mutilating them to death. The nobles overseeing this cheer and laugh in great excitement.

Anne cannot keep from screaming as she sees the violence from upon horseback. Three women yell to some young boys and chase after them, armed with a scythe and two clubs. Two dogs lick at the bloody head of a male toddler. One of the dogs grips the head and rips it free from the body. A little girl in a black dress lies nearby with her arm severed.

A horse trainer beats an old merchant repeatedly in the face as his old wife pulls back in terror on the ground. A red-headed woman hits her over the head three times and she falls silent. A bald fellow lies on the ground nearby curled in pain with a long trail of blood leading to his gut. Under him hides a frightened teenage boy.

Several soldiers in full armor, armed with swords and shields stand among dozens of shredded bodies. Two bodies hang from a scaffold behind them. Out of the second story of a building filled with cracks, men push a corpse out the window onto its head.

Beside a canal, a pile of thirty unclothed Protestants lie dead. Peasants kneel next to the pile, stripping corpses, then kicking them and tossing them with the others. The bodies float throughout the surface of the water, sickly bobbing.

On a bridge, an old woman and three young children are beaten by a gnarled-faced figure with a club and slashed by another with a sword. Several bodies of victims lay battered and bloody on the bridge. A servant pulls a body of a woman in a white dress by a rope tied around her neck and rolls her into the canal.

Within a wooded area, the noble stops the horse. He climbs off and helps Anne down with the mannerism of a gentleman. He tells her, "You should be safe. May God be with you."

Anne rushes down the street quite wobbly. She appears numb of emotion. Finally, she reaches the manor in which Charles and much of Thomas' crew are lodged. She knocks on the front door frantically. She wipes sweat from her forehead and knocks again. Benjamin unlocks and opens the door.

"Let me in!" she exclaims, pushing past him dizzily.

Immediately Benjamin compels her to enter. "Yes, this way," he says, leading her into the dining room.

Charles and several of Thomas' crew carry on loudly. They wave wine glasses in the air as they speak. Several pretty ladies laugh and engage in conversation. Anne sees Charles and rushes for him, shaken emotionally.

"Charles! You are all right!" she says.

"Of course I am. What is the matter?" he says.

Now that she is in full light they see the blood smudged across her face, from her chest to the bottom of her dress, and in globs upon her hands and up her arms. Her expression is aghast with absolute fear.

She vomits upon the floor and nearly faints. He brushes his fingers through her hair to calm her. She gazes around the room at those struck speechless, and exclaims, "You are all in the gravest danger!"

# 30

# The Hills of the Slaughtered

CHARLES CALLS TO BENJAMIN, "Go and clear the way to the city gates. I will catch up with you after I meet with Thomas." They pour out of the manor armed with light armor and various weapons. Half of the group leaves one way while Benjamin and the others follow Charles and Anne. The other women enter the house, lock the door, snuff out the candles, and hide.

Benjamin and his group see two villains ripping the clothes off of a woman. Another is raping a woman in the grass on the side of the road. Benjamin quickly stabs the two. The last one stands and half-fastens his pants. Two pistol shots send him down dead.

Benjamin yells to the women, "Escape into the woods. It is not safe here!" Though they only sit and cry, he follows the path once more.

The Duke of Guise, Besme, and three soldiers break open the door to Coligny's house and enter. Within the stark shadow, heavy footsteps storm up the stairs. The door to Coligny's bedroom is kicked open and Coligny calmly turns his head toward them.

"At last you have arrived to send me to heaven," Coligny says.

Besme charges and stabs his sword into Coligny, stabbing his left kidney. He then stabs him directly in the gut. Coligny looks downward at the wounds and feels the blood.

"It was not so bad," Coligny says, gritting his teeth.

Besme screams and grips Coligny with two hands, tossing him through the window. Coligny crashes through the glass and falls to the ground below. Besme and the Duke peer below and see Coligny's body draining blood, surrounded by broken glass. In the distance, a soldier yells to them. Many battle with pikes and halberds.

The Duke says to those under his charge, "Search the house. Make sure there are no survivors."

The Duke of Guise and Besme rush to join the battle. The Duke's soldiers kick open the door to the guest room. Thomas stands in the middle of the room prepared with a sword in his right hand. The three soldiers rush in. Lucy grabs a pistol and shoots the farthest soldier, killing him. Thomas slides out a second sword from a sheath hanging on a chair. He stands like a wild animal defending its territory.

Lucy reloads the pistol. The first soldier thrusts at Thomas, but he swiftly dodges the strike and sinks both swords into the soldier's lungs, causing him to wheeze and fall over dead onto the bed. The second soldier swings a halberd. Thomas dodges it, places his sword on it, pulls the soldier toward him, and stabs through his Adam's apple.

Four male citizens rush into the room. Two are armed with scythes, one with a club, and one with a butcher knife. They all rush Thomas and Lucy. Lucy shoots one holding a scythe in the face, causing him scream harshly and fall over dead.

The other with the scythe charges Thomas. He swings the curved weapon. Thomas leaps and rolls away, dodging the blade. The club swings just over Thomas' head as he tackles the one with the scythe, landing a sword in his gut. Thomas turns to the man with the club and decapitates him while he is confused.

On the balcony, Lucy and the man with the butcher knife wrestle on the ground. Lucy grips his wrist to keep the blade away from her face. She jumps back and slides out a large knife from a sheath on her boot. He swipes at her and she dodges. He grins and swings overhand as she stabs his fingers causing him to drop his weapon. She bores the tip of her knife into his throat. He squeals, "God! Please help me! No, please have mercy!"

Lucy says to him, "Tell your God that you have failed!" inserting the knife fully into his throat. She slides it downward, opening the flesh and causing it to gush blood. He screams in agony, gurgling through his torn throat and vocal chords.

"I hope that hurts," Lucy says, kicking him off the ledge. He falls to the earth below, making a faint wheeze on the way down. The body meets the ground with a loud crack.

On the ground below, five soldiers see him fall from the balcony and then spy Lucy above them. They are weary from battle, carrying gashes on their faces and other parts of their bodies. Their pikes drip with blood. One points to Lucy, calling, "There! Protestants! In that house!"

The soldiers rush inside Coligny's house and crash up the stairs. They charge into the guest room with their bloody pikes firm in grip, dying to sink those sharp blades once more into human flesh. Thomas and Lucy leap onto the balcony, fleeing the onslaught. Thomas slams the doors shut, locking them with a key.

The soldiers violently crash out the glass in a few windows. They kick at the doors and charge, breaking the lock slightly. A shot fires from the ground just missing Thomas and Lucy. Thomas and Lucy look over the edge to see if they can jump safely. The soldiers hack the door with their halberds, ripping it from its foundation. The doors crack and twist loose. They are nearly open.

The charging and chopping stop suddenly. A soldier's face crashes through the glass which stabs through his chin. Blood gushes out of his mouth and runs down the white framing. Another soldier screeches in pain and is thrust against where the two doors meet. His face is visible in the space between.

Charles' voice is heard on the other side saying, "Hey, open up! It is safe now!"

Thomas unlocks the doors and slides them open. The two dead soldiers flop to the ground with glass and splinters in their faces. Charles, Anne, and those who followed them stand victoriously. The room is filled with dead bodies.

"Charles! You are alive!" Thomas says, elated.

They share an embrace, warm and heartfelt. Charles steps onto the balcony and says, "Why does everyone keep questioning that? Let's go; they are waiting for us."

Torches along the walls give off a warm glow. Piles of citizens' bodies lie about. An especially high pile lies against the gate. Both rich and poor scramble upon the dead to climb over. They are stabbed to death by soldiers. A few men are agile enough to rush past the soldiers and shimmy halfway up the gate, but there is not quite enough grip to be had. Their feet slip continuously while their hands reach high, one after another. They are both shot dead.

Benjamin and those with him witness three people running from soldiers on the left side. These people are stopped in their tracks by the pikes of soldiers. Benjamin and the others charge and a battle erupts. The soldiers are far more accurate in their strikes, but they are outnumbered by more than double. Pikes, halberds, and swords wave in the air like a hellish forest of violence.

One on Benjamin's side places a pistol in a soldier's face and pulls the trigger. A hole opens and the body drops. A soldier with a bloody bandage around his forehead slashes three of Benjamin's, killing them all. Benjamin furiously rips the pike out of a soldier's hand and stabs him between the clavicles. At this triumph, they surround Benjamin's charge, slaughtering the soldiers in front of them.

The last soldiers are surrounded. The bandaged soldier stabs Leonard in the neck and swings his pike around, slaying two and injuring two more. Four of those commanded by Benjamin charge the bandaged soldier, cutting him through all sides of his body. He wails, saying, "You'll follow me to the halls of death!" then collapses onto the pile.

The last of these soldiers are pierced and shredded, but from the left side charge ten soldiers and eleven shoot out from the right. Benjamin marches upon the hill of dead bodies and takes a defensive position. Weapons rain down from both sides. Chaos of blood and clashing steel create confusion. Three grit their teeth and strike. Two are stabbed in the belly.

Thomas witnesses the battle from afar and rushes in. They surround the soldiers and stab them in the back as they duel with Benjamin's side. Several soldiers spin around and attempt to battle in several directions at once. A barrage of thrusting weapons fills these soldiers' bodies and quickly ends their lives.

"Good to see you all," Thomas says.

Benjamin says to him, "It is good to have friends in hell," laughing with his teeth glaring and other people's blood dripping down his face.

"Let's get out of here," Thomas calls to him.

"It seems we are locked in," Charles says, shaking the gate.

"Then we should climb," Thomas says.

Francis attempts to climb the tall gate. He struggles, pulling himself up the skinny metal bars. He sits upon the top and hollers down, "This is possible, but it will take a long time for all to make it over."

A team of mounted soldiers and nobles approach. From all sides, soldiers appear out of the blackness. Ordinary citizens, male and female, of vastly differing ages, appear also. On Thomas' side they number over fifty. Anne steps backward behind them, on the arms and torsos of the bodies, against the gate. She attempts to climb, but cannot.

"Help her up!" Charles yells.

Francis reaches down as Charles lifts her up. She is lifted and set upon the top frame of the bars.

"Go! Take care of her!" Charles says to Francis.

Francis climbs down to the other side, followed by Anne. She runs to the gate and calls to Charles, "Be safe! Oh God, please be safe!"

The mounted soldiers step forward. The captain of the mounted soldiers yells, "Engage them! Blow them to bits!"

Thomas yells to Lucy, "Now you! Up with you! Be safe!"

"I shall stand and fight," she says defiantly, sweat drenching her scalp.

He steps toward her and says, "I will assist you. I want to see you alive."

"Back!" she hollers, swiping at him with a spear atop the deceased.

"I have no time for this stubborn bitch!" Thomas says, filled with worry for her, returning to formation as he must.

A dozen soldiers stand in position and fire. Several fall. A dozen of Thomas' men shoot pistols. Two are shot in the face, one receives a shot in the leg, and two bullets hit the soldier's armor and bounce off.

Thomas orders at the top of his lungs, "Take ten with you and slaughter them!"

Benjamin and ten others rush the gunmen soldiers as they attempt to reload and lay pikes into them. Four are killed. The gunmen take out swords. One kills one of Benjamin's men, but all of the gunmen are stabbed to death. Ten soldiers and fifteen civilians rush toward Benjamin's formation.

"Return immediately!" Thomas calls out.

Benjamin, in the center of the cluster, defensively maneuvers backwards until they reach the rest. Three rows are set up on differing elevations upon the dead, allowing many fighters to thrust their weapons. The soldiers and civilians reach Thomas and violence erupts. Lucy finds her occupation in this fight as a slayer of civilians. As the men bear down against the masters of warfare, her nimbleness strikes through to the pockets of common folk. The disorganized manner of the soldiers allows them to be easily stabbed in the face, neck, and belly.

The soldiers are joined by six on horseback who take many lives as they stab their long pikes over the formation, directing fatal wounds. Three mounted soldiers blast pistols killing with each shot. The front ranks are repeatedly slaughtered as both the foot soldiers and the mounted soldiers pick them off.

"Ready your guns!" Thomas yells.

Thomas and several others aim.

"Kill the horses! Fire!" Thomas screams.

Pistols blast into the horses, causing them to panic or fall over dead. Three horses throw off their riders and trample the soldiers near them. Two other horses crumple. One horse runs backward in pain with its rider still mounted and bucks him off onto his head.

Thomas roars, "Charge! Kill every last one!"

Those in Thomas' command engulf the nearby soldiers and massacre them. Benjamin hacks into a soldier's throat repeatedly. Charles thrusts his spear into a soldier's belly and pushes him backward. The soldier causes others to be imbalanced. In the confusion they are instantly cut through.

Spinning around, Thomas hollers, "Those in the back, gather every corpse you can find and pile them high!"

They work together and toss bodies upon the top of the pile. All of the soldiers and civilians near them approach. Ten of them work together and carry a horse to the top of the pile. It now stands seven feet at its highest point.

The soldiers all charge. The murderous civilians follow just behind. The front ranks are gutted in the sea of blades, which flurry about and spout fountains of blood.

Pure blind violence engulfs all who engage the madness. The mass consists of a fifty foot wide sea of black-suited flashes of energy, among the drab, commoner cloth. They scream madly and strike without care. This horde is pure chaos, a porcupine's suicide.

Swords cut through the ranks on both sides. Screams of horror and of fury constantly fill the air. The actions of offense and defense are repeated unconsciously. Roger stabs a pike into a horse's eye, causing it to kick up, knock its rider off, run, and bash into others. Those distracted are immediately routed.

Shots blast and take down those on both sides. Two mounted riders charge through Thomas' side, killing many and causing them to break formation. Five are killed.

One mounted rider is stabbed in the back of the neck and falls dead. The other mounted rider flings his pike about, kills three, and returns to his formation. Thomas and Charles fight side by side in a blind fury. They yell, seemingly never ceasing, each slicing the throats of three adversaries.

Thomas, filled with hate and fear, erupts as if possessed, saying, "We must have their blood! Charge, for we are their executioners!"

Thomas and Charles storm the soldiers, massacring many. Blade points thrust all around as they charge harmoniously, roaring aloud. They take up pikes, and sink the points into a mounted soldier who escaped.

Thomas stands within the pile of bodies with the twenty-five he now has left. Numerous soldiers lie dead, intermingled with Thomas' fighters and civilians.

Thomas says, "Quickly pile them high. We are leaving!"

All of them work piling bodies on top of the mound. Five drag a second horse on top of the pile. Torch flames can be seen in the distance. Many soldiers arrive in view from the darkness.

"Hurry. Move it!" Thomas says frantically.

The closest climb the metal bars of the gate. One raises his hand, calling out, "Hey! Give us a hand!"

Those on top lower their hands and pull up the ones below, including Lucy. Now Thomas, Charles, and Benjamin are lifted. The soldiers near.

"Hurry, dammit!" Thomas yells.

A gunshot blasts a bullet into one standing on the pile, wounding him. Two more shots ring out, hitting one on the pile and another on top of the gate. One on Thomas' side shoots and kills a mounted soldier.

Those on top help the last up as two manage to climb on their own. One being assisted is shot in the back.

The one lifting him yells, "You can do it! Stay with us!"

Four nobles open fire and hit both, causing them to fall on opposite sides of the gate violently. On the other side, arms, legs, and heads of the bodies stick through the bars. A soldier lies moaning, near death a few feet within the pile. A woman at the bottom faintly moves, tries to speak, but makes no sound. A stout laborer on the left, near the middle of the pile, struggles, pleading, "Get me out of here—help me, please."

Seven soldiers appear and open fire. Three fall dead. Several shoot back, killing four. Charles tosses his torch through the gate, starting a fire with the cloth and human kindling. Charles kneels before the laborer stuck in the pile. Staring into his eyes, he says, "There is nothing I can do. You must understand you are a sacrifice."

Two of Thomas' companions drag one of the wounded. A soldier shoots one of those carrying him in the face. They fall in a pile. The fire is blazing bright behind the five attempting to climb the fence. Those on Thomas' side run away as over twenty soldiers stand on the pile attempting to rise over the tall gate amid the soaring fire. They run blindly through the darkness.

Francis calls out, "Hey!" faintly visible in the glow of the crescent moon.

He and Anne are huddled by a tree. They stand, and Anne wraps her arms around Charles. Charles hugs her and kisses her cheek.

They all run for miles and eventually reach a small town. A carriage with two horses stands on the side of the road.

"Take it," Charles says to Thomas.

"And what about you?" Thomas asks.

Charles says, "I am to stay."

"What?" Thomas says, his throat tightening from the shock.

Charles grabs onto his face, speaking to him seriously. "There is still a chance to make something of this great country."

"You're right."

"Stay here. Help us," Charles says in a heartfelt tone.

Thomas contemplates the question seriously. Finally he says, "I've got to find out if Diego's words about this Eden are true."

"Is it worth it?"

"Yes."

Charles nods, silently enjoying the breeze.

"Everything will be changed as of this moment," Thomas says.

Charles nods once again, wishing to speak, but not quite sure how to start.

"I hope we are not mistaken," Thomas says. "Are we sure what we are getting into?"

Charles clears his throat nervously.

"What is it? Something is the matter. I can tell," Thomas says.

"I fear for you," Charles says, his voice filled with sorrow.

"Perhaps I will waste my life. Or lose who I am. But I must do this."

"You will learn much among nature. I know it. Stay true," Charles says, patting his shoulder.

"You as well. Make this world right again."

"I intend to learn all I can from these people. I wish to be a statesman someday, and so I must take advantage of knowing them and learn how they work.

"But how can you?" Thomas asks.

"I will start at the beginning like anyone else. Perhaps I will have the chance to use my knowledge one day to create a society of goodness."

"You are the good one. I'll be off hoping to be a shadow of what you are—"

"Stop it—"

"I lost control and I hurt you. I want you to know—"

"I already know. That's why I said I fear for you."

"Life takes us far from that which we dream of."

Thomas feels an overwhelming emptiness wash over. They embrace, but it is not so tragic for Charles. His heart is already drifting.

"Life is only a series of pains," Thomas says, feeling very morose.

"It will not get any easier. Expect the worst and allow it to make you strong."

Thomas grips Charles' shoulders and says, "May you be victorious."

Charles nods, "I will. Rest assured I will welcome you if you ever return... Captain."

"There is no need to call me—"

"Goodbye, friend," Charles says, and pushes off. He smiles and waves to Thomas, becoming smaller and smaller in his vision every time he glances back.

# 31

# Heartache and Departure

**T**HOMAS HOLDS THE REINS, guiding the carriage through winding roads and long stretches framed by fields. Benjamin and Lucy sleep inside, overcoming the shock and soreness the battles left them with. A poor country house is on the side of the road. Three bodies lie beside it. A grape vineyard expands far into the distance. A dozen people lie dead among the vines. The sun glares down in Thomas' tired eyes.

From far off charge two horses, their riders firing pistols. Thomas pulls the reins and yells, "Ya! Ya! Ya!" Benjamin and Lucy wake and see the pursuers nearing fast. They grab pistols and fire, sending a rider to the earth. One of the carriage's wheels hits a rut in the road, cracking it through.

The carriage rolls down a hill and Benjamin is thrown out, injuring his arm. Benjamin is shot at, but dodges with a leap. A bullet grazes across his cheek, gushing much blood. Benjamin hears the horse hooves nearing. He sidesteps, and as the rider passes him, Benjamin slashes his sword across his opponent's throat box.

Sitting quietly upon his horse, the rider breathes with great caution as blood pours out of the slit. He feels the wetness and whimpers. Benjamin, still bleeding from his face, shoves the rider off of the horse onto his head. He mounts it and meets Thomas and Lucy as they run up the road in his direction.

"You are injured," Thomas says.

"It is nothing," Benjamin says, wincing.

"There is a house up ahead. Let's get you cleaned up," Lucy says, pointing off to the right.

Reaching the house, Lucy knocks on the door and fixes her hair. A woman answers and says, "Who are you? I thought it was my children."

"May we wash him?" Lucy asks, gesturing to Benjamin. "Our friend has been injured."

Thomas peers downward to the frail woman and notices she appears famished.

"Did you fall off a horse?" the woman asks.

"I was shot," Benjamin says.

The woman says, "Shot? Who would shoot you?" appearing shocked to hear the words.

Benjamin says, "Have you not seen the madness about all the country?" even more shocked to hear her words.

"We are very far off. We do not see much," the woman says.

Lucy asks her, "Where is your husband?"

"Husband?" the woman says. "He has gone harvesting and has not returned."

A serious look appears upon Thomas' face. He bargains with her, saying, "We will hunt for you if we can wash his face."

The woman shifts her gaze downward and stares at the ground in a dark mood.

"How many days has it been without food?" Thomas asks her.

The woman continues to stare toward the ground.

"Come in," she says.

Thomas, Lucy, and Benjamin creep through high weeds in light clothing, scanning the tree line for animals. Benjamin's wound is wrapped several times over by a long cloth that was pulled between his eyes and tied around his head.

"Perhaps I should keep her company," Lucy says.

Thomas insists, "No. I should not have the fear on my mind. It is not safe at all."

Clusters of bushes lie scattered throughout the wilderness. Through dense woods they search for game, twisting through the arms of the trees barricading their way into the old forest. Under the canopy, the shade cools their moist, perspiring heads. The breeze blowing through the tunnel of trees feels good.

A pheasant flutters off into a distant tree before they can react. Thomas and Benjamin give it chase, their fingers tense on the triggers of their pistols, their eyes set like those of a hunting dog on their prize. The shots ring out, yet nothing falls from the sky. Their bird has vanished in the smoke.

The sun feels more pleasant as it descends. Everything around takes on an orange tone. As they exit the wall of trees they come across a vast vineyard of gamay noir grapes. The three hunters decide to take a rest at seeing such a delicacy. Resting upon the earth, they pierce the skin of the black grapes gently with their teeth. They hope to treasure the sweetness, but only sourness gushes.

Suddenly, a slight rustling is heard. The unmistakable sound of clomping hooves beats the ground softly. Peering through the clusters of the aromatic fruits is a stout, full grown, male deer. Their hearts beat so heavily. Sliding their pistols free, they take aim.

At once the bullets fly and sink into the bristly fur. The dark eyes of this grand creature widen in shock. A lung is burst. The small intestine is severed, spilling free a bit of its contents inside the body cavity. It juts its gnarled antlers in a sweep of pain, then falls upon the green grass as its legs fail.

Thomas and Benjamin carry the carcass over their shoulders. Entering a meadow, Lucy picks wild red rhododendrons and milky white primrose. She places them in her hair, smiling happily. Walking down a worn path, they come across a clearing, encountering a sight they would have given anything to forget: Two rotting children hang side by side, twisting in the wind from an ancient tree. The young boy and girl float above the roots from a long rope, their necks strung tightly. Waves of despair flush through every particle within Thomas, Lucy, and Benjamin. Lucy breaks down and cries. She is paralyzed with sadness. The clothes hanging on the deceased seem to have been clean at the time of their death, but a moisture seeps into the material through the disintegrating skin. Their faces, green with rot, are soft and seem delicate as if they were sleeping.

Thomas says, "It never ends, does it?"

Thomas climbs the tree and cuts the rope. The dead children hit the ground making a sound like a sack of rotten fruit landing on a pile of garbage. A noxious odor fills the nostrils of the three witnesses. Benjamin heaves the contents of his stomach into a patch of long grass. Thin pockets of soggy skin burst black blood. Thomas drags the bodies by the end of the rope through the bushes to the back of the French woman's house.

Thomas and Benjamin sink spades into the earth, digging two small graves side by side. Solemnly, they place each child in their respective plot and quietly say a prayer. Lucy stands, looking in the other direction as they dump each shovel full on top of the bodies. The little boy's arm can still be seen poking through. The small hill of loose dirt is shoved, sealing them in. They pat it down hard with the soles of their shoes.

Benjamin cuts up the deer on the French woman's table. Thomas lifts one of the deer's severed haunches and has a strange gleam in his eye.

"What's wrong?" Benjamin asks.

"Nothing," Thomas says, stepping before the closed door. "She needs God's protection."

Thomas spreads the blood from the deer on the country woman's door. After two streaks are spread across, he goes back to helping Benjamin divide the rest of the animal.

After the meat cooks through, they all sit at the table. The woman serves Thomas, Lucy, and Benjamin venison stew filled with the aroma and flavor of fresh herbs. Everyone eats their meal by placing their bowl up to their mouth. The country-woman smiles. Thomas hands her a sack of coins.

"Thank you for taking care of us," Thomas says.

"What is this?" the woman asks nervously.

Thomas tells her, "If your family does not return, you are to use this and flee."

The woman appears confused and looks away.

"You will understand."

Early the next morning, Thomas wakes, rises, and peers into the woman's room. She is not there. He opens the front door, looks outside, and sees her sitting on the ground. She looks toward him with a blank, depressed stare. Her hands and all up her front are covered with dirt from the graves of her children. Thomas jerks back and rustles Lucy and Benjamin, waking them.

"We are leaving. Now!" he says, still alarmed.

They all quickly exit the front door. The woman sits covered in dirt.

"You will find a new life…" Thomas says to her while making his way to the horses, "in time, madame. Good-bye."

They ride the horses bareback through the heat of the day. The sun bears upon them until evening. The sun sets and they ride on through the night in the cool darkness.

Sea birds fly through the air. Merchants sell their wares. Children run about. Thomas, Lucy, and Benjamin stand by as the horses drink water from two buckets. Simon struts up the road and calls out to them, saying, "What are you doing standing around?"

Simon puts his arm around Thomas' neck and leads him.

"We've been waiting for you," he says.

Thomas hands the reins of one of the horses to a passing boy. Thomas and his crew board the Blood of God. The massive ship departs quickly from the dock.

"Is she not a beauty?" Simon says, patting the side of the ship with his hand.

"To feel the ocean breeze on my face again!" Thomas exclaims, hurling his doublet into the air. It flies high, catching a gust, then falls into the sea, floating on the waves. Staring at the land growing smaller and smaller, he says, "Let them squabble over their small sliver of land!"

After a moment Simon asks Thomas, "Do you think this place Diego speaks of is all he says it is?"

Thomas says simply, "We have nothing to lose. Isn't that right?"

Simon nods and seals his lips tightly.

The ship bursts with speed, sails wide open, catching the strong breeze.

Even among the tumult of the raging, unforgiving sea, Thomas' crew finds solace in the chaos. The blue expanse offers hope. Across this churning vortex lays the path of exile from the putrid, rotting cities of death and corruption. No matter how ambiguous Diego's claims have been, the land spoken of seems to be a gift for the strength they've shown through their recent hellish turmoil. Thomas is in rapture to have this boon. No matter what lies in that great unknown, through the black void that veils the future, have not their lives been spared for this blessed journey? They are to arrive in God's country, a land unmolested by the forces that have caused them sorrow all their lives. There they can create whichever life they desire. Such is the idealism that arose in the minds of those on this blood strewn ship.

# White Sand

**W**HITE SAND EXPANDS, shining like crystalline diamonds across the Hispaniolan shoreline. The Blood of God halts as it approaches the slope of land entering the sea; the sails are unsecured and tied down. The anchor is dropped. Eyes fill with wonder as they see these sights for the first time. Innumerable palm trees spread their fan-like fronds across the landscape in abundance. The green seemingly goes on forever.

Leaping from the deck with aching muscles, legs propel these weary sailors from this surface that is—thank God—not made of wood. Many fall flat and roll in the grains laughing like children. Others pacify their wonder in peering through the foliage—what wonders are to be discovered in this gorgeous place, this paradise? A short distance up the strand, Simon discovers a family of iguanas warming themselves on an outcrop of rock. The odd creatures seem to take no notice at all, even though these reeking beasts have invaded their country and block their sun.

"Come, come all please!" Diego says, waving the scattering multitude toward him. "There will be plenty to see along the way!"

"Thank you," Thomas says to Diego, taking him by the shoulder. "It really is all you said."

"I am grateful as well. I had only heard rumors," Diego says as they all disappear into the green.

After traveling a few miles through the forest, the party leaves the overhang of trees to see a large, half-built fort. The construction is built of heavy lumber and stands upon a lush, green hill overlooking the sea. Plain to see, on a white backdrop, flies the red cross of the Spanish flag. Explosions ring out, carried on the air as a caravel fires upon a smaller pirate vessel. Waves rush upon the hull as the craft nears the shore. Another blast opens a hole at the tail of the ship just at the waterline. Sea water rushes inside, gorging the cavity. The ship violently grinds into the rocks clustered there.

More than six hundred Spanish soldiers await the assault in battle formation. Lined before the gaping, unfinished wall of their fort, they stand still and ready. Suddenly, a wave of greasy rat-men numbering at least two-hundred leaps from the wrecked vessel armed with cutlasses and rapiers. Madly, they charge the uniformed soldiers of the Spanish army, slicing their blades wildly through the air. Steel upon steel the weapons collide. Shots ring out, filling the scene with gray clouds. Fighting at such odds, the pirates have no chance. Within an hour there is not one left standing. Bodies litter the beachhead. The ravaged ship rocks slightly, creaking on the rocks, as its destroyer so gallantly flaunts its victory before the noonday sun.

Diego waves to the soldiers as they return from battle. A captain, with a troop surrounding him, steps forward across the plain to the edge of the forest and addresses him. "Where do you come from! What brings you here?"

"I am to see Agustín. We are his guests," Diego says with a slight bow.

"Please wait while I verify," the Captain says respectfully.

"But of course," Diego says, waving the Captain off to allow him to do as he said.

Thomas appears apprehensive. He at once feels a fear, wondering just how safe they are among the Spanish.

"It will not be long," Diego tells Thomas. "Let's make ourselves comfortable."

In short time, Diego leads the sea-worn company to the comforts of meager civilization in the Spanish fort known as Fuerte de San Felipe. Accompanied by the blade-toting soldiers, Thomas follows Diego's footsteps to the quarters of Agustín de Zárate, their host in this far-off country. Under the shadow of the dim flicker of candlelight, they approach the crack of the door of the one they sought. Rising from his humble bedding, he beckons them to enter. Graciously, he lifts the wine at his bedside at seeing the face of Diego. Sitting up in his bedshirt, he pours for his old friend, a toast to old memories, a libation to religion and to friendship.

Diego takes the glass in hand and toasts accordingly. He takes a sip, as does the priest, both ritually recalling memories. Agustín mutters a long prayer with his hand on the back of Diego's head. Feeling the ritual past its purpose, Agustín calls out to Thomas, "And who may you be?"

Thomas, stricken with silence, is relieved as Diego speaks for him. "He has lifted me across the sea, far from my pursuers, those noose-men who lurk in shadow. I thought my feet had run their last when by chance I had run into his tiller-man, Benjamin. With but an ounce of plea, he granted me travel across the great sea."

"What was his stake?" Agustín asks.

"Wonder," Diego says. "He heard only a rumor from my lips and took action at the chance that it was true."

"To what, this jungle?"

"For peace. Peace of mind, peace of heart."

"Fine. It is easy to understand if one lives under the fire of civilization. What country did you originate from, sailor?"

"Scotland. Then later, England," Thomas says.

"It's understandable, given that our armada will make you our slaves."

"I hold in mind no lineage to them. I am my own person."

"You have in your making that of a priest."

"Except that I steal and hold a sword."

Agustín snickers. "And I? Surrounded by a grove of steel? I am not excused from this sin."

Diego says, "This is why we travel so far—to hope to find a world free of this."

"Yes. The Taino are free to some extent. It is well worth knowing—their ability to live in love as children do."

Diego and Thomas listen intently.

Agustín continues, "No matter your enthusiasm, it is hard to trust someone battered with Europe's hatreds to keep his hands free from blame. It is too often an overwhelming temptation when one's fathers were at constant war."

"Enough of that. What preparations are there for the jungle, if you know any?" Diego says.

"Your will must not leap from your grasp. Besides that, the usual food and clothing. What is worrying me is… Perhaps you will notice this island sparsely populated—strange it is, though they had ample time to fill it with their numbers."

"What then is the cause?"

Agustín answers more tense than before, "They did populate, ages ago… though since the arrival of Admiral Columbus they fell at such a rate! We think it must be our doing, but the reason is beyond our knowledge."

"Our doing?" Thomas says. "How do you mean?"

"As I said. It is beyond reasoning, and so we act as though we were at no fault."

Diego says, "Then perhaps we best not pursue them, lest we curse them."

"Much is a guess. Do as you will. I am leaving in a week's time to assist them in matters of their souls as well as their crops. Come if you will."

Thomas' party is unfavorable to the idea of waiting after being confined to the ship for all those months. Most pass the time with wine, allowing their minds to drift, for the idleness seems a form of torture in that they had counted on relief coming as soon as they reached dry land. The sight of the sea sends most into a state of revulsion; the sand is no better. On the third day, several of them take to hunting in the forest. Hour after hour they return with some form of life blown to pieces. Finally, they have something to look forward to. More and more take to this practice, and so the pile of carcasses grow to such a great height each day. Iguanas are stacked as high as the shoulder, barbecued and devoured. Sea birds such as seagulls, pelicans, and petrels are shot regularly. Some dive to the seafloor and drag up every crab and lobster they can see. Many varieties of sea turtles such as the loggerhead and the hawksbill are hunted and fish were netted hourly.

In this way they find solutions to their boredom, to amuse themselves by playing as aristocrats at their grand banquets that are held after the sun descends under the horizon. By the fifth day, game is scarce, and throughout the land not one animal is to be found. This is no matter, for they have had their fill of hunting. It has ceased to be amusing. Instead, they find lounging entirely enjoyable and look forward to their departure, which is to take place a day ahead of schedule.

Thomas wades, the mild waves lapping at the middle of his calves. The white glimmer of the moon plays off the black water. He stares off the way he commonly does, sinking inside his mind, saying goodbye to the sea that was his company for such a long time. Agustín sees Thomas' silhouette and puts forth his bare feet, stepping across the wet sand, enjoying the coolness as the ocean water fills in each footstep. He rolls up his pants and stands beside him.

"What are you thinking?" Agustín asks.

"What am I doing here?"

Agustín rests his hand on Thomas' shoulder and says, "You're searching for meaning."

"I don't know."

"This doubt is healthy. What lies in the wilderness, is it better than what you had before? That's what you're wondering, yes?"

Thomas nods.

Agustín says, "I have been there and returned. I will tell you that it is deep within those trees where you find who you really are. Away from the cradling supports of our cities, the laws and modes of conduct, our temptations claw at us to be acted out. The first of our men here, those who took the voyage with Admiral Columbus, they gave in and paid with their lives."

"I don't know anymore. I don't know if I want to know. It seems too much now. It seems empty here, and there's a vacant boredom. I don't know what to do with myself."

"I see it's got you already."

"Has it?"

"We forget how much of who we are is constructed by others. When we live among nature for a time, much of that fades and something else surfaces. There's a reason for our societies, I've come to realize. When we lose that part of us, the devils come calling. You must be strong enough to withstand them."

"I will be," Thomas says, forcing confidence.

"I hope so."

# 33

# A New Hope, New People

**T**HE SOLDIERS, thankful for the morsels freely given by Thomas' crew, bestow gifts in the form of extra clothing for all, for given the climate, it is sure to rain. It does rain in fact, six days out of the eight that it takes to reach the river known as Yaque, the largest on the island. As they canoe down the river, rain water needs to be scooped out by hand. Four days of traveling by river, camping on the bank at night so as to not blindly collide with rocks, leads them into the mountains of Ciguay.

Guiding his craft beside Thomas and Lucy's canoe, Agustín peers skyward and says, "There she is! The seat of their god, Yúcahu. If only our Jehovah chose such a lush seat, rather than that dusty Israel!"

Later that day they come across an embankment linked to small branches of the river. The water runs through a tropical glade surrounding a great towering rock, which becomes slender to a point above its wide base.

"That is their home," Agustín says, pointing to a formation of the mountain molded into an alcove so perfectly it seems as if God formed it from clay.

They ground their canoes, lining them in a vast array. They stop for a stretch, then continue following Agustín to the vault of trees. At a distance of around five-hundred paces within, two young women are seen. They are fully nude, washing themselves in the shallow river. Coyly they smile, recognizing Agustín, innocently unaware of the shock they build inside the men. The girls continue pouring the clear water over their bodies, beads collecting on their radiant skin. The only other skin the travelers from Europe know that is different from their own was that of the blacks that were shipped in and sold back home. These girls have different skin; it appears smooth like milk, although it is as if they have been filled with honey and chocolate. It is more skin than most of them have seen in all their lives.

The smell of cassava permeates the space between the rugged trunks. Its sweetness leads the way, making it no longer necessary to follow after Agustín. Their noses know well where to go. The darkness gives way to an open valley dotted with huts. Stepping into this, a whole world opens up, one never imagined by these who only know European housing, the barricaded fortresses of the rich and their own dilapidated structures surrounded by waste pools. Amid humble hives of straw and palm leaves, the brown people, this small cluster of humanity, go about nude. A strap of cloth covers the loins of some of the eldest, but those who presumably are as of yet unmarried, go free as a child.

With hearts aflutter, the company let their feet unconsciously carry them through this vision, which seems all but a dream. Agustín, light on his feet, bolts into the village with boldness, seemingly merry. Women tend a fire, roasting the roots that scent the forest with their aroma. Catching sight of Agustín, they smile wide, revealing their white-as-pearl teeth.

Thomas observes the activity within a rectangular court called a batey in the center of the village. Males take part in a game that is also called batey, scurrying to hit a ball into the air, careful not to let it touch the ground.

Eyes fall on the strange clothed newcomers, though at seeing them in the company of Agustín their care is relinquished. Thomas finds it strange that everyone seems to have the same haircut: The hair is cropped straight at the bangs, the black flowing clean, glistening, generally falling straight and loose around the back of the neck. To the newcomers, their speech is incomprehensible, though it has a sort of melodic charm as they carry on scrambling to hit the ball with various parts of their bodies—anything but their arms or feet.

Drums sound past the nearest cluster of huts. Flutes accompany the melodious bursting of voices in a chorus that follows after a single chanter of joyous phrases. The sound rings through Benjamin as if these players were their like-minded kin. It seems strange for this distant people to know how to stir the spirit of those of another world, but it is so. His heart begins to transform from a feeling of alienation into a yearning to bond. He claps his hands as clusters of Taino lose themselves in dance. Numbering at least fifty, they thrust their arms about and take flight upon the earth in carefree celebration of each other, seemingly of goodness itself.

Thomas is not as joyous about these people and their ways as many of the others are. He stands a way off, holding his nose at what is not filth, but the natural smell of this different people. Gazing over the crowd of dancers, he scoffs, thinking they must be stupid to lose themselves this way, as children do. He wishes somehow that he could be as simple as they, for it was his wish to be in this place that was hailed as being closer to the state of humanity at the time of creation. Their faces do not seem inviting to him; their flat faces, slanted eyes, and their dark skin keep him at a distance, bringing out a sense of disgust and a yearning for the familiar he didn't know existed. Their nakedness, and that overwhelming sensation at suddenly viewing all this flesh, causes him to reject them, branding them as shameless and savage.

Lucy is noticeably repulsed by the sight that surrounds her. To her, even peasants are despicable, and they still live in suitable houses and obey the proper customs of law and tradition. She had never imagined a people could be so low as these "wretched creatures," a term she feels compelled to utter incessantly.

She clings to Thomas' arm and hides her gaze from what appears to her as a grotesque tissue swaying between the legs of the men. The exposed organs afflict her greatly, as if they were lechers assaulting every part of her flesh. She feels greatly in danger, helplessly falling into a panic, caught in visions of them as loose animals likely to give in to the urge to rape and brutalize a new woman, this pale fetish in their territory.

"You are not liking this?" Thomas asks her with consideration.

She clenches her eyes, seeming to want to cry.

He holds her close and says, "At least we finally have something in common."

"Are you fucking stupid? What did you think this was?"

"I know. This was a mistake."

Peeking out from his shoulder, she now notices several clusters of women of all ages staring back at the gawkers.

"I want to go home," she whines.

Thomas decides it's not best to remind her of how far from that home they have traveled.

He says, "You said you had no life there."

"I don't care," she says, feeling the sadness strongly. "A whore in England is more civilized."

"For me that was hell. This could be no more than purgatory."

A brave, young Taino woman breaks from the line of females and takes the hand of an Englishman with short cropped hair and a blond mustache whom she finds attractive. This dispels the fear in several others, causing attempts at rudimentary conversation to be attempted, and a few enamored couples to wander off after finding there has risen an instantaneous mutual approval. Lucy sees the openness of these women and grows greatly afraid of losing Thomas to them.

Thomas is watching a woman as she bends low to pick up her child. As she turns the other way, he traces the curves of the muscle definition in her thighs and buttocks. A swelling of rage bursts within Lucy, and her fists fly out with all the might of cannon fire. She bloodies the inside of Thomas' cheek as her knuckles jam the soft flesh into his molars. He spits blood and lets fly a closed fist into the triangular nook in the softest part of her jaw. Kneeling and cursing, she is gripped by the back of her neck and dragged off by him to the other side of the nearest huts where they volley heated words.

A moment later, Lucy charges out screaming, "Then stay here! Live amongst the tree people! I'm going home!"

She heads straight for the tree line so furious that she is blind to the impossibility of her mission. Thomas chases after her to make sure she doesn't hurt herself.

"No! Don't come near me!" she says. "I don't need you!"

"You're not even going the right way!" he yells, catching up to her.

She circles around, attracting the attention of the mixed group of Europeans and Taino.

"You want to stare at naked women?" she says, hysterically tearing at her mud stained clothing. "I'll become one of them! That's what you like, isn't it?!"

She rips open her dress and begins to tear it off, slipping out of Thomas' grasp. She falls to the ground and wiggles out, then strips free of her underclothing all while striking at Thomas and writhing wildly.

Thomas screams so all can hear, "Come now! They are all naked. Should I go around with my eyes closed?!"

"Yes, close your eyes! This is not for you!"

He cannot think of a situation more destructive on the people's opinion of his leadership.

"This is what you all like! I know!" Lucy says with her small, pale sprouts of breasts exposed for all to see. Her left wrist is gripped tightly by Thomas, but when she loses the constraint of sanity, her limbs jolt and slip free like an antelope's can.

"Look at me! I'm one of you now!" she says screeching, running free shirtless, her back slick with mud and her hair piled in a matted web of knots.

Within the swelling crowd, Benjamin finds lightness in his heart. He spies a flute beside a tree on the earth and flies toward it. An elderly Taino with well grooved skin sees his want and bends, lifting the instrument gladly. Hesitation drifts away, as Ben knows well the gift is offered with heart. With a flash of a hearty smile, he offers his silent gratitude and lifts the wooden object to his lips. He fills the air with his Anglo rendition of a Taino orchestral movement.

Benjamin's feet lift his girth as if he was of deer lineage. The natives welcome this exuberant white animal within their circle as one of their own. Two women who must be past their fortieth year take to dancing opposite Benjamin. They rattle the shells tied to their wrists and ankles, prancing and spinning. One of the women even has a baby strapped to a board on her back. The baby seems not to notice, for it is already used to this.

Just outside the dance circle, two young ladies stroll with their mother, their petite breasts sitting high like apples. Their slender bellies lead to a short-cropped pubis. To see the soft flesh, the delicate slope to this parting of stark femininity, sends the males limping. Their gaits fail them, for the protrusions under their waists force them to walk taut and cause a hurt with each step.

The sisters, Assawako and Prockne, notice Ben's playing, leading them to daintily lift on their feet in dance. Hand in hand they skip in place in a girlish movement of hips and slender arms. Benjamin and Assawako lock in a gaze, their hearts lifting with amorous feeling. He steps closer, playing his flute gaily. Prockne pushes her sister toward Ben. Assawako, feeling overwhelming coyness, leaps behind her sister and gives her a punch on the shoulder. Hiding, she steps away, disappearing through the crowd to the comfort of her mother.

Agustín speaks to the chief, or the cacique, as the Taino call their leader, and the shaman, known as a behique. The cacique's name is Pandukuli. The behique is called Kadesh. They enter and remain in Pandukuli's hut for many hours, catching up and discussing the ramifications of bringing in such a number of newcomers to the village—Europeans at that. Pandukuli is an open-armed sort, but he also knows the danger in being too giving. He dwells on the idea for some time, finally telling Agustín that the newcomers are welcome as long as there is food for everyone. He includes that the amount of crops grown must be increased, and also that the Europeans must work like anyone else. Agustín nods respectfully to the cacique, saying to him, "Of course. I will ensure they will bring no hardship upon your people."

Pandukuli is pleased at this, though he has other matters upon his mind, "It is too common that people from your land look upon us as animals, because we do not have what they consider—what do you call it? Civ-al-iz-ation. These newcomers must respect us and the way we live. They must respect our women. It is understandable that males and females will naturally have certain desires and act them out. We understand…"

Agustín nods in agreement.

Pandukuli continues, "But as you know, at a certain point, if they continue, we insist that they marry."

Agustín tells him, "I fully agree that marriage should be insisted upon—lust will be no surprise. The ladies of your village are lovely in every way, so I do not expect any protest to the idea of marriage to them."

Agustín's journal entries:

April 24th, 1566

It was decided that five men should be appointed to each available hut until more space is made for them. This designation was made because there was not much else that could be done, and that the decision would make for a more speedily construction of new accommodations. They are elated to sleep in the hammocks. It is such a relief to not constantly sway on the sea. The fresh air is an incredible comfort compared to their mildewy quarters that were infested with rats, fleas, and maggots.

The immigrants find the work to be nothing at all, and even feel it's a joyous amusement as the Taino generally do, especially since song and dance accompany nearly everything that goes on.


May 6th, 1566

My friends from England have quickly felt a kinship to this people. It is wondered if they were created by God in a separate Eden—and if the Taino are closer to the state of innocence than they are.

Even Pandukuli greets them genially. It is not something they were used to, for a leader to be jolly and warm, speaking to his people like any other. He has free time as his people do, with little to attend to. Pandukuli lives in a large rectangular-shaped hut with his eight wives and children. His most frequent job consists of overseeing the celebrations and religious observances.

The neighboring Taino tribes are really like an extended family, so he has no serious matters to attend to besides rare problems with the crops or the invasion of Carib. The Taino, when discussing these people, say they are from a different "cave," as it is believed that their people originally ascended to their land from under the Earth. They speak of these people in a hateful tone.

June 16th, 1566

The predictions of lust spoken of in the chief's tent, of course, came to be. Some of the whites and the Taino girls find each other attractive. Pairs often break off, finding a spot to share their amorous feelings, and when the moment comes to pet each other—what else goes on needs not mentioning. The Europeans found that the Taino girls, when they find desire for one of their fellows, class was not considered. The fellow himself could be desired for? It was a striking shock. It seemed that they somehow bypassed a prerequisite of status to be loved. Once a girl decides that her boy is worthy, she makes sure that he is made to feel wanted. A girl ensures that her desired mate is cared for, that he knows that she is now one with him, though it is not official until their humble wedding.

If a girl feels that true, mutual feelings are present, she prepares for her sweetheart a guava fruit sliced and prepared on a clay plate. Or she may surprise him with a dinner of barbecued duck or another type of delicious bird if a member of her family has had a lucky find. It is strange to the men to be desired in this way, to be pampered. When the idea was considered, they realized that this was always the way this sort of thing worked: In Europe, such things as status in society or bombast gave the advantage to a male over other males. It is perhaps their advantages over the Taino males that give them a boost in the eyes of the women. Here, the Europeans came with deadlier weapons, and a forceful nature, which seemed to take hold in the hearts of the Taino women just as it had with women back home. Those who had the same advantage in that society were what they called "rich." The natural idea of status, they surmised, was what transferred the blessing upon them. Still, whatever the reason, the girls, once drawn to them, seem true. It seems this is what one calls love, regardless of their culture.

# 34

# The Intruder

DIEGO PRACTICES WITH BENJAMIN, running through swordplay techniques. They both hold a rapier in each of their hands. Diego appears confident and natural in his form, while Ben is somewhat unaware of what he is to do with this second sword. Diego says to him, "Think of the advantage you will have over your opponent using two blades, rather than one. You may block with your right and strike with your left. To be armed with only one blade is to be severely disadvantaged."

Diego tells him, "Strike at me," and parries the blow downward, away from himself. He strikes a false blow, stopping before Ben's neck.

"See the benefit of this?" Diego says. "Hold your right hand here like so," he continues, holding the blade above the outside of his right thigh. "We call this the coda lunga e stretta. You aim the point directly at your opponent."

Ben attempts to imitate Diego's stance.

"Very good."

Ben's stance is now much more convincing. He seems quite proud in this achievement.

"Now I will strike at you. Prepare to defend yourself," Diego says.

Benjamin nods. The blow is struck slowly. Ben strikes it downward just as

Diego had a moment ago, and follows through with his right arm, feigning a blow toward Diego's neck. Diego steps backward out of reach of the blade.

"Excellent," Thomas says, having viewed the whole exchange. "It is unbelievable how far they have come with your instruction."

Diego bows and says, "I am just as pleased. They have great heart to engage in the lessons; there is no more a teacher could wish. Besides, if it was not for them I would have no one to practice with and my skills would fall away."

"We must not let that happen," Thomas says.

"No, Captain. It gives me the greatest pleasure to engage in my most loved sport in this pristine weather."

"It is very fine," Thomas says, relishing in the breeze gently blowing past the palms, the scent of the mountain flowers rising in his nostrils.

Agustín's journal entry:

August 14th, 1566

At first, the idea of competing with the natives in the game of batey was quite intimidating. These men, and occasionally women, played with such skill as to cause the whites to wonder if it took a great many years to become similarly skilled. This game is played with a rubber ball constructed from the sap of the cupey tree, and also other plant fibers, to add to its solidity. The players are only allowed to use their head, shoulders, elbows, and most often the hips and knees. The aim is to send the ball to the opponent's side, over the dividing line. A point is scored once the ball hits the hard pounded earth of one's opponents half of the court, or lost when landing out of bounds beyond the line of stones surrounding the court.

The games are begun and ended with much ceremonial dancing and singing, which made the European's initial attempts at playing the game that much more embarrassing. There were so many eyes on them and such a show of discontent in their failure. Benjamin was intent on bettering his skill no matter how often he let his team down. He would aim for the ball with his head or his knee, often missing the ball altogether or knocking it straight to the ground. After weeks of constant failure, he devised a method that would drastically change his ability to play: A ball came sailing from above, and instead of attempting to hit it with his head, he backed up, briefly catching the ball with his girth, his gut if you will, taking the speed out of it. Now with the ball in his control, he laid into it with his knee with such a force that it collided with a player on the other side who could do little but watch it bounce off of him and hit the ground past the boundary line. Ben was in such a state of disbelief. Everyone was cheering for him, even those who he had just scored on. It was a spectacular shot after all, but to be honest, part of the cheer was a show of relief—finally a white had become a worthy competitor in the batey.

Ben, the burly, fiery-haired Scot, had found his place in the batey court of this hidden away Taino village. His mass hid away sinews of muscle that he put to good use. He is a fan favorite. This is due to his appearance being so drastically different and his never ending charm and exuberance in the game. He would often put on a show, hitting the ball with his rump, causing the onlookers in the stone benches to collapse in ecstatic laughter.

Assawako was no exception to this attraction to Benjamin. At first sight she had an unexplainable pull toward him. She had never seen another of similar appearance. His carefree attitude made her all the more attracted to him, especially due to the favorable reception of him by her people. She began to watch the games he played beside her sister. He noticed them for the first time since his encounter with her in the dance circle as he first arrived.

Benjamin and Thomas were discussing the best they could the game they had just played with the two best batey players in the village, the brothers Macocael and Yaguasa. The girls were standing fifty feet off, seeming to be transfixed with Benjamin alone, chatting and giggling. The four young men were praising the shining moments in their recent game, and also sharing a laugh over the most comical ones, though there was some struggle to understand in that they were just beginning to get a grasp upon each other's language—often using hand movement to illustrate a point. The brothers presented an alcoholic drink made from fermented corn they made themselves. Ben gave in to heavy consumption, as he tended to do, and eventually worked up the guts (also being prodded by Thomas and the brothers) to speak to Assawako. He waved her way, and by the time he made two steps in their direction, the two girls turned and disappeared, making him believe that he had made a blunder in his action.

Thomas is startled from sleep. He jerks to his feet, confused and startled as to why smoke is floating within his mouth, throat and nasal cavity. Outside he hears the sound of pounding footsteps and people choking. Upon sticking his head out of the hut, an orange glow hangs about and the rumbling crackle of the huts and forest burning is intense. Someone screams that the crops were destroyed. A mother is screaming that her children were taken. Others are frantic as well, asking if any had seen their daughters. "Carib" is the word spoken with horror. The Taino word for that people means "cannibal." The

Carib steal people away, slaughter them, and consume their flesh. The young women become slave-wives in a Carib village.

A crowd is gathered near the entrance of Pandukuli's home. The aged body of Naha Koboni, his mother, leans next to the entrance of the hut, the head nowhere to be found. The torso lies stiff, seemingly still warm, freshly killed, for the blood slowly flows from the gaping, raw, open neck. Pandukuli falls to his knees. Inconsolable, he collapses upon the muddy earth, thrusting his fists over and over into the ground. He writhes, showing his terrible emotional anguish while his eight wives stand behind him and weep sympathetically. He grips the left ankle of his mother, crying over and over for her, "Bibi! Bibi! Bibiii!"

A crowd bursts past within the forest in search of the guilty. Thomas and Benjamin catch sight of each other, nod, and rush to the forest in search of the invading Carib and their victims. Standing under the flaming canopy, inflamed leaves fall all around these two young men. Diego appears, forcing the thick smoke out of his lungs. The orange lights shift as the silhouettes of the Taino searching throughout the clusters of trees project their frantic forms as clear, razor-precise outlines. Even beyond the river, no sign is found as far as they know.

Pandukuli lapses into a state of boyish dependence. He collapses onto the ground, repeatedly being raised by those highest ranking in power. He tears at his face with his fingernails, an act that needs constraining, for obvious reasons. His wives and others closest to him speak to him in a sorrowful tone, almost humming the words of how his mother lived a full life, how the blessings bestowed upon her from the gods are evident all around. They proceed to continually fill the air with good tidings of the lady who lies at their feet, as a pyre is stacked higher one dry log at a time.

Kadesh appears with his train of young ones. Even Thomas, in his disdain for the shaman, is awestruck in the magnificence of their appearance. All stand against the backdrop of the dim firelight, their skin glistening with a shimmering gloss of red that glows when the light flashes their way. Streaks of black fall from each shoulder and plumes of piercing shades of blues and whites point to the sky from a leather band on each forehead.

They hold two bowls each. In approaching Pandukuli and his entourage, paint is applied liberally, allowing it to flow over the dome of each head. The red flows like thick blood, dripping onto the shoulders of each in this ritual. It is an almost sensual act in the intimate care which is put into each touch. Pandukuli and his terrifying warriors undergo this transformation like little boys, so obedient. Every so often, the chief loses control and allows a fist to come crashing into the earth along with his tears, but a light constraint reminds him of the importance of willful participation.

The women are likewise painted. They go into fits, feeling their husband's pain. They writhe and weep, beating their chests, clenching each other, relating to each other how they loved her and how they will one day be in her place. They wail for him, sending their feminine cries to the gods so he can hear. They moan for him in an effort to take the burden.

The painted ones look like demons as Padukuli's headless mother is lifted atop the pyre. The fire is lit. Pearly white eyes stare out from line of nobility. The white pierces in contrasting with the hue made from the dye mixture meant to represent a blood sacrifice. Pandukuli tears at his drenched locks of hair draped over his body and attempts to leap and save his mother from the wisps of fire melting her away. The fire rages, as do his closest who are involved in the wrestling match with Pandukuli. They must, at all cost, support his expression of grief, yet not allow it to overpower him and lead him to rush into the heart of the fiery element.

Kadesh begins a sorrowful chant that is joined by the whole of the tribe. It is a peculiar spiritual feeling that hangs on the air, for the tones and emotions hang so heavy on the heart. They even seem to mingle with the elements, in the air, in the leaves of the trees, and in the glow of the moon that carries across the sky. A vibration flows through every part of Thomas' body and culminates in the front of his head, tingling and pulsing stronger than it ever had during the singing of hymns in church with his mother. Here he can feel some sort of spirit, a connection with all these people.

When morning comes, there is a warrior tied to the great stone head before the batey court. His arms are strapped tight so as to cause him pain. He has his hair grown long, flowing straight and healthy. His skin is covered with designs painted with a red dye similar to the one the Taino used the night before, and his eyes are circled with black. He wears a necklace made of teeth with a longer crescent-shaped ornament in the center. Macaw feathers of red and deep blue are tied into his hair, while more feathers lie fallen onto the ground as if he was a bird himself, plucked and ready to be roasted. His forehead is flattened just as those of the Tainos are. He is also somewhat stronger than the average Taino. He seems like he has been honed for battle, as evidenced by his muscular build, rather than the Taino whose healthy appearances must be due to their diet and from their constant dancing and playing of batey.

The cacique and his five best warriors surround him with either a manaya or a macana in hand. The chief's second-hand man yells curses at the Carib, taking up the captive's bow, and severs the bowstring with his stone blade. Still uttering fierce words, he takes arrows out of the Carib's quiver and snaps them across his knee one by one.

A teenage Taino boy is brought forth. He is the one who discovered the Carib hiding in a tree the night before. Pandukuli, with his chest heaving, displays the rage for his ravaged mother hard across his face. He hands the young Taino a stone knife, which he takes gladly. The feeling of great purpose is evident on the boy's face. With great seriousness he stabs the jagged stone blade straight into the belly. The Carib screams. He shudders and convulses, tugging wildly on the ropes taut on his ankles and wrists, refusing to die. Blood pours over his abdomen from the small slit like juice pouring from the torn skin of a cherry. The deep red flows over the face of the great stone. The Taino erupt in cheer at their victory over the individual. Families of those who were kidnapped have tears running from their eyes and a certain gladness in this act of revenge. Thomas and the others from his ship appear shocked, for they had seen nothing but childlike pleasantness from these people before this violent act. Agustín, on the other hand, does not appear shocked in the slightest.


Later, Diego and Thomas drink liquor made from fermented cassava. A bright array of stars fill the sky. The Milky Way spreads in a great glimmering sheet of white.

Diego screams, "I find distaste in their thoughtless spilling of blood!"

Thomas replies, "Did you not kill men in the wars you took part in?"

"To kill one who is unarmed. It is a cowardly action," Diego says, throwing his arms about.

"He came into their village. Battle wasn't declared openly."

"Then he is a coward as well."

"Their way is different—"

"No! It is the same! You think you have escaped vice by removing yourself from the great cities? It is in all our hearts!"

"We shall see."

"Yes," Diego replies, drinking down the bitter drink.

"What shall become of you?" Thomas says casually.

"I have not yet made up my mind," Diego says, pondering the question. "Perhaps I will join my fellow Spaniards on the coast. I feel the desire for company of fellow soldiers, thrust into battle—that is my passion."

"There is a contradiction in that—you have killed needlessly, no doubt."

"Maybe. But it is for my country. I will fight for my country. I believe that God guides us."

"Who here can judge?" Thomas says, sipping his drink.

"None but God," Diego says solemnly.

"What will you do if you stay?"

"I will practice my swordsmanship. And enjoy the beautiful nature around us," Diego says, passing his hand as if presenting the trees and the sky.

"Won't you take a Taino girl for marriage? They are very nice."

Diego says sternly, "I made a promise to my dear Francisca. I swore to her that I would not touch another. I never go back on my word."

"You think you are so strong that you can contain your passion for a pretty girl? How about when she touches you? When she flashes you a smile and you smell her skin and her hair?"

"I will not! Besides, I have been tempted already. It is nothing."

"Fine. I wish you strength. But it will be hardest when you meet one who you feel for deep inside. When you find it impossible to remove her from your thoughts. When you contemplate if she or your wife is better. And when, if ever, you are to return home."

"Why push me on in this way?!" Diego says, trying to contain his anger. "I don't want to come to blows because I respect you, but you push me!"

"I don't say these words to anger you. I respect your intention to keep your loyalty to your wife true. But you must make a decision. If you plan on going home to her, then all is well, but if you stay here you cannot fight your nature. Think of it as a new life. You break your vow by not being with her."

Diego thinks deeply of the words Thomas has spoken. He clenches his fists in frustration and wanders off under the moonlight.

# 35

# A Vision and a Skinsuit

THOMAS BATHES IN THE RIVER under the purple glow of the early morning light. He holds a handful of crushed digo berries which contain a natural soap within the seeds. He rubs the yellow translucent fruit over his body, working up a lather.

Kadesh strolls along the riverside with his boy-behiques following in train. Five boys, three of them in their fourth or fifth year of life, just past their mothers care, are now bonded to Kadesh. Boys are chosen for this life if they exhibit a tendency to act effeminately, for this deviation from the norm is seen by them to be a sign of a special power to commune with that which is beyond the abilities of common folk. It is thought that they have a special connection to the great mother Atabeira due to their nature. Often a boy's posture and mannerisms will be noticed to be more like that of a girls, and if he naturally is inclined to have a strong desire to wear his mother's or sister's jewelry and a severe lack of desire to follow in the way of a man, the boy is brought before the behique. Upon rare occasions, after careful scrutiny, the behique may admit him. It is considered a high honor to have one's son admitted to this life, for it is believed that the fertility of the tribe is in his hands. It is believed that the spirits are kept in balance because of the behique, so he and his students are upheld with high honor.

Thomas dunks himself one last time, and exits the water as Kadesh instructs the boys on the medicinal uses for the fruit of the jobo tree. Thomas thinks it strange how Hutia, the eldest student of Kadesh, at thirteen years of age, sits so closely, intimately with him. The youth is effeminate in his facial build and his mannerisms to the degree that one would perhaps confuse his gender if he were not nude. The boy sits thigh to thigh with Kadesh, with his necklace strung with gold around his neck, coyly playing with his hair whenever Kadesh looks upon him while giving instruction.

Agustín's journal entry:

October 22nd, 1566

It is not a rare type of question I am asked, when the whites come to me for guidance or to share their thoughts, that they ask about Kadesh and his young initiates. In Taino society, boys who are of a natural effeminate manner are thought to possess added talents and connection to the spirit world. Those who are not accepted by Kadesh though, are often still treated as women. They are expected to fulfill women's duties, including, among other things, cleaning, cooking, and taking care of children. Whether a boy is initiated into the life of a man or a woman is really up to if he can hunt and wage battle successfully. If the tests are completed there is no question. If a boy desires to live as women do, there is often no test. He may also marry who he pleases and live as a wife in every sense. There are two in the tribe who live just this way: married to their husbands, preparing cassava, and taking care of household duties as the women do.

It is this sinful behavior that gives the whites such a revulsion. There are some that claim to have seen licentious behavior between Kadesh and Hutia. Also, it is the occupation itself that greatly angers the whites, in that it is Kadesh whose job it is to create the cemis, the idols that the citizens of the village pray to. More than once these carved representations of gods or spirits were found broken and left for all to see, to the fury of the Taino whose possession they were in.

Panic spreads throughout the village more and more since the night the

Carib laid waste to the majority of the crops. For weeks Kadesh is at work beckoning Yúcahu, Atabeira, any God who may bless the Earth with fertility. The people are hungry, and rationing the intake will only suffice as a method of survival temporarily. People's spirits are low; the Taino, for the most part, cut down on their activities that burn excess fuel and instead adapt to meditations inside their huts, praying to gods or to their ancestors for rescue from this calamity. The whites too go into fervent prayer, but Christ also fails to make the seeds spring earlier than their natural process dictates. As a result, talk begins to spread of leaving the tribe altogether.

In the absence of sufficient food, lethargy overcomes the village. A wave of activity springs up, then quiets down again as it never had before. They are out of energy. Some fall into the care of Kadesh, for they break out in a strange rashes and sometimes blotches of inflamed dots. This outbreak startles the tribe, for it is the sign of great evil coming upon a people. The sick lie helpless, daily becoming worse. Within a week, half a dozen are dead and many more are declining in health fast.

Word gets out that Thomas had had experience with expressing his spirit with Charles' mother. Thomas told the batey champs, they told other Taino, and soon it became common knowledge. Therefore, Pandukuli orders Kadesh to prepare for Thomas a mixture of tobacco and cohoba to enable his spirit to commune with the spirits that roam the Earth. The mixture is carefully measured and placed in a long pipe over a foot in length. None of the boys in training can be trusted with such a responsibility, and Kadesh cannot be sacrificed. It is thought that Thomas, bearing the strength and abilities of both a warrior and a shaman, may be ready for such a responsibility.

It is declared that the ritual is ready for Thomas to undergo, and so he is sat down on a soft cotton mat and handed the smoldering pipe. Members of the tribe stand over him chanting a solemn song, making Thomas feel very much on the spot.

"No use in keeping them waiting," Thomas thinks, placing the pipe to his mouth.

He sucks in the harsh smoke, filling his lungs to their capacity. After a few moments, a tunnel of gray-white smoke shoots upward as if he were a chimney. He coughs hard and deep, tears falling from his eyes, relieved to have that burning feeling leave his lungs.

Just as Thomas thinks the ordeal is over, Kadesh once again packs the pipe to the brim. Thomas, after inhaling three times total, is then provided a padded cotton pillow to rest his head.

After about a half an hour of resting, not noticing anything in particular, Thomas begins to feel a sensation: His fingers lying in front of him feel like soft bread dough. Even the tiny, jagged rocks that he rolls his fingers over feel like soft wool. In the cotton pillow he can distinctly smell the fibers of the original plant—the leaves and everything. He presses his face hard into it, huffing the scent aggressively, loving it. He is taken back to a forgotten memory, to the farm his parents worked on back in Scotland. He remembers hugging the lambs, the sweet newborn-fresh smell of their skin, and their soft wool.

Thomas, still lying sideways, staring at the blue-black dirt covered in shadow before his face, begins to explode in hysterical laughter. He picks himself up and crawls around half-believing he is a sheep and that his mouth has molded into a long snout. A flood of laughter bursts forth as if a dam had crumbled inside of him. He believes that he is bleating, but it only comes out as mad cackling.

He presses his nose against Pandukuli's thigh, breathing in the strong odor of his sweat. Pandukuli, well knowing that one under the influences of cohoba is apt to act in such a preposterous manner, is not alarmed at this, but finds the sides of his mouth curling, finally letting forth a burst of laughter. He nudges Thomas in a direction away from the crowd. To Pandukuli's amusement, Thomas crawls off in the direction he was faced, disappearing into the blackness of the forest.

"Will he be all right?" Lucy asks Pandukuli.

"He will have quite a journey," Pandukuli says grinning.

Lucy pats Thomas' forehead with a moistened cloth inside their hut. Pandukuli approaches and kindly asks, "May I come in?"

"Yes, please," Lucy says.

Pandukuli looks over Thomas and says, "Walking with the spirits takes a lot out of a man, doesn't it?"

Thomas nods.

Pandukuli says, "What did you see last night?"

"Some animal urinated on me. All over my legs."

"Oh?" Pandukuli says laughing aloud.

"This morning I had to wash it off. It was awful."

"Do you recall playing the drum this morning?"

"Drum? No, I didn't play a drum."

"Just after light broke you were beating on a drum in the middle of the batey.

We gathered around you to watch."

"What is that?"

"You were dancing and beating on a drum. Often your eyes went white. You were in a trance."

"Really?" Thomas says seriously, unable to recall the memory.

"A larger crowd gathered and you began urinating all over the ground. You sprayed all over your legs while you spoke words of nonsense and beat on the drum till your hand bled."

Thomas looks to his bruised, scraped hand, now without much option but to believe in the story.

Pandukuli asks him, "What from last night stands out to you?"

Thomas says, "Well... At some point in the night out of nowhere came my ship, sailing through the soil as if it were liquid. The ground rippled and waves crashed, carrying the bushes and trees in the wake as the ship cut a hole in the jungle. There were lights on the ship that glowed a luminescent green. When it came close I could see that the lights came from the feathers of great parrots that were dressed as sailors. The ship plunged its anchor deep into the earth as it came beside me. The parrots squawked in a wonderful chorus all in unison— and from the midst of them stepped the Carib, risen from death."

"The Carib?" Pandukuli asks, floored by Thomas' statement.

"Yes, his name is Amoika. His chest was still bloody from the wound that killed him. I saw it clearly as he looked down toward me. The green birds stretched out their feathers like long fingers. Those bright, glowing fingers picked me up like a baby and pulled me in, and we flew off across the sky. We flew among the clouds, and there I spent time with and spoke with Amoika for what seemed like weeks. He said he could feel my heart and sensed the love in it. With my heart, he said, he could seat his spirit and lead me to paradise—a land where the tribe may live and prosper."

Pandukuli contained his reaction, though he was exploding with glee inside. He nodded and left Thomas and Lucy, allowing Thomas to get some rest.

Later that day, as Thomas began to feel strength returning to him, he ventured outside his hut. There he found Pandukuli and Kadesh waiting for him, holding up the dried skin of Amoika.

"What is this?" Thomas says, surprised by their presence.

"You are to join your soul with Amoika. A journey lies in your future," Pandukuli says.

Thomas nods knowing his words to be true. He steps forward, accepting his fate. Thomas strips off the cloth covering his genitals and slips his legs inside the skin as the people begin to gather around. The Taino chant as he pulls the skin over his torso and slips his arms inside the arm skin one by one. Lastly, he pulls the face over his own—the mouth over his mouth, the nose over his nose, the eye holes around his eyes, Amoika's long, black hair cascading to Thomas' waist.

Agustín's journal entry:

December 1st, 1566

Once Thomas donned the skin it soon became his passion. After all, he claimed that sacrifice worked numerous times before to help him and his friends. Why should it not work now? I find it somewhat hard to believe that the Carib's spirit speaks to him, but if they believe in it, or even Thomas alone, that faith can be a great ally. I don't care if I live or die, after all. I have done all I wish to do in this life, so I observe the things around me in a detached manner if I cannot directly help.

The ancients found sacrifice as a very useful method—he would be a Moses to this people. The Lord led him here, he believes. The coincidences added up to be far too numerous—he was meant to be in this position: another one of his beliefs. He knows he will find something great out there in the unknown. "It will happen," Thomas declared, having the Carib's skin sewn tight, formed to his body. "God is on our side."

I, personally, have lost my hold on this world long ago, through the dedicated withholding of pleasure, as is the way of my priestly calling. Therefore, their squirming is but an amusement, only worthy of little more than the briefest lifting of my eyes from the page.

The Taino continue to live off the remnants of the crop that was not burned. They have no other choice but to hope for Thomas' success. If the Taino leave, what can they find elsewhere? They could find little benefit for all their trouble, and so they must be patient and endure. The crops have been burned many times, but not this badly in several generations. The only solution is to acknowledge there will be a high death toll, to hope to recover through massive planting, to borrow or trade what they can from neighboring tribes, and to hunt far beyond the bounds of the usual.

The whites are harder to win over. They know that a portion of the bounty won from their piracy is theirs and is sitting on the ship at the fort Fuerte de San Felipe. Can they make their way back to the ship alive? They had made their way into the innards of this green island easily, thanks to my knowledge, but can they make their way out again? The idea is further complicated when the problem of how they can find their way back is brought up—where exactly is that fort? And how can they return to any sort of civilization once they get there? Is there a sufficient navigational mind among them to return to England or any land that will hire them for their respective trades? Many think the idea of leaving is better than starving here. To stay is to choose to eat the available food of the starving Taino for whom they are guests. Most have heart for the Taino after being in their presence for nearly a year. It seems the most sensible, the most manly, and even the most selfish decision for some to leave. Eleven of the sailors left one day with the detailed instructions burned into their minds, as well as in script by my hand. I provided them a compass and told them to follow north until they had reached the sea. The route would take them, if all went well, once they reached the sea, around thirty to forty miles northwest to reach the coast and find their way to the Spanish fort.

The moment came for Thomas. Lucy of course, did not leave his side. She doesn't like the Carib skin. It is disturbing to her. She never realized how much her happiness depended on touching his skin until it was sealed in a wall of leather. No matter how bizarre it is, it is his voice inside, his heart. Though she has always criticized him, she has no other connection in these jungles.

The batey champs, Macocael and Yaguasa insisted on coming as well. It was not thought that their chances would be bettered by high numbers, so they finalized the party on the four of them and left with little announcement. Spirits were low already, which is why there wasn't much of a cast off. There was a goodbye to them, but the question remained as to who was to die—those who left or those who stayed? Who was to offer a prayer for strength and hope, when both needed it badly?

# Exodus

**T**HOMAS AND HIS PARTY leave in a southwestern direction as he insists this will lead them to his "fountain of life." The twin brothers are confident in their success, for they know that they can receive support from Taino tribes that they will pass along the way. The twins also know well how to find food in the jungle, so the three week supply of cassava cakes, corn, and fish will last far longer than needed, most likely.

They wander for three weeks. It is not such a hard walk, feeding on fruits, the occasional hunted animal, edible plants, roots, insects, grubs, and so on. It is a journey of mixed feelings, for no matter how disheartening the recent events were, life has always been disheartening.

They reach the place of the tribe once led by the great cacique Hatuey, now desolate. The time of his departure was the same year Pandukuli's father led his tribe to the hidden-away place they now live on the mountainside. Hatuey's people were assaulted with such force by the Spaniards that he knew they didn't stand a chance, and so he left to Cuba with over four hundred to gather fellow Taino for a full scale revolt. Being peaceful in nature, and having no evidence for the truthfulness of his claim, the Taino leaders in Cuba prepared no attack, and therefore were defenseless when the Spaniards came and burned many, including Hatuey, at the stake.

Here and there, skeletal remains lie sunken in the dirt, frozen in time, but beyond that only stone-hard food remains. Foliage overwhelms the once cleared village. The sacred batey is now a field. The huts are sunken in like sun-dried fruit. The four of them leave, not wishing to witness any more heart-crushing visions. The twins become afraid, for they previously heard this tribe spoken of as one who was very much alive. Perhaps they moved as Pandukuli's father had, though there obviously has not been anyone here recently.

They move on, passing farther into the wilderness upon the faint hope in Thomas' "dream." How could they keep moving when their original hope was tied in their belief that they would be welcomed by Taino peoples along the way?

"Thomas," Macocael says with his rough pronunciation. "We are fools to go on."

"What?" Thomas asks. "Don't be afraid."

Yaguasa cuts in and says, "It is not that we are afraid. You're not worth dying for!"

"Please trust me," Thomas tells them while strolling side by side. "We will find a new life for your people."

Thomas sleeps every night filled with visions that renew him with belief in his quest. The twins ask him if he feels that their search was in vain, if they should return to the village. He replies again and again that he feels they are very close, that they should believe more strongly. As time goes on, they become more unpleasant. They become more aggravated in their speech, that which is understood. The language difficulties are another source of aggravation. When enough time goes by that they are sure that people are dying in the village, and their own store of food is gone, they become quite irate in their demeanor in believing they were misled.

Thomas and Lucy never cease to help them in catching food, whether that means wandering through the forest in search of edible flora or striking down some swift fauna. Thomas and Lucy never let the twins far out of sight though, for they know the temper they are in—they cannot allow them the solitude to dissolve Thomas' face from their minds. Thomas knows that they hold great respect for him, and for that they remain in his company. He tries to keep them in a cheerful state of mind, but he knows and understands their complaint with him. It seems there is nothing he can do to make them fully believe. Still, he cannot let them go, because he and Lucy would never make it back to the tribe alive. He hopes that the twins hold them in favor enough not to abandon them in the night or as he turns his back.

Macocael feeds a fire. The orange-yellow glow casts a waving, warm light across the faces of the four of them. The leather cased around Thomas' body itches terribly. The dryness irritates his skin and the lingering sweat reeks. The Carib's long black hair hangs alongside both sides of his face, creating an ominous appearance in the fire-lit night.

"You have wronged us by leading us here," Macocael says.

"Calm yourself," Thomas.

"You have betrayed our friendship in this delusion of yours. Your dream was only madness, nothing else."

"I don't blame you for saying that. You cannot feel the power that I feel."

"Quiet! Quiet before you cause me to spill your blood!" Macocael says, slipping free his stone knife.

Lucy becomes startled by this threat. Thomas calmly lies beside her and says to Macocael, "Do not worry; it will not be long. Amoika speaks to me when I dream. He is glad to help us," Thomas says as the hunger cramps his stomach.

Of course, deep down Thomas feels a great fear that Macocael may be right.

"Maybe I am mad," Thomas begins to repeat to himself.

Even the most self-affirming leaders have their secret doubts in their visions. Without proof, it is difficult to even tell oneself that the devout affirmations are not repeated acts of insanity. Thomas' dreams are so real to him, on the other hand. He is the sort of person who, when filled with a surging of belief in his heart, it soon transforms within his mind into fact, into a grand prophesy. He wakes renewed each morning, his mind filled with blissful scenes of a valley overflowing with an abundance of food and life-giving waters. What the waters represent, he cannot say. In his dream the waters are sweet with overhanging boughs of guava trees and pearly-golden sunbeams shining all around.

One day, after the second month in the wilderness had passed, Macocael shakes Yaguasa from sleep. Yaguasa's body flops, his face staring straight at the sun.

Macocael screams in his own language, "Brother! Wake!" He strikes him hard in the back and finally Yaguasa's limbs animate. Macocael sits him up and Yaguasa's throat convulses in an attempt to vomit. Yaguasa bends and widens his jaw, croaking like a frog, yet only a dribble of yellow bile seeps out. He collapses onto the soil and closes his eyes.

Yaguasa is covered in sweat and moans horribly all through the day and night. Macocael stops at the first sign of disease and takes to comforting him. Macocael, full of fright, searches the forest for a cure and insists that Thomas and Lucy halt for once and give him a chance to wander for that needle in a haystack cure. They do wait, and while waiting for six days, taking care of Yaguasa while he intermittently moans and sleeps, Macocael, full of feelings of failure and desolation, returns with nothing but food that is divided sparsely.

"I believe he can still make it," Macocael says to Thomas and Lucy.

They both agree.

Macocael rephrases his statement, "What I mean is, if we leave back to the village, perhaps he is still not so sick that he will die on the way. If we leave now."

Thomas refuses. He says, "No. We are not returning while the end is near."

Macocael erupts, "What do you mean with this cold-heartedness?! He lies here on the edge of death and you deny him hope for life!"

"No," Thomas says, appearing like a demon wearing the still, leathery face and the long, black, wiry hair of Amoika, the Carib warrior. "I am his only hope," Thomas says resolutely. "To wander back would mean his death."

"I must try! You expect me to surrender while there is still—"

"I understand your feelings, but moving forward is our only path. It is the only way to heal your brother, as well as our people."

"How can I?"

"Believe in me. I know your heart was with me when you set out. Be with me now. We must keep our faith no matter how hard it seems."

On the seventh day of waiting, Thomas declares it is wasteful and dangerous. Macocael agrees that it will be better for them to be off searching as well. With little other option, they leave his dear brother lying on the cold earth of the forest to possibly die alone.

Macocael returns with a cluster of plantains he had found growing more than a mile off.

"Brother," Macocael asks, "have they not returned?"

Yaguasa, struggling to open his eyes, tells him he had not seen them.

They do not return all night, or the next day, or the day after that. Macocael, fatigued from his great hunger, lies next to his brother. He wonders if he can make the journey to the plantain tree and climb it so they can eat. He decides just to rest. He curses Thomas and Lucy, for his guess is that they found their way back to the village. They must have thought he and Yaguasa were too much of a burden. He feels very sorry for the way he spoke to Thomas, feeling shameful for his anger, no longer surprised when each day passes and they do not come back. He expects to watch his brother die, as his vision steadily blurs and the world around him spins. Only the faintest flicker of faith remains in his heart for Thomas.

Macocael awakes to the sound of slowly clomping hooves. His vision is blurry when he opens his eyes, seeing the outline of two great Iberian bulls, stout black beasts with horns reaching over two feet long from each side of their heads. Atop these massive animals sit Thomas and Lucy, one to each, calm as ever, as the bovine graze on the forest foliage.

"We have found it," Thomas says proudly.

Macocael cannot manage to say a word. His parched, cracked lips stand agape in wonder.

"Hop on," Thomas says. "Let us relish in our victory."

Relish in the victory they did. As soon as Macocael and Yaguasa see the vast field full of cattle numbering more than a hundred, their eyes show joy, something that was long abandoned. They have never seen creatures this size before. It is as if they are from another world. They roll off of the back of the bulls they are riding. Macocael leads Yaguasa, who steps like a geriatric, though raises his hands and has the joy of disbelief spread across his face. Their hearts leap, for hope is surging through them once more. They leap in the creek that crosses this valley, soaking themselves, drinking the clear water in, embracing each other, carefree like they were boys again.

Yaguasa's illness catches up with him, so he sits and relaxes. Macocael finds some jobo trees and plucks an armful of the translucent, golden fruit, passing them out for all to enjoy. The jobo calms Yaguasa's aching belly and also fends off the hunger some. Thomas calls Macocael over to assist him in slaughtering a cow.

The Taino watches as Thomas lets his sword fall, severing the spine of the brown and white spotted creature. They clean the carcass, separating the organs, the fat, and the meat. The body is dragged to a muddy clearing. Thomas' his hands are caked in a red, bloody syrup, the globules of fat and bile dripping onto the unblemished earth. He situates the cow's guts in an arrangement within its own cavity meticulously. Macocael at last receives a spark and holds aloft a bundle of blazing sticks. Thomas declares, gazing into the heavens, "Oh Lord! We offer the best to you as a show of thanks. All the choice parts of the flesh, the fat that covers the entrails, the kidneys, the entire fatty tail cut close to the backbone. We light this for you, this fragrant offering, this sweet smelling aroma made for you by fire!"

Macocael places the torch within the body and it feeds on the fat and other oils, quickly bursting into flames. Black smoke billows from the carcass and rises into the heavens. Thomas removes the skin of the Carib, first severing the stitching, slipping his arms and legs free, then tossing the leather suit into the fire. Thomas kneels and offers a prayer to the original owner of the skin, "Amoika. You acted nobly in acting as our guide. May your path lead you to heaven."

The four of them spend the night around the warmth of the campfire, sharing cheerful words, purging the toxins that had stored, inflicting mind and body for the two months previous. They fill themselves on steak, accompanied by healing herbs Macocael had found creekside. The tender, hearty meat seems to renew their strength fully. They sleep soundly this night like babes. When the light of morning comes, Thomas and Lucy take a bath. She washes the buildup of filth that had encrusted on his skin.

Two bulls and two cows travel with them on the journey back, both as vehicles and to feed the tribe, which the four saviors deem must be in the most desolate condition. The trip, now that they know the position of both locations, only takes a little over three days to complete. With sufficient sources of water and food along the way, it is really no problem.

When they reach the village, there are ecstatic reactions of both jubilation and fear. The initial fear was if the creatures they rode in on were demons or monsters and would possibly eat them. The fear subsides more as the villagers are told of the paradise that was found. As the people of the tribe eat beef for the first time, gladness spills over. Everything edible of the four animals is consumed, because the Taino were starving for so long. The organs, marrow, and the skin all disappear. Pandukuli cracks a skull open and eats a whole brain; Kadesh finds the eyes to be an exquisite delicacy; the four greatest Taino warriors have the privilege of eating a whole heart all to themselves; the intestines and the kidneys are sliced and consumed by many, a special treat when made crispy on the fire.

As the feeling of joy creeps back into their bones, people take to dancing. Flutes and drums carry their lively sound through the air as the singing begins. The chorus erupts, seeming to make up for the times of hunger when this activity was, for the most part, abandoned.

While the clacking of shell bracelets and anklets sound in a multitudinous beat, and the maracas send an irresistible rhythm to the hearts of all, Benjamin finds himself entranced. He thrusts his arms and legs about and writhes his body like a snake. Upon wiping his brow, a momentary break of the spell to catch his breath, he is caught under another spell: The figure of Assawako before his eyes, dancing carefree, yet so seductive. Her slender, smooth limbs sway to the music as gracefully as a deer's pacing through a valley. The warm glow of the fire plays on her skin, seeming to seep inside and draw out her natural tone of milk and honey.

Benjamin chokes back his fear and finds his legs unconsciously stepping beside Assawako. He is filled with dance once again. She sees him and smiles; surprised, he smiles back in gladness. Everything seems to slow for him. The sound is dulled, save for the pounding of his heart.

Pandukuli steps inside the circle of dancers and announces that the tribe will be moving permanently to the land filled with cattle. A unanimous cheer resounds from the throng. They celebrate doubly now, both in celebration of the boon that they enjoy this day and also for the boon that is to come.

Benjamin and Assawako, caught in the thrill of it all, fall into a deep kiss. Her father sees this, for his eyes are always on his youngest daughter. He steps from the center of the circle and pulls her away, barricading her in his home. She is not dismayed by this, and takes it as a challenge.

She searches around for the woven chest in which he keeps his things. Inside, under his feathered headdresses, under his many beaded necklaces, lies the manaya he owned since he was young. The weapon is stored in a humble wood sheath. Thrusting the manaya overhead repeatedly and tiring herself completely, she manages to cut a slit barely wider than her hips. She presses on the fibers of the wall so as to bend them upwards. Assawako passes through the narrow gap, scraping her torso a little, but otherwise escaping quite easily.

Careful to stay far from her father's gaze, she sneaks back to Benjamin's side and leads him to the cover of the forest. There they sit and enjoy each other's company, staring into each other's eyes, caressing each other's hair, and speaking sweet words that were held in for such a long time. Kisses are shared under the pearly moonlight with tender passion, with the warmth of each heart.

Morning greets Benjamin and Assawako as the light of the sun flashes in their eyes through the crisscross of leaves above. She wakes first, her fingers still intertwined with his. She sits up and stares into the yellowy-blue glow in this moment just after dawn. She shakes him, saying, "Wake dear, wake."

He does wake, but tucks his head once again. She shuffles his shoulders until his eyes open wide and his face shows of confusion and disorientation.

"It is such a nice morning. Let's not waste it."

"I am making much use of it," he says, falling back asleep.

She rustles him again, raising him at the shoulder.

"Fine," he says. "I give up. What shall we do today?"

Benjamin and Assawako venture to the edge of the Yaque river under the hanging boughs of trees.

"The river is nice," Benjamin says. "Its trickle is so calming."

Assawako says, "Look," pointing to the trees before them. The wide-spreading, deep green leaves create a fine shade and wonderful atmosphere for lounging. Round green fruit still remain on the highest branches.

"It is called guava," Assawako says.

Ben's eyes light up with the thought of this. With tongue extended from his mouth, he immediately springs to the nearest tree and climbs like a monkey to a cluster of the green-skinned fruit. Above him he can hear a nest of squawking hawk-chicks, guarded over by their mother. She is absolutely beautiful with her soft-feathered, gray underside and the brownish-gray top feathers. The beauty of her piercing eyes and the matching lemon-yellow of her sloping crescent beak causes him to pause and stare. She rises on her feet now, and the glare she gives Ben seems to say, "This is not your place here in the trees. Take what you came for and leave."

Ben plucks six of the green orbs, lets them fall to the ground, then climbs down himself. Once landing upon the flat, leaf-covered earth, he holds one of the fruits before Assawako and slices it in half with his dagger. The juice runs down his wrist as he slices one of the halves again, handing it to his focus of love. She bites the sweet, pink flesh, relishing in the taste.

His first bite is followed by another and another, spitting out the hard white seeds unconsciously. He had tasted strawberries when he was a child, but they were not fresh. Being poor, he had lived mainly on grains and what discarded meats he could find. Fruit to him was an absolute delight. It was in this that he felt his feet grow roots in this country. His heart is forever bonded to Assawako, but this taste is like that of another world. To him, it brings to mind what it may be like to be in paradise.

The lovers share the delicacy, feeding each other, sharing kisses containing the wet juice of the fruit. The indulgence in the fetish is carried on with no rush. When the six guavas are through, the sweetness being prolonged for such a long span, they wash themselves in the river and begin to be drawn to an irresistible urge for each other. Ben and Assawako spend the day resting in the mud on the riverbank clenching their fingers in an embrace, enjoying the pleasure of touching each other's skin. Time is theirs for the taking. To them, in moments like this, the world is cleaved off and they are only ones left alive.

# Jubilation



**AGUSTÍN'S JOURNAL ENTRY:**
February 21st, 1567

Within five days, the tribe had migrated to our new home. After eight days, volunteers had brought all the materials worth bringing through the jungle. The huts were set up relatively in the center of the valley, between the winding river and the wall of trees. Living in the open, under the warmth of the sun inspires a new pastime, that of laying oneself sprawled out in the field, sleeping half the day. If one could say they indulged in their free time before, now they are as cats. The joy that this life brings inspires in the people a fervent sense of civic pride. When one does set their self to labor, their production is at an all time high. With the destruction of their former village fresh in their memory, there is inspiration to fashion cruel weapons of war. The crops grow fat in this fertile plain, and people's labor is lessened in that the earth is soft.

The people take to being herdsmen, constructing a vast enclosure to ensure the cattle do not leave them. The Taino cannot consume milk, but the people of Europe drink it down and turn it into butter, adding it to the cassava cakes, greatly improving the flavor. The whites teach the Tainos to lead cattle in the plowing of the fields. Also, manure is used to improve crop yield. Now a bounty of meats and greens may be had at each meal. These advances in labor technology change the Tainos' perception of life, such as their former satisfaction with cassava. Now they have the luxury to slaughter one of the beasts and share the flesh before the communal barbecue anytime they want.

The introduction of these creatures means people have even more free time. Works of art are produced, and to Thomas' surprise they often take to carving his image in wood and stone. His monumental return to the village is captured in a popular form of iconography, that of the herdsman, typically a figure with hair hanging long in the foreground, accompanied by two bovine at his side, and more scattered far in the distance. This stylized impression of Thomas' journey can be seen decorating people's homes, as well as along the riverbank, carved directly into the sides of the trees and boulders lining it. This image became in a way a representation of the tribe itself, for as he led in the herd, he led the tribe to a renewed life out of doom and darkness. They feel so strongly for his sacrifice, and the special ability they deemed him to have, that of a seer, a guide, and a prophet.

Lucy spends each day curled in pain in a corner of the hut. Thomas attempts to console her, saying sweet words and massaging her sore muscles. Hourly he helps her to her feet to find a hole dug in the forest so she may push forth the watery feces welling inside her bowels. Momentarily relieving the painful cramps, they return to the tent where she shifts between sleeping and waking to vomit. Thomas, when he occasionally leaves her to take a stroll through the village, people offer their heartfelt condolences. They hand him healing herbs and the food, which stands in a great mound outside their home.

After more than a week of this, her sickness suddenly stops and she spends her days blankly staring out into nothing. This oddness causes Thomas to feel as if blood-lusting bugs are crawling up his back, nipping at his neck, and into the bones of his spine. He is told by many passersby that there is to be a celebration in a week's time in which he is the honored guest. He tells Lucy this good fortune, but she does not seem to notice. She only sits staring or sleeps. At one time she held her arms around him when he asked if she would be able to go, but he was not so sure that this action was any sort of answer.

As time goes on, she becomes more alert, but she is still reclusive. When she was ill she responded to caresses favorably, but now as she appears to be recovering she remains quiet and caught up in herself. She will wander off without a word through the village, or sit and fiddle with a sprig of grass or a dagger and aimlessly carve lines into the dirt. Thomas begins to lose patience with her, in that she does not seem to be herself. This queer behavior is almost too much for him to bear. He wakes each day hoping to find her returned to her old self. Each day she remains lost, almost a vacant shell, an imposter posing as the girl he loves.

Before leaving to the celebration, he kneels before her. She lies on her side once again. He touches her shoulder and she swats it away harshly. Hurt by this, he stands abruptly, and with a crack in his voice he says:

"I love you. I'll be back soon, OK?"

Pandukuli and his entourage lead Thomas to the festivities. Amid the darkness they step toward the blazing yellow that seems to hover. They place a wreath of palm leaves atop his head and a garland of flowers around his neck. As they near the commotion, his heart beats faster. The vibrations climb his legs and swim all through his body.

As Thomas steps up the ledge, he clearly hears the roar of voices, booming drums, and multitudes of squealing flutes sending their vibrations to the night sky. Up above, the shimmering stars seem to be caught in the same sort of dance as the entranced Taino, their sheet of white seeming as a glimmering reflection of heaven's hosts. The din is in full view now, as Thomas stands among them. Their throats call out to nature and to the gods in praise.

Pandukuli sits Thomas in a seat beside him, a great chair adorned with multitudinous assortments of feathers of every color imaginable, fitted as a spectrum like a vibrant rainbow. Eyes fall on him, and he feels the great weight of human care in his gut. He is handed a cup filled with sweet cassava liquor, which upon tasting immediately brings him delight and calms his nerves.

It is an almost a mad frenzy that fills the Taino, as if the spirits of jaguar were trapped in the bodies of deer. The myriad elbows and knees cutting through the air and whirling seem as one horrible creature, its life force compelled by the thunderous drums. In the center of it all, dancers find their bodies thrust into an ecstasy of narcotic-induced splendor. Their endless leaping and flailing of limbs inspires the rest to do the same.

Through the night, beautiful girls are brought forth before Thomas and the Chief to perform seductive dances. Their bodies absorb the warm softness of the fire light, sinking into Thomas' mind as liquid sexuality, flowing though his senses all at once as if they were a river of milk drunk directly into the mind. One after another, the girls come forth, sometimes in twos or threes, expertly trained to mimic the flicker of the tongues of flame that envelope their bodies in shifting orange radiance.

Caught in the magnificence of this union of humanity, Thomas leaps from his seat to meet this show of gladness. He meets each face surrounding the fire with a kiss, stepping slowly past. As his lips meet the faces of those he passes, hands softly grip him in a familial show of love. He passes people of all ages. He picks up children and feels their arms grip him as if he were their fond relation. He knows this is their way to let loose when sadness and doom has gotten them feeling down low. He remembers back to his old home with his mother and father and how they had lost hope. Gladness fills him in realizing this chance to experience soaring joy, when such a thing did not seem possible on the festering streets which he spent so many years.

After an indeterminable period of time, Pandukuli takes Thomas by the arms and leads him past the ecstatic crowd to his personal hut. Through the shadows, away from the pandemonium, tripping over stones in the darkness, bewildered to be taken away, his heart beating hard, his mind trying to adjust to the change in seeing lit torches lining the inside of the long hall. In the warm light Thomas sees half a dozen of the tribe's most beautiful girls reclining on padded seats of palm wood. Pandukuli exits and secures the door as the girls rise and lay Thomas on a bed of feathers, massaging his tired muscles. One girl softly plays a flute, the tones causing his limbs to fall limp, his mind flowing on a cloud of bliss. Thomas feels hands lay upon him, bringing an overwhelming rush of serenity. The pains and tenseness flow from him as they knead the tight knots, press into the flesh to refresh it with blood flow and stroke the toxins out of him. After an hour, while his body is tingling with pleasure, they lay their lips upon him. He is done. He is theirs. They enjoy each other's bodies through the night.

# 38

# The Cat Pounces

**T**HOMAS IS FURIOUS that the Taino are continuing to get lazier the longer they live with the luxuries and comforts that the valley offers.

He yells, "You want to be overtaken by the Carib yet again?! They destroyed your first village because you weren't prepared! What you do now is wait for them to build up a force and destroy us completely!"

He grabs a teenage Taino boy and drags him by the arm to the crops, impressing him to work.

"Do you not remember how it was? To have your food burned up? If it was not for me you would be dead! Do not take for granted this blessing. Enjoy it, by all means, but you must not forget—the better your life is, the more they will want it! They are not lazy. They are mad and will not stop unless we stop them!"

Thomas quickly gets the Taino working hard to produce crops and forming the cow skin into leather shirts to protect the warriors in battle. He means to fortify their position in this land. Diego leads the warriors in drills with carved swords of bone. He teaches his most deadly tactics, for instance, that of the strike and fly, so that the enemy will be wounded, but will not have a chance to retaliate. He teaches the feigned thrust, in which one's adversary reaches to block a thrust that is not there, but is stabbed elsewhere once their attention falls to the false attack.

Long spears are fashioned to keep the charging Carib at bay. The battles are planned to be fought in the close quarters of the forest to give the advantage to those with tactics over the blind assault the Carib continually wage.

Thomas sits in the coolness of the forest kissing a beautiful, doe-eyed Taino girl. In each other's arms they indulge in the feeling of each other's skin. Suddenly, she stops. Like a frightened cat she stares out into the forest, and seeing a strange dark figure approach, her legs take flight. Before Thomas can turn, hands in soft leather gloves twist his neck, nearly breaking it.

The shadowed figure whispers in his ear, "I've got you."

Thomas has a blade pressed into his back. He is compelled to step forward out from cover. He knows that voice, that raspy, yet eloquent way of speech that he heard while recovering outside the smoldering church in the town of his birth. How is it that he has chased him here? What sort of madman would come so far for revenge? He must have come to deliver repayment for the injuries he received and to take back his daughter. Thomas remembers clearly how the brickwork lay on Constantyne's right leg and notices now how he hobbles. He gives the Admiral a donkey kick in his bad leg, causing him to holler and fall to the ground. Out of a gut reaction, they both lunge their swords, both blades tasting flesh. Thomas flops like a snared animal and leaps backward, blood streaming from his chest, soaking his shirt. He readies himself to strike, but knows he must flee as he sees Constantyne's soldiers appear from the darkness of the forest and charge after him across the plain. Rushing for safety, he is not fast enough, for a few of them close in. He swipes in a full circle causing one soldier's Adam's apple to spit blood. He feels the blood rushing out and knows he must make it to safety, or this armored soldier will not need to strike true to end him. The soldier leaps upon Thomas. Thomas grips his wrist, fighting the blade from sinking into the flesh of his neck. He is strong and so well trained to secure Thomas' hands, wrestling him into submission. As the blade is set before Thomas' throat he sees the soldiers watching with glee. No struggling makes a difference. Filled with fright, Thomas closes his eyes and sends his will to the sky, begging mercy from heaven.

Thomas' body collapses onto the earth. He smells the strong smell of the grass of the plain. It envelopes him. He awaits a rush of pain, or the feeling of blood gushing from him and his organs beginning to fail. None of this occurs, to his unimaginable confusion. There, before him, two arrows are lodged in the neck of his attacker. The gore of red muscle and the throat box spills out the crevices, his helmet sitting neat on the earth beside him. Thomas' head pokes up from the tall grass and sees the Admiral's armored fighters off in the distance slaughtering the Tainos. Their swords cut through warrior after warrior.

The arrows of the Taino begin to dart out to little effect. The points ding as they collide with the steel helmets and plate armor. Only in having superior numbers do the Taino achieve a stalemate with their adversary, slashing through them with hatchet swipes. Dozens of Taino lay gutted open as the armored warriors retreat in order to devise a new tactic.

Only after the marauders are far in the distance does Thomas raise himself out of hiding and feel the fear his companions are feeling in seeing their brothers shredded so easily.

This sudden attack pushes the production of the tools of war to a frenzy. Long, stout spears are made, with cattle bone sharpened into skinny points like daggers, tied to the end of each long pole. Diego leads this action, setting in motion the creation of war technology through his knowledge of the art. A class of warriors are given sabers, each made from a long femur of a bull, sharpened and fitted with leather at the base to improve grip. Diego trains them not to just attack wildly, but to lay deadly blows in the throat and the belly which are unprotected by bone. Formations are instituted, tight lines which will be held while those elite warriors fitted with both spear and bone sword are more mobile. Atop the backs of bulls, they will tear apart the waves of Carib, create confusion, and sweep in with the spear before they have a chance. This status may only be attained by those whose fighting skill is most exceptional, and by showing a certain bravado, leaping upon the backs of one of these creatures and demanding their submission.

It is not long before the tribe is located by the Carib and is assaulted by a night raid. This is no victory for the invaders though, for a great number fall upon them as is their duty as part of a formal watch. This attack spurs the people to call for a war party to be sent. Diego leads this, and Thomas by his side. They march out the next day with a troop of twenty. A guide leads them to the nearest Carib village in which they burn completely and cut down those that confront them. The blind rush tactic the defenders use is suicide when the long poles of the spears split their bellies at a distance. Upon leaving, many of the warriors take a woman as captive, as is permitted by tradition.

Constantyne, with his wounded assassins, encounter a Carib foraging in the forest. With the use of clever hand signals, his perplexed face shows some understanding and he guides them to his tribe led by Nohi-Abassi. The village is stunned to see such a tall and imposing figure followed by armored blondes, gripping fearful creations of steel.

Constantyne is sat down with Nohi-Abassi, who by way of taking up and crossing the weapons of each people, handing him a finely made halberd, and gripping his fist tight around the chief's as to show his desire to conquer together, soon there is a military union enacted.

Constantyne leads the warriors the best he can. He sets those who know something in the way of military strategy to mold these wild tribesmen into regimented soldiers. Instead of resorting to their blind charges, they are taught the basics of striking and defending. By habit, the Carib break formation. Most do not respect the words of these foreigners, whose insistence on holding back seems to them an effeminate sort of behavior.

After four months of preparation, Nohi-Abassi insists he meet with Pandukuli. Assured of victory, he lets fly his advantage in the way of European generals and their tactics. He demands a formal war, which Pandukuli accepts with vigor, elated to see the power of his new war machine in action. In ten days time the troops are to arrive at a clearing several miles east, a place relatively midway from both tribes.

Throughout the morning hours, battle cries ring out through the valley. One would think great trolls inhabited the forests for all the unhindered bass rumbles resounding. As the sun makes all things visible, Constantyne is pointed out. Thomas catches sight of him, his form present on the hill past the parted tree line. He is seated upon a smoothed, wooden throne, placed into a carved-out portion of the hill. From there he may oversee the battlefield.

Diego holds his sword aloft as the call to battle is bellowed from both sides. Thomas, Benjamin, and most of the other whites who are not guarding the village, stand in line with the warriors girded in their steel armor. The Carib start off from afar, charging with their hatchets and war clubs, as Diego drops his blade, issuing the call. At once, arrows rain down with well honed aim, felling numerous Carib. Arrows fly from the hands of Carib as well, sinking deep into their victims. Bravery stays with them as the bull warriors are ordered to stampede and slaughter, bringing great confusion to the fierce, painted bloodseekers.

Each side stomps past their archers and the dead, seeing a vast field, their brethren at each shoulder, and straight ahead, enraged, demonic-faced adversaries. Several figures are clustered, always shifting. Which skull would be lined up for the first blow?

Finally the clusters fall into all out battle. The overwhelming numbers of the Carib prove to be deadly and intimidating. They charge with hateful ferocity. Many heads are cleaved or crushed by their heavy blows. The spears though, prove to be effective in putting them down. The long points constantly fly forth, consuming lives as the mass moves as one, the spikes jutting on all sides like an urchin.

The bull warriors pick off numerous Carib that continue to trade blows, riding with speed, dipping their blades in quickly as if spearing fish. Both the naked-torsoed Taino and Carib seek hiding among the cover on opposite sides of the battlefield.

Constantyne's armored soldiers, though only fifteen in number, seem to be unstoppable. The charging of the bulls becomes a predictable motion, four of the eighteen Taino riders being slashed through within the first minutes. As the animal rides by it can be dodged and the rider cut through the gut by a halberd. The tenaciousness of the beasts get the best of them, as a wall of blades point their way and seal their doom if they dare press toward.

In the end, after the bulls are cut down, laying in massive heaps of flesh, Thomas' fellows face death, seriously regretting leaving their armor upon the ship so far away. Taino and Carib once again regroup with their comrades, and the fighting is soon stopped. The armor reigns advantageous and Thomas' troops raise their hands in surrender.

It seems to Thomas that he has lost. His hands are tied behind his back, as are those of his companions. While surrounded, they sit. Far off on the hill, Constantyne discusses how he will punish Thomas and the other under his submission.

As the tense wait is endured, Thomas sits wordless in the plain with steel and stone blades pointed his way. Night falls, and still no change is made, save for long torches planted in the soil. A few arrows soar from the forest and land near the guards. One with a flaming tip ignites the nearby foliage. The flames are quickly stamped out. A troop of Carib are sent to chase away the archers.

Thomas, Diego, Benjamin, and Simon are led among other prisoners to the center of a ramshackle camp set up by Constantyne and Nohi-Abassi. The feet of every one of the defeated are tied, leaving them the ability to wiggle like worms as the only form of mobility. One by one, Tainos and white men are carried to a tree stump, their head is set upon it, and an executioner splits them at the neck.

Several flaming arrows are shot from the east. Some of the huts catch fire and the occupants hurry out. In this confusion, a wave of Tainos comes in from the north across the field. Their weapons clash as they enter the vicinity. They are cut down, but the beheadings must be delayed as more and more bands of Tainos and arrows snuff out the lives of the guards one by one.

Constantyne approaches Thomas angrily. Standing before him he says, "I will punish you. These savages are mere flies. Your life ends tonight."

Thomas replies, "So what if I die? I have had my revenge."

Constantyne composes himself, taking care to not lose his composure. He watches over his prize, careful to not let him slip away this time. All the while, his men strike down the waves of Taino warriors. Side by side the Carib, the spears, halberds and swords pierce the flesh of their attackers. Carib reinforcements come, and messengers are sent to order others in the village to scout and take out any Tainos they find.

A number of Taino dare to stop in their tracks, though arrows fall all around them, and shoot arrows of their own. Though they quickly die, several surrounding the captives perish. An arrowhead plunges through the eye of an armored soldier. The body falls with a metallic crash just beside Diego. After the initial shock, Diego takes the initiative, though at miniscule movements at a time, to near this newly dead adversary. Amid the shouting, no one is closely watching Diego's actions. Finally, he has arched his back over the sword, snug in its sheath. Taking the grip in hand, he inches it out. The cords that bind his hands are slid over the blade. With freedom in his grasp, in a flash his legs are free and the guts are bursting from the bellies of those watching over his fellows.

No one can compete with Diego. He is a tiger among lambs. Heads chopped clean, strike, parry, deflect and gore. Two blades now in hand, he kills numerous charging Carib with each blow. Graceful, yet ferocious, he dances around the less agile, causing them to back step and regroup. With this advantage he blurts to Thomas, "Lift your arms!" At this, with a swipe he severs the bonds binding Thomas' wrists, and Benjamin's as well.

An armored soldier confronts Diego, keeping him at a distance with a halberd. With the point of the weapon he charges and Diego backs away. The soldier whirls the curved blade in a great arc that Diego then smashes downward. Diego dips his other blade into the uncovered armpit of his attacker, piercing organs and ending him.

All of the sudden, with great force Constantyne lunges straight at Diego's core and quickly follows with a second blade falling hard. Diego feels his forearm slit and gush as he spins and rolls out of the great Admiral's far reach. A moment to think is not granted Diego as the dual blades strike and swipe his way. Even hobbling on his leg of wood and iron, Constantyne is quick. And although tendons in his left arm were damaged years before, his strength, size, and skill burst forth into reality in the form of dismembered adversaries.

Thomas and Benjamin free their legs and take up weapons. They quickly free a number of their companions and then lash out at those nearing Diego. Their distraction goes as planned, providing time for all to be freed and forcing Constantyne to confront the only man among them who can provide a true challenge.

Constantyne and Diego circle around each other, inspecting for style and flaw. As Constantyne sees Diego sway just slightly—in swipe several dips of the blades. Diego dares not attempt any haphazard attacks, lest he be caught trapped within Constantyne's long reach. Constantyne jabs at him and he will either step away or deflect the blade. After a number of rounds at this, Diego knocks the sword coming at him hard and darts his other blade straight for Constantyne's neck. Constantyne dodges and deflects in the same manner, charging the prancing Diego, who must also be on the lookout for those who wish to cut into his back. With swipes here and there the Carib are cut through—but then Constantyne is there to take advantage. At Diego's back and sides advance more warriors than before. With nowhere for Diego to run, Constantyne strikes his twin blades out in a flurry of precision. Dodge, parry, lunge, sidestep—and Constantyne thrusts an overhand toward Diego's head. Diego leaps into an angled somersault, rolling on his shoulder, knocking Constantyne's artificial leg aside as he spins back on his feet. As Constantyne's stance is momentarily spread too wide, Diego spins away, lacerating the back of Constantyne's injured arm. With a roar worthy of a jungle cat, Constantyne falls to his knees, but is then guarded by his many fellows.

The whole of Thomas' men and his Taino allies are free, holding before them weapons dropped from the slain. They step back, but then clash with Carib who lash out viciously. Through the air sweep their weapons of wood and shards of bone. Fury sounds on each side with growls and hateful curses.

Skulls are crushed, noses lobbed off, and bellies slit wide. Finally, Taino reinforcements come and shoot arrows into the distracted Carib. Both sides retreat and disappear into opposite sides of the forest.

It is within these trees that Thomas sees Lucy. She has her glare and attention transfixed far out where her father is.

Thomas tells her, "We barely survived."

She doesn't say a word. She only looks Thomas over, seeming overwhelmed with his presence.

"What do you wish to do?" Thomas asks.

She says, "I should go to him."

Thomas has no reply worth giving to halt her. "I tried," he says.

She nods, acknowledging his effort, though the thought of returning to civilization sounds like a blessing to her now.

"Go and do what you wish," Thomas says. "He's bleeding out there."

Constantyne overruns the Taino village. He and his comrades perch there, making it their own. He finds no sign of Lucy or Thomas, and receives no useful information, despite the liberal use of torture on straggler Tainos. Voyages into the wild forest yield no results, only footprints leading to slight signs, broken twigs, and foot impressions into nothing. More footprints may lead over hill, though gully after gully reveals only disappointment. The chase is impossible, it seems, for the Carib employed to find these uprooted Taino and their companions. Those they seek must be very far.

After five months of sending out scouts deep into wild nature, those closest to Constantyne speak of the developments going on, the small fortifications being raised along the neck of the newfound landmass of the Americas. They wish to go there, have a stake in the wealth.

"I will hear none of his," Constantyne says in response.

A loyal soldier tells him, "Your will is ours, but I ask you to consider our crewmen waiting on the sea for us. Our mission was to be a brief surprise attack. Perhaps if we spend the rest of the year here, Lexington's men will cut his throat and engage in pillaging without your order."

Constantyne considers this in solitude through the hours of the night. He grasps in the darkness, but his prey fails to register in his mind as it had before. In the morning he makes known his decision to relent and soon their supplies are packed.

They make their way back to their ships and head to the disorganized meeting grounds in places along the span of the land bridge of this new continent. They raid each fort or naked marketplace with fire and bloodshed, finally coming to a city called Panama. Filling each fledgling settlement with cannon shot till they give a ransom of money, food, drink, and women, they get what they want or else it is an all out Viking raid, a horror with all slaughtered by the hands of sailors too long at sea.

In reaching Panama, they have more than enough manpower. They storm the city, defiling the natives, robbing the Spanish conquerors before them of their jewels and gold. They spend the summer there as parasites, lounging on the shore, enjoying the fineries as vultures of gluttons.

As this game is an old tradition, those Spaniards which they conquered gave a certain loyalty to them while they reign, and join their forces at sea. As the organization of aristocrats simmer near their old strength and become a threat, Constantyne sets off with a renewed force of arms, a sea armada capable of raiding and renewing its own power continually. He now had the ability to consume Thomas' people several times over.

# A Spiritual Wound Is Now Festering

THE TAINO'S NEW SETTLEMENT lies far south, almost to the ocean, at the midpoint of the island. They lost the battle with their adversaries, but life goes on and is still fruitful. A plan has been set to celebrate this new life and shake off the loss in war.

Decorations in the way of feathers, shells, and flowers are woven and hung around necks, donned on foreheads, wrists, ankles, and across the many structures erected recently. The intensity of the drums increase as the day goes on.

As the celebrations fully bloom, Diego is congratulated by three chiefs: Pandukuli, and two invited from elsewhere, by the names of Gueybana and

Orcobix. They each bring their entourage to hail what they perceive to be a time of peace.

Before all of Pandukuli's people, and near fifty from each neighboring chief, counting their wives and closest family, leadership support, and guards, Diego is donned with numerous wreathes of flowers and is presented with Pandukuli's daughter Procne as a wife. He is overwhelmed by this roar of cheer and the deafening boom of the drum companies that raise the fervor in the crowd to a greater and greater swell, too caught up in this high, this dizzying surge of pride to contemplate what being married to Procne will mean. He is accepted in the royal circle, granted liberties for sure, but also he must contend with the oath he swore to his companions and to his dearest moral conviction, to God. In his heart he doesn't give up this promise to return to Francisca, his wife, but the taint now placed in him by this other woman causes a disturbance in him to branch and spread.

Next before the crowd is Thomas. He is approached by Pandukuli, who kisses him upon each cheek and begins the train of those who will don him with wreaths of vibrant, fragrant-rich flowers. That floral musk, along with the rising scent of the bovine being barbecued all across the valley, raises Thomas' spirits as if amidst the pinnacle of a religious sacrifice. He huffs this pristine incense deeply into his lungs.

After a day of drunkenness, of twirling Tainos, Diego is led into his new hut. There Procne is set upon her knees delicately on the earthen floor. Beside her is a thin matting of cloth prepared so that they may consecrate their bond.

As he approaches she begins to feel weak. The attendants leave, and in her fear she touches her face. She feels along the ridge of calcified tears at the corners of her eyes as Diego nears her.

Outside this hut her two servants hear all. These women had wiped Procne clean when she first was birthed from her mother. They had taught her humility and love. In her play with other children they were there to clean her wounds when she fell. Their ears heard her cares, of her loneliness and her want of closeness with her mother and father. In turn these women became aunts to compensate. And now they must hear her pleas for help and do nothing. Diego's words are a mystery to them, but his roaring hate pierces their insides. The cemi idols are heard crashing as he curses. Her arrhythmic gasps suggest her strangulation, being thrust into the earth and struck, and her body being thrust into viciously. It's an agony how long it goes on. Procne utters the cries of a speared animal being slit open while it is still alive.

Thomas is uplifted in his chair of entwined vine. He is deafened by the roar, the wall of surging power from the lungs of the Taino. Gone are his petty games at imagining a chorus of angels in the court of heaven. His idea of what fervor and power is possible from humanity is surpassed tenfold. The pressing on his flesh from these voices is like that of wolves' teeth, the only equation of force he could pull together in his mind to illustrate how it binds him so forcefully. Wolves' teeth, with their hard composition, press without mind or care, but with a pearl-like front that imposes on him, forming his body into a tight frame.

He is lifted up, still in this constriction, inflicted by this heralding of his name. It is of no comprehension to him. Upon this chair of wooden wires he is lifted up, his body and form is shown to all upon the backs of the strongest Taino. The crowd screams, many tearing their throats, beckoning this idea that is so new to them, this unstoppable force of societal momentum.

Suddenly Diego steps forth, his nude form presenting itself before the people. They tear into him and raise him up, sending his form into the cyclone of bodies, of arms, of sinews, of hair, and beating hearts. He is thrust head over heel, helpless. He is their war-maker, pouring glory and affluence into their compound net of nerves. To those now spoiled on satiation, he has delivered even more. His Taino companions spread the word of his magnificent slaughter of the enemy. Though surrounded, the story is told that it was not he that cowered, but he that confronted the enemy like they were rodents. This tale of pride and glory makes the idea of defeat seem an error. And now he is one with the Taino, bonded by marriage and consecration. The rapist is the gilded knight of God, the one who shall pierce through the shade of mystery.

Two days into the celebration, Thomas breaks free and returns to Lucy, who is frozen cold, pressed against the wall of her hut. He cups his hand around her, but she doesn't move. She seems healthy, quite more alive than before, but even though her abdominal swelling seems lessened, her mind has wandered off to some other place. Lucy is unbreakable like an iron implement.

He sits with her, letting the empathy slather off, letting the humors relax of their piteous titillation. She lies caressed and fed by her black-haired womenfolk. They come every day and clean her.

# 40

# Barbarism Shows Its Face

DISEASE BREAKS OUT among the Taino like never before. The whites seem unaffected by the blight, as was the case in the first affliction. Babies, young children, and the old pass away daily, and a great pillage of vitality sweeps the people. The curse is a mystery, the only sign being an appearance of reddish-pink nodes that appear on the skin. The red wave sweeps over roughly two-fifths of the native population. Many of the healthy are set to netting new hammocks, which are lined in an out of the way place so that the sick may rest among the quiet.

A few days after the outset of the breakout, Pandukuli shows the typical signs of the sickness on his cheeks. He immediately senses a desire for a coup among those closest to him, who stand to benefit from a breach in the stability of leadership. At all times around him is a circle of those he feels he can trust—those paid with the best material compensation—with weapons at their sides.

Kadesh announces that a cure may be found in an herb that lies in the northwest. Diego volunteers to be his guard. He takes pride in this important mission, though trusts no one in this time of turbulence, and so takes Procne with him.

"I am worried about her," Diego says to Kadesh, with Procne trailing behind.

"Trust in nature. It has provided the cure I spoke of," Kadesh says.

"Are there any structures that we may rest in?" Diego asks. "I fear she may be feeling effects of the illness."

Kadesh stops and inspects her. He notices her complexion has become paler and her mind distant, and so he agrees. Her eyes are dark and sunk in, signifying a decrease in health. He tells Diego that there are many rudimentary huts along the way built by others for temporary stays that will serve their purposes.

They spend the day resting in a shack drinking a fragrant tea made with a mixture of herbs and the bark of a tree which tastes much like a combination of a nutty mint and cinnamon. Diego tests the solidity of the structure by being forceful with it. He rattles it from all conceivable angles and pounds his fist into the wood. It seems solid enough, the mild warping from rain damage showing that it must not be much more than a few years since its construction.

Diego serves Procne in all ways, fulfilling his oath to chivalry toward women. She lies prone. He cooks and serves her food with added care—adding sweet words to ease her in her suffering. He pours her drinks careful not to spill a drop. He strokes her hair and skin when he feels the love rise up in him. Her heart dies in this way, in this horror blanketed in softness. She is bored out like a gourd, the falseness evident in his stammering-adulation. His shameful attempt to use feathery words, to speak of her fire flickering within and other such poetic talk, is oppressive to her. Sleep is her savior, for there she can be numb.

Kadesh leaves in the morning to search for the herbs he seeks by the name of Koh. They are an often-used plant, boosting the immunity in the body, imperative in a time such as this. It spreads across the forest floor, multiplying the flare of magenta from the soil, tapering off and shelved by leathery, deep green fin-leaves on each side of the spines that rise no higher than five inches. Its effects are often abused for its ability to numb the limbs to the point of tingling and play upon the mind a state of giddy-drunkenness of shifting states of stupidity, manic impulses, and ecstatic bursts of joy, intertwined with unpredictable states of lucid depression.

Procne sleeps through the day, rolling over as she becomes aware of a spear of sunlight poking through a break in the regularity of the timber. Suddenly she is shaken harshly. Diego stands above her, displeased.

"Get up," he says abruptly. "I have things for you to do."

She does as he says. For some reason she looks around for a counter-argument, then realizes there is no use in it.

Diego says, "I need you to wash me. The priest left some of his potions. Go look and find something that may cover up this smell."

She does as he asks. Looking through a ratty, reed-woven bag, she examines a number of small leather pouches until she finds one she recognizes by appearance and smell to be a mild cleanser. Mixing that with a small bit of water creates a substance they can work with. He strips and she washes, or rather perfumes his skin to cloud the musk. Saturating a cloth, she sops it under his underarms. A light lathering of his back and chest follows with a soaking of his genitalia, the hair, and in the hidden away ravine of his backside. She soaps this with a distance of mind, imagining her footsteps taking perch on invisible steps within the air, escalating a stairway which runs upward and sideways at the same time, while her hand feels the runoff of the filth accumulated from this man, this disappointment, her husband.

Diego feels her rejection of him and rises up. His nude torso drips, showing of brown tight-sewn battle scars on his shoulders on skin so white it seems like octopus meat. His form is baffling. It is so pristine it is a joke. The black hairs spread over muscle defined almost foolishly perfect, one may decide that it belongs more on a statue than something made of flesh.

Diego stares upon this woman with disdain, then noticing a fatness around her belly button. The skin is tight and extended outward. This is strange, for she is of the utmost slimness usually. His mind cannot quite wrap around what that may entail.

Diego asks her, "What is wrong with you?" pointing to the protrusion.

She looks down at it, cutting her gaze off from him.

"I asked you a question," he says.

Her eyes peer downward, fearful of him and wishing to be away from him and the creature he planted inside of her.

"You keeping secrets? Is that what it's come to now?"

His hands clamp around her neck without his own notice. They tighten without his conscious nod. She doesn't resist. "Do it," she challenges him. "End me," she begs, but he cannot do harm to a woman, and he cannot go unwanted. She falls limp after her blood is choked from her and drops to the earth floor.

Kadesh returns a day later with a bundle over his back and a strap clasped tightly with both hands. The shaman enters the hut and sees them intertwined in the nude. He retracts from the doorway in a jolt. Diego calls him back. They sit there still, but what difference is there from purposeful nudity and casual nudity among the Taino? Procne slinks her arms around her husband's neck, seemingly in an impulse of love.

"She is not prepared to go," Diego says.

"Is she not?" says Kadesh, stepping forth and feeling her skin. It is a bit hot to the touch. A lack of life is evident in her as well.

Kadesh takes a few sprigs of his herb and grinds it with a mortar, then mixes it with a bit of water he stored for the journey home.

"Give her this," Kadesh says. "It will surely heal her."

He then wanders to the door, pulling it open. Amid the glare of light he says, "I trust you know the way back."

Diego nods.

Kadesh continues, "I cannot be delayed to help one if I am to heal the people."

He closes the door without the slightest stall. The massive sack full of herbs pulls through just as the fiber hinges swivel the couple into solitude.

Diego and Procne spend day after day returning to the jungle on their strolls. She teaches him what she knows of edibles and what cures what. Sometimes they sit and wait for a creature that may pass, always a wonder to see, especially to Diego, as if this configuration of form and mannerism materialized for the first time before his eyes. She remains with him on his hunting excursions. While in wait for a beast, she gathers what plants may suit for dinner. She climbs the shorter palms and gathers the nuts that resemble a larger form of hazelnuts. Those provide a hearty, warm buttery flavor along with any edible vegetables she finds and what animal he hopes to catch. The first day, after firing his shots, only by luck he tosses a dagger at the last second at a small black bird and hits his target. This small amount of meat is more than enough with her compliments, the end result becoming a flavor-rich mix. It consists of the contrasting tastes of robust oils in the nuts and their granule texture with the rich greens that have a hint of sour and bitterness. It's all ground into the flesh of the bird, the subtle juice combining with hints of all the rest.

They live this way, arguing terribly as Procne wonders why they do not return to her village. She sees the vindictive side of him gradually increase in the way of a lurching devil, the kind he told her about, the one he accused her of worshiping so many times. She sees the devil reemerge in him, into a creature formed by duties he speaks of across the ocean.

His mind unloosens and the words spill out. "Don't you see—I have a wife! A wife I love. And I made a mistake. I got angry and stabbed a man. I thought too much of myself and didn't back down. But now you're here complicating things… I need… time away from temptation… to repent… get right with God."

He locks her in a great chest of rain-worn palmwood. He weeps and thanks her for being a good woman, how he considers nothing to be of higher worth in all existence. He takes the key he found stashed in the back of the rickety cupboard and seals her, crushing her limbs forcefully amid her mad pleading, blocking it out as he has whenever ravaging innocents. He presses her shins into a place in which they can press tight into her face and belly. He turns the key on the woman with the rounded spine. The chest sits silent. No one is inside. No noise utters, so moral judgment may be more easily regained.

Diego takes the steps back to the Tainos. He feels the sorrow in his heart. He feels for the loss of a woman, of a woman who gave her heart to him, put her special care into easing his wants. But she could not compare to his Francisca. Procne is a devil, bred from this devil people. Her demonic gods he smashed, but still she holds them in her heart. She calls to them secretly when she wanders out of sight sometimes. Her face is flushed when found out and knows a sore punishment is coming. Her devils are dead and no mimicry of a good housewife can cover her evil. She is an animal, bares herself naked like an animal, and is so regarded with the carelessness of morals when considering an animal.

Diego finds tears gushing from his eyes uncontrollably all the way back to the tribe of the Tainos. He finds himself fighting this urge, in crying for a demoness, crying for the one he lay beside and kissed so tenderly—no! He resists his impulse, his desire for sympathy. He wanders toward a palm with all its serrated arms outreaching and grips one frond. This he yanks every which way, finding its green stalk fighting against the strength in his arms. He finds that if he pulls down harshly, gripping the teeth that spread from the edges, his grip may fasten. Feeling the knot of self loathing spreading in him like roots of a great tree cracking his foundation, he hopes to emulate the Franciscan's cure in this time of sorrow. He reacts hysterically, pulling down the skin of the frond, laying his weight upon it, goring his palms and torso as he grips the serrated edge. All life in him is persistent in this wresting match. As the fibers of the trunk give way the length of half a forearm, he sets the muscles of his calf pressing down on his talus, thrashing with his heel as the tendinous flesh of the plants give way. When the fibers remain only a half an inch wide, he cuts it away with his knife by stabbing through violently, gripping the handle with his gored hand.

He grips the spiny palm frond and whips himself across the face for hours at a time. He is forever disfigured. To change it up, he whips across various parts of his body, his chest, his belly, his genitals, and his thighs. He enables the tiny spears to punish him, the way the monks taught him long ago. He lets the weight fall in with the toleration of an expert. Taking in the pain he absorbs, the surging throughout his body begins in the gut and strikes through his lower and upper torso simultaneously. This happens at an uncountable rate, a terrible gnawing occurring in his hands where he bleeds, but in considering how all things are connected in one way or another, he feels the writhing he perceives every half second.

After two days of this, he steps into the tribe full of pride. No one gives him an exclamation of congratulation, to his surprise. Several Taino guards support his body as he stumbles. Common people stand around, feeling pity and worry, wondering what may have happened. They lay him within his old hut upon a bed of leaves, his sense of self having long before left him. In his own mind he is conscious of a swirling of his meat, feeling a shredding never ending. He cannot see, save for a flash occasionally, which is often composed of a face whose features should be recognizable, though he cannot place it. He screams for Procne, but he only sees her as a body torn of life. Questions come of her whereabouts, but he only blathers like a fool. Pandukuli insists on an excursion to recover whatever is left of her, and since Diego only speaks of a small space of land, his hopes of recovering his daughter is feasible

Diego is laid in a cart, while Pandukuli and several of his closest ride on bulls ahead, armed and ready for battle. As they reach the cabin spoken of, Diego shrieks aloud. He sits but does not speak. The caravan disembarks before this shabby construction of poor quality wood. Diego stares within the gaping wide door.

Diego flops off the cart. His serrated rib meat mashes hard into the stones and soil, causing several Tainos to gasp. Still, Diego drags himself on toward the door. The rawness exposed across his belly leaves a sludge of pus-laden blood on the earth. Despite the pain, he sacrifices for his progress, though only in inches. Clawing at the soil, he believes his fight is imperative for a sort of ambiguous heroism. In his mind he is bloodied in battle, sword in hand, the blur in his mind disguising the evil that has ravaged him and his love.

Diego cries, "She is in there! The savages locked her within that chest!"

Pandukuli and his closest rush in, but cannot open the box of wood and leather. Very soon they realize a key is necessary, and look to Diego, who they expect knows more than he has admitted. He points immediately to a cupboard which holds the key.

Procne is found as the lid is lifted. A gust of poison air wafts up. Her form is rigid as death, and all the skin is flaked and dried as an onion. The servants raise her, place her out of the container, and set her just beside it. She is a mollusk, the meat of an ocean nymph. Her hair is plastered tight as one mass of mussel-teeth, stuck to a soul sure on suffocation, too late for this up down children's world. She tries to speak, feebly, though in revealing the inside of her mouth they realize her tongue is only a raw, meaty lump left in the back of her throat. The blood still gathers. They feed her water from casks. The liquid drains but she does not understand the concept, though the physical construct of her being knows a use for it.

Pandukuli points to Diego's pitiful form and declares, "This is not the way of the Carib! This is the way of a coward! Our people will hear of his crime and I will slice out his guts myself!"

The march stops at an in-between point one day's walk before where Pandukuli has stationed himself and the settled people. Procne, despite the torture she received, hangs on to life. Diego latches by her side, sticking to the story that Carib committed the horrors she underwent.

Resting on a bed of leaves, she endures a day-long labor and births a son small in size. Diego is beside himself with pride and joy. He cleans the newborn, and not long after, lies beside Procne, cuddling their baby.

Upon reaching the outskirts of the village, Pandukuli senses something is amiss. Within him the fear had been building since the morning the day before. He calls for the train of people and wagons to stop. He ventures forth on his own, wandering with a clouded mind and a limp due to the worsening of his illness. A sturdy servant rushes to him and supports his wavering weight. Gazing across the landscape, where there was once the fervor of a happy people, are now mounds of the dead. More are being carried and dropped into massive pits all the time. In other places, full mouths burst flames as if something had bored these holes into an inhospitable underworld. The smoke rises as a vortex from each, tornadoes born from the earth bearing the yellow light. The matter that is burned, the oils and the gasses, rise to mix with the clouds. Pandukuli's heart beats faster, more so every step, as he senses his populace reeks of burnt hair and human flesh.

As the winds change, he feels the smoke ride down his nostrils and the heat swim past his skin. There in the square, where the recent ceremonies of joy were held, he sees his eldest son Zinato and Kadesh draining the blood out of the neck of a bull into a great stone bowl created for the purpose. Beside them lie three other bulls flayed, the flesh being cut free and placed in bins. When these are full, they are dumped on sacrificial altars in which fires are fed, that pierce through openings and bite at the meat.

Zinato and Kadesh look to Pandukuli. Though this beaten-down chief is still very much capable, in the eyes of the superstitious the weakness of a chief signifies something very obvious: the connection to his weakening health and that of the sickness of the people. The only remedy is to place a fresh, healthy chief in the seat of power, and the only way to do that is to remove the former from this life.

Zinato's mother, Tureygua, an elite among Pandukuli's numerous wives and concubines, steps forth. She calls for her servants to take the arms propping up Pandukuli away. The chief is left by himself, among the tunnels of smoke from the burning cattle and Taino people. His mind fades and his knees weaken. A knee drops to the floor of mud brick. At this, the attendants, numbering in the dozens, take his quivering body and drag it to a construction much like that which was built to collect blood during sacrifices. Two pillars of stone stand tall on each side of a molded bowl. Pandukuli is too weak to fight as his arms are pulled and tied harshly. He knows what is to come. He accepts it the best he can. It is the way things have always been, how he gained his position. A chief must be healthy, no question.

Kadesh approaches, his face bearing no sign of emotion. It is his sign of life and vigor, the purposeful contrast of the weak one soon to die. Here is nothing of ill intent shown on his body, presented to the people, to the chief as a salve, so he may leave this plane of existence without, or rather, with a minimal sense of vindictive intent from those he cares about. Kadesh slips free the ceremonial knife shaped from an amber-colored, transparent stone, glowing with more life the closer he approaches the flames before the sacrifice. As the fire takes its form under the legs of the Chief, Kadesh's appearance changes to that of a kind, loving elder. He radiates care and adoration as he chants a tune full of buzzing, vibratory utterances, while slipping in the skinny knife, in and out, in and out, sawing through the meat under Pandukuli's ribcage, slipping the blade in and cutting through the rubbery arteries.

The Chief takes the pain as proudly as he can, attempting to transport his mind as he witnessed his father do. Forcing himself to indulge in the beauty of the shape of the green hillsides of his country, the heart drops free. He kicks and convulses as the blood gushes and his brain begs for the red bath. Pandukuli is soon gone, yet the body still shakes, spilling its overflow into the fire, clothing him in a cloud of darkness. The people fall into a catastrophic upset. Zinato calls for his father, though it was him that instigated the testing of his weakness. His wives give in to weeping, and the common Taino wail in this loss of their closest love.

# 41

# The Source of Lucy's Suffering

IT HAS BEEN RAINING for the past eight days. Thomas returns to Lucy after spending his waking hours filling pits with the dead and torching the bodies. He lies beside her and notices her expression blank with varying states of exhaustion and grief under the guise of stability. Moisture in the air causes his nostril to tingle, so he sniffs suddenly and rubs the sensation out.

"Do you feel any better today?" he asks her.

She lies motionless as always, trying to not let his pondering let loose too many black thoughts at once.

He goes flat on his back as she is, his gaze aimed at the pinnacle of the hut's dome, all the fibers spiraling from this stone-in-the-pond. His eyes dance over this simple wonder he never noticed before. The skeleton framework of the palm leaves dressed in the interwoven dried grass seems a beauty, as when viewing the form of nature's creations glazed with wind and light. This roof is of nature as well, but is also crafted with the care and skill acquired from numerous generations of Taino, the ones who placed these now likely deceased. Thomas thinks upon these folk, their vibrant energy, their amazing spirit, how it has affected him in these past years. He is always in a state of shifting opinion about them, between awe and revulsion.

"They are a dying race," Thomas says.

Lucy coughs in order to speak. She lets out a, "Hm?" cocking her head toward him ever so slightly.

"There will be very few of them left. So many leave us every day."

The rain provides a patter, a percussion which accompanies their meditation. A chill blows in, causing her to roll over and lay her arm over Thomas for warmth. She presses her cheek into his chest, resting her head on his shoulder, gripping him tighter.

They lie still for a time, both collapsing into sleep. When Thomas awakes it is still light out, the rain pelting the soil harder than before. He feels her breath on his neck, feeling a great comfort, especially after seeing constant horrors on a daily basis. It is a relief to him that she is opening up to him, especially after being so bereft of spirit for so long. He wishes for peace, to leave her be and to soak in this moment for as long as circumstances allow, but he notices something alarming about her odor. It is something he cannot put out of his mind now. It chokes him. The stench would not be so terrible, as he admits that he is not the cleanest representative of humanity, but her smell is so foul it is on a whole other level. It is reminiscent of a gangrenous wound. He worries that a part of her is dying.

Thomas shakes her gently in a hope to capture her attention, yet retain the calm that has been created. He knows his questions may greatly shatter this, but he believes there may be something serious which is not being properly addressed. Her eyes open slowly and a look of confusion, a "Why did you wake me?" expression shows on her face.

"Sorry, dear."

"What is it?"

He attempts a careful choice of words, "I noticed something. A—are you well?"

At first she has no idea of what he is getting at, and simply nods her head.

"What I mean is—are you well down there?" he says patting on his own crotch.

She hides her eyes in his shoulder. She utters nothing, only breathes, revealing great contemplation.

He allows her peace by remaining silent for a time, but rouses her from a half sleep with his words, "Can you tell me?"

As his questions open up visions and feelings in her which she had dammed up, tiny bits of moisture develop from her tear ducts. She swallows hard more frequently and breathes deeper the more the sadness is released. Tears stream from her eyes from a vision transfixed into nothing, instead giving way to her focus on images of terrible memories passing by her mind's eye.

Thomas asks no more questions. He leaves her be and they lie together through the night.

Lucy awakes and peers outside, surprised to have a break from the rain. A bit of yellow pokes through the haze of clouds. She rocks Thomas' shoulder and his eyes open just to the point of being slits. He sits up, noticing the brightness outside, and looks to her with one chosen eye expanding just wide enough to see. His hair is a mess.

"Good morning," he says.

"Good morning," she replies, fighting to be stoic. "I'm ready to show you."

"All right," he says, at first not understanding what she meant. His mind is still getting used to being out of the dream world.

"Outside," she says standing. "It's out there."

"It?" Thomas says standing, quite perplexed.

They step out together. As they make their way from the hut she corrects herself. "Her… Bridget, I mean."

Thomas is at a total loss. Lucy freezes, shuddering, yet trying with great effort to smile and keep her emotions in.

"Our daughter. We have a daughter," she tells him.

Thomas lightly rests his arms around Lucy. He cannot think of what to say, in that it is strange that she doesn't make much of a show of what should be an overwhelming moment.

"I couldn't tell you," she says.

They are both absolutely defenseless. All the sorrow of their lives pours forth as they grip each other in the tightest embrace. A light sprinkle of rain begins and covers them both.

She tells him, "I'm sorry. I can't think of touching the place where she came out. I know it smells."

"Don't worry. I just thought you were sick. Everyone's dying, you know?"

"Her blood is still on me. It hurt really bad one day. I just laid there and knew something was wrong. I kept bleeding and I had to push her out."

She takes him to a clearing in which five old trees sit side by side in the shape of a crescent. There, in the muddy earth, before the center tree, a rectangular, wooden box stands half out of the soil, crooked with its lid unhinged out of place, revealing just a crack of the darkness within. It must have been carried out of its original position by the days of constant flooding.

"You didn't have to keep this in!" he says embracing her full of dread, his eyes tingling. "I will be there for you. Never again like before, you hear me?"

She nods, looking into his eyes.

"I'm growing up," he says. "This isn't fair for you. You put your trust in me and I—"

"I asked for it," she says.

"No, you haven't. You did nothing to deserve—"

"I've been a bad person, bad to you. After this I can't be a little girl anymore."

The rain drenches them they and continue to hold each other. Thomas looks to the box holding the little girl of his that didn't make it far into life.

"This isn't right for her. She needs a proper burial at least."

Thomas kneels in a spot of mud to the right of where the box lies and pulls out handful after handful of mud. The job is not hard, for everything is saturated. His hands work as shovels, creating a hole that soon reaches the depth of a foot, then two. He pulls out thicker mud as the rain falls in. Lucy looks upon his effort and is proud to have him. Half his torso now in the hole, his fingers scrape, making grooves, loosening more and more that is released and tossed out. The hole is about four feet deep.

"I'd better stop before too much rain gets in," he says.

Despite the reservations he has of touching the box, he knows he must. He digs his fingers through the mud and wrenches it. Water tinted with red sits within the box to the brim. Small fragments of material from the placenta float on top. Thomas pours this into the hole, then when the trickle stops he closes the lid and latches it, setting the box carefully at the bottom.

Thomas mutters aloud saying, "She is unblemished. Never will she suffer as so many do." He presses his hands upon a hill of mud, but stalls and says, "Can we really pour mud over her?"

Lucy unfastens the necklace she wears around her neck which bears a black cross. She reaches down into the hole and places the object carefully at the level of where the head should be. "So she can go to heaven," she says.

She pushes an armful of mud into the hole, covering the cross and the box. They both perform this act, while patting down the top every now and then to make sure it's compact. They end with a mound pressed down with shoe prints, then smoothed over by hand.

Their hearts are heavy, but they are getting numb to the thoughts and the emotional pain that is swollen in their chests.

"We need to bathe," Thomas says. "It will do us good."

She nods in agreement. They return to their hut to get the jobo fruit they will use as a cleanser, then go off among the trees and strip.

A weight is released in the removal of clothing. For a time they do nothing but embrace, body against body, while being pelted by the water. Thomas reaches down, takes a fruit in hand and rubs it between his palms, working up a lather. He reaches around her back and scrubs, then in the armpits and all over her arms, causing her to crack a smile and jump a little due to ticklishness. He kisses her a few times on the neck. They scrub each other's hair, working out all the caked dirt and other things such as small sticks and leaves.

They continue this way, kissing a little, recalling how long it's been since they could bear their hearts in this manner. He kneels down and washes from her female parts what material has not yet washed away. Blood had run down her legs and dried. Her pubic hair is plastered with it. He takes his time to help this to loosen without being too rough. She stands shivering with her arms crossed, a bit shy in having that part of her seen in such a condition.

# Revenge

WHILE THE TAINO GATHER in their hastily made housing, they are pelted with cloudburst. The enemy could be there any moment. That fear dominates the annoyances and miserable situation of having stones in one's back each night and near constant showers soaking everything. Underlying everything is, once again, the lack of food. The bulls and cows taken along to their new village, out of desperation, are killed and distributed. Every action begins to lose its meaningfulness as the rituals of everyday life are more and more neglected. Hope is a luxury that can barely be recalled when hearts have sunk so low.

Every day, every hour, Procne's boy cries. Diego gave him a Christian name, Gabriel, but she does not call him that unless Diego is around. The presence of this man, this creature who ravaged her and carries no heart of worth in his chest, pulls the life from her. No matter how hard she tries, she cannot love this child. It is of the seed and carries the face of the one she despises. It is not her son. Nursing it is a chore, and its cries she quickly dampers with a cloth stuffed in its mouth. No remorse at all.

Assawako comes to visit, and they have a friendly chat as best they can, despite Procne's gored tongue. Of course, the subject of Diego's cruelty is expressed in the form of Procne's furious sign language, of her time stuffed in the chest, cutting down her range of expressions to little more than showing rigid hate. Gabriel cries through the cloth.

Hours later, Diego enters the doorway of leaves, greeting his wife. "Where are you?"

"Here," Procne says, approaching with her sister.

"Where is my son?" Diego asks.

"He is sleeping," Procne mumbles with her tongueless mouth.

Diego relaxes, sitting in the sole chair they have.

"What is that smell?" he asks.

"It is a share of the pig caught last week," Assawako says.

"It is lovely."

"It was a noisy pig, a very ugly sort, but just enough fat," Assawako says.

"It's being fat which counts for a pig," Diego says, settling in his chair, resting his forearms behind his head in a nice stretch.

"It's been simmering for some time," Assawako says. "Care for some?"

"Yes, I'm starving," Diego says, sitting straight now, facing the small table made from freshly cut forest wood.

A shallow tin dish is placed in front of Diego, which contains chunks of meat along with greens from the forest and a swirling pool of fatty broth.

Diego sips the flavor from the water, then lifts a chunk into his mouth. He chews, delighting in the amount of fat in each bite.

"This doesn't taste like any pig I've ever had," he begins. "It is the best, I have to say. Not rough or strong in any way," he says, chewing two morsels, one on each side of his mouth.

From the cooking pot Procne lifts the gelatinous head, the hair still hanging from the dome of her son's scalp. Sticking it on a metal spike, she places it on another thin tin serving dish, distended facial features and all, and steps forth with her sister and places it before Diego. There they stand to glimpse the face of the man as he registers what he had just eaten. Still on his tongue, the lipids draining down his throat, the initial chunks of the boy he loves already digesting. The eyes stare gray, cooked through, of he who Diego created through brutality, and led to this horrible end through the unjust torture of the innocent mother. While he is still locked into a chamber of shock, the sisters shoot out the doorway.

Procne and Assawako charge across the plain, away from Diego with all their might. Thomas and Lucy cross a parallel direction, always assaulted by trees and foliage. They see the girls up ahead for a while, until they disappear into a clearing. Diego cuts through after them, hacking into another cluster of trees with his saber, briefly jerking his head back to see Thomas and Lucy following.

They all thrust into the arms of flora growth, diving under and around, leaping over stone and green-plume. Diego's silver blade is out before him, hacking at the vegetable life he comes upon in hopes to murder the slayers of his boy.

Thomas finds himself caught in a web of winding branches. In between he sees Diego closing in. He's pressed himself up against the girls. They must be saved, but Thomas knows not how he can make use of himself. The girls back away closer and closer to a ridge that is only backed by blue sky. It is a drop-off that declines sharply into jagged, tooth-like rocks, pushing out of the sea below. There the sisters pray as heartfelt as any he had ever seen. Thomas, frantic, glances at Lucy, and shoves himself through every abrasive, gnawing bit of friction, and though bloodied from face to shin, stands before Diego.

Thomas grips his blade with all his body and mind can focus into the tendons of his hands and arms, though the girls are gone. Diego has gone white-faced, staring into the sky above him, as two small birds, a swallow and a thrush, struggle to beat their wings. After several unsteady dips, they adjust and flutter off.

Diego sinks the tip of his sword into the loose soil. He tells Thomas, "I wasted my time. My love waited for me, yet I violated that. I hurt her in my show of emotion—in my show of my blade. I killed myself that day and ruined many more."

Diego glares his eyes and lobs his body headfirst, blade in hand, off the cliffside to crush and decompose alone on the wave-worn cove, hundreds of feet below.

# Despondency

**T**HOMAS DECLARES TO ALL, "I have decided... that there is nothing left for us here. And we must be on our way, back to our ship."

A look of surprise shows on the faces of many. One young man approaches Thomas and says, "Wait just a little more... please. My love... she's sick and needs to recover."

"Your place is with her," Thomas tells him. "I brought you all here so that we could find some sort of new life. If you've found that, regardless of terrible things that have come to pass... you're free to stay or come with me. But we're leaving in a day's time. That's all."

Thomas turns and leaves the anxious crowd.

Later that afternoon, Agustín peeks his head inside the opening to Thomas' hut and asks, "Hello? Mind if I—?"

"Come! Sit down," Thomas says as he sees his face. "I'm just rolling up this cassava," he says, referring to his small, personal ration.

"That's not enough to survive on," Agustín says, kneeling so he can see Thomas eye to eye.

"So you heard we're leaving?" Thomas asks him.

"Yes, and I will be by your side."

"I'm surprised," Thomas says. "I can't imagine you anywhere else."

"I can't help them any longer. They've... closed up to me."

"What I feel is the... depression. It just goes on and on."

"Yes. And whatever direction they're headed. They've got to figure it out themselves." Agustín stands and heads for the opening. They each nod and Agustín says, "See you in the morning," as he exits.

Thomas dwells on the Taino all alone in his hut. In his hate for society he had hoped to find a people free of corruption. In the end, the Taino proved to be all too human. He feels the most intense fear welling in his throat, in his chest, drowning in the feeling in knowing he is soon to enter society again.

Benjamin asks Thomas where Assawako is. He does not appreciate Thomas' insufficient answer, that she and her sister transformed into small birds and fluttered to freedom. He perceives it to be an attempt to save him the grief of hearing gruesome details, though he repeats his question again and again, more earnestly each time. Quickly he loses all respect for the cruel false-empathy Thomas is fronting as truth.

"Enough of the act," he tells him.

They have known each other for a long time, and he knows truth is valued in him more than a peaceful state of mind. It enrages Benjamin as they are ready to set off into the forest to leave the Taino forever. He begs him for the truth, for a moment that he may be directed to the spot of her resting place. He only wishes to see the burial mound, or the remains, as he suspects the girl he loved met an unfair and violent end.

Diego's image presses itself on his mind. The one he introduced to Thomas; the one that led him here to his love; the one who abused Assawako's sister Procne—the negligence of allowing such wrongness to continue led them to dull the truth in their minds, and so evil went on being acted in complete freedom. The cruelty overflowed to such a degree, effecting so many more, leaving their lives torn, ravaged.

"Show me where she is," Benjamin begs Thomas, as the party steps deeper into unfamiliar territory. "Did you bury her?" Benjamin asks, begging for some kind of answer. "She deserves dignity."

He imagines his love cut through by the blade of that maniac. He imagines so many scenarios. All fall into his mind at once like a bladder full of liquid, his brain overfilled. If Diego is gone, then what occurred was not something soft and innocent. Benjamin closes his eyes, lets his companions wander ahead, and lets his guilt attach itself to a vision of her.

Their time living amongst the natives of this environment gave them great ability to forage. Therefore, their travel is survivable. Still, the leather wrappings tied around their feet do not make for suitable shoes. The moisture turns the flesh between their toes to mush. Rot afflicts many. Mosquitoes pester them incessantly, and soon disease takes the life of at least one a day. They must keep moving. To be soft out here is to be prey for that beast known as wild nature.

After around a month of traveling, the terrain gives way to a series of hills that provide new perspective and a drier environment than the humid layer under the canopy of trees. A gorgeous valley winds like an oak leaf no more than a mile out. A deep grey-blue filters through silky undulating clouds that gradually drift overhead. The rain that falls is pleasant. Not far along is it till another valley comes into view. But this one has been planted with sugarcane. The pitch-black skin of slaves can be spotted right away. They hack at the full grown stalks and pile them high. As Thomas and his companions wander further along the ridge, the great number of people at work comes into view. The black and milky brown forms work along the ridge of the crop in a winding line as far as eyes can see.

Agustín stops suddenly. As others pass by him he calls, "Thomas!"

Thomas turns and soon backtracks to see what the priest wants.

"Here," Agustín says, handing him his compass. "I'll not be needing it."

Thomas says, "I see…" knowing just what he means.

Agustín says, "You will have no trouble. The ocean is north, and from there head west to the fort."

"Yes. We will be fine."

Agustín asks, "Did you find here what you were looking for?"

"No… but I'm forever changed."

"I as well. And it will continue…" Agustín says.

"Farewell then," Thomas says, and with a nod the priest makes his way down slopes and ledges to the floor of the jungle.

It is one more month of continuous travel till they reach the sea. Following the coast, eventually they reach the fort which their ship is docked at. It appears in the distance, and their minds struggle with the idea of returning to the complex business of the civilization they were once immersed in. Such fatigue and sickness must be contended with first. While being nursed, or rather, allowed to lie and recover, all at once the dread of the crowds, of the confines of the instituted order, of the chaos of money and labor come in remembrance to Thomas. Also, the luxury they may have in the way of variety, of foods, of sights and sounds, of notions that have come to society while they were absent fill him with want.

They feel weary in greeting the Spanish soldiers. A week is spent before they are privileged to talk to the man of authority, and already they are sick of the feeling of being confined, by being forced into a set of rules that are made with little care for sense or logic.

In the meantime, Thomas brings further annoyance as he begs to ask for assistance in drawing up a navigational plan. A number of different maps are compared in order to study rough streaks and swirls of ink drawn through the blue Atlantic in order to designate which direction is best to flow with the currents.

In great anxiety Thomas and Lucy sit before the gruff secretary. Two coal-black sets of handcuffs hang from a nail on the wall behind him, tools of the trade for this fort serving as a pirate prison. He sneers at them and begrudgingly shuffles through papers scattered on his desk to locate the notes that prove the Blood of God to be theirs. Finally the forms are authorized and they are told to take their grime-caked boat and leave at once.

All there is to do is wait on this span across the ocean, and that is a horrible thing for a team already in foul spirits.

The boat reeks. The moldy wood and decomposed material have to be scraped by all. This business of lifting putrid material is not so bad when compared to the alternative: going mad with nothing to distract the mind at all. At least this distraction is ever present.

Benjamin never recovers from his sorrow in losing his love. He asks Thomas countless times—and Lucy too.

"You think I can't take the truth?" Benjamin hollers.

His days before knowing her were often carried along, softened by the saving grace of alcohol. It caught his depression and transformed it into joviality, but now he has become a great barrel of a man, a reservoir in which their vats of rum flowed into. Once he was a shy but cantankerous boy. Now he is nothing. The character that carried his companions through hardship due to his steadfastness, trustworthiness, and kind nature, has disappeared. He is now a waste.

His skin is baked daily. Red, deep red. It has an oily shine and is a taut, wrinkled, blistered-over, full body sore. When approached and told to rest on his mat in the deck below, he thrashes at the incoming sound, only wanting his misery. In being continuously drunk to the point of nausea, his hair from the top of his head to that which is sprouted from his face is knotted and matted with gelled remains of rum and saliva. The constant skin sensation he feels is absolutely on par with the feeling felt when one is tortured by having a red hot iron rod pressed into their skin. All of the self-hatred, the numbness, the thriving on pain... Nothing is more true to him now.

All of life is a lie, and only pain is honest. Such is the sort of idea that he repeats to himself. Only this pain can help him understand what Assawako and Procne underwent. Most of the time his thoughts are nil, the self-abuse arising from sub-rational bursts of anger. At other times, moments of clarity flow through, bringing slivers of catharsis. He repeats the words and views the images that shift in this way. He dedicates this funeral service in the form he feels is appropriate. Absolute annihilation of comfort and logical thought is needed at times for him to reach out and mourn properly.

# 44

# The Floating Coffin

WAVES OF DEPRESSION wash over the crew. They drink warm beer and rum to numb the pain of boredom. First they sit in their soggy, sea drenched shoes. Then they go barefoot, many of them suffering from splinters implanted from the long neglected deck. The agony is near intolerable. Full grown, they still complain like babies, unable to take the torture of the wooden quills boring deeper and deeper into the tendons in the bottom of their feet.

Benjamin plays a slow, somber song on his old lute and quietly sings along. The crew stare blankly into the waves, deeply entrenched in their inebriation. They lie passed out on the ground as a frail, bony companion whistles a tune. They all cover their ears and yell at him to stop.

For months it goes like this. For months there is nothing much to stimulate the mind, until the day a lookout hollers for all to hear, "A ship! I spy a ship out yonder!"

Thomas takes out a telescope and sees the enormous vessel.

"This fat beast shall be our prey," Thomas says, relieved.

Several minutes later, they near enough to see it clearly. It is a giant barge—a slave ship.

"Are they blind? Why do they not fire?" Benjamin says.

The sails are secured and they slowly glide toward the slave ship. Benjamin guides the rudder so the boarding can be done gracefully. High above in the rigging, ropes are tossed, secured with hooks to the top of the gigantic hull. Thomas and Benjamin shimmy across first, grasping the sidewall of the neighboring ship. They then climb aboard, followed by the rest of the crew.

Twenty slavers sit nauseated on the top deck. Thomas' crew steps around them, resulting in only slight glances. Vomit covers many of them, as well as much of the deck.

"Toss them over," Thomas orders.

Teams of two work to lift members of the sickly crew and toss them overboard. Most are consumed immediately, never to be seen again. Two weakly wave their arms for a slightly longer period, but sink regardless.

Entering the deck below, the crew of the slave ship lies about on the floor. Thomas and his companions step over them as they cross through. They wander from one end of the dining hall to the other. They pass three slavers sitting at different spots at a table in a sickly state with bowls of soup before their faces. Vomit is caked all around. They descend the stairs. Two lie dead. A wide room stands before them, visible through an open door. They step through.

Four dead slaves lie limp, still chained to their stations. Their skin is dried like leather. It seems their labor was to wash cloth. A long tablecloth lies in a pile next to buckets of water harboring islands of mold. Maggots churn inside a gaping mouth. Flies hover around the head and tunnel through rotted-out eye sockets. Thomas and the others move swiftly, for the stench and the awful visual horror overcome them.

They pass through a series of doors and rise up a set of stairs, coming into what appears to be the slave captain's main hall. A grand table laid with a partially eaten pig swarms with flies. There is porridge of some sort, and various other dishes that appear to have been, at one time, filled with delicious sauces and sweet meats, but are now all dried through and covered with a shell of green and white molds. A golden-baked goose, its hind quarters partly eaten, reveals a writhing mass of maggots in the sunken husk of the bird. Spider webs cover the length of the room. Flies are spread throughout in an unbelievable number, all sucked dry. One of the killers, a fat, eight-legged fellow, makes for cover.

The heavy, fibrous webs are torn down and set aside. Dozens of spiders of various varieties make their escape to cover across the planks. Through the clearing, as if prisoners in the web-womb, sits a wretched half dozen sucked-up figures of humanity. In the center of the cluster sits what appears to be the captain. He would be deemed dead by most, in that he seems to be without the slightest animation. Though, if one concentrates hard enough, one may see his chest rising and falling slightly. Their eyes stare straight ahead, paying no attention to the intruders into their hovel. Flies eat away at their skin, boring into deep, red crevices, most likely preparing these hosts to be a nursery for their young, similarly to the carcasses at the dining table. Swollen red spots dot their clam-skin, which do not seem a reaction of fly nips, but of sickness.

A sailor at the left of the captain has a deep gash in his shoulder, revealing the horrible redness of the meat inside. Every rare moment, he goes into a convulsion to shake the congregating flies free. It does seem as if all of them are suffering from a battle. They are all severely cut up and bandaged.

"How can the food be more rotted than their wounds?" Thomas asks rhetorically. "The time it took for the spiders' webbing to become so concentrated and the extent of the rot that has overcome the food… Their wounds are not so old as all that. They must have, in their madness, struck at each other, then set themselves down in agony and futility."

The captain's eyes move to Thomas under his stringy, greasy hair, and his broad-rimmed hat. The eyes freeze and the captain's breathing becomes heavier. The sunken, bony jaw quivers as if he were trying to speak. To the disbelief of Thomas' crewmates, Thomas steps forward before this decrepit skeleton. Near death, breathing out poison air from dehydrated, papery organs, Thomas leans in to hear. The long, wild beard shakes, as his lip vibrates like one lost in a Baltic winter. He is trying to make out forms of speech. Thomas is almost touching him as he hears the struggled-for words sputtered, "Do not think you may be so smug."

"I believe I can," Thomas says.

Feebly trembling, the captain is overwhelmed by this small exertion, and feels as if his soul is crushed in feeling so pressed down by Thomas' vigor. After a spell of quivering, he manages to steady his lips to mouth the words, "You may judge me, but you are not so different."

He is lost to the world.

"Is that so?" Thomas says, gripping the captain by his shoulder, ripping him from his seat. Immobile, the weight of the human frame falls hard on the bony neck like a duck carcass tossed into a garbage heap. The body writhes like an injured bug, unconsciously twitching, limbs in motion in no rational manner. Blood and mucus drains out of the orifices of the face, running in an irregular stream, flowing with the rocking of the ship.

A bewildered sailor of Thomas' crew bursts into the room, screaming, "Come now! You have to see this!" The sailor rushes from one end of the hall to the other, waving them on. Thomas moves slowly behind.

"Slow down. What could it be?" Simon asks.

After following him to the lowest section of the ship, he opens a door, bewildered at the wretched smell that leaps forth. Everyone holds their noses and mouths. Four vomit immediately. Thomas' eyes water as he spits and dry heaves. In between gags he complains, "The deepest bowels of hell have spewed forth, surely!"

They cautiously step closer and closer toward the open door.

Wooden supports hold more than four-hundred chained Africans. Fecal matter, vomit, and urine fill the floors and drain down the beams. Feeble black bodies lie chained in small openings. Visual estimations find around three-fourths of them to be dead. Many peer out from their slot weak and helpless. Many dead lie beside the living.

"What do we want with this floating coffin?" Thomas asks, sickened terribly.

Simon says hesitantly, "We are low in numbers, Captain."

"We bring these cursed souls on our ship; we inflict ourselves with the demons they were born with," Thomas says.

Simon stares at a corpse covered in maggots. He says, "It is no matter to me."

"It should be interesting to allow them revenge," Thomas says. "Let them loose to torture their capturers. Let them choose a captain for themselves and find their way home."

Simon holds back from vomiting. Thomas ponders his thoughts intently, saying, "And choose some healthy ones to scrub our deck."

# 45

# Thomas the Tyrant

**T**WENTY SLAVES SCRUB THE DECK and work various chores. Simon and three others watch them with pistols at their sides. The heat beats down heavily. Thomas keeps guard, yet appears delirious. He loses his balance, catching himself on his knee. A slave with an Arabic notch on the bridge of his nose scrubs the deck strangely, as if sick. Simon taps him with his stick, but his quality of work still does not improve. He bends before the slave and pats around a bulge in the man's pocket. He slips his hand in and retrieves a stale piece of bread. Simon hits him with a stick and yells furiously. Thomas steps forward and asks, "What did he do?"

Simon says, "He's a thief," holding forth the bread.

"Stealing?" Thomas asks. "Get the whip."

The slave is tied to the main mast. Thomas whips his back furiously. The slave wails in terrible pain as the tongue flicks in faster than the eye can see, drinking up the layers of skin and meat. He whips and whips, his arm arcing hard. Thirty lashes. Forty. The slave hangs limp against the rope in a semi-conscious state. Blood gushes in cherry rivers. Thomas takes a cup out of a crewman's hand and spills out the ale. He collects the cascading blood from the slave's back in the cup. To receive more, Thomas presses the lip into a gash. Milking the black skin with the metal rim, he presses harder until the wound opens wide, like a blooming flower, exposing the red rawness inside. Thomas seems drunk, lost in ecstasy. The gaping wounds, so numerous, lie open and seeping like a rugged mountainside, the craggy terrain moistened with the flow of great waterfalls.

Thomas, in a trance, turns with a blank stare and approaches the door to his quarters. He drips some of the blood onto the door and smears it with his hand. He then pours the blood onto his shoulders and over his head.

"Blessed be God!" Thomas bellows. "Full of everlasting love. Thou shall not steal. Did no one tell you of the laws of Moses?!"

No one dares approach him.

Thomas falls to his knees and stares into the sun with his hands folded in prayer, smiling giddily. The crew, including the black crewmen, all kneel, fold their hands, and stare at the sky as Thomas does. Thomas allows a slight giddy laugh to break through and screams into the sky, "Praise be to our God who provides such a pleasurable life!"

Lexington stands on the fore of his ship as two merchant ships approach. A tubby merchant waves to him. Lexington calls for a crewman to climb to the top of the mast and wave a flag about so both ships may know they may approach.

As the ships come closer, the merchant loudly says, "We are carrying gold to England. Would you serve to protect our Queen's property—these are not safe waters at all!"

"Quite true! I happen to be pirate hunting as we speak. Thomas is the name of the ruffian who is said to haunt these waters," Lexington tells him.

Lexington mutters something to one of his sailors, then turns back to the tubby merchant saying, "If you like, you may accompany us for a time."

Admiral Constantyne hangs on the side of his ship. He appears very haggard and shows the signs of old age: deep set lines around his eyes and an unmistakable feebleness in his limbs. The wind blows through his gray locks of hair as he stares diligently into the sea. The crewmen show great signs of fatigue. The sun blares hot upon them as they fan themselves. Several hang weary onto the edge of the ship. Some sit or lie down and drink. A morose sailor approaches the

Admiral and nervously says to him, "They grumble incessantly. We have been out to sea far too long."

The Admiral clenches his teeth slightly and says, "I will hear no such talk."

"Be sensible!" the morose sailor says.

The Admiral turns suddenly and places his pistol against the morose sailor's head. He announces to all, "Any who find this voyage cumbersome shall be relieved of his burden—and shall be sent to the next world!"

Thomas stands in the doorway next to an agitated sailor with bloody gums. Several lie in their beds, moaning in pain.

"Captain, we need a doctor—a real doctor!" the agitated sailor says desperately.

Thomas appears serious. Finally he speaks, "Yes, you are right. I will seek treatment in haste, though your prayers shall serve you for now."

"Now! Now, you fool! We suffer so!" the sailor says.

Thomas grabs him by the collar and tells him, "I will deal with you soon, don't you worry," and pushes him against the wall. Thomas steps past the sickly fellow. The agitated sailor stalks behind him and says, "It is a strange sickness. Their minds go mad with pain. We bleed constantly from our gums. It is unbearable!"

Thomas turns to him and says, "I sympathize, for I feel it coming on as well."

Thomas peers toward an obese teenager quivering in pain in his bed with a mouth full of blood. Two sickly crewmen emerge from the shadows with drawn swords. Thomas stops, alarmed.

One of them, an angry brute, says, "I propose we elect a captain who will see to our needs."

"What do you intend to do with that blade, sailor?" Thomas asks.

"What I intend you will soon find out," the angry sailor says.

Five more emerge from the shadows, leering at Thomas.

"What a fun game you propose!" Thomas says, letting out a long maniacal laugh. He removes his sword and confronts them. "What I shall find…" Thomas says glaring, "is your blood strewn across this floor here, see? Am I not a worthy captain?"

They take a step back as Thomas grows mad.

Thomas says, "Funny. I never questioned that! Let the strong survive, I say! Ha ha!"

Thomas slashes through the angry brute's throat, spilling much blood, as he tries to block the strike and misses. A shot rings out and bursts into Thomas' shoulder, which gushes blood. Swords tear through the air and rip into Thomas' forearm as he dodges and rolls away.

A blur of blood and steel erupt as the pain-filled screaming clouds the air. A sword breaks through a sailor's gut, spilling out blood like a fountain. He yelps like a beast and falls to his knees. Lucy stands in his place. She holds the handle of the sword lodged into his back and stomps on him, pulling out the blood-drenched weapon, clenching her teeth furiously.

Sailors stand beside Lucy with blood strewn up their arms. Thomas stabs his sword through an attacker's gut and dodges another's blade. Thomas kicks the agitated sailor into the pile of bleeding and dead men.

Thomas orders him, "Move to the top deck immediately."

All stand around the main mast, which the agitated sailor is tied to. Thomas stands stiff with an axe at his side.

"Forgive me Captain," the sailor says. "I am sorry. The sickness went to my head. I did not know what I was doing at the time."

The sailor weeps terribly.

Calmly Thomas tells him, "Compose yourself sailor. You served me well for quite a number of years, though just a moment ago you meant me to die."

Thomas slams the sharp blade through the Agitated Sailor's neck. Blood gushes in great torrents from the body, and from the head as well, as it knocks upon the deck and rolls toward the crowd. The shocked sailors disperse as the head rolls with the rocking of the ship and bleeds. The corpse hangs limp, still tied to the main mast.

# Showdown with Lexington

**B**ENJAMIN NOTICES SOMETHING IN THE DISTANCE. He walks up to the poop deck and takes out his telescope. He sees two merchant ships as well as Lexington's.

"Oy! Ahead lie three vessels!" he calls out.

Thomas approaches him, takes the telescope, and focuses on the details of the ships. He says, "Lower the sails. Ready the cannons, arm yourselves, for this time we fight for real!"

Moments later, the Blood of God approaches Lexington's ship and the accompanying vessels. They are approximately one hundred yards away.

Benjamin asks Thomas, "Are you prepared to kill?"

"If they stand in my way," Thomas says.

"Do not expect them to pause to consider your life. We must do the same."

"I have killed before and I will do it again. It seems this is the life fated for me."

"For me as well."

"Raise the flag!" Thomas yells.

The red flag is raised. He drags Lucy and pushes her into the captain's quarters.

"Stay here," he tells her.

He locks the door and realizes that he is missing a pistol. He pats the holders and scans about, suspecting all.

Thomas' voice calls out to the merchant vessels, "We will not harm you if you surrender immediately! But if you mean to strike at us we shall have no mercy upon you!"

A cannon blasts from the closest merchant ship, dropping far before Thomas'. Another shoots and Benjamin watches it fly, missing the ship just beyond his station.

Storming across the deck, Thomas shouts, "It seems they want a fight—and so we must give them one! Do not fire until I give word!"

The Blood of God sails smoothly.

"Sail around their aft! Let's disable it if we can. A good shot in their hold means no money!" Thomas calls out to Benjamin.

Benjamin yanks the tiller and the Blood of God sails around the back of the merchant ship. Lexington's circles around beyond the other ships.

"Aim!" Thomas howls, waiting for the right moment. He stands solid, watching his opponent like prey. Finally he calls out, "Fire!"

Cannons blast into the aft of the other ship. Figures can be seen scrambling. A hole is broken at the base and water pours in. The ship slowly tilts as it sinks little by little. Thomas' crew erupts in cheer. Fearful hollering is heard across both decks of the merchant ships.

The Blood of God sails toward the second merchant ship. People cling on until the last moment as the first ship sinks. Others leap to the water and cling to their lopsided, bobbing vessel. Lexington's ship sails toward Thomas' and the two come in close contact.

Thomas calls out, "All on the main deck! Prepare for attack!"

Benjamin has a half-filled gun powder bag tied with a lit fuse. He throws it in the middle of the opposing crew. Several scream and leap overboard in order to escape the blast. Others panic and run toward Thomas and the rest. It explodes, decimating many.

Thomas slashes into half a dozen with his sword, flaying body parts and slaying them all. Two sailors surround Thomas. Thomas stabs one in the neck with a knife and Lucy shoots one in the back. Thomas glances at her, overflowing in gratefulness and surprise. She flashes him a grin and says, "You think I can't break a lock?" and takes hold of a blade.

Simon jumps on the other ship and slashes with his shorter sword, stabbing a sailor in the guts. Roger empties out two guns on one sailor, then takes up another set of guns from his side and shoots more at close range while screaming. David jumps over to the other ship and is stabbed through his throat. Blood gushes forth as he screams and falls into the water below.

Thomas cuts through sailors. He swings at two sailors' rapiers, knocking them both down as he sends his sword through one of their skulls. Simon cuts the other sailor's head off. Nightmarish screams gurgle out. Blood covers them all, as well as the deck.

Benjamin strikes with fury, sinking his rapier, piercing body after body. Lexington's marines are no match for his furiousness.

Robert swings at a sailor, but is shot by another. He falls as Benjamin blasts both sailors in their faces. Benjamin grabs Robert and realizes he is alive. Holding him, Robert speaks while struggling for breath, "Glm... No—I didn't even see him. I didn't know it happened till I hit the ground."

As Robert's eyes begin to close, Benjamin speaks from his heart, "You did all you could. You lived a good life. That's all we can ever do."

Amid a swarm of swinging swords, Thomas and Lexington confront each other.

Lexington speaks smugly, "You are despicable."

Grinning, Thomas says, "I know! It is a great life!"

Lexington cuts across the air and Thomas dodges. Thomas stabs and slashes violently with sword and dagger as Lexington blocks each attack with skill. Lexington swings at Thomas' head and Thomas rolls out of the way. Lexington swipes with might and Thomas, on his knees, crosses his blades and blocks the attack.

They both push with all of their strength against the other. Suddenly a dagger pierces Lexington side. His strength is sapped and he stumbles backward. Lexington turns to see Lucy standing before him.

"We came to save you, dear," Lexington says to her, his body wavering. His sword drops from his hand.

"Do you remember me? Let's go home," he mutters as his face loses its color.

She slides out the dagger. It releases dark blood. She then stabs him several times in the gut before he grabs her wrist.

"Let's go," he says weakly. Finally he kneels and settles his back against the gunwale. Fingering the narrow slits across his belly he tells her, "It makes me sad. We've gone through so much to find you."

The boys finish off the remaining sailors and toss them over the edge. The sailors shriek as the fall. A mess of bodies and limbs litter the deck. Blood flows back and forth as the ship rocks. A white flag flies over the last merchant ship in the distance.

Thomas calls to them, "Sail beside us! We will not harm you as long as you lay your weapons down!"

The two ships meet side by side. The losing side stands along the far side of their ship as Thomas' crew boards. Their weapons sit in a neat pile in the center of the deck.

Thomas speaks to them all. "Why would you risk your lives for someone else's gold? Grip a sword with gnarled fingers after laboring long years for another's gain?"

Thomas strolls along the line, continuing, "You may leave as you wish or join us and share in the winnings. It's your choice."

A brief time later, ten sailors from the merchant ship stand lined up on the deck of the Blood of God.

People pour out of the lower levels and see clearly the gore on Lexington's bloodied deck. Women cry as they see the aftermath of the carnage. People from the demolished ship beg for ropes to be dropped, but Thomas denies them for the cannon fire they sent. They swim to the ship covered with blood and attempt to climb. Thomas orders those who scramble to be shot dead.

Thomas speaks to his new crewmen, "You must swear to follow every word I say and dedicate yourself to my ship. And if you steal or commit any sort of crime against this crew you will pay with your life, you hear?!"

"Aye sir!" they say simultaneously.

"Now, help transporting the cargo!" Thomas orders them.

A sailor tugs the material on Admiral Constantyne's shirt. Lexington's ship lies drifting free. Sailing closer, the carnage that took place becomes apparent. The dead line the deck—their soggy, decaying flesh melting off of the bone under the sun's intensity. Even fifty feet away, the stench of the rotting human bodies causes a chain reaction of nausea across the Admiral's ship. Intestines and hacked up limbs ooze blood and other substances. Faces of sailors lie cold on the deck, many still holding the same expressions of horror frozen in death as they were in their last moments of life. Lexington is strapped into the rigging onto a sail with his arms extended against the material as if crucified. Blood is smeared across the white sail. Seagulls snap at each other as they feed from the large hole dripping blood from his gut. His head lies limp, bloated, and morose.

Eyes stare, but not a word is uttered.

# It Unravels

A SLIGHT BREEZE BLOWS OVER THOMAS. He wakes next to Lucy and readies himself, putting on a shirt, a pair of coverings of sheer material over his legs, pulls black pants over and says, "I'll go and observe the activities of those at work."

At once he sees eighteen of his crew, including Benjamin and the slave he whipped, lined shoulder to shoulder across the deck. They stand cautiously at the points of swords extended from a sailor known as Anthony, who seems to have taken a position of leadership, along with four others at his side, and three perched on the poop deck. Half of the blacks are part of this mutiny. Thomas steps out and a shot blasts from up high. The ball collides just before his feet. He jumps back inside at once and takes up his sword leaning against the bedside. He slides the tip in the door's hinge space, letting it close him in.

"What is the matter?" Lucy asks. "Was that a shot?"

"Keep calm and be ready," Thomas says.

Outside, Anthony is heard ordering those at his mercy to head below deck into the sleeping quarters. Thomas takes a key from the back of his wardrobe and locks the door. He sits beside Lucy and strokes her hair.

"Okay!…" Thomas says from behind the door. "Who are you… and what do you want?!"

"I am Anthony! What I want is power—and power I have!"

Thomas asks Lucy, "Do you remember an Anthony?"

She shakes her head.

"Anthony!..." Thomas calls.

"Yes?" Anthony answers.

"So, what do you want? What will you gain being in power?"

Anthony pauses. He discusses his next words with his companions.

Anthony's words suddenly cut sharp, "I… will bring justice back to this ship! There will be no borders of class, besides merit!"

"This isn't fun anymore. It's not worth it," she says.

"I know," Thomas says.

They sit and wait for hours. Every now and then nervousness arises as someone rattles the door and discusses how best to open it. Bodies crash against the wood barrier for hours, then stop, an unsettling experience for the couple within. From Anthony's perspective the takeover has gone quite well, in that he had been successful without needing to take losses.

As the glow of light fades from around the door, Thomas and Lucy know that the entire day has passed. They slip into their sheets, trying not to let anxiety get the best of them. The darkness of night makes the mutiny seem as if it did not mean the threat of murder.

Deep in the heart of darkness, a light tapping stirs Thomas from sleep. He sneaks, closes to the door, lifts the key from the paneling, and asks, "Who is it?"

"Ben," the voice replies. "It's Ben."

Thomas takes the key and turns it practically as slowly as vegetables raise in growth. If only his companion was not of such a large size he would not be such a risk, for Thomas is forced to allow the creaking to resound its full breadth so Ben can enter.

"Tell me," Thomas says.

Short of breath, Benjamin tells him, "When it was still dark they stood in attack formation. We had absolutely no warning, so we were unarmed for the most part, and not mentally prepared to strike back at they who threatened our lives."

"What of the others?" Thomas asks.

"They sit below. No weapons of any sort, not even a pole or eating utensil remains. Their plan was fairly thorough."

"What do you hope to find here?" Thomas asks. "Why not rush the mutineers when they are off guard?"

"We have no—"

"For God's sake, why leave my men while you are still able to lead them?"

"They have no heart. There is no spirit to inspire. That is what opened the others to succeeding at their revolution so quickly."

"What shall we do?" Thomas asks him.

Lucy cuts in, "Whether we fight and die or we drown ourselves, I don't care. I can resist fear longer than any. Let them try me. Either we take up arms with what we can find, or—if we have no courage left—if our spirits are thoroughly eaten by rats, we should die."

"We shall take them now," Thomas says.

"No," Benjamin says, cutting in. He takes Thomas' hand and lays it upon his sleeve.

He feels it is soaked through.

"I was cut, but not badly," Benjamin says. "Most of the blood is that of a lookout's. Even my way here cost the death of a man whose heart's desire is not far off from ours."

"We should not leave," Thomas says.

"Yes, although they are low in numbers, they are well placed. It's not worth it," Benjamin says.

"We have no food and no water," Lucy says.

Benjamin says, "Those who would defend us can only rush out of the long staircase. It is too easy for those guarding the hole to blast through their skulls. They'll be like a hare, yawning and stretching, greeting the morning sun, only to be torn apart by a fox."

Thomas says, "We have no hope then. No matter how many prey run at the predator. They have made us feeble."

"It is as I said," Lucy says. "We must sink ourselves. Fortune is not in our favor, but who cares for the rules? We play this game how we want—shove the pieces off the table. Bore a hole straight through this hull and sink their victory."

Thomas and Lucy are the only ones with daggers in their possession, so they take it upon themselves to press the points into a place halfway between their bookshelf and the border of the room and gnaw the wood away. With overarm chops and deep thrusts, pushing their pelvises and legs, inch after inch is broken through. Benjamin takes over, thrashing at the hole like a mad lumberman.

As exhaustion makes itself known, they push through the sensation that tells them they have no strength left, through all the aches in their muscles, hearts, and lungs. They continue chopping, for it is all they have.

In the morning hours the door is pounded. They continue grinding their hole. The mutineers know not how pounding could be a threat to their goal, so no further action is taken. It is an annoyance and is thought of as nothing more.

Daylight shines through the slits around the borders of the door. Still they grind their weapons, and chop, and jab, until half of a sword may be swallowed. Finally… the whole blade pops through. Air from the deck below streams in. The voices of the men imprisoned there call out.

"Who's poking through my ceiling?" Simon yells.

"It's your captain!" Thomas calls to him through the hole. "At once we need you to—"

"I beg you, Captain, but I must know if Ben is with you!"

"He is, and he's fine."

"Ahh… fuckin' right! Good one, brother!" Simon cheers.

Benjamin climbs over and puts his face to the hole. "Hey!" he yells. As the men below cut in with cheers, Benjamin shouts again, "Simon! You gotta listen!"

"What is it?" Simon returns.

"We gotta make this thing dip. Those fuckers out there have us beat as far as positioning goes. We gotta knock 'em off balance."

"Knock 'em, what? What'ya suppose we—?"

"Just the way we bored to you, friend. I don't suppose you have any source of flame down there…"

"No, of course not. It's like the depths of the underworld."

"Then we'll be descending this single candle to you. Don't you let it snuff out or it may mean our lives."

At that, a shred is stripped from one of Thomas' ragged, old shirts. It's tied to the single candle and lowered into the hole. Slowly Benjamin lets the way and flame scrape past the uneven grooves. There the flicker wavers. Into the darkness, the life of the crew floats in the yellow. It is faint, but alive.

From below it is grasped and calls go out to signal so. All pupils within the hold shrink at the sight of their hope.

From above comes Benjamin's voice, "As I said… We bored to you, now you must bore to the sea. The weight of the water will lay an imbalance upon our enemies that we will take advantage of."

"Yes, Benjamin!" voices calls out, one after another.

Feeling his power diminishing, Thomas pushes Benjamin aside and says, "I believe you have no blades. Axes would be preferable, but daggers will do. In time they'll break to the sea."

Another strip of cloth is cut. With this the daggers are lowered below deck one at a time.

All the while screaming and pounding occurs violently at the door to the captain's quarters.

Every once in a while a challenger or two charges into the hold below. The danger for them is just as much as it is for those below charging upward—so they are murdered with blunt objects. At this failure the assaults stop.

The fire is kindled with scraps and the hole is helped with the daggers. In time smoke lifts up the stairs and those who dare to look in are chased back with jeers and the appearance of blades.

Simon raises his hand, signaling the others to have patience. A pool gathers. The weight amasses, setting the ship off just slightly. The spaces filled with this excess cause the momentum of the vessel to halt. Its aft drops to such a degree that the drag makes movement little more than bobbing.

What was once irritated knocking upon Thomas' door has become a frantic pounding of hard, heavy objects.

Now Thomas, Lucy, and Benjamin are holding on to candle holders implanted into the sidewall. Books drop from Thomas and Lucy's library, as do the fellows outside. The collisions of their bodies sound with booms against the separating wall. Heavy stomps and hollered arguments can be heard outside.

Thomas decides it's time to slip out the key from his pocket and unlock the door. He does so and cautiously slinks out of sight. Taking up his sword, he spears it overhand into the necks of those terrorizing him.

The blood of the mutineers sprays with gravity's help as Thomas strikes wildly, and Benjamin after him. The bodies of those struck spring suddenly through the door into the far wall, crushing. Above Thomas sees the mutiny-men perched high upon the perches of the sails, hanging on for their lives. Everything is on edge. One falls, then another, some breaking limbs. From below, reinforcements take up arms from the injured and deceased and hack through these broken traitors. Shots ring out, each side trading casualties, but the advantage is by far on Thomas' side.

Anthony, seeing his loss is soon coming, falls to his knees. He begs his captain for forgiveness. Thomas drags him by his hair across the deck and into the flooded room.

Thomas screams, "You threaten my friends' happiness?"

Thomas drags Anthony through the dark, smashing his fist into Anthony's face if he ever dare speak. At the end of the hold he shoves Anthony's head under water, despite the thrashing. Into the hole Thomas shoves Anthony's head. The wavering of his hand quits soon after Thomas stomps the neck, crushing the pipes, and lodges his skull firmly in the breach through several hateful blows to the bottom of the jaw.

The body, anchored, floats, and so Thomas takes in oxygen, wading with his head butting against the ceiling as he drifts upward, peeking at his companions and the dead from the angled doorway. He swims, dragging at the water until he can walk. Climbing the length of the hold, he sets to executing the rest of the rebels.

While at this business Thomas speaks, believing the sentiment is unanimous. "We've been out too long. Let's set to fixing that hole properly, and remove the water one bucket at a time, so we may be done with this agonizing voyage. We almost didn't make it this time. Let's get ourselves home before any more chaos occurs."

# 48

# Home at Last

LUCY IS BLINDFOLDED. Thomas holds her close, leading her by the hand. Before her stands a manor house built in an older style, reminiscent of King's College of Old Aberdeen. Oriel windows jut from the stonework, mullioned and framed at the top with a bold white parapet that extends across the length of the uneven sloped roof. Twenty-six acres of gardens and woodland extend from the property which stands atop a prominent hill in town overlooking the seaside.

"What is that?" Lucy calls out. "It's—I smell apple blossoms!"

Thomas removes the blindfold. Lucy smiles with excitement.

"What is this place?" Lucy asks.

"It is our home," Thomas tells her.

Lucy turns around, her eyes gazing in wonder. She kisses him.

In the kitchen a cook teaches a slave woman to boil beef. He stirs a pot of long-simmering stew and adds herbs as she observes. As Thomas and Lucy enter, a nurse approaches Lucy.

"How are you feeling today?" the nurse asks her.

Lucy smiles and says, "I am fine."

"Just tell us if you need anything," the nurse says, meeting another nurse in the drawing room.

Thomas and Lucy ride up a bumpy road in a carriage, crossing the Ayr river over Auld Brig. They pass through the town, waving to all the happy folk who find their Percheron white speckled ponies delightful. They find curiosity in the strange Celtic carvings preserved beside newer constructions. Upon entering a meadow filled with lush, green grass they nod to each other.

"This looks fine," Lucy says to the driver.

"There is a creek. How nice. Driver, please stop," Thomas says.

The driver pulls the reins and the horses come to a stop. Thomas takes a small bowl filled with soup and Lucy carries a cup of apple juice and a blanket. They step over the soft, green grass. Lucy straightens out the blanket and they sit.

Lucy takes the spoon and jabs it in Thomas' mouth. He laughs, trying to keep it in. She attempts to feed him again and he laughs, pushing it toward her. She moves in to swallow it. She peers upward at the gray clouds above.

"Looks like rain," she says.

Benjamin, Simon, and three other of Thomas' friends drink beer at a nearby pub wearing fine clothes. Benjamin downs his empty mug and pats the bar. The bartender fills it, sets a new mug before himself and gulps it down.

"Settle down over there!" the bartender yells to some rowdy fellows in the back.

The three rough-looking sorts from the back stumble to the bartender. The one who seems to act as leader says, "We are sent to find a pirate. Goes by the name of Thomas. Word is he took roost in this town."

Benjamin and Simon look to each other nervously.

The bartender hollers to them, "I haven't seen any pirates, so why don't you calm yourself down?"

"If you see 'em send word out. There is a noose with his name on it," the leader says, stumbling out the door with his mug in hand and companions in tow.

It is raining hard outside the manor. Thomas and Lucy enjoy tea, surrounded by dimness, save for the flicker of firelight. They both sip, feeling carefree. Benjamin steps in with the others, appearing serious. Thomas and Lucy look toward him, surprised.

"What is it?" Thomas asks.

Benjamin whispers in his ear. Thomas jolts and spills his tea in his lap, patting it quickly due to the pain. Thomas stands and says aloud, "Rouse everyone."

They all rush outside into the cold. Rain pours upon the heads of Thomas, his crew, and the black crewmen. Lucy wraps her arms around Thomas and gives him a hard, passionate kiss.

"Do not let him get me," she says.

"I promise."

They embrace as the wind blows and the rain pours hard upon them.

Thomas sails through the stormy night. Nothing can be seen, though as morning comes they spy the Admiral's ship far off in the shipyard. They lie and wait like a leopard, waiting patiently to pounce on their prey. Several ships come and go as the day arrives, and still they wait. Evening comes and Constantyne's ship leaves port.

They follow as the rain crashes down and waves pummel, tossing it about. The sun sets. For three days they follow like this. For three days they wait for the right moment.

Finally, in the darkness of the third night of pursuit, Thomas gives the order to close in. They near the Admiral's ship, reaching about a fifty yards distance, becoming only visible as the lightning strikes.

Cannons blast from the Admiral's ship and soar toward Thomas'. The slave with the Arabic notch tackles Thomas to the ground as a cannonball flies over them and mutilates a sailor's face behind them. Thomas looks to the slave, astonished.

"Fire!" Thomas roars.

Cannons blast from Thomas' ship into the Admiral's. Chain shots spin through the air, tearing up the sails. Thomas' crew cheers all at once. Those on the Admiral's ship are seen scurrying about.

Thomas' ship halts suddenly with a great crash. Wood cracks at the base. The crew flies about, colliding hard into the solid structures of the ship. A gunner flies and collides into the next cannon over. Another flies off of the ship and is swallowed by the waves. Thomas runs toward Benjamin at the tiller and screams as loud as he possibly can, "Move it! What is the problem?!"

Benjamin spins the tiller, but the ship doesn't move. The sails blow in the wind, but the ship does not move.

"No! How can this be?!" Thomas screeches madly, tearing at his hair.

Voices call, desperately hollering to hear information on who fell off the craft.

They must wait out the storm on the ship, hearing the boards crack more and more, all while Constantyne is out there in the darkness somewhere.

# Iona

THOMAS' CREW ASCENDS THE STAIRS to the top level and looks out. A lush, green landscape stands before them. The ship's hull sits planted on a shore, much of it ground and shattered among clusters of rocks that spread far out to sea.

They bury two who died the night before: One was killed by the cannonball, the other broke his neck in the collision. Two graves sit side by side with small sticks tied together as makeshift crosses at the head of each. They bow their heads. Thomas turns his head to see the slave with the Arabic notch praying with his hands folded.

Thomas and a group of ten crewmen stroll over green hills. The slave with the Arabic notch follows beside Thomas. Thomas writes something in his journal. Iona Abbey is seen in the distance. Eventually they near the base of the high, worn, gray walls of the structure. Around the perimeter, three Benedictine monks pick weeds out of a potato garden. The toppled remains of crushed stone crosses lie on either side of the entrance. A monk looks up and stares as they pass into the building.

The solemn monks do not seem to be bothered by these invaders. They do not even interrupt their prayers to take notice of them. Thomas and several others pass under the wooden beams which support the floor above and frame the center yard. Intricately designed stained glass windows line the walls. Two are broken, letting sunlight shine through. It is an almost perfect worship space.

Thomas and his companions kneel at the altar beside large pillars. A great cross stands before them and a thick bible lies open with the figure of crucified Jesus illustrated in bloody, torturous detail. Thomas turns his head to see the slave with the Arabic notch kneeling. Stripes of fresh blood are soaked through his white shirt.

Thomas and his companions travel upon the sand, waves lapping upon their feet. Thomas halts. The others stop and turn to him. Thomas kneels before the slave with the Arabic notch and folds his hands upwards toward him, shaking.

Thomas says, "I do not know if you can understand me, but I am shamed for what I have done. I have learned nothing in all my life, for I have become who I most hate!"

The slave places his hand gently on Thomas' face. Thomas slowly peers upward, afraid to look him in the eyes. He tells Thomas, "You saved my life."

"It is not true! How is it you speak our tongue?" Thomas asks him with tears in his eyes.

"I was a captain, sailing a small vessel in Spanish waters," the slave says, "picking off ships to feed mouths waiting at home. I heard many manner of speech upon the waves."

"What is your name, proud sailor?" Thomas says, now standing.

"Ibrahim."

"And what sad circumstances brought you upon that hellish ship we plucked you from?"

Ibrahim breathes a heavy sigh and finally tells him, "I was sold by traitors on my own ship, by whom, I could not see. I was tied and gagged as I slept, and I found myself breathing the stench of death. I was sure I had died, flung into the rotting bowels of hell."

Thomas places his hands over his eyes, saying, "And all your struggle… to escape to the pain of my whip!"

Ibrahim tells him with a smile, "The whip is nothing, for I may breathe sweet air yet once more. Hope is alive, praise God!"

"Such forgiveness!" Thomas says.

Thomas removes his shirt and soaks it with sea water. He lifts Ibrahim's shirt carefully and removes it, attempting to make the process as painless as possible. Thomas cleans the caked blood from Ibrahim's back, dipping the shirt in the ocean once again. Blood flows in the waves as Thomas cleans the gashes.

As three days pass, the men of Thomas' crew decide they have had enough of being stranded on this treeless island. They steal three tables from the churchmen, muttering threats of violence all the way. At once they go to fashioning planks that will be nailed over the crushed hole in the side of the ship.

Nearby, a bearded sailor bowls a small cannonball down the beach and knocks over nine out of ten small tree branches which serve as bowling pins. A crowd of bearded sailors yell and cheer. Ibrahim leaps and shouts with a smile.

# 50

# A House for a House

THOMAS ENTERS HIS PROPERTY wearing ragged clothing and donning a full beard. Lucy is pushing their little boy William in a carriage. She is alarmed at seeing this haggard vision enter, though rushes to meet his embrace as she recognizes him. Thomas kneels and picks up his son. He smiles, lifts him into the air, grinning, then pressing the child close. He kisses Lucy.

Lucy takes him by the hand and directs him to the study. She opens a drawer and hands Thomas Charles' letter.

"This arrived shortly after you left," she says.

Thomas spends his days in splendor. He pours his heart into his little son, giving him what he never had. Sometimes he feels a tear starting to break from his eye when he remembers that he is not in a dream. This little boy is all he has worked for his whole life: To see him smile when, as a boy, he could not. To fill his son with happiness is to live again, to live his childhood again and think it splendid.

Days are spent waking as early as the child wakes. In the yard, among the people Thomas teaches his boy. William learns to say the name of his black-haired puppy.

Days are spent simply, engaged in activities such as Tom reading to his son and strolling with him through pleasant nature on nice, sunny afternoons. William takes great interest in books with rich illustrations of animals. Thomas sees him taking his first steps in trying to reach his favorite, a page with a little black dog drawn on it. William falls, but still his parents erupt in applause. Laughter flies from his throat as he crawls the remainder of the way and looks down, still peering at the little black dog, laughing.

They all take a stroll in the garden. Thomas watches from a distance when William reaches for a rose and smells it. He first hears his son speak this moment when a bee buzzes by and William points his little, stubby finger toward it and says in the most innocent voice, "Bee."

Ibrahim converses and laughs with two servant women and a sailor as they enjoy tea. Thomas approaches with a sack full of money and places it on the table.

"What is this?" Ibrahim says.

Thomas says, "You are to leave the first thing tomorrow morning."

"I do not understand. What did I do?" Ibrahim says.

Thomas places his hand on Ibrahim's shoulder and says, "Your family needs you. I thank you for your sense of honor. It is inspiring."

The sun begins to set. Thomas and Lucy ride down a dirt road in fine attire. The driver holds the reins with a bright smile. Flowers fill the trees on each side of the road. They approach a house as several people enter dressed nicely.

. . .

Figures creep from out of the woods behind Thomas' house, some carrying torches.

. . .

Thomas and Lucy are welcomed at the doorway and greet several with smiles. A glass of wine is handed to each of them. A flute and a lute are heard playing a strange, archaic tune in the other room. People sit on pillows upon the ground with filled wine glasses in their hands, some with arms around each other. The room is decorated in Scottish fashion, despite four dancing women dressed in Romanesque attire with much rouge upon their cheeks. An eighteen-year-old boy is wearing a white Roman style cloth with a crown of leaves upon his brow. He is also painted with heavy rouge on his cheeks and stands in the middle of the room as they prance around him.

They play their instruments in a fury. The women amorously stroke the youth as they pass. They feed him grapes and he smiles, and hold up a small branch of a tree abundant in leaves.

. . .

Figures in shadow raise their torches and alight Thomas' house. Flames catch and spread up the walls.

. . .

One of the women brandishes a fake dagger and pretends to stab the youth. Fake blood drips forth abundantly.

. . .

In the cover of darkness, three of Constantyne's men toss a bloody sailor down the stairs. Blood pours from his throat.

"He is not here," the one cast in shadow says.

The tall, strong figure of the Admiral stands in the moonlight. The back door is heard shutting. They run to it, find it is locked and kick it forcefully until it opens.

. . .

One woman rips the cloth from the youth and bares his chest.

. . .

Figures in the shadows catch up with to two black servant women and stab them to death as they scream just before they reach the tree line.

Three servant women escape, one with William in her arms. They pass multitudes of trees, dodging branches and leaping over roots with agility.

Several follow the Admiral into the woods and see Roger kneeling in a clearing praying. His head is pointed upward, his hands are folded, tears gush from his eyes, and the moonlight shines brightly upon him. The Admiral kicks him directly in the face.

. . .

The women slice with the false knives. As they feign to slay the youth, imitation blood squirts from a hidden pouch and streaks across his chest. He lets out an effeminate scream and falls to the ground, pretending death. The women continue to revolve-dance around him to the music.

. . .

The Admiral slices a deep laceration into Roger's arm. Roger hollers as blood gushes forth. They stab him repeatedly as he writhes in pain, screams in agony, then finally lies still.

Thomas and Lucy ride to the house and break down in sadness and fear for what they see. The house is charred black, fires inside still churning. A dead sailor and a dead servant woman lie stiff, heavily burned in the doorway. The three servant women, horribly shaken with tears dripping, bursting with words, run towards them with William. Thomas and Lucy rush to grab their son. They hug and kiss him with all they have.

"Praise God he is alive!" Lucy says.

"How many were killed?" Thomas asks the slave women.

One says, "Tonight my sister... she no longer..."

"Why did he wait till now?" Lucy says.

Thomas looks toward the smoking house and, reminded of the immediacy of the danger, calls out, "We must gather what we need and leave immediately."

# 51

# Purge

THE BLOOD OF GOD ROCKS IN THE WAVES. Thomas purchases a smaller ship to sail beside it. Lucy cries as Thomas holds his arms around her. They kiss passionately, knowing well that it may be for the last time.

"You must go," Thomas says to her. "Protect William for me, my love. Be safe with Charles far away from here!"

Lucy says, "I cannot! My heart will wither and die without you!" pressing her head into his chest, her bawling half-muffled in his jacket. She soaks the material with her tears.

Thomas, his lips clenched in bitterness, kisses her down her cheek and neck repeatedly.

"It was a good life," he says.

Thomas pushes off and climbs aboard. Lucy is forcefully pulled aboard the other ship. She stares at him as he addresses the sailors, "Hear me now! Any whose fear shakes his bravery—leave now and save your life!" He paces, telling them, "You are free, if you wish—take your promised gold and live out your years, cowering under the power of one tyrant or another."

Several do, feeling somewhat cowardly, but liberated.

The two ships sail out to sea. Thomas keeps a close watch, for they mean to chaperone Lucy and William until they are a safe distance away.

The day passes slowly. The ships continue to sail deep into the vast ocean. White-beaked dolphins feast on a school of fish off the starboard side. Sea birds dive into the sea to hunt as well. Gloom as well as determination shows on every face. Their hearts beat uncontrollably in anticipation.

As day breaks, three ships appear on the horizon. All remain silent as Thomas peers toward the small figures on that distant vessel, awaiting his destiny.

He slides his sword out and cuts his forearm, letting the blood drip down onto the deck. He then lets the stream drip free into the sea. Thomas kneels before his bloody sword and calls out to the heavens, "Lord, I pray you give us strength today. Death seeks our blood to be spilled: us, fortunate few, chosen to cut down evil in this world. This we do proudly!"

Thomas slowly stands and strikes his sword in the direction of his second ship, calling out, "Full sails! Depart at once!"

A sailor on the other ship waves and yells to the crew. They open all of the sails fully at his word. Thomas turns to Benjamin with a tear in his eye. He says, "Friend. Turn us around."

Thomas' ship sails toward Constantyne's at full speed. Upon nearing, his ship crosses past the broadside of the two closest ships. The two burst forth their cannon balls. Several splash into the sea. One hits the aft of Thomas' ship, sending several of his crew off their feet. Another rips through the main sail.

Grape-shot crushes into a group of Thomas' sailors. One catches the object directly in the belly, causing blood to burst from his mouth, crumpling him in a heap due to whatever broke inside of him. Thomas raises his sword with a vicious smile.

"Sail around to their other side!" Thomas yells.

Benjamin turns the tiller sharply. They sail close to the fore of one ship.

Thomas bellows, "Let's send them under the waves! Fire!"

Shots explode from the cannons on Thomas' ship and burst in a concentrated area where the fore of the other ship meets the sea. A hole opens up and the ship plunges. It floats with the fore bobbing in the crashing waves, sinking farther every moment as the crew run about in a frenzy. Thomas' crew cheers as though mad. The Admiral's ship sails apart from the others and opens fire. Those on Thomas' scream with fury.

"Get down!" Thomas screams.

A mysterious sailor stumbles as the ship rocks violently. This mysterious figure holds its large hat on, covering its face as the sea sprays and heavy wind blows its scarf in the wind. Several sailors fall and tumble.

"Hurry with those cannons!" Thomas orders. "Double time! Ben! Clear us of that cannon shot!"

Benjamin turns the tiller hard to the right and the ship soars through the massive waves. It cuts at an angle horizontal toward the aft of the other ship. Cannons blast from the other ship and one collides into the edge of Thomas', sending splinters through the air. The Blood of God sails beyond the sinking ship and juts out broadside. Thomas waits nervously, yet determined, until his ship nears close to the other.

"Fire!" Thomas yells.

Cannonballs explode and crash into the hull. A small opening at the waterline under the main mast bursts open. Grapeshot heaves across the deck, goring sailors as it flies through them, crushing their bones and insides. The dead line the ship, bleeding. Benjamin laughs heartily as he turns the tiller. Thomas' crew celebrates with screams of cheer. Thomas smiles viciously. The mysterious sailor stands, the shadowed grin under its hat.

The Admiral's crew panics, holding a nervous gait, some climbing the sails and opening them wide.

"What do we do Captain?!" the Admiral's helmsman screams in terror.

"Get in there you worthless sea scum! I want an open shot!" the Admiral answers him harshly.

The second sinking ship tilts in the direction of its damaged hull. They scurry to hold on as others slip off headlong. Thomas' ship hides behind it with its fore peeking out. The Admiral's ship rides at full speed, surging through the wild sea. Thomas' ship is visible, parallel to the sinking ship.

"Ready on my word, you ninny women!" the Admiral says.

"Captain?" a sailor says, surprised.

"Fire!" Admiral Constantyne says, filled with fury. "Blow them to hell!"

Smoke fills the sky as the cannons release their contents in a great, deafening blast. The large black balls launch, three of them carving into the hull of Thomas' ship, exploding a great hole. The Blood of God tilts into the waves and drifts into the other sinking ship. A lookout dangles on the rigging, swinging with the last of his strength until his fingers can grasp no more.

"Come show us what you got, you rotten scoundrels!" another says, hanging just beside where the other was.

Those on each ship exchange curses, shaking fists and weapons. The ships near and swords slash across the divide, clashing and cutting flesh. They jump from ship to ship, chaos of blood and bared teeth on each deck, as men duel with sword and pistol. Each ship bobs as they slowly descend into the sea.

Benjamin and Thomas fight side by side, slashing at sailors. They cut through the other's ranks with ease. Thomas heads in the direction of Constantyne as swords clash all around. He juts his blade downward into an opponent's thigh. The fighter motions to lunge as Thomas kicks him in the stomach against the main mast and decapitates him. Those on both sides lie slaughtered as others battle atop them.

"Rout them!" Thomas screams. "Run these worthless vermin through!"

Thomas' remaining crew, though much fewer in number, carve through any who approach as they retreat. Fear leads to guns being fired haphazardly. Many dodge, though several on both sides are struck and lie incapacitated. The mysterious sailor removes her hat and lets her hair fall low. Lucy is revealed.

"No! It is you, my love!" Thomas calls to her, "Flee from here!"

She kisses Thomas and says nothing.

Constantyne bends on one knee and leans over the edge of the ship with his arm extended. His voice carries to her, "You live! Beautiful Lucy—my lovely daughter! Come to me, my dear girl. My baby!"

Lucy stands defiant upon the other ship. His ship sails, nearing their sinking vessel. Thomas and the others stand firm, guarding Lucy.

"Sail back to the wretched hole where you came from, lest we spill your guts asunder!" Lucy says to her father with two swords in her hands, prepared to attack.

Thomas' crew grip their swords, ready for the oncoming fight. A pistol shoots out and sends Simon dead upon the deck. Several other pistols fire and bodies fall on both sides. Brave ones on both sides leap across the divide to hack their enemies. One of Thomas' falls into the sea as he is pushed off. Thomas' allies suddenly charge and hack the faces of the others, sending several gushing blood onto the deck and into the sea.

Screams of fury are called throughout the cluster as glimmering swords and heavy blows are exchanged. Lucy slashes through torsos. The Admiral stands motionless, filled with shame.

Several of the Admiral's team up and rout Thomas' fighters. Benjamin is confronted by four. He slashes through the first two but is cut through the throat as he defends the blow of the third. He shoves his sword through his killer's gut and cuts out the other's throat, sending him flying. Thomas holds him as he chokes up blood and bleeds profusely from his neck. "My last and best friend!" Thomas hollers.

"Get up! Leave me be! It is no matter! It was a good life, alas!" Benjamin says choking up blood.

Several sailors confront Thomas and he cuts them through in turn. Thomas receives two gunshots and falls to his knees. He stands and is cut across the chest. He stabs one in the gut and decapitates another. He is weary, trying to keep balance, covered in blood. Several confront Thomas as he lunges for the Admiral. Thomas breaks their defenses and slashes through them. He cuts down hard and the Admiral blocks the attack, sending Thomas to the deck. He is overwhelmed and scurries to the side of the ship. His blood pours out in torrents as the Admiral confronts him.

"You cannot defeat me, trash," the Admiral says to him. "I live through all the ages, hanging over your kind."

"No!" Thomas screams defiantly, pushing himself onto his wobbly feet and stumbles toward the Admiral. The Admiral waves him to come closer with his one good sword arm.

"Come! Claim your revenge!" Admiral Constantyne says, baring his teeth like a wolf closing in on a kill.

Constantyne and Thomas exchange strikes, blocking and dodging constantly. Those remaining circle around. Constantyne's hobble and lame arm make him an odd sight in a swordfight, but his strength and skill make up for it. He lunges, causing Thomas to fall. Just as he does, the Admiral slashes wide, bearing down at his prone adversary. Thomas braces his sword before him, the blow pinching his wrists painfully. As the blade sweeps upward, it tears open a gash on Thomas' shoulder. Trying his best to block out the pain, he rolls free and stands once more.

Thomas strikes and gashes the Admiral's face. Thomas dodges a strike and gashes the other cheek. The Admiral wails in pain and becomes angered. He strikes at Thomas, and Thomas dodges and slices the Admiral's fingers, causing him to drop his sword.

"Curse you!" the Admiral screams.

Thomas lunges and stands over the weapon. The Admiral tackles him and throws his weak body to the side, picking up the object of death-wielding. The Admiral charges, and Thomas backs away with each strike, up onto the edge of the ship. The Admiral limps toward him and strikes overhead. Thomas blocks with his last energy. Thomas becomes disoriented as his blood flows out of his wounds, down the length of his body. He falls, delirious.

The Admiral sinks his blade into Thomas' side, sending forth much blood and watery fluid. Thomas wails in horror, covered in blood and quivering in pain. Like a wounded deer, Thomas crawls away. Lucy takes hold of his arm and drags him. Satisfied laughter is heard from a few sailors. Lucy holds him and attempts to stop the blood from leaving his body. Pulling him onto the edge of her vessel, she wails as the ship sinks deeper and deeper. The Admiral and his sailors stand on the edge of the other ship, peering like hawks. Lucy bawls horribly as Thomas loses consciousness.

"Come, leave that criminal. He is dead, finally. What he deserves!" the Admiral says, mocking him.

Lucy holds her face against Thomas, as his head leans lifeless on the scum-tinted boards. She says, "No, it is you who have been dead all along!" She weeps bitterly. The ship dips suddenly and floats away. Constantyne reaches his hand out and begs her to come to him, "I only wished to give you the best. Forgive me—I beg you!"

The ship sinks more and more. Water fills much of the interior and allows the water level to rise.

"Get her!" the Admiral yells.

Two sailors move to reach the other ship.

"No. No!" she says, slipping a pistol from her side and placing it to her temple. She sobs and closes her eyes. Her hand shakes as she cries bitterly and pulls the trigger. With a blast like thunder she falls dead. The spray of blood across the deck shocks the witnesses, freezing their emotions. Constantyne says nothing. His breath is choked as his eyes take in the image of his still daughter.

Thomas and Lucy—their bodies lie where they fell, arms splayed, her neck crossed over his shoulder. The two corpses, with their stuck faces and innard trails, finally taste the salty water. As the liquid encapsulates them, they bloom in a rush of blood. It is there in the murky depths they greet the seaweed and the other slain.


# THE END

Thank you for reading!

**Jacob Kilgore** grew up in Southern California, but now resides in South Korea where he is teaching English. He studied creative writing at the University of California, Riverside. The desire to write started in high school when he would write poems and write songs for bands he was in. Later, the requirements in screenwriting courses pushed him to write longer works. That's what *Vagrant Prince* developed from. From there sprung the many things that make this novel unique: characters being both hero and villain at the same time, a twisted narrator, the connections to events and struggles of people today, and the commoner or warrior as a shaman. We gain nothing, Jacob believes, by gaining the acceptance of the mob. Only by taking chances and honing our skills will we rise above.

www.thegrandphilosophy.com